MUSTIQUE ISLAND

MUSTIQUE ISLAND

A Novel

SARAH MCCOY

THORNDIKE PRESS
A part of Gale, a Cengage Company

LIBRARY OF CONGRESS CIP DATA ON FILE.
CATALOGUING IN PUBLICATION FOR THIS BOOK
IS AVAILABLE FROM THE LIBRARY OF CONGRESS.

ISBN-13: 978-1-4328-9961-5 (hardcover alk. paper)

Published in 2022 by arrangement with William Morrow, an imprint of HarperCollins Publishers

Printed in Mexico
Print Number : 1   Print Year : 2022

Para mi abuelita Mama Maria Norat Esparra, for raising daughters and granddaughters as boldly unique as the stars

All good things are wild and free.

— Henry David Thoreau

God caused every tree that is both beautiful and pleasing to eat to spring up from the ground.

The tree of life was also in the middle of the garden, along with the tree of the knowledge of good and evil.

— Genesis 2:9

■ ■ ■ ■ ■

PART 1
WILLY MAY

■ ■ ■ ■ ■

CHAPTER 1
GODS OF PARADISE

January 1972
Mustique Island, the Grenadines
The bow of Willy May's boat, *Otrera,* cut the waters like a butter knife, winking along the waves. Willy May's first glimpse of Mustique Island had not been of the palm groves dancing in the breeze or the ivory beach wrapping the three-mile isle like a satin ribbon. Her eyes had been cast down into the deep blue, and she wondered if she had been brought here on a fool's errand. Her new British friend, Davey from Trinidad, had convinced her to come.

One night while a soca band played a calypso beat and tiki torches lit up the Port of Spain harbor, Davey had turned to her and said, "How about popping by Mustique to say hello next week?"

As if Caribbean islands were everyday homes in an everyday neighborhood.

Davey knew a guy on Mustique — Arne

13

Hasselqvist, a celebrity Swedish architect, who was causing quite the hubbub among those who had the means to own a piece of paradise. But that's the thing with Shangri-la, only the elite are invited. In Mustique, like most places, money and title were prerequisites.

The sunlight shimmered like a crowning aurora. The closer they came to the shore, the calmer the sea, reflecting a rippled image of Willy May on the glossy surface. The sea spray held her hair's natural wave in place. She'd worn it in various styles throughout her life but now, at forty-five, it was shoulder length and honey blond with a little help from Clairol. Her cheekbones V'ed prominently, making her look perpetually on the verge of puckering to speak or laugh or blow a kiss — whatever the viewer wanted to believe. And once soft as a cream rose, her skin had been sunbaked to a nut. Sailing had changed her in that way and many others.

It'd taken three years to circle the entire earth, starting in Bristol Channel and moving eastward. The drive to attain the goal had fueled her every moment. But having done so, the thought of another rotation made her tired. So, she'd gone in the opposite direction — west to the Caribbean, for a respite.

Now, as she looked down into the watery mirror, the pouches beneath her eyes stood out. The crow's-feet at the corners were new, too. She frowned at herself, and then stuck her hand straight through the middle of her face to see beneath the surface.

An inch separated *Otrera*'s hull from the coral. Mustique was laced in a massive reef. Like porcupine quills, it kept the island safe. There was only one entry: Britannia Bay. Davey had warned her that an attempt to dock at any other location would result in the ship's grounding.

The island was in an amphidromic point. Tideless, in essence. But if the earth shrugged one way or another, if the balance of water to air hiccupped, ruin was inescapable. Such was life, Willy May knew.

Before her first mate, Ronnel, could secure the boat to the dock piling, two men in blazing-white suits, espadrilles, and straw hats welcomed her to the pier.

"Ahoy, ahoy there!" they greeted in a British clip.

One took off his hat and waved it excitedly, exposing a tanned bald head.

"Welcome to Mustique!" said the other.

Willy May shielded her eyes against the glare.

Otrera kissed the landing and Ronnel knotted the hitch. Willy May would have been more comfortable tying the dock lines and placing the fenders herself but fought the urge. A woman of means would never do that, and first impressions were everything. So, she pushed her shoulders back and pressed her lips together. Old lipstick from the morning pulled dry at the corners. She went without a lot of things as a sea woman but never without color cream on her lips. She'd feel more naked without it than the emperor in his new clothes.

Davey gestured to the slender man with the bald head. "May I introduce the master of ceremonies, Mr. Colin Tennant, heir apparent to Baron Glenconner."

"Please, just call me Colin." Colin bowed in Edwardian fashion. "Delightful to have you on our island."

Oddly charming, thought Willy May. Like a grown-up version of Peter Pan, sprite-like while homely human. Unsure if she was supposed to curtsy in theatrical return, she put her hands on her hips instead.

Colin turned to the man at his side. "This is Hugo, my business partner. We were chums at Eton. Hugo knows everything about everything so if you want to know anything, he's got the encyclopedia in his

16

noggin."

Hugo nodded hello.

"I presume you haven't eaten," Colin went on. "But even if you have, you can eat again. The heat stokes the metabolism. It's one of Anne's biggest complaints — the incessant sweating. But when she's home in Scotland, her dresses fit like a glove without girdle or tights. Have you seen the new hosiery at Selfridges? Fabulous. I love a costume, don't you? We put on our own dramatics, you see. I ordered a whole case of different-colored tights, polka dots and animal prints, during Princess Margaret's last visit. Naturally, it turned out to be the hottest summer on record, so nobody was in the mood to wear them. We strung them on fishing poles as streamers instead . . ."

He rambled a soliloquy as he led her down the wharf. Over her shoulder, she caught eyes with Davey, who put up both hands as if to say, *What's to be done but go along?*

A golf cart parked at the edge of the beach where the sand turned to crabgrass.

"Princess Margaret is building a château — at the southern tip of the island. We gave her the plot as a wedding gift. Better than any of the bric-a-brac usually dispensed at weddings — Waterford vases and Leavers laces," he singsung. "One never really knows

17

what to do with the stuff. Instead, we offered a piece of the Garden of Eden!"

He gestured for Willy May to sit in the passenger seat, which she did. Her mind whirled on his chatter and the thrill of knowing that the rumors were true: Princess Margaret was a resident.

"Hugo, Davey — hurry up!" Colin called back. "We don't want our Texas beauty queen wilting in this heat!"

Willy May had won the Limestone County Beauty Contest in 1942, which automatically made her the queen of Central Texas. It came with a twenty-five-dollar prize and a year's worth of milk from the local dairy sponsor. Her parents, William and Gretchen, were day laborers. Sometimes her mom cleaned houses. Sometimes her dad did carpentry or plumbing. They were a Jack and Jill of all trades and masters of none. The mention of her past made her earlobes sweat. Willy May hadn't told Colin about her history. But that was the thing with money, it bought you secrets. Yours and other people's.

Hugo and Davey slid onto the back bench of the golf cart and their foursome took off with a jolt over flattened bamboo and fallen manchineel leaves. A large sign warned: POISONOUS. DO NOT EAT THE SMALL GREEN

APPLES. DO NOT STAND UNDER TREES WHEN IT RAINS. AVOID TOUCHING THE FLOWERS AND SAP. AVOID BREATHING POLLEN. TOXIC. LETHAL. AVOID.

Willy May felt a tightness in her chest and realized she was instinctually holding her breath. The men made no mention of the poisonous grove blanketing the island. Was it too late to get back on her boat and sail away? The wheels of the golf cart sprayed sandy dirt as Colin pressed the acceleration and they sped onward.

Behind her on *Otrera,* two island men collected Willy May's luggage off the deck while Ronnel tied down the sails. He would sleep in the crew bunk and stay on to keep watch. Part of her was jealous. *Otrera* had become home since her divorce. She'd created it with her own hands.

Boatbuilding had started as a hobby. On a lark, she and her ex-husband, Harry, had built another vessel named the *Stingray.* They used it for holidays and annual family sails, going as far as Shanghai. Her daughters, Hilly and Joanne, had been small then. They'd easily fit into one bunk and loved sleeping head to toe, toe to head. They'd been glued at the hip at those tender ages and shared a root attachment that seemed to transcend even her own to them. Willy

May found their sisterhood fascinating. She and Harry hadn't much experience with sibling bonds, both being only children.

Harry's mother was the daughter of an earl whose pedigree was heavy but bank account light. She married an aging tradesman, Philip Henry Michael Sr., of the vastly successful Michael & Boutler Brewery. Harry was the blue-blooded prince of his household, the sole heir.

As a father, Harry knew little of raising girls. Truth be told, neither did Willy May. But she kept that to herself. She was their mother. Her choices were their choices. Her daughters were part of her, sprung from her deepest hope. She wanted them to experience the world and rise to be part of it. And look how well they'd turned out.

Hilly was a model and actress, and Joanne was studying to become a musician. Willy May was proud of them both. They were artists, the heroes of their own lives.

To onlookers, the cardinal sin in their family had been the divorce. Such a sordid affair. She hadn't expected Harry to cut her out of everything. Especially when he'd been the unfaithful one. She didn't deserve to be treated so shoddily. So she'd hired a young, whip-smart attorney. The judge had awarded her far more than she would've received had they negotiated the settlement privately. Harry's response had been ugly. She'd been ugly right back. She took full responsibility for her rancor.

On a practical note, had the Michaels done a better job with the legalities of the brewery, her lawyer wouldn't have found the loophole entitling her to such a large settlement of the family's assets. If Harry not been so miserly from the beginning, the whole thing, and possibly his own death, could've been avoided. He knew she hadn't any means of supporting herself but refused to allocate any income toward her well-being in the settlement — so she fought back.

Willy May came to England without formal education and knowing no one, which Harry hadn't cared about at first. She was a novelty item. When they wed in June 1943, she'd been sixteen. The marriage certificate said she was eighteen, but everyone falsified their age back then. There was a war on.

Royal Air Force pilot Harry Michael had been training at the British Flying Training School in nearby Terrell, Texas.

"This is Willy May Corbel. Our Central Texas beauty queen," her girlfriend had introduced them at a Saturday night USO dance.

"Enchantée," Willy May had said.

She'd heard Vivian Leigh use the French word in a newsreel. While she wasn't entirely sure what it meant, she knew that celebrities said it.

"A pleasure. I've met a lot of eminent people, but never a queen," Harry had replied with an accent dripping of knights and fair maidens.

Afterward, her friend pulled her aside. "He likes you, and he hasn't looked twice at any girl in Texas. You'd do well to like him back — he's rich as Croesus!"

She'd thought Harry cute but money made everything golden. Willy May put on her best nymphet act, using all the tricks she'd seen employed by Rita Hayworth, Veronica Lake, and Betty Grable in the Hollywood films. To her surprise, they worked. Soon enough, she was on her back between the cornrows of old Mr. Brown's field, husks in her hair, Harry inside her. Tipsy on beer and moonlight, Harry didn't notice her distant expression. It was not her first time. Months earlier she'd been curious to try it with someone who wouldn't expect forever from the act. So, she'd given herself to a sweet cowboy on his way to Amarillo with his father's herd. He was tender and young and she could tell it had been his first time, too.

But still, she let Harry believe that she was a virgin. It was what men wanted to believe. He'd reverently handed her back her blouse, caught on the leafy arms of a nearby cornstalk, and asked if she was okay. She'd demurely buttoned the front and nodded, "Gosh, I hope I don't get pregnant." She'd looked up at him from under her lashes. "They say it only takes the once. I guess that's how love works."

They didn't wait to find out. A week later, she and Harry eloped at the Limestone County Courthouse. She thought her parents would be proud of her. Harry was a military officer, the only son of a wealthy British family. They wouldn't have to worry about her future anymore. But they'd been appalled.

"He's not even American." Her mother had balked. "Where will you live?"

"In England."

That was one of the reasons they'd married quickly, so she told them. Harry had finished flight school and would be returning with his squadron.

"His family has a big house. I think they might even have two! Plenty of room for us."

Her mother had shaken her head in disbelief. "Our people have been in Texas since the first American flag was stuck in the dirt. Nobody ups and leaves. We can't — *you* can't."

"She won't, if she knows what's good for her," her father had threatened.

Willy May had already made up her mind but his challenge lit a fire in her belly.

"You'd rather I stay here in Nowhere, Texas, marry some local nobody, have a bunch of going-nowhere babies, and die an old shriveled nobody like all my people before me?"

Her temper lit his. Like father, like daughter.

"We ain't good enough for you, Miss High and Mighty? Then go on! Good riddance!" He'd ripped down the bedsheet that separated their bedroom side from hers and thrown it at her feet. "I didn't raise no Judas daughter. If you go, you gone. Don't let me find a hair of you left." The door slammed behind him as he marched out of the house.

"Mama?" Willy May asked, as if for some reassurance. "It's my chance to be somebody. I know you want that for me."

Her mother had lightly touched the curling leather edge of their family Bible. " 'Put no trust in a neighbor; have no confidence in a friend; guard the doors of your mouth from her who lies in your arms; for the son treats the father with contempt, the daughter rises up against her mother . . .' The book of Micah." She'd wiped a tear that threatened and turned away. "Best get you packed."

Willy May knew there was no going back. They didn't ask if she loved Harry. Love was not their way. They'd never even said as much to her. To be honest, she wasn't sure what love looked, sounded, or felt like. She'd seen it in movies and read about it in books but being admired, complimented, and respected was the closest she'd actually experienced. All of the things she felt for Harry Michael. It must be *love,* right?

So Willy May put all her eggs in one basket, ready to leave her people for a foreign land with a husband she barely knew, only to discover his family would never fully accept her. When she first arrived in England with a marriage certificate and little else, her mother-in-law had greeted her as if she were a strange insect her son had brought home in his suitcase, and she wasn't sure whether to pin her to an entomology board or use a swatter.

"What do we have here?" she'd said as way of hello and then, "Oh dear."

Mother Michael said that having the couple sleep together in Harry's bedroom across from hers was distasteful. She suggested the newlyweds move into the family's carriage house and instructed the housemaid to put their luggage there. The carriage house was spacious but a junkyard of sorts, full of antiques that had been rejected for the main house. Her mother-in-law had walked her round the cluttered rooms, explaining the history of each piece of furniture as if it were a privilege to sit on their splinters.

But just because Willy May came from nothing didn't mean she was content with nothing. She'd nodded, smiled, graciously accepted her mother-in-law's tutorial on housekeeping, and then didn't lift a finger to perform it.

Harry was bequeathed his grandmother's wedding band for his new bride, a simple ring but pure gold. Willy May marveled at its shine under the sun. She swore then that she'd never take it off, and she never had. Divorce and widowhood didn't change what the ring meant: a new beginning, a precious thing to remember. Her mother didn't have a wedding band. She'd told people that she donated it for the war efforts but really, she'd never had one. Willy May's father never could afford it. He said keepsakes didn't do a living person a lick of good. He'd never been one for sentimental appreciation — of his wife or his only child. They were things of worth so long as they made themselves useful.

In England, however, wives and children had power. They were social embellishments that embodied the future, and Willy May quickly learned that the English were obsessed with cultivating the branches of their family trees.

During the early years of her daughters' lives, she and Harry had been bonded together by unquestionable, undeniable love. Whatever the holes in their marriage, the girls filled in the gaps. But that's the thing with love, it wasn't a concrete material. It needed room to grow. Cemented in place, it died.

Looking back, she saw that's what happened. Once the girls were older, she and Harry had nothing between them but a partnership of polite white lies. Sometimes through the lonesome lens of night, she caught clear glimpses of their past, and it shamed her. She wondered if something inside her was broken, defective, or at the very least, twisted up. She'd manipulated Harry into marrying her. Had he been a tougher sort, he might've left her in Texas, felt a pang of remorse for her perceived lost maidenhood, gone home, and married whoever his mother approved. But like a fish in open water, he thought privilege was pervasive and boundless. It was his fatal flaw. Seeing it, Willy May had seized her opportunity.

From the moment they met, she'd tricked Harry into believing that she was someone she wasn't. She'd moved into her mother-in-law's house, put on lipstick, heels, an heirloom ring, and the role of self-assured British housewife; hoping to make up for deception done in service of a greater good, hoping that by being everything Harry expected, he would come to genuinely love her.

She told anyone who asked that her kin were landowners in Texas. Her mother was a lady of the house. Sometimes a lie did good. One could believe and spread that kind. She was sure of it. Eventually the good lies would manifest. That was her thinking. She assumed the spell worked both ways. When others called her "Mrs. Michael," she'd hoped it would dispense on her the happily-ever-after she longed to achieve. And it did, for a time. Her life in England had been far better than it ever could've been in Texas.

So, when she first learned of Harry's affair with the Viscountess Mary Hailsham, she didn't know what to do. It hurt her. But confronting his deception would mean confronting her own, going all the way back to her sixteen-year-old desperation to get the hell out of Limestone County.

At the time of the affair's disclosure, the girls were in primary school. She weighed her options or, rather, she asked herself the question at the crux: What did she hope to accomplish by kicking up a fuss? Divorce at that stage in her life would've made her a single, uneducated mother of two with no family, no house, and no income. A one-way ticket back to Nowhere, Texas. That was the opposite of what she wanted. She needed the Michaels, and they needed her as the mother of the family's heirs, if nothing else. That was worth the emotional sacrifice, she told herself. So, she turned a blind eye to the infidelity and over time, the lies became easier to believe. It meant they could go on living peaceably.

Then Harry went and botched it all up. He got caught. Not by Willy May. He was coming down the steps of the Queens Hotel with Mary Hailsham noodling his arm. His indiscretion was a result of three scotches when he usually only drank beer. Willy May had been on a shopping trip with the girls in London. Harry hadn't expected to bump into his mother's oldest friend, Lady Lizzy Fitzpatrick, and three wives of title leaving a charity dinner at the hotel. All members of the same social club. The scandal was a feast for the gossip starved. Everyone pretended to be shocked but hid knowing grins behind their palms. Harry and Mary had been an item since they were schoolchildren. In their minds, Willy May had always been the interloper.

All of English society was staring and talking. The scandal was out. Hilly was turning eighteen and Joanne, sixteen. After nearly thirty years of dutiful marriage, the law was on Willy May's side, and she saw no reason to stay in the union. They had been young when they met. There had been a war on. It had been another time and place. They'd made a good run of it for three decades . . . two beautiful daughters as evidence. But one could probably argue that it had been over before it had even begun. She'd tried to do right by him. A divorce seemed the kindest action. It meant Harry could do as he pleased with Mary and she was free to do the same.

Less than a month after the civil court

proceedings concluded, Harry had a heart attack.

"It was the stress of the divorce . . . *that* woman killed him," her mother-in-law had cried at the wake, though it was common knowledge that her own husband, Philip Henry Sr., had died of a stroke at nearly the same age. Heart disease, the doctors said. It was genetic.

Despite the medical truth and Harry's faithlessness, the social stigma stuck. It was a far better story in whist circles to name Willy May the villainess. Mary Hailsham came from a noble pedigree. All of Cheltenham knew her parents and her grandparents. She was respected. While this Willy May . . . what was her maiden name? No one even knew. They blackballed her.

She couldn't shop at Premier Supermarket without catching side-eyed glances. So, she'd gone over to the Gloucester shipyard with a blank check and a big idea: *Otrera.* She'd fallen in love with the sea on her first voyage. It was everything she'd never had in landlocked Texas. The breezes of distant places kissed her, and she could taste the freedom in them. Salty. She set her mind to ace her Skipper Practical and surprised herself at what a good study she turned out to be. She'd never been particularly interested in schoolbooks, smelling of chalk dust and clammy fingers. Learning to sail was different. It was tactile. She learned by doing: tacking, jibbing, steering, adjusting to the give-and-take of the elements. It was a dance between two partners of equal determination: Mother Woman and Mother Nature. It was relational. It was impassioned. It was unconditional acceptance in a way that she hadn't experienced in her life up to that point. So, when her marriage ended, it felt natural to run to the sea's embrace.

She hired a construction crew and channeled everything she had into building a boat that was exclusively her own. It was her escape and the only home that carried no condemnation. She launched with a two-person crew.

As long as she kept reaching forward, she kept going. Three years later, she was one of the few women who had successfully sailed around the globe. Mission accomplished, she sat down to write her girls and found herself unable to answer *What now?* She didn't know.

On her first night docked in Trinidad, at the end of those three years, she'd awoken panicked. Sweat made the back of her knees stick together painfully when she'd tried to stand from the boat bunk. The taste of soured mango stuck in the back of her throat. The sound of the waves lapped incessantly, *thunk-thud, thunk-thud, thunk-thud.*

She'd poured herself a glass of water and gone out on the moonlit deck. The dark horizon went on and on, making her feel small as a speck of stardust. By the time her glass was empty, she was sobbing over things so far removed that it seemed ludicrous. She was missing her girls, remorseful over Harry's death, regretful of the lost years, lost family, lost dreams . . . so much loss. The problem with wanting to conquer the world was that it kept moving, changing. One had to make a choice: chase it forever or stop, root, and see what grew. She'd tried the former and it'd brought her to this moment of drifting sorrow. It was time to try the latter.

The next day, she'd met Davey through the Trinidadian harbormaster. A British expat and seasoned captain, Davey had just come off a chartered yacht. He was warm, welcoming, and seemed to be friends with everyone. He was the sort of person who put you at ease no matter who you were or what the circumstance. Trustworthy. When he suggested Mustique — a mysteriously exclusive island that boasted freedom from scrutiny — she wanted to believe such a place existed. She wanted to believe she could belong.

Chapter 2
Civility

The Cotton House was originally part of the island's murky history, a failed plantation back when the Caribbean was another arm of the global cotton trade. Built on the bluff with its rear facing the sea, it now operated as a luxury guest lodge for affluent friends of Mustique's current owners, Colin and Anne Tennant. The famed theatrical designer Oliver Messel had personally remodeled it from floorboards to pitch, but the couple had insisted on retaining the building's name. Given its origins, Willy May wondered why. Was it lack of creativity? Or some kind of warped colonial nostalgia? She would soon find out.

Ushering Willy May to his not-so-humble abode, Colin parked his golf cart — his *mule,* as he liked to call it — at the Cotton House pool patio. He preferred the seaside entrance.

A wall mirror trimmed in lustrous shells

hung directly opposite the entry, reflecting the ocean so perfectly that it tricked the eye into believing, if momentarily, the illusion of stepping out on the waterline. Willy May's knees impulsively gave, but she reminded herself that she was on solid ground.

The house was a triumph of theatrical opulence. The veranda was wide as a proscenium with louvre doors along the sides so that the sound of the breeze flowed through as an unbroken woodwind note. The roof was pitched high and grand as that of an auditorium. Sofas and chairs had been upholstered in refreshing blue and white linen with iron patio furniture painted in bright green.

"We've trademarked the color," said Colin, running his hand over a chair arm. "You know Majorelle Blue — well, this is Mustique Green."

It's like Kermit the Frog, Willy May thought, but what she said was, "It'd make a pretty nail polish."

Colin lifted his chin with a smile. "It would, you know." He turned to Hugo. "Write that down. The Mustique Company is launching a fashion brand to go with our island-grown cotton."

It had been a throwaway remark on Willy

May's part, but it seemed even the outlandish was taken into consideration here.

"A woman does use many cotton balls when getting a manicure," she added, just to play along.

"Indeed." Colin smiled.

An islander in linen shorts and matching tunic approached with lowered eyes and hands dutifully at his sides. "I'm sorry to interrupt but Lady Anne is waiting."

On command, Colin shuffled Willy May forward through the double doors into the palatial heart of the Cotton House. The communal lanai was adorned from corner to corner with eccentricities: a narwhal tusk hung from one wall with a taxidermy menagerie on the floor below. Colorful birds perched eternally on their stands beside a fountain made of giant clamshells. Bits of iridescent sea glass hung overhead from fishing lines, tinkling as they refracted colored pastels on the tile floor. Towers of leather-bound books and a vast army of brass-bound trunks lent gravity to the otherwise wildly embellished, nearly childish decor.

At the far end, where the windows opened to the palm fronds, a rainbow of foods sat on a long table. Around it was an intimate luncheon party dressed in such similar tunic style and in such similar repose that Willy May had a hard time distinguishing the men from the women.

A lithe figure with an Hermès scarf tying back ash-blond tresses sipped a finger of whiskey on a single ice cube. Colin gestured to her ceremoniously.

"May I introduce Lady Anne Tennant."

Anne swung a long leg from its crossed position so that she could lean forward. She was dewy with sweat from nose to toes, and what Willy May initially took as a healthy flush was, close up, a prickling heat rash. Her cheeks were streaked scarlet, without a stitch of makeup, but she didn't try to cover up her flaws. Was it humility or hubris?

"Welcome to Mustique. Call me Anne." She extended a hand into the patch of air between them where the sunlight cut through the palms. "No formal family names. We prefer to keep it casual."

That was how she introduced herself, with the gems of her rings glittering, an assertive grip, and a smile that made her eyes turn into crescents.

"Nice to meet you, Anne."

"That accent. You must promise to keep it. Texas, correct?"

Willy May's Texan drawl had dulled considerably from years of living in England, but it seemed that Anne fancied herself a sociolinguist.

"Yes, ma'am," Willy May said, indulging her.

She'd learned early to accentuate her positives. If being a red-blooded American made her an exciting novelty, then she would use that to her advantage. Clearly, Colin was a collector of exotic things.

"Have a seat. Are you hungry? We're having egg salad in cucumber boats. George, our cook, is amazing. The eggs are from island hens. The cucumbers from our gardens. He makes the mayonnaise from scratch."

Anne pushed the platter of vegetable boats forward, taking one between her fingers and biting. She licked the smeared mayo and egg from her bottom lip. "Otherworldly, trust me."

Colin snapped his fingers in the air, more celebratory than commanding. An islander across the room answered.

"George, my good man, would you make our honored guest a . . ." Colin tapped his chin with a fingernail, long and buffed shiny. "What's your pleasure, my dear?"

"A club soda on the rocks."

"Are you one of those American prohibitionists?" asked Anne.

"I have nothing against booze except that my ex-husband owned a brewery. I learned early to never start with it. Goes down like a Joe Frazier punch."

Anne laughed. "Fair enough. I'll drink yours for you. Make mine a double, George."

George dropped ice into tumblers with satisfying *clinks.*

"So" — Anne leaned closer to Willy May — "Davey tells us that you've been traveling awhile but are looking to settle. Is that right?"

Had she said that, or had she only thought it? Memory was hazy. George handed her a highball glass full of iced soda. "Thank you." Willy May drank.

"We have builders on the island and our own construction crew," said Colin. "No need for anyone from the outside. The locals love the work. Finer craftsmanship I have never seen — except back home, of course. But you can't build Buckingham on an island."

"Yet still, you try!" said Anne.

"Yes, well, we can't live in native straw huts," countered Colin.

George picked up glasses. A shadow seemed to pass across his gaze, but his grin remained unchanged. He caught Willy

May's stare and held it a beat before exiting. She watched him go, more curious about him than anyone else in the room.

"Let's speak candidly." Anne turned to Willy May. "Colin is selling plots to selective buyers. By that, we mean *quality* families. You see, Colin believes he's building a new Eden here on Mustique. I'm not as convinced as the Princess that he'll do it." She smoothed the silk scarf at her temple. "Personally, I prefer the climate of Scotland. Humidity is wretched on my hair. Frizz is an indomitable enemy."

Willy May laughed. Anne had a sharp tongue. That was a greater sign of intelligence than all the refined talk in the world. It also made her equal parts charming and treacherous.

Anne set down her glass and stood. "Come, let me show you."

She took Willy May to the open window at the front of the house, overlooking an expansive green lawn and the island beyond.

"See the white construction beams." She pointed. "That's the Princess's home, Les Jolies Eaux, on the other side of Toucan Hill."

Willy May saw it winking through the jungle.

Without retracting her arm, Anne swept

41

her finger to the right. "Do you see that cliffside? The one facing Britannia Bay, where your boat is docked?"

Mustique was but a mile wide and three miles long. The Cotton House sat on the northernmost hill with a clear view of everyone and everything. In the distance *Otrera* floated on the blue sea, and Willy May nearly believed she could pinch her fingers and pick it up. Directly adjacent to the bay was a rocky butte with a flat jungle ledge.

"That could be yours," said Anne.

"At a pretty price, no doubt?"

"Everything has a pretty price, my dear." Anne put her hand on Willy May's arm. "The question becomes, what's the pretty price to you?"

Colin shouted behind them and wielded a banana like a sword, challenging Oliver Messel to a duel. Clearly Anne had not been the only one indulging in double whiskies.

Anne leaned in close so only Willy May could hear. "I'm sorry about your husband."

Willy May shook off the kindness. It pained her, though she knew it oughtn't.

"Me, too. I wanted him divorced, but not dead," she replied. "We'd been at odds for years."

"Aren't we all at *odds*?" She dipped her

head toward Colin. "Still, I'm sorry you had to go through that unpleasantness — with the affair and then his family — and to have him die on you." She tsked. "There are many who thought you handled it all quite bravely. No matter the majority opinion back home, everyone here sympathizes."

There it was, her past catching up to her. Gossip was the life-blood of the upper crust. Especially when *The Sun* covered it. You were your reputation, even thousands of miles and over three years away. In England, the old-world rules governed. In England, they would've discussed the topic of her past before she arrived and then not ever directly with her. She liked that Anne had come to her forthright and addressed the proverbial elephant in the room.

Mustique felt like a new beginning. The support of someone of social class surprised Willy May. Few people had come to her corner.

Off the Cotton House veranda, the horizon line was straight and smooth, an underscore on a blank page.

Mustique and its landlords wanted her and being desired was an alluring quality in love and in real estate. One that she hadn't felt in some time. Never mind the obvious: this was paradise. No one could argue that the island wasn't one of the most picture-perfect places on earth. If she was to fit in anywhere and belong to any group, why not here? There were worse places and people. Far worse.

"I could take a look at the property," she told Anne.

It couldn't hurt.

Anne smiled. "Good. Tomorrow, then."

CHAPTER 3
BEAUTY

After a late lunch the next day, they ascended the hill. The climb through the jungle to the cliffside plot was more untamed than Anne had let on the day before. Kenton, a local youth, led the way. Apparently, there had been a road once. Colin cut it to allow his mule carts to easily pass. But like a man's beard, the jungle had simply grown over the shaven strip. A mile from the site, the caravan had to abandon their mule carts and walk the rest of the way in single file.

Thick vines, banyan roots, and bamboo branches tangled into a web of living green, through which only Kenton's machete could penetrate. The air pressed down like hot irons. Sweat pooled in the soft divots of their flesh. Colin had been conversational at the start but now, even he plodded silently, flicking beetles off his shirt and swatting the daytime mosquitoes that swarmed at his open collar.

After an hour of trekking, they arrived at the flat terrain that Willy May had seen from the Cotton House porch. The turquoise sea stretched out to a leaden storm cloud on the horizon. The colors reminded her of her daughters' eyes. They shifted depending on the weather. Bluer on some days, greener on others, and ombré when their thoughts were tempestuous.

She reached down and clasped a handful of dirt, smoothing the particles between her fingers to get a feel for its texture, rich and sandy. She'd put in a garden here. Bougainvillea bushes and hibiscus shrubs. Lemongrass, turmeric, and cilantro did well in the tropics. Jasmine, ginger, and angel's trumpets, too. The more the better. The plants would help with soil erosion and anchor the house to the hillside. It had been so long since she planted something. She began to make a mental list but was interrupted by Colin and the architect Arne Hasselqvist dragging sticks across the dirt.

"The foundation would need to be built on the rock like this," Arne explained, gesturing.

"What do you think, Anne?" Colin scratched a smattering of red bites at his neck.

"The veranda of the house must face the sea." Anne turned to Willy May. "Don't you agree?"

Willy May looked over the cliffside. The waves tumbled on the white sands below. The wind swept up from the feathered spray and brought with it the echo of dolphins and the scent of algae. In a blink, she could see it: her ivory tower. She would tier it like a wedding cake and crown it with flowers. It would be everything she never had in England or Texas. *She* would be everything she wasn't there, too. A home to be proud of. A sanctuary. She would bring her daughters.

"Yes, facing the sea. But not just one veranda — three, at least," she said.

Anne raised an eyebrow.

"A terrace. Multilayered. With a glittering pool right on the edge. I want this house to be unlike anything that's been before."

Anne smiled and nodded. "Did you hear her, Oliver?"

"It's ambitious." Designer Oliver took off his hat and batted it to cool himself.

"Good thing this is an island of ambition," said Anne.

"A crew up here won't be easy work," he replied, "but I have a design in mind."

He began making a foot trail of how the

house would be set.

Colin spotted ripe mangoes dangling from a tree and instructed Kenton to fetch them for a snack.

"So, do you like it?" he asked Willy May. "This is one of the few times I've not had an American give a rowdy opinion!"

"I like it," Willy May said simply. "It's paradise as it was intended without the riffraff of the polluted world."

"Colin only allows beautiful people on the island. Anyone wishing to buy land must submit a photograph for his approval." Anne laughed alone.

Willy May ran her hand through her wavy hair so that it fluffed at the crown. She pulled her shoulders back out of habit and stood as tall as her five-foot-two-inch frame would allow.

"Sorry to burst your bubble, but my beauty queen days are long behind me," she said.

"Honey," Colin feigned a Southern accent, "money is always beautiful."

Willy May thought his imitation quite good and somehow, more befitting than his British accent.

"*Beauty* is deep and abiding. A blessing and a curse. It's in my family lineage, you see. Inherited from the Wyndham side —

48

passed down by my grandmother Pamela to two of her sons, my uncles Bim and Stephens."

"And your father?" asked Willy May.

"Skipped," said Colin. "But it picked right up again with his progeny."

Willy May's eyes rolled instinctively, and she feigned interest in a passing gull laughing overhead.

Kenton sliced the mangoes into cubes. The yellow flesh protruded from the skin like teeth. The cloying ripeness stuck to everything. Colin tore a piece free and ate.

"I like my fruit a little softer." He licked the juice from his lips before continuing, "The physical features don't entirely matter."

At first, she thought he meant the mango but quickly realized he'd returned to his philosophical soliloquy.

"Beauty is a separate quality. It's the essence of original paradise. It holds the power of destruction and creation. God is beauty incarnate, and we are made in God's image, according to the Scriptures. So why not an island exclusively of it?"

"But beauty is subjective. Who decides what is and isn't?" asked Willy May.

Colin chuckled to himself. "Those in power decide, of course. The universe is like a giant clock. Beauty abides by the same rule as time. It can't help but move forward according to chronological nature. A rose buds, blooms, and withers. That's its science and its magic. I've never been one to partition the two. They coexist as two sides of a balanced scale.

"So, simply apply the same universal rule: We have the beautiful on one side and everybody else on the other. The saved and the damned. Them and us. Balance. See?"

It was madness, but before she could reply, Anne called her to the rock precipice.

"Willy May" — she gestured — "look."

The hovering sun reflected rippling gold flames in the bay. They stood together in silence, watching the sea extinguish the light, glimmer by glimmer. The end of day. The beginning of night.

A blink before the sun disappeared, a fluorescent green flash on the horizon, caught her eye.

"What was that?" she asked Anne.

"Mustique's 'good night.' It's a mirage. A bona fide one. If you stick around, you'll see it every night." Anne smiled. "There's a kernel of truth to even the most beguiling things. Colin's not entirely off. We're all trying to attain the unreachable. Is it a piece of nirvana or everlasting beauty? I'm not sure.

But Mustique's as good a place as any to give it a go."

True, thought Willy May, *but what was the price?* And this time, she didn't mean money.

The last of the sun dipped into the water. From hidden nooks rose tiny living embers.

"Fireflies," whispered Willy May.

"Yes." Anne reached out a palm to one hovering between them. "It's the height. Nothing but mosquitoes down at sea level."

"I'll name it after them."

"Too late, Mustique beat you to it. It's the French for 'mosquito.'"

"No, not the mosquitoes." She stomped the dirt with a foot. "I'll call this Firefly."

Anne nodded with approval. "Princess Margaret is calling her home Les Jolies Eaux — 'the beautiful waters.' English is the official language here, but French makes everything sound so much more *magnifique, oui?*"

"It does."

She turned her gaze to Princess Margaret's villa, where the white walls caught the rising moon and glowed.

"Then that settles it. We'll all be neighbors soon," Anne went on. "Princess Margaret is coming for her winter visit. She's officially moving in — bringing her things over. Well, not everything. Her husband, Tony, the Earl of Snowdon, he's staying behind."

With that, she turned to the rest of the group. "Let's get back to the Cotton House. I need a soak before dinner." She eyed the armpit stains on Colin's shirt and wriggled her nose. "Everyone could benefit from the same."

When they returned from the plot, Willy May found Davey sitting casually on the veranda with a hot-pink cocktail in hand.

"I didn't take you for a Pink Lady drinker."

He pushed the drink toward her. "The locals call it sorrel. They make it from fermented roselle hibiscus, ginger, cloves, and rum. They say it's good for digestion."

Two empty glasses sat beside the one in his hand. He noted her gaze.

"The first two were medicinal. This one is pure pleasure." He raised the glass and gulped. "So," he asked, "how was it?"

"I think I'm going to stay awhile."

Davey nodded. "I thought you might. I saw the shine in your eye." He stood with a slight list to the left. "Ronnel and I will take the early ferry back to Port tomorrow. Need anything before we leave you?"

"No."

Everything she owned, everything she

needed, was on *Otrera.* Except for two things.

"Actually, will you send a telegram to my daughters when you get back to Trinidad?"

HAVE NEW HOME ON MUSTIQUE ISLAND. ARNE HASSELQVIST IS BUILDING. I'M HOLDING THE DOOR OPEN FOR YOU. LOVE, MUM

CHAPTER 4
TANGLED

Willy May had insomnia that night. Her mind wheeled on the decision to stay and how much of her savings it would cost. The divorce settlement had provided a sizable nest egg. Minus the cost to build *Otrera,* she'd touched very little of it during her three-year sail. She needn't worry about the girls. They were taken care of through the Michael family's trust fund. So, on the one hand, what else was she to do with the money if not establish herself somewhere with it? On the other, the sum cost of the plot, plus construction materials, plus labor, could snowball into something bigger than her ability to manage. It was a risk but such was life. The probability of going broke was just as likely as being hit by lightning and sinking in her boat. She juggled the pros and cons, cons and pros, back and forth until she felt nauseated from the topsy-turvy thinking.

The heat of the island didn't help. She hadn't been able to breathe and felt as though she'd been poached like a pear.

Outside her window, nightjars squawked. Frogs croaked. Bats clicked. Furry hutias whistled from the branches. It was louder than the London Zoo. In delirium, she rifled through her medicine kit and found a sleeping pill. It did the trick — too well.

At quarter to noon the next day, she was still asleep in her guest bungalow. A rapping on the front door forced her up from her bed.

"Coming," she muttered.

She hadn't a robe nearby, so she twisted the sheet around her.

A lithe island woman puckered her lips in hello. She wore a crisp uniform. Her dark skin was accented by a shock of white hair combed back in a neat bun at the nape of her neck.

"I didn't mean to disturb you, ma'am. I'm Candace, one of the housekeepers. I'll be attending to you during your stay." She cleared her throat. "Your breakfast has turned to lunch. I worried."

"Please, come in. I'm sorry," said Willy May. "I couldn't sleep last night. The heat."

The woman's large brown eyes took in her bedraggled sheet. "May I?"

Willy May stepped aside. With calculated dexterity, she opened the north and southeast windows, and closed all the others. A cool, briny breeze flooded the stagnant room. Willy May turned into the air current headlong. The sheet swept back, exposing her body, but for once in a very long time, she didn't move to cover herself.

In her youth, she'd celebrated her curves and narrows. She'd learned to accentuate them from the pinup girls and actresses she admired. It had been empowering to show a bit of cleavage here, a glimpse of a thigh there. That changed after Hilly and Joanne were born. Harry had pointed out her *wobbly bits.* He suggested she might do well to join a gymnasium like the one to which his mother belonged.

The older she got the more her mind chose what it wished to recall without her having a say. This, for example: she remembered the *wobbly bits,* but not the sound of Harry's voice saying it. Strange.

She shook off the memory and the shame of not remembering better. The breeze against her bare skin felt like a hundred butterflies. Free.

Candace pointed to the shower. "You best get in while the water pressure is good. It'll go to a trickle by midafternoon when the kitchen begins preparing dinner."

Willy May wasn't accustomed to being waited on. Candace's demeanor was so courteous that she couldn't imagine not doing exactly what she said. Willy May didn't want to offend her.

In the time it took to suds and rinse herself, Candace had made the bed, folded the towels neatly, swept the bungalow, replenished the vase with pink ginger flowers, and vanished. Willy May thought she'd left for good but then she returned, pushing through the bungalow door backside first.

"Your meal, ma'am."

A tray of fried eggs, sliced ham, pineapple rings, a short pitcher of milk, and a bowl of dry cereal. She placed it down on the coffee table between the rattan chairs.

Still in her towel, Willy May sat and picked a purple O from the bowl. "What are these?"

"Sir GrapeFellow cereal," said Candace. "Colin has it flown in."

"Odd."

Willy May forked a flimsy piece of egg. It was cold, congealed, and smacked of lighter fluid from the stove. She couldn't blame the cook. The meal had been made hours before when the rest of the household took their breakfasts. She set down her fork and poured the carafe of milk over the purple

O's. One sour bite, and she spit them back into the bowl.

"The milk's gone off."

Candace lifted the pitcher to her nose, sniffed, and nodded. "I keep telling them, fresh milk got no chance on Mustique." She went to the window and threw it out. "Powdered. That's all I give Ada."

Willy May ate the pineapple but had little appetite. "I have two daughters. Hilly and Joanne. Is Ada your daughter or granddaughter?"

"Not by blood, but family just the same."

Candace poured tea that had been steeping and handed her the cup. Willy May accepted it gratefully.

"I never carried a child of my own," Candace confessed. "I married a good man, God rest his soul, and he loved me enough to make up for the lack." She pursed her lips briefly again.

Willy May swallowed her tea. "Oh? I'm sorry, I assumed . . ."

When you assume, you make an ASS out of U and ME, the proverb came to mind. Profanity was an excellent mnemonic for elementary school spelling bees. More than three decades later, the message rang even truer.

"Ada came to me as a baby. She's fifteen

now," said Candace.

"I remember when my girls were that age — it can be challenging."

Candace pushed the plate closer to Willy May. "Eat the ham. It's got vitamins and keeps off the mosquitoes."

Willy May wasn't sure if that was medical science or an old wives' tale, but she ate the ham.

"I hope I get the chance to meet her."

"It's an island. We're all tangled together . . . in knots, one could argue." Candace hesitated briefly before continuing, "Ada helps me after school." She picked up the full tray. "Tomorrow, I'll bring banana buns and papaya from the staff breakfast. You try that and see what you think."

"Thank you," said Willy May.

Candace smiled deferentially and left.

Willy May didn't hurry to finish her tea or to dress. She thought about Candace's response: *We're all tangled together.* She wondered what exactly she meant.

That afternoon, there came a knock on the door. Willy May was finishing her day log on a piece of Cotton House embossed paper, a force of habit. She was dressed by then with her hair combed smooth and a swipe of lipstick. Despite the fashion trend toward makeup-less, bra-less women's emancipation, Willy May appreciated the support of a girdle. She liked the way she looked with rouge on her face and welcomed all things Revlon. She didn't believe that liberation meant she had to go without her favorite accoutrements. It meant that she was free to decide for herself.

Hilly and Joanne had tried on Flower Power briefly. "Hippies in heels," she called them. Hilly contracted impetigo following a free-spirit assembly at Hyde Park. Seven days of infection oozing from her arms, she quickly crossed over to soap, clean clothes, and topical antibiotics.

"I only really like the music and rainbow peace signs," Joanne had innocently told her.

Willy May assured her that she could still fully enjoy the Who and the Beatles without psychedelics. It had been her roundabout way of asking if they'd experimented with drugs.

Hilly had remained notably silent.

While they were with their tutor the next day, Willy May went through Hilly's bureau and found a plastic bag with four cigarettes rolled inside a set of underwear. Hiding things was not one of Hilly's strong suits.

Willy May broke the cigs over the toilet and flushed the leaves, then left the knickers unfurled in the drawer. They both went on without mentioning it.

They were only cigarettes. It wasn't like she'd found illegal substances. *That,* she would've really done something about.

Willy May did not condone recreational drugs. She'd seen how quickly one became five and then ten. Her father had been a hardworking, proud Texan who loved his country, his pickup truck, and apple pie à la mode. But then he hurt his back and the doctor prescribed a "salt pill" to help manage the pain. Benzedrine. By the time Willy May left home, he couldn't go a day without his tablets. He was jittery all the time and prone to flares of irrational anger. He spent most of his wakeful hours collecting newspaper clippings related to the war, convinced there were secret Nazi conspiracists in Limestone County planning to take over America. So consumed was he by his Benzedrine-induced delusion and persistent back stiffness, he barely worked. Her mother took on an extra job to make ends meet and nursed her husband's addiction like an overwrought dog that was only calmed when you fed it treats.

Who could blame Willy May for falling in

love with a self-controlled, confident brewery magnate? But the solution to one extreme was not the other extreme. Soon enough, she'd realized her mistake. Willy May wanted to believe that life could be balanced between the two, but she had witnessed little proof of that equilibrium. One couldn't be a little bit dry or a little bit wet, a little bit sober or a little bit drunk. Not really, right?

So perhaps she should've made a bigger deal over the matter, confronted Hilly or, at the very least, told Harry so he could. But motherhood, like marriage, was a continual replay of how it could've been done differently. If she believed in reincarnation, she would've made a mental note to try the opposite in her next life: discovered the wrong, made a clamorous scene, threatened, punished, and then moved along knowing that the lesson was learned. Maybe she should've been more of *a force to be reckoned with,* as her own mother had described her father. Maybe that would've resulted in a family who didn't leave her as soon as an opportunity presented itself. Harry for another woman. Hilly, jet-setting across Europe. Joanne to Mother Michael's alma mater.

She wondered if every woman grappled with the gnawing feeling that she could've been a better daughter, a better wife, a better mother . . . just *better.* What she knew for certain was that men were encouraged to confidently act and never second-guess, even when they really ought to have. Colin Tennant was showing himself to be a prime example.

"Ma'am?" a voice called. "Mr. Colin asked that I bring you fresh flowers."

"Oh?" Willy May was surprised. Candace had just brought her pink ginger.

She opened the door to a wisp of a girl with star freckles on her cheeks, hazel eyes, and copper curls pulled into a ponytail. She carried a nosegay of white frangipani.

"Hello, I'm Ada." She held up the flowers. The honey scent perfused the air between them. "Plumeria are my favorite. I hope you like them, too."

There was an innate sparkle about her that made Willy May exhale in reply — a kind of laugh with no sound.

"I do. Thank you, but" — she pointed to the vase — "Candace just brought me those."

Ada nodded. "Yes, those were the morning flowers. These are the evening ones. Mr. Colin says there's nothing so depressing as a dying flower so we are to change them twice a day."

63

"I see," said Willy May . . . even though she thought it nonsensical. But that was entirely Colin.

Ada went to the vase, took out the pink ginger flowers, and slipped in the white ones with yellow centers. "Besides, plumeria smell strongest at night."

"They do?"

"Yes, to attract the moths, you know."

Willy May didn't. She thought the saying was *moths to a flame,* not *moths to a flower.* She supposed anything was possible on Mustique, though.

"Well, it's nice to meet you, Ada."

Ada beamed briefly and then went on straightening the room in the exact manner as Candace a few hours before.

Willy May stood awkwardly aside. She didn't think a girl Ada's age should be attending to strangers. She should be at home, reading fashion magazines and complaining of boredom. That was what her girls had done in England. She didn't know what girls here did.

She cleared her throat. "It's awfully hot. Reminds me of Texas. Is it always like this?"

"I've never left Mustique so I can't compare." Ada shrugged.

"You've never left the island?" Willy May knew that kind of isolation. If not for Harry, she might still be in the same house, same town, same *same*. An island in the middle of Texas.

"Not that I can remember, at least," said Ada. "I came to Mustique when I was a baby. I was left at the clinic and Naomi, she works there, called Mama Candace asking if she knew of any pregnant women at the Cotton House. Mama Candace is from St. John's but came to work on Mustique when word got around that the Tennants were offering full-time staff housing in addition to wages. She knew everybody living on payroll at the Cotton House and nobody was expecting a child. So, they figured my birth mother must've come over from one of the other islands.

"The only thing they found on me was a name pinned to my blanket: *Adaili*. It's from the Arawak legend of the sun god. Technically, it's a boy's name. It could be my father's but nobody knew any Adailis. So, I became Ada."

Ada spoke with neither pride nor shame. Her life story was the way it was, and she was who she was. Simply Ada. She wasn't looking for someone to give her answers to unanswerable questions. It gave Willy May hope that perhaps on Mustique, she could be simply Willy May.

"I would like to travel abroad," Ada continued. "One day."

Willy May knew that feeling, too — being on the cusp of adulthood, yearning to grasp beyond without knowing how.

"Well, maybe we can help each other. I've been a lot of places, but I'm putting down roots here. Building my home, Firefly, on the beach cliff overlooking Britannia Bay. I'll tell you anything you want to know about traveling and you can give me tips about living on Mustique. Does that sound like a deal?"

"Yes, ma'am."

"Good. I'm going to need a guide."

Ada smiled, showing off a dimple in one of her cheeks, and Willy May thought her even lovelier for it.

CHAPTER 5
THE NATURE OF GIFTS

The islanders and colonizers scuttled back and forth between the Cotton House and the docks, between the bungalows and the kitchen, between the old sugar mill and the vegetable gardens. Even Arne's construction crew stopped work on Firefly in anticipation of Princess Margaret's arrival.

All were put to royal preparation: trim the lawns, dust the furniture, shake the rugs, polish the silver, shine the crystal . . . and that was just at the Cotton House. Colin also had a number of entertainment venues constructed, stages and sound systems. Portions of Macaroni Beach had been swept so clean that it looked like shag carpeting. Elaborate tents were pitched.

"I want the island to be a carnival!" Colin declared.

Oliver suggested that they string the trees with fairy lights. Colin loved the idea, but they would've had to order the lights months ago. There was really no way to come by them at such short notice. Despite the implausibility, the fairy light rumination went on for over an hour at dinner.

Finally, Anne said, "The Princess knows it isn't bloody Christmas. Don't be daft, Colin."

And that was enough to pull him from his compulsive banter. He moved on to the flowers and food. He had an arsenal of blooms brought over from a greenhouse in Trinidad: lilies, gerberas, violets, amaryllis, chrysanthemums, orchids, and heaps of perfect roses — a tribute to Princess Margaret's middle name, Rose.

George stocked the kitchen pantry from the Cotton House vegetable garden, chicken coop, and local anglers.

"Should we serve fish?" Colin fretted on the heels of the fairy lights.

"It's an island. Of course we serve fish," said Anne. "So long as it isn't fishy."

"No fishy fish, George! Do you hear?"

No response from the kitchen.

Colin continued in his mental checklist, "We have plenty of Famous Grouse whiskey. So, if the food isn't to the Princess's liking, a drink will suffice. Oh, if only we had those fairy lights . . ."

"Stop twittering like a goose. It will all be

perfectly as it should be. You're complicating things for the sake of spectacle and there's nothing so distastefully common." Anne dropped her spoon in her half-eaten dish of vanilla pudding. "Princess Margaret is coming here for peace. You'd do well to give it to her — give us all some."

"I think it sounds lovely, Colin," said Hugo's wife.

Colin's business partner Hugo had wed a second time to a cheerful young woman named Jinty, the cousin of his ex-wife, Penelope. Penelope and his three children remained in England, while he and Jinty had relocated (aka been socially exiled) to Mustique. Arne's wife, Anita, had explained the forked family tree and skipped the details of the forking.

"You know how that goes," she'd said.

It tore at Willy May. Jinty was the other woman while Willy May had been the faithful wife . . . until she became a divorcée. Now they were equally scandalous.

"It's late. I'm going to bed." Anne rose from the table. "I don't want to hear another word about fairy lights."

The wives followed her out, while the husbands took to the patio for cigars. Willy May sat alone at the table and continued to eat her pudding.

She'd been spending her days at Firefly's construction site or with Candace and Ada in her bungalow, laughing and telling stories. Candace and Ada had been so helpful in teaching her the day-to-day know-how of living on Mustique. How to: spray a mixture of vinegar and soap to keep off the mosquitoes. How to: plait her hair to keep cool. How to: place peacock feathers in jars by the windows to scare off lizards.

In return, Willy May showed them how to: tie a Hercules knot. How to: add starch to depleted sugar jars to make the sweetness last longer — a trick she'd learned from her mother and used during the war rationing years. How to: dance the Mashed Potato. Willy May knew these lessons were less practical compared to theirs, but Candace and Ada seemed to enjoy them, nonetheless.

Sometimes, when Ada tilted her head just so or scratched her cheek with her knuckles, Willy May saw Hilly or Joanne. It was the way she moved, limbs lanky and free, that reminded Willy May of the girls when they were younger. Ada and Candace actually felt like friends. So, while she ate her meals and socialized with the upper crust, they were the company she longed for.

The delineation of power made it impossible for her to know if they genuinely liked her or were kind out of duty; but she found herself wanting them to like her. The relational paradox could not be stamped out. Her mother-in-law had been adamant about having household staff. Growing up, her parents had been the household staff. She knew well the impenetrable wall between employer and employee. There was a boundary. No matter which side of the divide you were on, scaling that wall was tricky.

When Candace had been occupied preparing the sovereign cottages the day prior, Ada had brought the afternoon tea and fresh flowers. Willy May insisted the girl stay and have a sultana scone. Soon enough, Ada was telling her about the preparations.

"They wash the Princess's towels and robes with Persil laundry detergent and rinse them with rosewater. Not once, but *thrice,* on Colin's orders."

According to Ada, the items were then pressed with hot irons and spritzed with essence of lavender. Tins of digestive biscuits and ornately shaped marzipan were laid out in a long line on the royal dinette alongside wine, liquor, and fizzy tonics. Under the sunlight, the bottles reflected a rainbow across the floor and up the walls.

"The bottles are even prettier than Mr.

Colin's last birthday party when cannons shot confetti up to the sky!" Ada had gushed. "We made a game of it — catch a piece, make a wish, and blow it out to sea."

Now, thinking back on the conversation, Willy May remembered a jar of colored sea glass that she'd collected from various beaches. She'd fetch it from *Otrera*. Ada didn't need royal bottles or cannons to catch a wish — just someone to encourage her passion for the world. The sun, the moon, and Ada herself would do the rest.

"You about finished, ma'am?" asked George from the door.

His forehead was dewy. His eyes were red from the heat of the day and the burn of his stove. He looked tired, and she realized she was holding him back from finishing his chores and closing the kitchen.

She brought her empty dish to him. If her parents taught her anything, it was to clean your plate.

"Thank you, George. That was the best vanilla pudding I've ever had. And please, call me Willy May."

He brightened. "It's my *maman*'s recipe."

"She taught you well. I tried making box pudding for my daughters once, but it was runny and completely inedible."

"Use coconut milk. That's my secret."

"Aw, so that's it!"

It was a small thing. Vanilla pudding with a fresh ingredient made all the difference.

A new moon cast no light, so she walked by starlight down to the dock, being careful to circumvent the manchineel grove. It was a surprisingly shorter and easier walk than the mule carts let on, with all their whirring and sputtering.

The moored *Otrera* bobbed empty on the waves. The low snore of its hull rubbed against the dock piling, calling her. She lit an oil lamp inside and snuggled into the hammock bed. The weight of sky above and water below seemed to balance with her as the fulcrum. Her boat still felt so much safer than anywhere else. The ability to shove off from anything displeasing, to turn a rudder and sail in the opposite direction of danger, to protect herself inside the vessel she'd built. She'd never been lonely on *Otrera* but she had been lonesome. She missed the sound of her girls' laughter and the smell of salt in their tangles of hair.

Hilly and Joanne had shared a bunk on the *Stingray* and liked it so much that they insisted on pushing their twin beds together back home in Cheltenham. Harry and his mother thought it peculiar, but Willy May didn't see the harm. Sometimes at night, she would leave her cold bed and crawl into theirs, where she'd hold a sleeping girl in each arm. *You are mine,* she would think to herself. The words filled her with such bliss that she'd point her toes until her calves cramped. Silent joy and pain knotted together.

Expressing one's sentiments was not the forte of her Texan kin or her husband's. She didn't know how to communicate love without it sounding ridiculous to herself. The closest thing she could think to *I love you forever* was *you are mine forever.*

But as with every living thing, forever was incalculably long and unexpectedly short at once. She had not been able to keep anyone forever. Hilly and Joanne had grown to see each other's strengths and covet what they lacked.

For Hilly, it was the very thing she cherished about her sister: Joanne's unswerving loyalty and congeniality. For Joanne, it was Hilly's beauty and passion. Both were right and both were wrong. Willy May tried to make them appreciate what they each possessed, but appreciation couldn't be coerced any more than morality. When suddenly, they weren't little girls anymore and their minds were fixed, they believed what they believed about themselves, each other, and the world's view of both.

They separated their beds, and eventually launched on their own courses. The space between them continually expanded. She hoped that by rooting herself on Mustique now, she might give them a shared tether, a place to belong.

The hammock swung gently with the boat's rise and fall. A rhythm so familiar, it nearly seemed her own breathing. She longed to stay and sleep, but Candace would come early with breakfast. She'd worry if Willy May wasn't in the bungalow and her worry would trickle down to Ada. It was strange to feel attachment after knowing them so brief a time. But everything on the island seemed magnified. One of the sun's better tricks.

She pulled herself up, ignoring the twinge in her knees, and found the jar of sea glass: blue, green, coral, clear, and colors so in-between that she couldn't say what they were. She held it to the lamplight and softly jangled the stones. A kaleidoscope spun on the ceiling and round the walls. A glossy flash from the corner cabinet caught her eye. A figurine made of polished volcanic rock that the girls had given her on the Mothering Sunday they'd spent in Greece. Out of the many gods and goddesses, they'd selected Otrera for her and to honor that, she'd christened her boat after the goddess.

She collected the statue and the ship's journal. Writing had become a daily ritual. It was difficult to sleep without emptying her head of the who's and what's and where's. Since arriving, she'd been scribbling on stationery from the bungalow's desk. The pages would be slipped into her journal in chronological order. Skipping dates made her anxious. A sailor's superstition. The ship might've stopped moving but time hadn't.

With her arms full of treasures, she snuffed out the lamp and made her way back to the Cotton House grounds.

"There she is!" she greeted Ada the following afternoon.

She'd spent the morning watching Anne and Colin battle it out in an aggressive game of lawn darts while Paul Simon LPs echoed across the manicured grounds. Oliver and Arne showed her the Firefly architecture plans during lunch, and she'd been in her bungalow waiting for Ada ever since.

"I brought you some things." She presented the sea glass and the statuette.

"Otrera is queen of the Amazons, a tribe of warrior goddesses. She was born an orphan in Greece and became a housewife in an arranged marriage. Her husband mistreated her so she trained herself in secret to use the tools and weapons of men. Then she taught those skills to other wives in her village. One day, Otrera and the women rebelled, overthrew their husbands, and went from village to village liberating other women. They were so strong in number that they moved together to a new land."

Ada held the rock goddess close, examining the details of her face.

"My daughters gave this Otrera to me. I named my boat after her."

Willy May had talked about Hilly and Joanne so much that it was almost like they were here — out on a swim or collecting coconuts from the grove.

"They'll come to Mustique soon," she told Ada, told herself. "Maybe for Mothering Sunday."

"Mothering Sunday?" asked Ada.

"Yes, they have Mother's Day on Mustique, right?"

"We do, but . . ." Ada shook her head. "I can't take this gift."

Willy May needed to brush up on her knowledge of gift giving in the Caribbean. "Really, my daughters wouldn't mind, if that's what you're worried about. And that's the nature of gifts, yeah? What we do with

77

them is what matters. I want Otrera to be yours."

Ada looked into her face, searching for what: assurance, kindness, authenticity?

"Thank you," she said after a cautious beat and then, "If the nature of a gift is that I do what I wish with it, then I wish to give it back to you." She handed the statue back and Willy May felt a sting of rejection. Then, without warning, Ada leaned into Willy May. A side hug. Brief but nonetheless, surprising.

Despite being American, Willy May had never been a hugger. Her own parents had been patters. A pat on the back was praise. A pat on the knee was comfort. A pat on the hand was love. Even in the intimate ways between husband and wife, Harry was reserved. The dry English peck was standard practice. The girls were keen to the fact that their father was a person who preferred his space. She didn't blame Harry entirely. She'd witnessed firsthand that despite doting on her son, Mother Michael was notably reserved in her tactile affections. She rarely touched her son or her granddaughters. Willy May couldn't recall ever being skin to skin with her mother-in-law. Not even for a handshake. She'd grown accustomed to the dearth of physical tenderness . . . which made this feel rather remarkable. Especially given the situation. On the surface, it did not appear an appropriate context for affection — a gift rebuffed — and yet, the magnitude of Ada's gesture nearly brought her to tears.

She took it as a sign that a person could change and maybe, hopefully, the transformation had already begun.

CHAPTER 6
ROYAL WELCOME

February 1972

"Margot is a clever one. Coming before Valentine's Day to avoid Tony," Colin mused on the veranda the day prior to Princess Margaret's arrival.

Anne had invited Willy May to tea, and she was surprised to find it was only the three of them. A series of articles had appeared in the British press weeks before making scandalous accusations on the state of the Princess's marriage. Colin's lawyer had shipped a box of newspapers and Captain Tannis had just delivered them. Already oxidizing around the edges from sea air and days of travel, they unfurled across the lunch table in a patchwork quilt of venomous headlines.

The stories alleged everything from domestic violence to extramarital affairs. The Princess and the Earl of Snowdon were a hot topic and that, as they all knew, displeased Queen Elizabeth II. There was friction between the sisters. Only the Princess could stare down the Queen and light a cigarette. Because Margaret knew that despite all she did or didn't do, and surpassing all other relationships, Elizabeth would be on her side. It was the unsaid of the thing. They were apples from the same tree — different colors, naturally.

Willy May hadn't any siblings and so had known from the start that she wanted multiple children. She'd ignored Harry's appeal for them to wait until Hilly was school age before having a second child. She worried that she was a sunflower, blooming once and never again. A weed in masquerade. She got pregnant with Joanne as soon as Hilly was weaned.

Much to her dismay, her firstborn had not taken warmly to a sibling. Hilly either cried for attention whenever her baby sister was in the room or ignored her altogether. It wasn't until Joanne's first birthday that Hilly seemed to settle into the idea of being a sister. It meant twice the fairy cakes, tiara parties, and a sidekick to confide in when no one else was paying attention. After that, they got on like sisters should, and Willy May was relieved to see it.

She'd wanted to have a third baby and

would've done so if Harry hadn't moved into a separate bedroom. He said it was so he could sleep. Willy May was up every few hours to nurse Joanne. She hadn't let it trouble her. Even Queen Elizabeth and Prince Philip slept in separate rooms. That was the norm for people of a certain social status, which she was now. Her daughters made her irrevocably part of the Michaels' ancestral tree, and her marriage had never been happier. Harry and she came together through the girls, if only occasionally in their nuptial bed. The whole of their family's love was greater than the sum of its parts.

Still, she yearned for another child and often speculated that the sibling dynamic would've changed had there been an eldest, middle, and youngest instead of an eldest and youngest, first and last. She thought the same for Princess Margaret and Queen Elizabeth. Had there been one more sibling, perhaps it would've balanced the scales of justice. Then disagreements wouldn't have come down to one against the other.

"Princess Margaret is not avoiding Tony," Anne snapped at Colin. "He declined the invitation. She's doing exactly as she has done every other winter. Don't make it more dramatic than it is."

"Perhaps we should invite Picasso." Colin

smirked. "They've always got on terribly well."

Anne frowned. "You would have the Queen come down on us? Her private secretary is already insinuating that we are the bohemian influence — well, *you*, Colin."

"Bohemian? I'm not sure if I ought to be offended or flattered. Bohemia is *en vogue*, my dear."

They spoke to each other as if Willy May were not present. She fidgeted with the straw in her pineapple juice, hoping to call attention to herself and remind them. Gossip was ugly. She no more liked it here than in England.

If Princess Margaret and her husband were having affairs, it was none of her business. She felt strongly that the only dalliances one should speak of were the ones under your own roof. That was a big enough fishbowl. No need to cast lures into the pond.

"I'm drowning out here," Anne said suddenly. "This climate is diabolical." She folded up one of the newspapers and used it to fan herself.

Willy May was at the bottom of her glass and accidentally slurped. The sound caught Colin's attention.

"Willy May." He turned to her. "We asked

you here to ensure that you're comfortable."

She'd been a guest in the Cotton House bungalow longer than she liked. "I'm hoping the construction on Firefly moves quickly. I appreciate your hospitality."

Anne waved a magnanimous hand. "Of course. But this is regarding protocol. Have you ever been received by a royal before?"

"No."

"I didn't think so," Anne continued. "It's quite simple. The Princess comes to Mustique to be anonymous. It's the only place on earth where she's guaranteed the right to simply be. We are committed to confidentiality. Nothing she does or says is repeated. No one she engages with is revealed. Here, she is an ordinary woman of preternatural esteem. Breach of trust would result in destructive consequences. Do you understand?"

Willy May nodded. Her glass was empty, but she was still thirsty. Sweat beaded on her upper lip, and she tasted the salt of it.

"Good. I knew you would," said Anne. "Oh — and address her as 'the Princess' or 'ma'am,' but only after she has addressed you first, and curtsy, of course, but that's *sine qua non,* right?"

"Sine what?"

"It's Latin — for something one absolutely

must do."

Willy May didn't think curtsying belonged in the same category as breathing and eating (in Latin or English) but she'd play along.

"Is walking backward when exiting the room *sine qua non,* too?"

Subjects were never to turn their back on a sovereign. It was an earnest question. Anne found it humorous.

"Only if you wish to fall off the veranda!" She laughed and wiped tears from the corners of her eyes. "Willy May, you are a hoot. Princess Margaret is not one for the pomp of court. She leaves that for her sister."

"The Princess is more like us. Only *not* like us," Colin chirped. "You'll love her. We all do!"

"She's arriving on tomorrow's ferry. We're assembling at noon for the welcome."

Like so much of what Anne said, innocuous statements doubled as commands. Willy May was expected to be there, and at the strike of noon the following day, she was.

"What in God's name?" she gasped.

"I know," said Jinty, Hugo's wife. "The first time I saw, I thought it a film set for a new Hitchcock." She stood in the shade of a palm tree, smoking a cigarette.

On the beach before them was nearly every Mustique islander dressed in mix-matched Edwardian costumes. Men in corseted gowns that flared at the waist like lily trumpets and top hats embellished with red begonias. Women in black-and-white-striped trousers, silk blouses, and plumage festooned with peacock feathers. Parasols opened wide like lace jellyfish under the searing sun.

"It's Colin's idea of a royal welcome." Jinty flicked her cigarette ash forward, and then took another long drag.

"They look ridiculous," said Willy May.

A laugh popped up Jinty's throat, emitting a puff of gray. "Don't let Colin hear you." She hid her grin behind her clutched cigarette. "It's rather like a nightmare masquerade, eh?"

Jinty's eyes skimmed the waterline to where Colin stood with Hugo, Arne, and Oliver. Willy May followed her gaze. The men wore the same blazing-white suits that they had when welcoming *Otrera* to dock, winking like shooting stars. Colin flittered from islander to islander, adjusting costumes.

"Why do they do it?" asked Willy May.

"Colin pays them double their daily for the show."

These were people, not puppets, thought Willy May. Candace, Ada, George . . . an island community indulging their crackpot sovereigns. They had to think this farce as deranged as she did.

Anne sat with Arne's wife, Anita, under a beach umbrella facing the water, unengaged with the procession on the beach. The only movement was the flapping of their cream caftans in the breeze.

"Colin likes to buck tradition," Jinty continued. "But deep down, he's really obsessed with it. Hugo says that he had the trunks from a dead cousin brought over from England when the Queen came in sixty-four. He recruited volunteers from the village and paid them to wear the frocks for the Crown. I suppose it was quaint then. The Queen was gracious, as she always is, and Colin thought that meant she approved. Of course, despite what he says, he always gives the Princess equal ceremony as her sister." She shrugged. "And so, tradition was born."

Willy May blinked away from the men in white to the islanders, trussed up in costumes. She couldn't help thinking that if someone else had purchased the island lock, stock, and barrel, none of Colin's mad traditions would exist.

Seeing the ferry, Colin took off his straw hat and waved it wildly, then paced about in the sand shouting, "Curtain up! Let's welcome our lady!"

The ferry chugged into port. As soon as the dockhand tied the rope, Colin gave the signal and a villager with a violin began playing "Rule Britannia."

Up from the deck of the ferry popped three heads: two women and one man. They waved good-naturedly, and Willy May tried to place which one was the Princess. No one looked like the photographs she'd seen in the newspapers.

Finally, a brunette bouffant and a pair of white-rimmed sunglasses rose into sight. The others parted. The residents on the beach formed a greeting line: Anne and Colin, Oliver, Anita and Arne, Hugo and Jinty. No one had told Willy May where to stand so she assumed rank at the end.

"Princess." Colin bowed.

"Welcome back, ma'am." Anne curtsied.

The others did similarly, cascading like dominoes, the last being Willy May, who battled the unaccustomed twist of her knees. If she had to hold the pose one more second, she was sure she'd fall head over tail.

Luckily, Princess Margaret gave a rushed

sigh. "Hello, hello. Enough with that." She cupped her fingers in the air the way one would to an obedient dog: *up, up, up.* Then she leaned forward to kiss Anne's cheek. "You are looking far too well for yourself, darling."

"Said the pot to the kettle," replied Anne.

"Don't say that too loud or some might report that I'm actually enjoying myself." A smirk crossed over the Princess's mouth.

"Are you not, dear heart?" asked Colin.

Princess Margaret scowled. "Of course not. Every paper in England is lambasting me."

"Oh yes, that unpleasantness. I'm so sorry." He hung his head low a beat, but then picked it back up. "Mustique will protect you from that boorishness!"

"Hmm." Princess Margaret turned to Oliver. "Hello, Uncle."

"Your Royal Highness." Oliver took her hand and kissed it.

She cocked her head at him. "I pray you aren't here to spy for your nephew."

He raised an eyebrow. "Only if you wish me to inform your husband of your activities, ma'am darling. My loyalty is consummately to the Crown — and the theater, but I hope you don't hold the latter against me."

Princess Margaret gave a hen cluck.

"Sometimes I wonder if I oughtn't to have married you instead."

Oliver shrugged. "Alas, I hear that from many. But as you know, Princess, my penchant is for an inamora*to*. We would've been a comedy and a tragedy in one act."

"Said like a true thespian." She moved on down the reception line. "Anita, lovely to see you." She kissed her cheek. "And Arne. How's my house?"

"Complete. All it needs is a woman's touch."

"That's why I have Oliver." She walked another pace. "Hello, Hugo."

"Welcome, ma'am."

Jinty curtsied again. "A pleasure to be here during your visit. It feels ever so long since —"

Princess Margaret pushed a windswept strand of hair behind her ear and walked on before Jinty had finished.

"And who is this?" She paused in front of Willy May.

"Our newest resident," said Colin. "May I present —"

"Thank you, but you may not. I think she can present herself. Don't you agree, Miss . . . ?" The Princess extended her hand, and Willy May took it. Her fingers were petal soft and warmer than expected.

90

"I'm Willy May. From Texas." She felt the need to establish her origins.

"Aw, an American. I love the Americans."

"Willy May's late husband was Philip Henry Michael Jr. of the distinguished Michael & Boutler Brewery," said Anne.

"An entrepreneur. Your kind are the true pulse of our global economy. Don't let any of the fusty patricians tell you differently. They'll rally in celebration of a good pint more than their family crests. That's the God's truth of it."

Anne pointed to the construction site on the rocky bluff. "Willy May is building her home there. It's called Firefly."

The construction crew had begun framing. Wooden beams poked through the jungle like chopsticks.

"A neighbor and a beautiful one."

Willy May wasn't sure if she was complimenting the house or her or both.

"We'll have much time to get to know one another now that Les Jolies Eaux is finished." She leaned over her shoulder. "Jean, have the boatman unload the packing crates first. I don't want any of my furniture ruined by salt water."

"Furniture?" Oliver frowned.

"Don't be a spoilsport, Oliver. Just a few things to make me feel at home."

She moved to the beach, where she waved congenially to the islanders: "Thank you all."

Colin skipped to her side. "We decided to go with an avantgarde motif — mixing up the frocks. Do you like?"

"Hmm."

"Oliver says it's the new thing. He's going back to London at the end of the month to work on one of those 'rock operas.' "

"Hmm," she repeated. "Well, I doubt they'll be performing it in a thousand-degree heat." She turned back to the islanders. "I'm very honored! Thank you! Now, please . . ." She leaned into Colin and whispered, "Get them cold water to drink. Half look near to fainting."

Colin clapped his hands. "Refreshments!"

But who was there to serve the servants? A handful of them came from the coconut grove carrying jugs of water and coolers of sodas. Willy May searched for Ada but didn't see her. *Good,* she thought.

The costumed islanders gave a low moan of relief as they packed the antiquated regalia back into the trunks. The violinist nearly walked away still wearing the top hat. One of his friends pointed it out. He took it off, removed the begonia, and set it back into the trunk with the others. Then, carefully, he placed his violin in its case and carried it off — violin in his right hand, begonia in his left. Clearly, they were the most valuable and belonged to him.

"This way, ma'am darling." Colin ushered the Princess toward his cart.

She turned to the group — "See you up" — and then marched on with Colin chattering at her heels.

The rest of the royal party disembarked. Anne introduced Willy May to the entourage: Jean, the Princess's cousin; Janie, wife to *Queen* magazine's owner; and Patrick, the Earl of Lichfield, a professional photographer.

Patrick was sporty lean and handsome as the devil. His hair was flaxen and feathered back against the wind like wheat at full harvest. He stood wide-legged confident in khaki pants and a white cotton shirt as if he'd just debarked an Admiral's Cup–winning ship and not a pedestrian ferry. He gazed at her boldly and smiled, which she could tell was genuine and, therefore, genuinely flattering. It was hard not to be attracted to his kind. The Earl of Lichfield was like the hero on the cover of a romance novel come to life . . . and he knew it.

"Hello, who do we have here?" He extended a hand, and she caught a whiff of smoke and mint, tobacco and aftershave.

"I'm Willy May."

"Willy May?" he repeated, rolling each word over his tongue for a taste. "Brilliant."

"She's an American beauty queen." Anne winked.

"Of course she is." He held a thumb in the air between them, like a painter smudging a line on canvas. "Look at those cheekbones." He lifted a camera and snapped.

"Move along, Patrick. There's plenty of time for that," said Jean. "The boatman needs to unload, and we've got to set up the Princess's temporary quarters while her house is being furnished."

Willy May couldn't imagine what they'd need to do. The staff had been working on the royal cottage for a week. The island men carried the luggage to a flatbed truck while the guests loaded into waiting jeeps. Arne and Oliver stayed on the beach to manage the furniture crates. Patrick stayed behind, too, taking photos of the islanders. Removed of Colin's ancestral trousseau, they laughed and posed naturally, holding up peace signs with their fingers and flexing their biceps for his camera.

Willy May watched Patrick from the jeep until the bush and banana leaves hid him from view. Only then did she turn to see

Anne, Jean, and Janie watching her. Anne cast a side-eye to Jean and then Jean passed it along to Janie.

"She really needed this," said Jean.

Janie nodded. "A breath of fresh air."

"Mustique's specialty," said Jean.

Willy May looked straight ahead, her pulse racing, though she told herself they were talking about the Princess not her.

CHAPTER 7
MACARONI BEACH

The next morning was a Saturday. Ada was
off from school and so came with Candace
at breakfast. They no longer waited for Willy
May to wake. Instead, they entered at
daybreak while the banana buns were still
warm enough to melt butter.

The early smell of them reminded Willy
May of days when her mother would bake
before the Texan sun had begun to scorch.
She'd leave the sourdough breads, fruit
turnovers, and dessert pies on the windowsill to cool so that the sweetness permeated
the house from tin roof to pine floorboards.
Willy May thought of seasons by the smell
of baked fruits. Strawberries and rhubarb in
the spring. Peaches and cherries in the summer. Pecans and apples in the fall. It made
her nostalgic for her childhood in a way that
didn't reflect its reality. The mind, once
again, choosing which parts to skim from
the surface and which to let sink below. She

96

would remind herself that those seasonal bakes were few and far between. Most days, they ate potatoes cooked in the pig tallow not used for candles. Perhaps the sour smell of the everyday made the baking more cherished.

A month after VE Day and two years after she'd left Texas, Willy May received a call from her parents. Despite alarm bells in her mind, her heart had alighted on their voices.

"Mama? Daddy? How did you get this number?"

She imagined them hunched ear to ear over the clunky black handheld in the living room.

"We asked the Guardsmen in Terrell," said her mother. "Told them that Airman Harry Michael married our girl and took her to England, and we needed to get in touch. Wasn't hard to track you down."

It wasn't? Then why hadn't she been worth finding sooner? Years had passed. Harry had not been deployed to the front, but he'd still flown defense missions, leaving her alone in Mother Michael's carriage house for long weeks at a time. She'd often had to bunker down through blackouts, food rationing, and air raids. She could be dead for all they knew.

Tears had welled, and she steeled herself

to keep them in check.

"I wasn't hiding."

She didn't expect an apology. She understood that she'd never get one. She merely wanted her parents to care enough to take the next step — to ask after her, her husband, her new life. She wanted to tell them that she managed the war with Texan courage. She'd planted a victory garden and contributed seven pairs of nylons to the women's auxiliary forces. That was more pairs than her mother had owned in a lifetime. Her marriage bed had Irish lace linens and down pillows, and she ate at a table that once belonged to a duke. She wanted to make them proud. She wanted to feel their pride — their love — across the miles. And later, in private, she wanted to tell her mother about the miscarriages she'd had. She was desperate for advice and motherly reassurance that she wasn't broken.

But what she got was her father: "We need money. Three hundred dollars."

He'd never learned to catch flies with honey.

"We'd pay you back eventually," her mother had said, ever softening his verbal blows.

"We owe property taxes," he'd gone on.

"They'll take our house if we don't pay."

"Right," she'd said. Money. "I can send a check."

The amount didn't matter. She'd tell Harry it was a charitable contribution. Not entirely a lie. Not entirely a truth. The Michaels regularly gave to humanitarian organizations. Her parents' welfare was as human as it got.

"Anything else?" she'd asked.

Please, stay. Say something, she'd thought.

There was a pause and her pulse filled in the beat with expectation.

"No," said her father, followed by a longer pause wherein everyone held their breaths.

"Thank you," her mother exhaled.

"That's what family is for." Willy May had cleared her throat. "You have my contact information now so . . ." She'd left it open.

Maybe this call was the beginning of a broader conversation. So many different elements. They couldn't mix oil and water and expect a cohesive outcome. So, she'd take care of the taxes and the next conversation, they could speak of pleasanter things.

When she hung up, however, she'd felt like a cracked egg on the verge of spilling out of her shell. Harry had come into the room then.

"Who was that?"

"No one. It was nothing. Could we go out for dinner together?" She'd reached for him, but he'd kept his hands in his pockets. Her own slid down his forearms and off.

"Can't tonight. I'm meeting up with friends — old chums from school. Bore you to tears. I won't subject you." He'd kissed the side of her head, practically her ear. "I promise not to be late."

He'd left and she'd stared at the phone for a long hour, broken.

The next time she heard from her parents was via the Limestone County clerk's office eleven years later. The office had sent copies of her parents' death certificates. *Car accident* was listed as the cause. Apparently, a sudden storm had flooded the roads. Their Chevy truck had been swept over an embankment. The certificates came with a notice explaining that all of her parents' belongings had been liquidated to pay off debt. To add insult to injury, the county was requesting an additional payment of $55.39, the outstanding balance. Such a trifling amount in comparison to all she'd lost.

Alone in the butler's pantry with the certificates clutched to her chest, she'd given over to the mournful tears: shock turned to anger turned to regret. But she'd been in the midst of packing for their first family voyage on the *Stingray*. Hilly and Joanne were young and arguing over how many dolls they were each allowed to pack. Harry would be home from work in an hour and her mother-in-law had insisted on hosting a send-off dinner for them later that evening. She hadn't the emotional capacity to introduce and mourn grandparents the girls had never known and never would. Better to stick to the schedule and sail on.

So, as planned, she'd pulled out flour, baking powder, and sugar, and made the batch of breakfast scones to take on the boat. She wouldn't bake again for over a decade. Bread was easier bought. She never sent the $55.39.

Now, the olfactory memory of her mother's kitchen and her own made her eyes water as much as her mouth. She pressed her face into her pillow until the emotion was absorbed.

"Good morning, Miss Willy May," said Ada.

She lifted her head. "Morning." She wiped her eyes of sleep and such.

Candace set the breakfast tray on the coffee table. "Lady Anne says sleeping on your face causes wrinkles. You should sleep facing up."

Willy May grinned. "Do *you* sleep facing up?"

Candace motioned for Ada to take the tea over to Willy May. "Can't say that I do but I always thought wrinkles were a sign of a good life. As a rule, I think it unwise to make rules about sunshine, smiling, or how to sleep. You're lucky to come by those in any amount."

"I put three sugar cubes in," said Ada.

Willy May took the tea and winked. "You know I like it sweet enough to catch flies. Thank you."

Ada smiled.

"What's today's royal agenda?" asked Willy May.

"Do as you please this morning," said Candace. "Princess Margaret stays in bed listening to the radio and reading her newspapers until eleven o'clock. Then she takes a bathtub soak for an hour. I imagine she'll be lunching about one o'clock, if you plan to join."

With that, she gestured to Ada. "Let's leave Miss Willy May to herself now."

Willy May started to object. She had no intention of either sleeping or sitting in her room until noon. But she couldn't think of an excuse to keep them there and thought it equally indulgent to demand that they stay. They were paid staff, not her companions.

So, she let them go, ate, dressed, and took a borrowed mule cart up to Firefly on the dirt road that Arne's construction crew had cleared. The newly opened ground smelled mineral. The roots of the deforested trees stuck out at awkward angles, making the cart's wheels sputter and kick unsteadily.

Arne greeted her at the top of the construction site. "G'morning, Willy May. What are you doing up here?"

She parked and turned off the engine. "I came to help."

"Help?" He scratched his cheek. "I never had a client want to help."

Willy May picked up a hammer from the toolbox and pointed it at Britannia Bay. "I built my ship down there."

She went to the side of an island man lifting a doorframe. Surprising him, she took hold of the other side, leveled it, and nailed it clean with a measured smack.

"She's got a good arm," said the man.

"That's one of the best compliments I've ever received."

"It's your house. You're the boss," said Arne. "Welcome to the crew."

She spent hours beside the men. She'd forgotten how therapeutic working with her hands could be. She was hammering herself into the land and building a home where she might have a chance to do things differently from the past. She imagined Hilly's dark hair blowing in the wind on the balcony; Joanne playing her music in the living room; bumping into each other as they cooked in the kitchen. She dreamed them into every nail and plank. Even the crooked ones.

Two days later, Colin sent the staff round the island to report that Princess Margaret was caught up on sleep and ready for entertainment. Willy May hated to leave Firefly but thought it best to make a good showing. Despite all her maverick bravado, she was a pleaser. She'd always been a woman who deep down longed for acceptance.

Growing up, she'd been overlooked because of her family's poverty and gained praise for her attractive looks. As a wife, she'd been snubbed because of her parentage and earned respect through her daughters. Now, she might've been an expat to all nations, but on Mustique she was acknowledged as someone. Even by Princess Margaret, albeit transitorily.

So, despite her druthers, Willy May put down her tools and took up her beach towel. Three hours into the excursion, the heat of the day had cast a soporific spell. Hugo and Oliver discussed the civil servants strike in Great Britain while Jinty read a Violet Winspear romance. Beneath a fringed beach canopy, the Princess and her ladies-in-waiting appeared to be napping all in a row. It didn't feel odd or out of step when Patrick tapped her shoulder.

"I'm going to take some island photos. Care to come with me?"

Willy May was grateful to do something. She'd never mastered the ability to lounge. It seemed to be a cultured art on Mustique.

"Point the way," she said.

Macaroni Beach was an alabaster cove that curved like a noodle against the sea. The scorch of the dry sand burned bare feet and made the pair bend their path closer to the cooling waters. Willy May and Patrick walked in silence. The cresting waves played a comforting rhythm. His camera clicked out the harmony, lens moving side to side, up and down, ocean to jungle, sand to sky. Like a conductor's wand. He paused while she walked a few paces. When she turned back, he clicked his camera.

"Did you take my photograph?"

"I did," he said. "I'm a better portraitist. The landscape of a person is most interesting to me."

She put a hand on her hip and kicked a leg forward. It happened in the company of attractive men: her beauty pageant pose.

He clicked again.

She raised her hand to block his next shot. "Wait a minute. You asked me to come with you while you took photographs of the beach, not me."

"I lied," he said.

She huffed — or attempted to anyhow.

The flirting surprised her. He was an earl over a decade younger with his pick of beauties. She knew she oughtn't indulge in his flattery. But if their roles were reversed — he, the older divorcé, and she, the young artist — the flirtation would've been accepted, even encouraged. *So why not,* she thought. It wasn't like it would go any further. It felt nice to be attractive and be attracted.

"Indulge me?" he said from behind the camera.

She ran a hand through her windswept flyaway hair.

"Fine. But promise that these are only for you, not for publication. My girls. I don't want them thinking I'm . . ." She scratched her neck, trying to find the right word for whatever it was she didn't want to be thought doing but clearly was.

"Enjoying your life?" asked Patrick.

That was exactly what she didn't want Hilly, Joanne, or anyone else thinking. It was the unsaid Eleventh Commandment, reinforced daily for three decades by the Holy Church of Cheltenham Proper: *Thou shalt not indulge in unearned happiness without recompense.* She knew she needn't abide by it anymore. Harry was gone. But the old ways within a person were hardest to shake.

"I don't think the blue bloods would approve. You know how Colin is about photographs leaking to the press."

"A conspiracy theorist. He thinks cameras *are* the press."

"Exactly. I'm surprised he let you ashore with yours."

"I'm blood. That trumps peerage."

"Ah, yes. I should probably curtsy to you, sir."

He cleared his throat and let the camera lens turn to the sand.

"My mother is Queen Elizabeth's niece. Queen Elizabeth, the Queen Mother."

Willy May nodded. "So your grandmother is the Queen Mother's sister, which makes you . . ." She did the algebraic biology in her head. "The Queen and Princess Margaret's cousin."

He bowed. "At your service."

"So how did you end up a photographer? It seems an occupation beneath someone of your station," she teased.

He shrugged as if shrugging were a definitive answer. "We all do what we feel compelled to, I suppose."

A privileged response, albeit honest.

"Sort of like being here, right?" he said.

"How so?"

He came to her side. Their arms brushed lightly against each other. "If Colin and Anne hadn't felt compelled to buy Mustique, it would belong to someone else, and we'd never know each other."

"I didn't think anyone today could buy an island just for themselves." She swatted a mosquito. "It isn't right, is my point. There are other people to consider. Who did Anne and Colin buy it from?"

"From the three Hazell sisters," Patrick said matter-of-factly. "Come now, you know this story."

She shook her head. No one had told her.

He took a knee in the sand and shot her from below, *click-click*. "The Hazells were a wealthy Creole family from St. Vincent in the mid eighteen hundreds, descendants of an English dynasty."

He circled round behind, *click-click.* "Mustique was passed on to them through their mother's side, cotton and sugar traders. It was abandoned for practically a century. Most of the local people left for the more developed islands."

He brought the camera close to her mouth, *click-click.* "But when the sisters came to collect on their family's inheritance, there was a sudden influx of jobs, commerce started back up, capital began to flow and brought everything back to life."

He stopped to clean the sand from his lens. His eyes finally met hers directly. "The sisters turned Mustique into their private playground. They celebrated holidays here, raced horses, hosted shooting parties, grew elaborate gardens, danced, ate, drank, made love . . ."

The way he said *love,* in that knight-like British lilt, his body smelling of sea and sweat — it washed through her like an ocean wave. Her breath caught.

"Whatever they wished. The sisters didn't adhere to precepts of propriety and didn't judge each other. On Mustique, they lived in the moment as liberated women long before liberation became à la mode."

"If it was all so grand, why'd they leave?" Willy May picked up a shell with vibrant blue striations, wondering if the coloring had come inherently or been achieved through some worldly outside influence.

"Much like everything, time changes us. The island was the same, but it became a financial burden. The Hazell sisters put it on the market and moved to New York. Anne and Colin were visiting Trinidad in 1958 and heard it was for sale. Who has their own island, right? Colin couldn't pass on a chance to live the mythological. Anne relented."

Willy May laughed. It was ludicrous to think that anyone could rightfully set up their own kingdom. It was the twentieth century, for God's sake. Then again . . . the danger was underestimating absurd men.

"Colin's been developing it ever since. Hugo and Arne joined as stockholders a couple years back. Oliver came to design. They formed the Mustique Company to make it lawful and to sell the plots. But Colin can't maintain it all on his own. He needs citizens of the realm."

"Citizens of the what?" She balked and turned to see him slyly grinning. She put a hand to her chest and shook her head. "Firefly might be on Mustique, and I might've married a Brit, but I was born in Texas. Americans don't bow to nobody."

"God love you Yanks." He flipped his camera back up to his eye with a smile. "Walk into the sea for me."

It was said with commanding gentleness — a request.

"My suit's in the changing tent," she told him.

"Who said a suit was required to swim?"

"Well . . . ," she began to argue, but realized she hadn't an answer.

Who had made that a prerequisite? So many rules made by other people. What if she took a cue from the Hazell sisters and simply lived? No judgment, condemnation, spite, or shame. Just a woman partaking of God's creation. How could that be wrong?

She slipped the straps of her dress over her shoulders and held it over her breasts a beat, Harry's words — *wobbly bits* — resurfacing. She closed her eyes and listened to the tumble and crash of the cresting waves until the sound drowned out all thoughts. She let the dress drop then and walked forward into the surf. Bubbles tickled up from her belly button. The wind swept her hair back and kissed her lips briny. She put her arms out to either side, barechested to the horizon. The sun spread over skin that had never seen its light and warmed her like a giant ember.

You are beautiful, she thought to the sea, the heavens, and higher.

So lost in the moment, she'd forgotten Patrick until his shouts drew her to the shore.

". . . too far!"

The water's roar and the thudding of her heart made it hard to understand what he was saying. She turned over her shoulder to hear better.

"That's it." He'd come in knee-deep, angling his camera. "Stay like that."

The waves crested frothy over the coral, fizzing up like champagne. She reached forward to let the bubbles buoy her and liked knowing Patrick was behind. He wasn't an anchor like Harry had been. Rather, he felt like the halyard on a sail. The sand beneath her feet gave, and she sank into the silkiness of the current's push and pull.

"I got it!" he said.

But she remained facing the blue on blue, transfixed by a beauty that had nothing to do with her. This was something bigger. Beauty that could not be reproduced. Beauty that defied lineage and surpassed human comprehension. It overwhelmed her with its power and for the first time in her life, she honestly prayed.

Thank you, God.

"Willy May!" Patrick called. "Willy May, you're drifting too far out. The undertow!"

For a split second, she thought how easy it would be to give over to it all. Let the beauty take her wherever it wished. But she had tethers — Firefly, her daughters, wrongs to be righted. It took willpower to pull her feet free, turn, and trudge back to land.

On the beach, she dressed while Patrick politely cast his gaze away, photographing shells at his feet. She wasn't sure if she appreciated the gesture or if the old modesty brought old awkwardness. Her sundress tugged uncomfortably. The wet salt caught between the material and delicate skin.

"The camera loves you," said Patrick.

He spoke as if it were a living thing.

"You promised," she reminded him. "I don't want to walk into a gallery in twenty years and see my old bum beside some quote about graceful aging."

He held the camera down, finger still on the shutter release. A position of habit more than action.

"I promise, only for my eyes."

He inclined toward her, or her to him, or neither. It could've been the wind.

"Hello there!" someone singsung.

Patrick straightened up with a showman's

smile and waved.

"Jean. Janie. Out for a stroll?" He lifted his camera and click-clicked a seagull gliding overhead.

"Oh, don't be silly. We came to find you, darling," said Jean.

"It's been over an hour," added Janie.

Had it? Willy May reflexively reached for her wrist, but she'd stopped wearing her boating watch. Without it, time did as it pleased.

"Princess Margaret returned to the house. We've packed the tents but didn't want to leave you stranded."

Fickle, thought Willy May. Only an hour ago, not a soul would be moved. While Princess Margaret was on Mustique, their lives were at her command.

Their foursome took the last mule cart up to the Cotton House with Patrick at the wheel and Willy May beside. Janie and Jean sat behind them in heated discussion over the canceled group dinner. The Princess preferred chicken salad in her rooms. Janie was perturbed at having spent a better part of the morning ironing out wrinkles in her silk Thea Porter dress only to have it go unworn. But their chatter was background noise. Willy May was too busy trying not to catch Patrick's side-eye glances — trying

114

not to glance at him in return.

As soon as she reached her bungalow, she took the hottest, longest bath possible. She hoped the heat would steam all romantic notions clean out of her head. She came out drowsy and dew-skinned in her robe. Supper plates had been delivered unceremoniously. Chicken salad for all, it seemed.

She thought the knock on her door was someone sent to collect her tray already. She'd been in the bath too long.

"Come in," she said.

Patrick entered and shut the door behind him.

"What do you think —"

Before she could finish, his lips were on hers.

Instinct told her to push away and she did. But then, like a magnet flipped, she couldn't draw him close enough. It'd been so long since anyone had reached for her with such unbridled passion. Sure, she'd been with other men since Harry. A headmaster in Gloucester and a Menorcan mariner. Both confirmed bachelors with whom she felt safe to spend an evening with. There was the shared assumption that tomorrow they'd go about their business without remorse, recompense, or requirements. She didn't ask who shared their beds and they didn't ask who shared hers. They kept their ties severed by day so that they could entwine by night.

As a divorced, widowed mother of two adult children, remaining romantically unbound seemed the wisest course of action . . . until that moment. She hadn't remembered how good it felt to have someone *burn* for her and she for him.

She didn't stop to think or allow her discriminating conscience to wag its finger. She pulled off his shirt and threw off her robe, took him to her bed, and rolled onto him like a wave. His lips tasted of cool peppermint, his skin of hot salt. His hands gripped her thighs and pulled her closer, deeper as their bodies moved. She closed her eyes and imagined she was underwater, swimming through layers of ocean currents. She was burning and chilled, tingling within and numb to the world without. Behind her eyelids, the black gave way to a myriad of colors folding into each other. She stopped fighting the tumbling, fell into it willingly, and when the wave crested, she held on to the riptide with every flexed muscle.

Minutes later, they lay breathless beside each other. Her night scarf was caught higgledy-piggledy on her head and hung over her right eye. She took it off, suddenly bashful, and used it to cover the stretch marks on her stomach while she stood. Patrick didn't notice. He let his hand trace the small of her back as she rose and retrieved her robe from the floor. She slipped her arms into it quickly and tied the waist.

There had been an unspoken code of conduct between her and Harry, even in their best lovemaking. It was controlled with the expectation that they'd have a digestive biscuit afterward, brush their teeth, and go to sleep. She'd carried that responsible lovemaking into her dalliances. Once energies were spent, they'd wordlessly pulled on shirts, trousers, and socks; waved an amiable hand and exchanged a casual, "See you."

She had no idea what Patrick expected now. He lay there, naked and unmoving in her bed, and she couldn't say she was entirely bothered by it. His body was tanned and smooth like beach sand after the tide. Still, she handed him his trousers.

He took his pants. Message received.

"Well, that was unexpected," she said to fill the silence while he dressed.

"Yes, it was." He stood shirtless, pulled her to him in a kiss, and then cupped her face in his hands and stared.

It made her extremely uncomfortable.

"Okay," she said, patting his bare chest, and pushing out of his grasp.

"Wait." He stopped her from turning away. "I need to tell you something important. I don't want you to feel that I've . . . 'tricked' isn't the right word. 'Misled' is better. I want to be honest." He plunged both hands into his pant pockets and shuffled his feet like a schoolboy. "You see, that is — I'm engaged."

"Engaged?" She stepped back and crossed her arms over her chest. A flush dampened her upper lip. The last thing she needed was to have unwittingly entered into a messy love triangle. "Then what are you doing here?"

He shrugged. She sarcastically shrugged back.

"I felt something between us." He cleared his throat. "I needed to know if it was real or if I was imagining."

He said it boldly as if his saying it made it right. The entitlement reminded her of Harry. Neither one meant to be outright pompous. As men, they simply believed that their wants and needs were universally understood. He stepped toward her, and she put up a firm palm.

It might've been customary for the aristocrat set to have casual affairs but it wasn't for her. She felt something for Patrick. That was real. But they weren't debating if what they felt was *real*. Two lonely people caught up in a moment was as real as the idea of two soul mates aligning for eternity.

Willy May was a practical woman. In this minute, she needed to appraise the situation, and that was best done on a full stomach.

"Sit," she instructed.

She gestured to a rattan chair and the dinner tray on the table.

"Tell me about your fiancée."

She took a seat on the opposite side and forked chicken salad onto her cold toast.

CHAPTER 8
THE VILLAGE

Patrick's fiancée was Leonora, the Duke of Westminster's daughter, he explained. While they were a far cry from days of arranged marriages, unions between royal lineage remained a parochial affair. Leonora had been eighteen when they were introduced. She was twenty-four now, and a wedding date was still being debated. The Westminsters and Lichfields blamed the hippie youth culture — all of this free love and liberation. For the union to be stable, hot blood needed to cool.

Patrick claimed the match hadn't been his idea, but he couldn't break it off. The families were too involved. It was destined to happen. They just didn't know when yet.

"I don't deserve the girl. She's too good for me."

"Poor you, saddled with a too-good woman."

Willy May wasn't falling for his noble

victim act. He was a thirty-four-year-old bachelor earl, not some lily-bud-of-the-valley. They found themselves attracted to one another on a secluded island. No one had been mistreated, maligned, or misused. They were responsible adults.

Patrick was forthright with her, after the fact, and she sympathized, to a minor degree. But nothing in her reality had shown her that love was built for endurance. *Ever after* was a fairy tale for a reason. It allowed people to believe perfection was sustainable, if only in the realm of make-believe. The minute the story ended, the rules of the here and now took effect. That was humanity. The everyday world did not correspond to the heart's yearning.

Everyone wanted to be seen as beautiful, but not everyone was. Everyone wanted to possess special talents, but not everyone did. Everyone wanted to be the princess and the prince, but not everyone could. The End.

"So . . . ? You've been quiet. What do you think?" Patrick finally paused to ask. He paced the room, fired up on adrenaline. It was nearly four o'clock in the morning.

"I'm glad we talked," she replied.

The talking felt as significant as what they'd done in bed. She and Harry never talked.

"But I think it best we both sleep now."

She bid him good night, good morning, and goodbye, and then hung a beach scarf on the door — the DO NOT DISTURB sign for staff — before falling into bed with exhaustion.

She awoke after lunch with dread. How was she going to handle this situation? She'd have rolled back under the sheet to hide if Candace hadn't set down a plate of baked noodles with a too-loud *clunk*.

"They had macaroni pie at the main house." A bunch of cold grapes on the side.

Ada was already finished school and still in her uniform, an emerald jumper that brought out the gold in her eyes. Her curls were held back with a matching green headband.

It reminded her of when Hilly and Joanne started at Cheltenham Ladies' College — so smart in their hunter-green tartans and matching sweaters. She momentarily recalled Hilly being written up for rolling her skirts and Joanne lamenting that the wool sweaters were awfully scratchy. She blinked away those complaints and saw again the clean lines of their blazers with embroidered school crests. She'd have been proud to attend such a prestigious institution. She never even finished public high school. She

122

was still ashamed of that, and it made her glad that her daughters never had to hide their education, Ada either.

Candace had mentioned that Anne had reestablished the school on Mustique and brought in a teacher from the University of Winnipeg. The teacher's salary, student supplies, uniforms, and even a substantial library had all come from Anne's pocket. Underneath the polished, guarded exterior was a woman of real heart. Given Colin's showy extravagances, Willy May imagined such a practical and unselfish act might go unnoticed. But she noticed.

Ada went around the bungalow emptying the vases of dry flowers and replacing them with pink hibiscuses. She put a vase on Willy May's bedside table, tenderly cupping the petal trumpets as if to direct their fragrance.

"Are you sick, Miss Willy May?"

Her hair flopped uncombed across her forehead. She'd yet to dress. "No, just tired." Willy May smiled.

It was true and not. She'd slept long but not deep. Something was gnawing at her, like when she finished a good book: the melancholy longing to return to the beginning and read the story for the first time. But once read, knowledge changed a person.

Patrick was engaged; he was a two-timing man.

She took a bite of her macaroni. The cheese was pasty in her mouth. She set down the fork. "I'm afraid I don't have an appetite. Indigestion. I was up too late." She held out the grapes to Ada. "Care for these? They'll sour in the heat. You'll be doing me a favor."

Ada paused and looked to Candace, who puckered her lips. "They'll go to waste if somebody doesn't eat them. Besides, they're better than Gobstoppers." She made a face at the girl, and Ada laughed.

Accepting the grapes, she placed one in her mouth, chewed, and swallowed with a smile. "Mr. Colin gives out Gobstoppers on birthdays, but Mama Candace and I prefer fruit."

Candace smoothed a loose curl back from Ada's forehead. "That's right. Candy is the same if you eat it today or tomorrow, but a grape is now or never."

Willy May had never thought of it like that: perishability making a thing precious. Hilly and Joanne would choose candy over ordinary grapes on their birthdays or any other occasion. When had inferior replication become the preferred tradition?

To some extent, she'd done the same in

life. She'd imitated film starlets to win her beauty crown and used her beauty crown to attain her husband; married her husband to produce her children and in them, she saw herself reflected. But really, all of it was an attempt to reconstruct love. None of it had succeeded, because like Candace and Ada pointed out, you couldn't substitute an imitation for the original. Mother Nature was an uncultivated surprise. A Gobstopper would never be a grape.

"Maybe I'll have one after all."

Ada passed her the bunch, and she savored the sweetness with new appreciation.

"Best leave Miss Willy May to eat and ready herself," said Candace. "The Princess is swimming again today."

Willy May moaned. The thought of another day of princess-ing in the hot sun made her want to pull the bedsheet back over her. She needed to clear her head so that when she saw Patrick again, she would know what to say.

"Can you take a note to Lady Anne?"

"Yes, ma'am." Candace brought her pen and paper.

Dear Anne,
Forgive me. I must go into the village to pick up a few odds and ends — personal

125

hygiene and such. A woman's got to keep fresh, even on an island. Please give my regrets to Princess Margaret.

— WM

Like everything else on Mustique, it wasn't a lie, just a different shade of the truth.

An hour later, Anne sent back a message, delivered by a young man Willy May had seen in passing at the Cotton House.

Dear Willy May,
  This is Titus. He'll give you a lift to Mustique Village. Come to Macaroni Beach if you get back early. If not, we'll see you at dinner. The Princess has decided that the postponed show of last night should commence this evening.

— Anne

Willy May tossed the note into her wastebasket. She was not keen on company. It meant she'd have to make good on her excuse. She'd hoped to slip down to *Otrera,* write letters to the girls, and enjoy a few hours to herself. Now, she'd have to go to the village and buy something.

"I'm sorry you've been given chaperone duties," she said to Titus as a means of of-

126

ficial introduction.

He stood respectfully outside the front door.

"It was actually Candace's suggestion to Lady Anne. She wanted to make sure you didn't get lost."

That surprised her.

"It's an island. How lost could I get?"

"How lost do you want to get?" He shrugged. "That's the more prevalent question — at least on Mustique."

"Is that so?" she answered without answering.

He smiled — one of those infectious grins that makes one smile back. Up close, she gauged him to be in his early twenties. His muscles flexed smooth under his white linen shirt, and he smelled of green pineapple. There was not a single wrinkle across his high cheekbones and wide forehead. Youth was divine.

"Are we walking or driving?" Willy May tied a silk scarf around her hair.

"Neither." He gestured to a motorbike parked on the dirt path. "Do you mind riding? It is the fastest way."

"I didn't realize the Tennants had motorbikes."

"They don't," said Titus. "It's mine."

"Of course."

Anne and Colin might've owned the island, but not everything on it belonged to them.

Titus's bike was one of those Thunderbirds that Marlon Brando and James Dean were photographed astride in the 1950s. The handlebars and seat were frayed from use while the pedals and engine had been refurbished with shiny parts. She'd ridden plenty of horses, driven cars, sailed ships, and been caddied in Colin's mule carts, but this was her first motorbike.

Titus got on and nodded to the seat behind him.

"Here, please, ma'am."

"Willy May. Call me Willy May."

He smiled again. It was incorrigible.

"Yes, ma'am."

She pulled her purse strap across her body to secure it and kicked a leg over the seat. "Should I hold on somewhere?"

"To me, yes."

She put her hands cautiously on his shoulders as if peeking over a hedge. She knew it was ridiculous. She'd never seen anyone ride a motorbike in such a position. Gently, he took her hands off his shoulders and moved them to his waist, solid without a smidgen of middle-age cushion. The muscles of his stomach flexed at her touch.

"Better if you hold here. I do not want you falling off."

"Yes — I mean, no, that wouldn't be good."

He laughed kindly. "Surely not. I have fallen and it is not good!" He turned the ignition and the bike roared to life beneath her.

After a bumpy start, they found flat surface. She kept her cheek pressed into the shield of his back to protect herself from the force of the wind whip. Riding, flying, or sailing, who could tell? The jungle, sky, and water slid into each other. It spun her queasy. She closed her eyes until she felt the clutch ease.

"We are here," said Titus.

The village was constructed like a scene from an Annette Funicello film. Willy May half expected Frankie Avalon to appear for a musical number — the "Merry Mustique Melody" or some other alliterative tune. Young coconut trees peppered the path. An ornate marble fountain gurgled in the plaza center. Brightly painted stucco huts formed the main street in a rainbow of neat Easter eggs. Willy May couldn't help the compulsion to follow it. Because while every adult knows that there's no such thing as a pot of gold waiting at the end, the childlike hope remains long past the illusion.

A wide concrete sidewalk wove serpentine from shop to shop. Each had a wooden sign in front specifying its trade. The general store was next to the bakery across from the jeweler and the spirits shops. Park benches separated the Cotton Boutique and the Mustique Company office at the end. Tidy to the point of unreal, it was obvious that this village had not organically sprung to life. The glare of the whitewashed concrete under the tropical sun made her squint.

Titus parked the motorbike and turned off the engine. "Welcome to Mustique Village."

Willy May got off. The muscles in her legs trembled. Her ears rang. Her skin tingled almost painfully. The vibration continued through her bones. A latent rush of euphoria. She understood the adrenaline draw. Her pulse raced and her mind with it.

"Where would you like to start?" asked Titus.

She should've come up with a list before leaving. On the spot, she said, "The general store."

He escorted Willy May inside, where a local woman in a bright red madras skirt, off-the-shoulder blouse, and matching head scarf greeted her with a broad grin. A calypso drum track played overhead. The store smelled of new paint and sunscreen. Everything was brand name. There were boxes of Kellogg's cereal, Coca-Colas, and Wonder Bread on the shelves; *Rolling Stone, Cosmopolitan,* and *Reader's Digest* sat on the rack.

"Hello, ma'am, I am Naomi. Welcome to the Mustique General Store. How may I service you?"

"Do you mind if I look around?"

"Please, take your time."

Willy May walked the shelves, picking up a bottle of L'Oréal shampoo, a can of Aqua Net hair spray, a bag of Tudor Crisps, and some witch hazel for mosquito bites.

"Do you have cotton balls for application?" asked Naomi. "The Mustique Company cotton is the finest."

"I don't — that would be terrific."

Naomi tossed the cotton balls into a brown bag with the rest of the items. "How else may we assist you?"

It was the collective pronoun that made Willy May pause and reconsider the scene — to really see this time. Naomi's nails were painted with bright red polish. She wore fashionable fake eyelashes, a gold wedding band on her left hand, and matching loop earrings. She was a modern woman.

Willy May felt foolish for thinking otherwise; and truthfully, she had assumed Naomi was part of the Mustique mystique. Because part of her had wanted to believe that she could leave the trappings of reality for a simpler time, an island dream where the people wore beautiful costumes and the streets were candy colored. All while retaining modern luxury, of course.

"Will that be all?" asked Naomi.

Before Willy May could answer, a little boy opened the door to a back room and the jingle of a children's cartoon program spilled out. The boy wore a T-shirt, jean shorts, and plastic flip-flops.

"Ma!" he called. "Can I watch?"

The theme song of *The Flintstones* sang from a television.

Naomi shooed him into the room. "Yes, yes, go on now, there's a customer."

She shut the door and turned back to Willy May. Caught between the fact and the fiction.

"A modern stone-age family," Willy May sang. "My girls used to watch that."

Naomi nodded. "My son's name is Fred, so naturally he thinks he and Fred Flintstone are somehow related." She rolled her eyes with a smirk. "I only let him watch on Saturday mornings if his teacher says he behaved for the week."

Was it Saturday? Willy May had lost track of the days.

"Sounds like a good deal. I should've bartered that same with my kids. They'd probably be better off for it."

Naomi smiled — a softer, warmer thing than before — and tallied the purchases. Willy May paid. Just before leaving, she looked back over her shoulder to see Naomi pull a magazine from under the counter, *Jet,* with singer Dionne Warwick on the cover. She hadn't seen that on the general store's magazine stand.

Outside, Titus carried on: "Would you like to visit the bakery for some of our island breads or the spirits shop — nothing like Caribbean rum! Perhaps you'd prefer to see our island fashions at the Cotton Boutique?"

Willy May planted her feet. "This isn't a real village, is it?"

"Real?" Titus scratched his chin. "What is really real, eh?" He smiled.

She crossed her arms over her chest. "There is real and there is fake. I don't like being played the moppet."

Only after she said it aloud did she realize how infantile she sounded.

Titus nodded for her to follow him down

the pedestrian walkway.

"The Tennants need a place where Cotton House guests and residents are comfortable shopping," he explained. "It's a smart investment. People come from other countries and spend money here on Mustique instead of St. Vincent or Trinidad or one of the larger commercial islands. Colin wanted something similar to the Polynesian Village at Disney World."

"The theme park in Florida?"

"He greatly admires Mr. Disney."

"So, it's a tourist trap?"

Titus laughed. "Call it what you like. It's a place where you can get your souvenirs, snacks, toiletries, and . . . it's pretty, right?"

They stopped in front of the plaza fountain, carved with angel-fish that spouted water at varied angles.

"The Mustique Company office is here. Someone comes once a week to check in but mostly, it's the biggest sign."

"Advertising."

He nodded. "Real estate, cotton manufacturing, fashion, consumables . . . our newest venture is in hospitality. At first, the Tennants were not enthusiastic about renting Cotton House rooms, but it ensures the Mustique Company retains year-round capital."

"You're a businessman," said Willy May.

"I have a business degree." He grinned.

She had no degrees but being married to a brewery baron had rubbed off a little. While Harry sat in the cushy office chair, her mother-in-law had run the books, and Willy May had paid attention. Titus's acumen was impressive.

"If this isn't a genuine village, where do the islanders live?" she asked.

"Many, like Candace, live in staff quarters on the Cotton House grounds. The remaining few, like Naomi, live on the south side of the island. That's where my wife and I had a home."

"You're a married man!"

"Once, yes." He slipped his hands into his pockets. "We are divorced."

He seemed too young to be married and divorced. But then, age was an enigma on Mustique.

"Marriage is hard. I was sixteen at my wedding. I'm divorced, too."

When going through her own separation, she'd disliked it when people responded with the apologetic *I'm sorry.* There could be valid reasons why Titus and his wife ended their marriage. Who was she to assume? She'd known woeful long marriages and very happy divorces. Not every union

135

was a good one and not every split was bad.

He raised an eyebrow in interest. "I was told you are a widow."

"That's how the higher-ups sell me, but technically I divorced my husband before he died so . . . you can't be an ex-widow, now can you?"

"I suppose you can be anything you wish." He shrugged. "I'm sure you had your reasons."

His words, so similar to her own thoughts, made her feel able to acknowledge the truth.

"I didn't love him." It was the first time she'd said it aloud. "Not in the way he deserved to be loved. Not in the way everyone deserves to be loved."

"That is a tragedy." He frowned.

Yes, it was.

"I wanted to love him at the beginning. I was young. I wanted to be in love, and I wanted him to be in love with me. But he wasn't. Not really. And I was too afraid to ask why not. It wasn't fair to either of us."

Deep down, she was sorry. Sorry that she couldn't go back and tell her younger self to be less narcissistic or her middle-aged self to be less of a coward. But youth was ego and life made cowards of everyone. She couldn't change either of those women, but she could change the woman she'd become.

"I know what you mean," said Titus and the look in his eye told her that he did.

"It's your turn to bare your soul. Why did your wife divorce you?"

He clasped his hands together. "It was more of a mutual divorce."

She raised an eyebrow. Were divorces ever *really* mutual?

He cleared his throat. "She was a girl from Trinidad who wanted a husband to give her a house, children, and a dinner table to sit at every night — you know, the traditional life. I was a student at the university on St. Vincent, and I wanted . . . *more* than that. The problem was that I couldn't say for certain what that *more* was. For two years she waited for me to find out, but I still hadn't. So, I had to let her go."

He smiled a little sadly.

"She remarried. A good man. They have four children. Two boys and two girls. She is very happy and I am glad for that. But St. Vincent is a small place. It was hard to see them always together. So, when the Tennants advertised for a business manager on Mustique, I sent my résumé. It was an easy job to get. Not too many people want to move to a place like this. Not forever."

Willy May shifted uneasily and Titus doubled back:

"Not islanders, I mean. Mustique — the Cotton House — it has its ghosts, as you can imagine."

She could and had. The old sugar mill had never been refurbished. The stone tower stood in the middle of Colin's croquet lawn with its pitched roof arrowed to the sky. A silent reminder of the property's origins and the community bound to it. The community still bound to it.

The sun slanted their shadows. The day was going fast with evening activities ahead.

"We should head back," said Titus.

They returned to his parked motorbike, but she didn't feel she could return without asking . . .

"Since we're being candid," she began, "there's something I've been wanting to bring up to Candace for a while, but I never knew how."

Titus tied her brown bag to the back of the bike. "Yes?"

"Everything about Mustique appears, on the surface, so beautiful. A utopia, right? But I can't not see that nearly all the staff are, well, black. Actually, I don't think I've seen one white staff member."

Titus narrowed his gaze on her. "What are you asking, ma'am?"

Willy May had grown up in Central Texas

and seen enough black men and women locked into patterns of perpetual exploitation. Dr. Martin Luther King Jr. had been in the grave less than five years and the United States was still engaged in hate and segregated warfare.

"Is working for Colin and Anne something you all chose, or . . ."

A handful of sandpipers raced by daintily on pencil legs.

"Yes, but like all choices, it's complicated, ma'am."

"Please, no more 'ma'am.' I appreciate it, but I'm no royal. I'm an ordinary person."

"I thank you for your honesty," he said.

The sandpipers skittered back the way they'd just come, leaving tear-shaped prints zigzagged in the dirt.

"But if you're asking out of pity," he continued, "please know, it's unwarranted."

"I —"

"Really. Everyone on Mustique has chosen his or her path here — the trajectory is our own making. I think the question that you're truly getting at is, where do *you* want your own to lead?"

Willy May cringed. Titus had seen the buried secret she'd been unable or unwilling to disclose. She'd feared revealing that truth would make her weaker, more vulnerable.

"I'm just trying to be . . ."

She didn't know how to finish her sentence. Maybe that was it. Maybe *trying to be* was all there was. Acknowledging that she didn't know all the answers was surprisingly empowering.

CHAPTER 9
THE KARMA HAND

Titus dropped Willy May at her bungalow before proceeding up to the Cotton House, where there was a commotion of activity.

In her room, Willy May found a note containing the reason for it:

Dear Willy May,

The Princess has given permission to have her portrait taken by Patrick. She insists that everyone on Mustique be included. Quite an honor! You are enthusiastically invited to join us on the Cotton House lawn at exactly six o'clock this evening. Patrick would like to take the photograph at six-thirty so as to make use of the sunlight. Dinner will follow at seven o'clock. While you may wear whatever you wish, we do want to show well! Everyone has a role to play and costuming to match. Might you wear something American — a cowboy hat or cowboy boots perhaps?

Never fear if those are not on hand. Oliver and I will fashion you.

Cheers, Colin

Colin had called in the troupe for the camera. A cowboy hat and boots? She should show up in chaps. Just chaps. It would serve him right. She wasn't naive as to his manipulations nor was she a guest obliged to play his games. She was a resident who'd paid a pretty penny for her home, which stood half built while everyone played theatrics.

It bothered her. *Really* bothered her. She'd gone from casual compliance to repulsed irritation in a flash. Her gut instinct was to march into the Cotton House, throw the note at his face, and say she refused to dress up like John Wayne's stunt double.

It was her fatal flaw — a quick temper. Cool as a cucumber, and then, in a flash, ready to burn the world.

Her bungalow was steamy hot, too, despite the windows being opened at the appropriate angles and the overhead fan clicking round. Her head swooned. Her brow beaded with sweat. She thought she might vomit from the nausea. Her anger had brought on a hot flash. They were growing more frequent. It was to be expected. She was a woman of a certain age.

She needed a cold drink. There was no ice in her room so she left her bag of village sundries on the bed and went up to the kitchen. By the time she entered the scullery, her underarms were sopping. The room was swollen with islanders preparing dinner.

"Where are the turtles?" George yelled at a boy who'd come in the back door.

"The men are scared to break the law. I told them turtle soup is tonight's menu, but they pointed to the beach sign: TURTLE FISHING IN OFF-SEASON FORBIDDEN." He raised his hands. "How to argue with that?"

"The Princess is the law and she wants turtle soup. You tell those guys to fish them turtles!" George commanded.

The boy exhaled with frustration.

Turtle soup. The thought of hot reptilian broth was all she could bear. Her vision tunneled. Her knees gave. She put a hand on the wall to steady herself and knocked over a fry pan hanging from a hook. The crash of it brought her back to her senses.

"I'm sorry." She picked up the pan.

"Feeling poorly, ma'am?" George came to her, dabbing perspiration from her forehead with his chef's towel. It smelled of tarragon and onion.

"It's my fault," she said. "I shouldn't be here. I was looking for a cold drink."

"Titus!" George shouted.

Titus came from the veranda. She was awash with relief to see him again.

"Is she . . . sick?" asked George.

Titus frowned. It was the first worried look she'd seen on him. He put a hand to her forehead and his face unfurrowed.

"Overheated. We were at the village and riding in the sun. She needs to hydrate. I'll take care of her."

George nodded and Titus half carried Willy May out of the kitchen to one of the cushioned lounge chairs facing the breeze on the lanai. In the distance, a little storm cloud misted a rainbow no bigger than her thumb. It quietly moved across the milky horizon like the colored marshmallow cereal her girls used to eat. It brought her a Saturday morning kind of peace. The beach palms whispered *breathe . . . breathe . . . breathe* with each gust, and she obeyed until the pounding in her temples slackened.

The communal living room was empty. Colin's bric-a-brac relics looked more cluttered in the vacancy. When there were bodies in motion, the dust had less time to settle. Now, the ancient books, garish decorations, and ornate mahogany furniture looked lost in time, out of place, and lonesome for it. She picked up a nearby figurine. A woman with four arms, one of which held a flower stretched forward.

"Lakshmi," came a raspy voice.

Princess Margaret leaned over the open window railing and lit her cigarette with a golden monogrammed lighter, the likes of which Willy May had never seen. She was pink-skinned and dewy from the beach, her washed hair was pulled back in a head wrap, and her face was naked except for a swipe of pink lipstick. She wore a cotton shift in a matching flamingo hue and feather-tufted sandal slippers.

"Ma'am," said Willy May.

The Princess flicked ash off her cigarette, then pointed with it to the statuette. "Lakshmi is the goddess of prosperity. That's her karma hand — flowering love and emotional fulfillment."

Willy May set the ivory down, searching the veranda for Jean, Janie, or Anne. The Princess was never without a lady-in-waiting and yet, here she stood. Alone.

Titus rolled in the bar cart with a bucket of ice chips.

"Read my mind. I try to conjure this heat when I'm freezing to death in London. Frigid place. I only really like England in

June, July, and August — and only if it doesn't decide to rain that whole time. My love is conditional." She grinned and then turned to Titus. "I'm hoping you're a chap who can make a proper drink. Jean just pitches it all in a glass."

"I can try. What would you like, ma'am?"

"It's early. Something light — gin and tonic on the rocks. Willy May?"

"Tonic only. On the rocks. Lots of rocks. A mountain of them."

In under a minute, Titus had mixed, poured, and garnished with fresh limes, handing the drinks to the women simultaneously. Willy May let the Princess sip first.

She did, leaving a bubblegum lip print on the rim. "That's about the best gin and tonic I've ever had. What magic did you use in this?"

"Gordon's gin, ma'am," he replied.

"Gordon's — in the middle of the Caribbean? Finally. Someone who knows how to get things right! We could use you back home. A man like you could run the kingdom."

Willy May took a long guzzle, sucking ice into her mouth to melt on her tongue.

"Better?" asked Titus.

"Yes," said Willy May. "Much. Thank you, Titus."

146

"My pleasure," said Titus.

Despite Titus's earlier words of assurance, Willy May could no longer blindly indulge like the rest of the guests. The knowledge of real and unreal, truth and pretense, had changed how she saw the staff and how she experienced every minute at the Cotton House. Candace had called them *tangled.* She understood better now.

"You should try George's Bloody Mary," said Titus. "Or perhaps, the Bloody Margaret?"

"The Bloody Margaret?" The Princess grinned cunningly. "Is there such a thing?"

"Indeed, ma'am, I believe it substitutes gin for vodka. George knows the recipe better than I."

"How perfectly delightful." Princess Margaret gave a genuine giggle.

It was a glimpse of her softer side — of the girl that Willy May had watched grow up in the newspapers and heard on the radio with her sister, Elizabeth. She rather liked this Margaret. If Willy May forgot the rest of the world, she might've imagined them as friends.

Anne came up the side stairs, exasperated. "I looked everywhere for you."

"Clearly not. Here I am," the Princess answered. "Having a drink that doesn't taste like it was siphoned from a distillery tank."

"The ladies are ready to dress you for the portrait." Anne gestured to the horizon. "Unfortunately, we can't command the sun to wait, and Patrick needs the dusk light."

Willy May's stomach twisted. Nausea returned briefly. She'd have to face him soon.

"Right." The Princess took a drag from her cigarette. "We'll save those Bloody M's for another time. Do remind me what your name was again?"

"Titus."

"Titus." She turned to Anne. "You've got a good man here. I'd pay him double."

"Yes, ma'am," said Anne. "We're very lucky to have found him."

Princess Margaret nodded and finished her drink in a single gulp.

Titus gave Willy May a knowing look and left the women on the veranda.

Two hours later, they assembled on the lavish lawn of the Cotton House. Colin brought in a horse adorned in full dressage regalia, a white chaise longue for the Princess to rest upon, jeeps washed and waxed, a giant dead sailfish, a sewing machine, a chalkboard, a white clock, and a collection of other set pieces that made little sense to

Willy May. The pièce de résistance was a private plane parked casually beside it all. Then, like arranging flowers in vases, he clustered people in twos, threes, and fives around the yard, fussing over how best to bunch so that the resulting design was pleasing to the eye. It seemed a vain effort to Willy May. Didn't Colin see? Mustique would always outdo his efforts.

In the background, the verdant hills rose and fell like a colorful song. The sky yawned the perfect hue of baby blue. Then, to prove a point, billowing clouds rolled overhead casting majestic purple shadows like a herd of passing whales. They garnered the upward awe of everyone . . . to Colin's chagrin.

"Now we have this lingering over," he griped. "Nothing worse than bad lighting."

Anne swatted at early mosquitoes. "It's just a photograph, Colin. Let's take it and go to dinner."

"It's not *just* a photograph. Don't you understand, my dear? It's got to be beautiful. The sunshine will take ten years off our faces — and some of us need it. Not you, of course, darling. Hopefully, these clouds will pass quickly."

Instead, the minutes passed and the clouds idled.

Colin thrashed his cane at the ground

angrily, bits of grass and dirt flying up, before hurrying off with Oliver to do one more costume check: the local police with shiny badges, the servants in their best liveries, the band with their shiniest instruments, the construction crew with hard hats, the island schoolteacher with two uniformed pupils . . . the butcher, the baker, the candlestick maker. He wanted as many professions represented as possible so that future generations would know that his was a civilized island.

Willy May hadn't a cowboy hat or boots. She'd worn a simple beige frock and hoped to escape Colin's theatrical costume shop. Not to be thwarted, Oliver had suggested that she change into a pair of American Keds. She'd thought he was kidding.

"Ridiculous," she'd told him. "No woman would wear plimsolls to a dinner party — on an island — in a thousand-degree heat." Never mind that her feet would never be seen in the photograph, given how far back from the royals she had been placed.

Still, Colin had insisted. So she wore the damned shoes and felt like a clown for it.

Her only consolation was that Patrick was too far away for them to have the awkward just-seeing-you talk. She was glad to put that off for as long as possible.

As soon as the clouds broke, Colin came to the foot of Princess Margaret and raised his hat. Patrick steadied his camera on the tripod and readied his trigger finger.

"Wait, wait — no!" said Colin. He covered his bald head from the shine, readjusted his stance. "Patrick, you tell me what angle? I want to look my best."

"For God's sake," Anne huffed. "Take the bloody photograph. Everyone is restless, and I'm about to eat the ringleader."

At her command, Colin counted. "Three, two, one . . . smile!" He lifted his cane high into the air.

Patrick click-click, click-clicked a few times and the deed was done. There was a collective sigh of relief as the sun sank into the sea. No light, no insistence on retakes. They were finished and everyone headed back to reality: the band, to the stage; George, to the kitchen; the construction crew hung up their hats; the horse was barned; the fishermen put away their nets; and the rest of the staff went straight to their nightly chores, the dinner service with accompanying entertainment.

Earlier, Candace explained that she'd refused to bring Ada to the photograph.

"Mr. Colin may own the island, but he doesn't own us. No matter what games he plays with guests." She'd moved about the room, dusting the windowsills. A fine sea salt was perpetually settling on everything. The wind carried it.

"He pays extra for the dress-up," she'd continued. "A man who turns down a fool's gold is the bigger fool. And nobody working on this island be a fool. Just because you put a glitter crown on your head don't make you God and king."

She'd turned sharply, seeming to catch herself, unguarded.

"I'm wearing his silly shoes and he didn't pay me. What does that make me?" asked Willy May.

Candace offered a reassuring smile. "A nice person." She shook the feather duster outside the open window. "Ada's in the kitchen shelling peas for tonight's mash and then she's going to do her schoolwork. Best she learns now that she's worth more than a snapshot."

The implication being that they were worth more, too. Willy May wished she could join Ada. There was nobility in a simple task done well. She could still feel the sensation of running her thumb down the center of the green pods. The gratifying roll of peas. It was one of the chores that she'd enjoyed as a child.

Willy May and her mom would sit on stools by the cellar to shell, pull corn silk, and unskin sticky tomatillos. She liked freeing the inner goodness of a thing and making use of the outer waste. Her mother let her take their kitchen scraps to the pig farmer, who gave her a nickel a bucket. She was always tempted to buy Red Hots from the five-and-dime with it but saved her money instead. It was her first semblance of making her own way in the world. Cash was king. She liked seeing the silver grow in the jelly jar hidden behind the pickled radishes in the root cellar. Her dad loathed radishes but her mom preserved everything that she could grow in the Texas dirt. Some drought years, that meant nothing, which made the jars even more precious. Willy May had decided it was the best spot to keep her fortune.

If only she'd known then that she'd end up trading all her nickels for a Toni perm that promised even waves but left her hair chemically frizzed. She'd have told herself to buy the Red Hots.

Now, Willy May walked with the rest of the guests over to the Cotton House. Waiters Joseph, Leo, and John served strawberries carved to look like decorative roses alongside puffs of Crab Rangoon and saucy

153

shrimp skewered into hollow pineapple rinds. Food dioramas. She wondered if these had come from the mind of Colin or George. The genesis would change how she enjoyed them.

Titus poured sorrel into glass mugs with cinnamon swizzle sticks. The island concoction had grown on her: a hibiscus tea with a spicy kick. Without her having to request it, Titus made Willy May's without rum. She hoped it made a difference to him that she was in the milieu but not of it. Mustique wasn't a holiday for her. She wasn't here to let loose and then return to some punctilious home abroad. She was rebuilding her life and that took measures — measures she wanted to take versus measures she was told to take. There was a great distinction.

Three hours and four courses later, Willy May was the first to leave after the coconut sponge cake was eaten and everyone rose to the disco beat of Tom Jones's "She's a Lady."

Full on the day, she hadn't the stomach for a late night. The inebriated laughter would quickly turn to carnal proposals. The deck of cards would be shuffled, each king and queen going home with another suit. At breakfast they would all be re-paired appropriately — heart to heart, spade to spade. Willy May was too tired to play.

The melody of the calypso drums, guitars, and tambourines carried her down the stone pathway, around the shimmering garden ponds to her bungalow door.

Candace had turned down her bed and left a small lamp on. It welcomed her like a lighthouse. But as she stepped onto the porch, Patrick rose from the shadows. He'd been waiting. Seated on the far side of the banquet table U, she hadn't spoken to him during dinner.

"Hi," he said.

"Hi." She sighed.

They stood in awkward silence. He swayed his shoulders to the rhythm of the distant band. Willy May worried she might be stuck here all night if someone didn't break the stalemate.

"Did Colin's photographs come out well?"

"I never know until I develop the roll. By then, the magic's gone. It's the possibility between the lens and subject that matters most to me." He gave a rakish smile.

Willy May yawned. It was too late for double entendres. Her feet hurt. Colin insisted everyone stay in costume for the dinner — to keep things festive, he said. But the Keds had rubbed a blister on her big toe.

"Great, I'm so glad." She pushed by Patrick to her door.

He leaned an elbow on the frame, blocking her entry. She sighed again with extra gusto.

"I'm tired, Earl Lichfield, and I want to go to sleep. Alone."

He moved aside so she could enter. "Can we at least talk?"

She couldn't endure another of his all-night soliloquies and sat heavily on the edge of her bed, unlaced the sneakers, and kicked them off.

"I really don't think there's anything left to discuss. You said enough." She inspected her toe. It was purple and swollen.

Still standing in the doorframe, Patrick crossed his arms over his chest and shifted his weight. "Are you angry with me?"

Whatever Mrs. Robinson fantasies he had, she wanted to make it clear that she was no Anne Bancroft and he was no Dustin Hoffman. They had a one-night fling. She was not looking to be harnessed in a long-term romantic affair . . . of any kind. She had to handle this appropriately so there was no bad blood between them.

She patted for him to take a seat beside her, which he did obediently.

"Listen to me," she said in the same

inflection she would use with Hilly or Joanne. Mother-like. "You are engaged to marry a lovely woman who is faithfully waiting for you. I respect the sanctity of marriage. Equal to it, I respect a man's or woman's choice to remain unwed. I have made that choice."

"I'm not —"

"I don't want another husband, real or in practice. I'm too old to be a kept woman and too set in my ways to shack up with anyone even for a short while." She laughed as she said it — so farcical an idea — and a wounded look crossed his face.

"Patrick —" she began again, but he put a hand behind her neck and drew her forward into his kiss.

She let him. Just one more. You couldn't build a life on a kiss. That was fairy-tale stuff, not reality. When they parted, she looked at him squarely.

"Thank you, that was sweet, but it's time for you to go home."

Home to his room, his fiancée, his titled life. He took her meaning.

"Trust me, it's for the best. I'm not like you all."

She had tried to be for nearly thirty years as Mrs. Harry Michael, turning a blind eye to his dirty secrets and sweeping who she was under the carpet. In the end, she'd tripped and nearly broken her neck on that lumpy rug. There were no carpets on Mustique. The soles of her feet tread on cool stone. The grit of sand between her toes reminded her that while her life in England was dead, she was not.

Patrick left without trying to change her mind. He could've made a scene but he hadn't, and she thought better of him for respecting the truth.

CHAPTER 10
FEVER SPELL

Willy May and Patrick were like two magnets orbiting without touching through beach swims, lavish feasts, and dinner shows. The days formed a pinwheel mirage, sunrise and sunset turning head over tail. Even Willy May forgot the day of the week, the week of the month, the month of the year, and she was sober as a judge.

Princess Margaret liked her booze and legal smokes. Drugs besides those were publicly disallowed. Still, there were guests who pretended their little pills were breath mints; others excused themselves to "powder their noses"; everyone seemed colorblind to the pink-dotted sugar cubes dissolving at the bottom of cocktail drinks. No one expected the Princess to be held accountable for what her subjects did in secret. The courtiers operated under the edict of *what she doesn't acknowledge can't hurt us.*

When someone keeled over during Colin's Triton-themed cocktail hour, Willy May suspected that the guest had succumbed to the secret stash of stimulants. She steadied herself for how the guest would mitigate the situation. It was not a guest, however. It was Leo, the waiter. He'd been serving thimbles of lobster bisque.

The pink creams had splattered across the tiled floor. Bits of it speckled stiletto heels and exposed toes, strings of lobster meat dangling in Hugo's ankle hair. He stomped to release them. Everything smelled nauseatingly fishy. No one had much of an appetite following. Still, Colin insisted that they proceed to the dining room for the grouper while Leo was put to bed and the staff cleaned up. But therein lay the rub. There was no extra staff available to clean up.

"They're all unwell," explained Colin.

"Unwell?" Princess Margaret lowered her cigarette and frowned. "How so?"

"A little bug is going around the domestics." Colin waved his hand. "Not to worry. We're taking good care, I assure you. I sent the prop plane. Medicine is being flown in."

"*Flown in* — what?" Anne balked in horror. "You should've informed us immediately!"

160

But they all knew why Colin had not. He would've done anything to avoid ending the party.

Princess Margaret tapped a ringed finger against her empty whiskey glass: *tink, tink, tink.* "What is it?" Her disapproval was penetrating.

To avoid the Princess's glare, Willy May found herself studying the floor tiles, glazed terra-cotta with a slight leaf pattern.

"A fever," he explained "They happen."

"Colin!" Anne was angry.

Princess Margaret raised an eyebrow high. "You don't fly in medical supplies for common sniffles. Do I need to summon the clinic doctor or would you like to tell me what's really going on?"

Colin waffled and wiped his forehead with a cocktail napkin. *What's really going on* was not his specialty. "It started with one or two a few weeks ago."

"One or two weeks?" Jean gasped.

"The doctor says, worst case, it's the dengue."

"Breakbone fever?" Anita turned to Arne with an incredulous look. "Did you know about this?"

He put an arm around her and pulled her close, whispering, "It will be fine."

Jinty flung herself into Hugo's arms with

161

a birdlike cry. Panicked murmurs spread down the banquet table.

"We should leave," Jean said to Anne.

"No need to be rash. It's under control!" Colin smiled but they all knew he would proffer the same grin while a tiger ate his feet. "The ferry isn't working this time of night anyhow."

"Of course she didn't mean tonight. Tomorrow," Anne snapped. "You should've told us at once, Colin. The Princess's health is nothing to take lightly. You'll have the Queen to answer to if the Princess catches her death."

At that moment, a mosquito landed on Margaret's arm. She smacked hard, killing it, and then raised her blood-speckled palm to the guests. Patrick handed over his napkin wordlessly.

"Thank you, Patrick." She wiped her hand clean. "I think it wise to retire to our rooms." She turned to Anne. "We'll take the early ferry."

Anne nodded, and then glared at Colin. After the Princess and ladies-in-waiting left, the room erupted in a cacophony.

"A fever!"

"Damned mosquitoes!"

"I told you I've felt off . . ."

"Check my head, am I warm?"

They scattered from the dining room leaving a platter heaped with fish filets untouched. Colin marched out flanked by Hugo and Arne.

Only Willy May and Patrick remained. He moved closer to her. It was the first time they'd been alone since the night she dismissed him from her bungalow.

"We'll be all right," he comforted. "Best pack up for the morning."

"I'm staying."

"What do you mean?"

"I'm not here on holiday, Patrick. I live here."

One of Colin's antique cuckoo clocks chimed in the main room: eight cuckoos. The violin player entered on the eighth. She hadn't seen him since the royal welcome on the beach. Was that a week ago? A month? She was ashamed of how easily she'd ridden Colin's decadent merry-go-round.

The violinist had been instructed to perform for the dinner party, but the room was empty. Not one to shirk his duties, he raised his instrument and played a slow, haunting melody.

"Don't be a cavalier American," said Patrick. "The dengue could kill you."

She understood the gravity, but she was committed to Mustique.

"Arne's crew has finished all the major construction. I'll move up to Firefly."

He reached out for her hand. She didn't pull away.

"I can't force you to do anything. But promise me that you'll take precautions."

The violinist finished on a strong note, then lowered his bow, nodded to her, and walked out. The silence was immense as the night ocean. Without ears to absorb them, the strains of his bow echoed through the Cotton House. Only then did Willy May feel the emptiness.

The staff was the lifeblood. The place was tomb-like without them. Tomorrow, the Princess and her courtiers and hangers-on would be gone, but the islanders would remain. She was defining herself in that moment.

"Have you seen Candace?" she asked.

Colin had hosted a series of elaborate brunches that week so housekeeping had forgone their usual service routines. Willy May had assumed that Candace was busy elsewhere but now, she worried.

"Who's Candace?" asked Patrick.

She rolled her eyes and pulled free from his hold. "Go pack."

Quickly, she returned to her bungalow, where she found her bed turned down as usual, but unlike every other night, eucalyptus had been placed around the windows.

"Ada?" she called.

The girl startled with hands full of branches. "It keeps the mosquitoes away," she explained. "The doctor said that they brought the fever."

"Is Candace sick?"

Ada dropped her chin to her chest. Her bottom lip trembled. "Mama Candace told me not to come near her. She doesn't want me to catch it. Everyone in the Cotton House staff quarters is sick. I'm staying at Naomi's house."

Willy May sat in the rattan chair so that her face was level to Ada's. She took both the girl's hands in hers. "Look at me."

Ada's tearful eyes shimmered. She was a beautiful child, even in sadness.

"She'll be okay," she said, even though she wasn't certain that it was true.

Ada gulped but couldn't hold back a sob.

Willy May wrapped her arms around her, surprised at how easily the gesture came. Ada was smaller than her daughters had been at fifteen. Her bones were delicate as a hummingbird's. "You know more than anyone else how strong your Mama Candace is."

"I know she's strong, but nobody is strong

enough when they're sick. You should leave with the rest of the guests, too," she cried.

"Well, I'm not," said Willy May. "I can't. I've got no place else."

For the first time, panic rose inside her.

"But I can tell you this, I am getting the hell away from Colin's. Will you help me pack?"

Ada nodded. "Where will you go?"

"To Firefly. It's secluded up the hill and there are fewer mosquitoes."

The task seemed to give them purpose. Together, they quickly moved the contents of the bureau into a trunk.

Willy May worried about Candace. She wondered if she ought to go to her — to aid in some way — but suddenly realized that while she knew the general vicinity of the staff quarters, she didn't know which one belonged to Candace. It illuminated once more the disparity between the relationship she thought they had and the one they actually did. Even if she found her house, showing up at a sick woman's doorstep asking, *What can I do?*, would be more of a burden than a help to Candace.

It was easy to blame Mustique's mosquitoes, but fevers didn't pop up on an island in the middle of nowhere. Diseases spread when mosquitoes bit infected people. It was more likely one of the foreign guests who'd arrived by ferry that brought the virus to their shores. Now that it was here, they needed to contain the exposure.

After packing the room and seeing Ada off, Willy May lay down in bed and draped the mosquito net over herself, praying she would find rest, praying everyone remaining on the island would.

Early the next morning, she ate a wild guava picked from a tree on her way to where the Cotton House guests had assembled with their luggage.

"No need to crowd. There's enough room for everyone," Colin was saying. "The Princess and her ladies go first."

"It's like the *Titanic,*" someone murmured.

"Hugo and Jinty are staying," Anne said calmly. "So, it isn't quite like the *Titanic.*"

"It's not *at all* like the *Titanic!*" Colin flailed his arms.

It was exactly like the *Titanic,* thought Willy May. They were jumping ship and leaving the crew to fend for themselves.

"It's a basic virus that will run its course and be gone by the time we return for our next visit," he assured them.

"*If* we return," said Jean.

"I've moved my furniture into Les Jolies Eaux. I'll come without you, if necessary," the Princess snapped, and Jean cowed at the reprimand. "Colin is correct. We're only leaving for precautionary measures. No need for hysterics."

"Colin and I will close up after you all go," said Anne. "We should be getting back to Scotland anyhow. I left the children with Nanny Barnes. The twins are still on the bottle, you know, and we missed Charlie's birthday last month."

Willy May had no idea the couple had children. To hear that Anne had infant twins was shocking. The oversize caftans and mood swings suddenly made sense. Willy May hadn't been able to leave Hilly or Joanne for more than an hour until they were weaned. Even then, her milk came if she so much as heard a kitten mewl.

The Princess's jeep arrived and Colin took over at the wheel. "Give my goddaughter Flora May a kiss from me. Amy, too."

"I will," replied Anne, and Willy May saw the flicker of tenderness between the two friends. "Come to the Glen soon. You'll see how much the children have grown. We'll throw a hunting party."

"Let's." Princess Margaret took a seat. "Be safe flying home. You know how I feel about propeller planes — terrifying contraptions."

"We're not fond of them either, but we do what we must." Anne looked regretfully at Colin.

"Carry on then, dear. See you." Princess Margaret waved.

"See you," Anne replied with a little curtsy.

Arne and Hugo pulled up in jeeps, and the rest of the contingent boarded.

Patrick came down last from the upper rooms, slinging a backpack over his shoulder and handing a slip of paper to Joseph by the door.

"That's my number in London. Don't hesitate to call if you need anything."

Joseph nodded. "Thank you, sir. Much appreciated."

It warmed Willy May to him.

Patrick made a beeline to her. "You're really staying?"

"I am," said Willy May.

He leaned close to her ear and her heart beat fast despite her firm commitment to disinterest.

"Promise to take care of yourself." His concern was earnest.

His lips brushed her cheek. Peppermint and smoke. He pressed a folded slip of paper into her hand, and she curled her fist around it.

"Go," she nodded, "or you'll miss the ferry."

After he'd gone, Willy May opened her palm to find a note with his London address. He'd written:

I'll keep my promise: you are only for my eyes. Now you keep yours: be safe. — P

"Willy May!" someone called, and she tucked the note into her pocket.

Titus. It was good to see a friend.

"Thank God, you are well. I heard about Candace."

He nodded solemnly. "And I heard you are moving up to Firefly early. That is wise."

The trade winds had picked up. The smell of fish and must dabbled the air. Rain was coming. Titus tilted his gaze up to the overcast sky.

"You should stay there until this passes."

■ ■ ■ ■

PART 2
HILLY/GALATEA

■ ■ ■ ■

CHAPTER 11
THE IMPOSSIBLE DREAM

October 1972

The only way to and from Mustique was aboard a ferry that shuttled passengers to the islands peppered between St. Vincent and Grenada at the southernmost rim of the Caribbean Sea. A salty old seaman named Captain Tannis was at the helm and treated passengers and cargo as equals. He pushed the small vessel at such a speed that the bow clapped against the oncoming waves, rocking the boat to a nauseating degree and allowing the waves to crest the sides. Hilly gathered up the hem up of her cherry-red caftan to keep it dry. The seawater was already to her ankles, ruining the designer sandals she'd been given at her last photo shoot.

It was the fall of 1972. She'd left Paris iced over in its first frost. The world felt dark and she, a wandering shadow, lost and unseen.

173

Images of the Vietnam War dominated the nightly news no matter what country she was in. The Olympics had become a massacre. Bloody Sunday was followed by Bloody Friday. G.I. Joes were a best-selling toy. Director Stanley Kubrick ruled the theaters. Bowie, Zeppelin, and Pink Floyd LPs spun, and everybody was humming along to Carole King's "It's Too Late," whether they knew it or not. The world was a black hole of bedlam. So, she'd set out to find her starlight.

In an attempt at reinvention, she'd changed her given name. *Hilly* was a contortion of her mother, Willy, and father, Harry. The name felt like a noose. She could never live up to her parents' lost dreams. She'd chosen the name *Galatea* outside the Piccadilly Theatre in London.

Her father had just died after her parents' divorce, and it was her eighteenth birthday. Months prior, Grandmother Michael had purchased tickets for her and Joanne to see *Man of La Mancha.* For once, her grandmother and mother had put aside their rancor and agreed. They insisted the girls get out, which Hilly welcomed. After her father's death, their house felt . . . . oppressive.

London was gloriously alive. The buzz and

laughter of the crowded West End streets. The twinkling lights of the theater marquee. Her sister, Joanne, and she walked arm in arm, darting between people, letting themselves forget together that they'd never see their father again. Freeing themselves to laugh and be light. But when Don Quixote took center stage and sang "The Impossible Dream" with the spotlight growing bolder and brighter until the set was awash in white and the theater seats trembled with the force . . . it was her avalanche of the soul. Hilly had wept irrepressibly under the weight of unbearable sorrow.

"We're okay." Joanne had threaded her fingers through Hilly's own in the theater and squeezed. "Look — it's so beautiful."

It was and it wasn't. Beauty and suffering felt equal to each other. Hilly could only squeeze her sister's hand in reply and hope she, if no one else, understood the wordless depths of her meaning.

After the show, they'd stopped at the corner pub for fish and chips, and her eyes fell upon the name: *Galatea*. It was a Theatre District advertisement for an upcoming production of *Pygmalion and Galatea* that had been plastered to the brick alley wall. The play told the story of a beautiful sea nymph carved of ivory and so adored that the gods brought her to life.

Galatea. A new birth year, a new name. She would reinvent herself the same. She took it as her supernatural sanctification.

Call it karma, fate, fairies, or Jehovah. There wasn't a person on earth who didn't seek out the miraculous. As her mother said, dig down deep enough and you'll find the obverse. At the bottom of the sea was earth. Underneath the earth was water. Reach up to the sun and you'd find ice. Go down through the ice and there was fire. Humans were hardwired to search for the missing, even when they didn't know exactly what was missing. To everything was an equal and an opposite. That was science. That was faith. Not a revolutionary concept, but Hilly gave her mother credit for it.

Her father was an enigma. She never really knew what made him happy or sad. Some days, he would look at her and smile. Other days, he'd do the same and frown. As a child, she'd even gone so far as to keep a log of what she was wearing, eating, doing, saying, and the mood of her father in the hopes of tracking his happiness. But no matter what she did, there seemed no consistent pattern.

Her parents were like a playground teeter-totter. When one was up, the other was down. That was marriage, at least the marriage she'd witnessed at home. The joy of being up high couldn't exist without someone digging their heels into the dirt.

Truthfully, when Hilly heard the news of the divorce, her first reaction had been pride. *Finally,* she'd thought, *Mum's done something about it.* They'd known about Viscountess Hailsham for years. Joanne had been the one to tell her.

Hilly had been fifteen and Joanne thirteen when Joanne beckoned her into their shared bedroom one dusky afternoon. Willy May had been coloring her hair with an at-home box of Clairol Frost & Tip and their father was working late at the brewery offices. Joanne told her that two of her Girl Guides friends had overheard their mothers discussing Harry Michael and Viscountess Hailsham.

Hilly had gripped her Beverly Cleary *Jean and Johnny* copy so tightly, a page tore. "Liars!"

"They wouldn't lie about something like that." Joanne had gingerly taken the novel away and placed it on her bedside table. "Almost all my friends said that their parents have fooled around with other people. It doesn't mean anything . . . I don't think."

Joanne had always been instinctively decorous whereas Hilly was instinctively indecorous. Naturally, that made Joanne the family favorite. She was sensible, intelligent, and beautiful in that painfully pale way venerated by the Brits. Petite and prim. Her hair was the color of winter straw, her eyes like lapis stones, her cheeks like fresh-churned butter.

By comparison, Hilly's hair was the color of summer mud. Her eyes were more of a midnight blue, and she had a cascade of freckles across the bridge of her nose that she hid under thick powders. Tall and reedy, she'd sprouted awkwardly to five feet eleven inches by the age of fifteen. She felt like the Giant and the Beanstalk. Grandmother Michael said it must've come from her Texan kin . . . *everything is bigger in Texas,* wasn't that the saying?

"My English and American roses," their father had once called them side by side.

It was meant to be complimentary, but Hilly couldn't help feeling slighted. They lived in England, after all. And she was not deaf to the comments her grandmother made about Willy May's lack of refinement.

Joanne had taken after their father in personality. Her response to the affair was an example. She seemed to calmly accept their father's infidelity, while Hilly burned with rage. First, at her father, then at the viscountess, and last, at her mother, whom she felt ought to have given some acknowledging response. Instead, she'd feigned ignorance, which Hilly found more disgraceful than actual ignorance.

It was around the same time that Hilly's breasts blossomed. Her hips rounded, and she developed curves from front to back. She liked the power that these feminine qualities bestowed. Women were on the streets demanding equal pay, equal rights, and fair ownership of their bodies. The Women's Liberation Movement was all over the telly, validating her inner whispers that there was more to life than washing nappies, braiding hair, and turning a blind eye. There were sparks of that power in her mother, too often wrapped in temper and disregarded as petulance by her father. But she saw Willy May most clearly in those moments — when the veil was drawn back. Inside them both was a shared strength, and stifled rage.

So, at eighteen, she'd set her mind to be seen. She wanted the world to recognize Galatea.

On the ferry to Mustique, a male passenger sitting across ran his eyes up her exposed legs. So fixated on her parts, he didn't notice that she was staring at him staring at her. Beside him was a woman under a straw hat. She elbowed the man, and her silver wedding ring caught the sun. When he didn't respond to her jab, the woman huffed angrily in Hilly's direction: "This is a public transport, not a boudoir."

Hilly thought about dropping her hem and letting the silk be ruined by seawater but then, why should she? The man's wandering eye was not her problem. The wife was acting affronted while Hilly did nothing wrong. All that frustration should have been directed at her husband, who sat like a dope with his tongue lolling out.

Why was it a woman's job to be ashamed of so very much while men were ashamed of so very little? The memory of Paris resurfaced yet again and moved like a storm cloud. She put on her sunglasses, and the ocean turned from blue to gray.

She was glad when the couple disembarked at Port Elizabeth and she was the only one left aboard. Captain Tannis invited her into the covered helm, safe from the wet deck.

"Headed to Mustique?" he asked.

"That's right."

"Got business there?"

"Yes, my mum."

He scratched the stubble of his cheek. "Some people say that's where Princess Margaret keeps her harem of men. I know a fella. Said he was sailing by and saw it with his own two eyes. Solid guy. Known him since we was kids. I have a mind to trust his word."

Solid or not, the eyes could play tricks on a person. Dehydration had a hallucinatory effect. "Well, my mum is single so maybe it's the perfect place for her."

The captain squinted. For a moment, she assumed it was a look of disapproval, but then he threw back his head and laughed.

If only he knew my mum, Hilly thought, *then he wouldn't laugh.*

She could still vividly recall the coldness of their family's breakfast table. They went over to the big house for most of their meals. Grandmother Michael had a large kitchen and cooking staff, while their carriage house only had a toaster oven and an icebox. Grandmother Michael always sat at the head of the dining table; Hilly and Joanne to her left side; Father and Mother to her right. Only the sound of them chewing echoed round the table. Her father had the same thing every morning: two soft-boiled eggs, canned baked beans, one pat of butter thinly smeared on one slice of toast. For special occasions, he'd jazz it up with a bit of black pudding. But always black tea, no sugar. Granted, her mother was not a good cook. Eating at Grandmother Michael's probably saved them all from habitual gastritis or starvation.

But she and Joanne knew their mother's secret. She could prepare unconventionally delicious things. She did so every time their father took one of his weekend trips. Then, they would not go next door to Grandmother Michael's. They'd stay home in pajamas and eat in the kitchen. Willy May would buy hot buns from the neighborhood baker and add extra brown sugar and butter to the squidgy middles. Or goat's cheese on fresh figs from the Saturday market. Or she'd whip up frozen toaster waffles with maple syrup, which was their particular favorite. Whatever it was, they'd eat off the walnut cutting board, plucking pieces with their fingers, laughing and feasting until they'd licked every crumb and no evidence remained. Her mother had a gift for taking whatever little they had and making it feel ten times more.

"It's our breakfast club. Ladies only," she told them, and they relished having the confidence of their mother all to themselves.

Looking back, Hilly wondered why Willy May needed to conceal those happy mornings or why she never included their father. He might've enjoyed them — been amused, at the very least. When they started taking holiday sails and it was just their foursome, her mother still denied him the secret. No waffles, figs, or hot buns from the galley. Two boiled eggs, canned baked beans, slice of toast, pat of butter, black tea, no sugar. By giving him exactly what he asked for, Hilly often felt that her mother was punishing him. Because even she knew that sometimes what you ask for was not what you really needed. Considering his genetic heart disease and future heart attack, lighter fare might not have saved his life, but it would've done him a bit of good.

The dynamic between her parents — between men and women — was fraught with inconsistency and contradiction.

Captain Tannis's ferry lurched forward. The wind was fiercer in the direction of Mustique. A large wave crashed onto the deck and Hilly was grateful that he'd allowed her to move inside the wheelhouse. She anchored herself against the wooden banister and held the rope tied to the wall.

She'd grown up on her family's boat, the *Stingray.* Her parents had built the vessel together and used it for the family's twice-a-year vacations, summer and winter. She hadn't particularly liked boats then either and the *Stingray* had been a far studier craft than most others. It had a plush interior cabin, track lighting, a roomy shower, a queen-size bed for her parents, a bunk for them, and even a built-in hi-fi, which was Joanne's favorite part. But it was the intangible that bothered Hilly.

She'd never been fond of going to sleep in one place and waking up in another. Something about the body moving without consent triggered chronic nightmares. One of her recurring terrors was that she'd been left behind at a foreign port or Fortnum & Mason. The location was inconsequential: the feeling was the same. A terrifying realization that she was utterly alone, abandoned to the world. She'd cry out in her sleep, "Here I am! Here I am!", and awaken to find the summoning had worked. Her mother and sister were there.

But like all fears, the more one indulged them, the bolder they became until one day, they stepped right out of dreams into reality.

Her father was gone. Her mother moved off the family estate to a rental flat by the marina. Her sister would be going soon, too.

Grandmother Michael had offered to pay for Joanne's musical training if she agreed to her alma mater, Dartington College of Arts — in Devon! No such offer was extended to Hilly. She wasn't like Joanne, naturally skilled in some way that could be honed and sharpened. Hilly panicked and got the impulsive idea: *she'd leave them before they left her.*

She'd been eighteen, fueled on emotion with a handful of modeling gigs under her belt and the pressing knowledge that her clock was ticking. Beauty faded. Her mother was living proof. Like the sun, what was glorious at dawn was burnt out by midday. So, she accepted a modeling job in New York City. At first, just the one. But while there, her mother launched out on *Otrera,* and she knew she'd been right to go. There was nothing holding her to Cheltenham. No reason to return.

Following New York City, she went to Paris, Milan, Rio de Janeiro, and everywhere between. She'd figured out the trick to tricking the nightmare. She didn't sleep on boats or planes or anything transitory. In fact, she barely slept at all. She was too busy chasing her spotlight to face the darkness.

But now, at twenty-one, her light seemed snuffed. Her mother's telegrams had come in her darkest hour.

The ferry chugged into Mustique's Britannia Bay sooner than expected. On the dock, she recognized her mother standing in perfect pageant pose, her coif of golden hair shimmering under the sun.

"Welcome to Mustique," said Captain Tannis.

Hilly inhaled and held her breath as the ferry coasted to the dock. They'd exchanged sporadic letters, telegrams, and phone calls, but it'd been years since she'd seen her mother in person.

"Hilly!" Willy May welcomed.

"It's Galatea now, Mum," she corrected and immediately felt bad for doing so.

Her mother meant well, and truthfully, she didn't mind being called Hilly in private. It was as much her name as Galatea. But in public, even a public that consisted of one briny sea captain, she wanted to be called the name she'd become. She was proud of it, and she wanted the respect of the honorific.

"Fine, fine, a rose by any other name, as the saying goes. Let me look at you." Willy May put her hands on either side of Hilly's cheeks and held her a beat too long for Hilly's comfort. *Little but fierce;* Shakespeare must've known her mother.

186

"You didn't say your mum was Willy May," said Captain Tannis and Willy May released her.

"I — I didn't think you'd know each other."

Captain Tannis set Hilly's paisley-print suitcase on the dock. "Do you need me to carry this to the beach for you?"

"It's all right," said Willy May. "That's my calisthenics for the day."

Captain Tannis barked with laughter. "I'll be sure not to challenge you to an arm-wrestling match!"

"Go on." She waved to him. "The cross-winds are picking up. Don't want you to catch them on the water."

"Much obliged," he said, eyeing the sky. He tipped his hat and started the motor.

Willy May lifted the suitcase.

"I can carry that, Mum."

"Light as a feather. You didn't pack much."

Hilly shrugged. She hadn't much to pack, but this wasn't the time or place to get into all that. Right now, she wanted the world to condense down to two pinpoints: her and her mother.

Willy May nodded to the beach. "I got a cold Fanta in the cart."

Hilly followed Willy May down the pier.

187

She was exhausted. She'd traveled so far, and though her luggage was light, her heart was heavy. When her feet hit the sandy beach, her knees went weak. Her head spun. Her stomach dipped.

"Whoa there, honey." Willy May reached out to balance her, but Hilly shook off the wooziness. "I haven't slept. Long trip."

Willy May narrowed her eyes on Hilly. The way she'd done all Hilly's life. The intensity of that gaze had the power to see right through, a mother's X-ray vision. Hilly hoped she couldn't see everything. She wasn't ready to explain.

"We best get you home." Willy May turned toward a golf cart parked under a palm tree. "Come on, Hilly."

"Galatea. Please, Mum."

It was said out of frustration, fatigue, and the itch of wanting to be treated as separate from her mother, a grown woman, Galatea! Unfortunately, the protestation only made her sound more childish, even to herself.

"Right." Willy May loaded Hilly's luggage into the cart and handed her the Fanta. "Drink this. And when we get home, we'll get some food in you. You're too skinny, even by Twiggy standards."

Hilly had only eaten a bag of peanuts with a glass of wine on the plane, and the ferry wasn't the kind of vessel with a snack bar. She was hungry and queasy on an empty stomach.

"Okay." She popped the can's tab, sipped orange sugar bubbles, and felt a little better. She slid down in the passenger seat so that her neck rested on the back cushion.

Willy May started the golf cart and drove, letting the wind be the voice between them. Hilly closed her eyes and laced her fingers over her ribs, the bones like a birdcage holding in the last six months, holding in the heartache and hoping that family might be the remedy.

CHAPTER 12
GUYS AND DOLLS

Hilly had been in Paris, working for *Vogue* magazine with legendary photographer Guy Bourdin. He was French, an artist, and twice her age. Praised for shooting marketing campaigns like gallery exhibitions, he was known for idolizing his subjects — be it a face or a collar ruffle. His ability to turn a shoe into a provocation could make even the strictest puritan lust after a buckle. He was volatile in his moods and unapologetic in his emotional outbursts as only a Frenchman could be. When he was happy, his whole body laughed. When he was angry, he raged from head to toe. He was so different from every other man Hilly had known.

The magazine had put the models up at the Four Seasons Hotel George V off the Champs-Élysées with a panoramic view of the Eiffel Tower.

"Welcome to the historic Golden Triangle," the concierge welcomed, as if Hilly should know what that meant. She'd thought it had something to do with the decor. The walls were flanked in mirrors reflecting triangular chandeliers, spinning the rooms in a golden glitz kaleidoscope.

Vogue brought over a crew from New York who set up in the living room of the Royal Suite playing the Beatles, the Bee Gees, and Bowie while doing Ziggy Stardust makeup and a teasing hair so high, the models were a foot taller. There were five of them, but Guy chose her as his muse. It wasn't a competition — no sashes or titles to claim — and yet, it absolutely was.

Dressed to the nines in haute couture, Guy took Hilly to the heart of Paris at dawn on the first morning of the shoot. The smell of French bread and coffee pressed down on the early hour, making her feel as wide awake and vibrant as the new day. All around her, tourists stopped, gawked, and edged closer, whispering to each other, "Who is she?"

"Belle!" he shouted. "Gal, you are incredible! Amazing! Radiant! Turn your cheek so they can see your magnificence. Arch your back so they can feel your love! Smile — no, no, look away — make them ache for you!"

The rapid *click* of his shutter was electrifying. The other models slunk to the sides of the frame, consuming madeleines and champagne to pass the time. While Galatea rose up in front of the camera. Guy saw every angle and called her beautiful.

How could she help but fall in love with him?

She'd never been with a man before. Three *almosts* with boys at school; but each time, she'd been struck with a wave of virtuous guilt and given them head instead. She'd never gone steady with anyone. It was the one secret she had withheld from everyone, even her sister. She let the world believe the fantasy and so they treated her as the vixen. She paid for it with her heart.

The affair ended terribly. They spent three weeks in Paris. When the shoot was over, the crew returned to New York. The other models went back on their diets and flew on to their next bookings.

Guy disappeared without a goodbye. He left a thousand francs on the bedside table with a note saying that everyone got a bonus and for her to take care of herself. It upset her more than it ought to have. She spent most of the money on international calls to her agent in California. He told her what she already knew. Guy had gone home to his wife and children.

She'd been wholly seen and wholly unseen in the blink of a camera shutter. Then came the double punch. Her agent explained that *Vogue* was going in a new direction. Modern, practical magazine readers wanted easy, adaptable style.

They were doing away with all the seductive models, including Galatea. On top of that, she had auditioned for a major film role just before boarding her flight to Charles de Gaulle Airport. The movie studio cast someone blonder, fresher. The Kodak girl: Cybill Shepherd.

Modeling was a means to an end. Being an actress had always been Hilly's goal. She'd been in Ken Russell's historical film *The Devils,* which garnered her praise as a "minor but powerful" character. Her agent said it was Hollywood's door swinging open. She'd screen-tested for Columbia Pictures' *The Last Picture Show.* Everyone said she was a shoo-in. Cybill, the model that the director had seen on a *Glamour* magazine in a supermarket, got the part.

She'd been rejected personally and professionally.

"Why didn't they want me?" she'd cried in the empty hotel room. The question clotted the air.

Heartbreak was a living plague.

She collected her forwarded mail from the hotel concierge before checking out and there was a telegram from her mother:

NEW HOME. MUSTIQUE ISLAND. LOVE, MUM

She didn't even go back to California for her things. Instead, she sold a pair of Manolo Blahnik heels that had been left behind with a wad of gum on the sole. With the money, she bought a ticket to St. Vincent and then on to Mustique by ferry, wearing castoffs from the shoot. Costumes were all she had.

"Oliver Messel designed the house," said Willy May while walking her through the villa.

"The stage designer?" asked Hilly.

Her mother ran her hand over a cascade of pearlescent decorative tiles. "Yes."

Oliver Messel had done the sets on *Suddenly, Last Summer* with Katharine Hepburn, Elizabeth Taylor, and Montgomery Clift. He'd won an Academy Award for Best Production Design. It gave her new perspective on the house.

"I named it Firefly," her mother continued. "Oliver put little nods to the name here and there. See?" She pointed to a corner where a floor tile had been stamped with a little winged insect. "It's like a game. Every room has one somewhere."

She could tell her mother wanted her to play. Willy May always tried to rally her daughters to contests. But at the heart of any game had to be the player's desire to win. Hilly hadn't the desire. She was exhausted. In her caftan's pocket was a blue pill that she rolled between her forefinger and thumb. It brought her comfort. Sleep. Merciful, paralyzing sleep.

The house was tiered like a wedding cake from a slick magazine. The ones that looked too good to be real because they *were*. Made of wood, Styrofoam, and hardened sugar paste: cakes for having, not eating. Willy May pointed out all the home's novelties from the colonial porticos to the bohemian-chic light fixtures. Hilly was too weary to feign admiration. She'd just come from Paris, glitteringly exotic and dripping with trophies. What was most attractive to her was the way the windows framed the island, like the curtains of a proscenium opening to a production of *South Pacific*. She stopped to stare and hummed a bar of "I'm Gonna Wash That Man Right Outa

My Hair" to herself. It soothed somehow, so she stayed there while her mother walked on. The slanting sun rippled across the lagoon, producing a school of leaping rainbows mirroring the fish below. A trick of the eye. She blinked but the breeze only multiplied their colors.

"I wanted to show you the kitchen next." Willy May had circled back to find her. "Make you a plate of cheese crackers?"

"Can it wait? I'm so tired, Mum."

"Of course." Willy May put a hand on Hilly's backbone and rubbed up and down the knobs of her spine.

She closed her eyes and breathed deep, smelling honey and ginger spice, warm as tea. She couldn't say for certain if that was Mustique or her mother.

Stay close, please, Mum, she thought.

But Willy May dropped her hand. "Go to bed. When you wake up, I'll fry eggs. Put some protein in you."

She guided her up the stairs, and Hilly saw that the rooms on the upper landing were grimy with concrete and plaster dust. Paint cans and ladders stacked haphazardly. It was more like a construction zone than a home.

"We're going to have to share for a bit," said Willy May.

In the master bedroom were two cots. A gauzy mosquito net hung from the ceiling. It looked like one of the living room tents she and Joanne constructed over their tufted velvet sofa and dusty wingback chairs as children. They'd pretend the webbing was a magic veil, transforming Grandmother Michael's antiques into the rooms of *House & Garden* magazine, transforming them, too.

"I moved in as soon as I could," Willy May explained. "Arne is doing punch-list stuff. Spackle and paint mostly. You came in time to help put the place together. We need furniture — starting with beds." Willy May popped the metal buckles on her suitcase and opened it wide. "Are your pajamas in here?"

She lifted the spaghetti strap of a sequined dress. Emerald sparkles flashed. Still holding the dress, she picked up a black lace lingerie top.

"Well, these won't do. The mosquitoes will eat you alive. 'Mustique' comes from the French word for mosquito."

Hilly took the garments out of her hands, put them back in the suitcase, and shut the top. She was too tired to cause a scene, but she didn't want her mother going through her things. She was all grown up now. She would choose what to show and what to hide.

While testing camera lighting, Guy's assistant had accidentally snapped an image of them leaning so close to one another that their lips nearly touched. Guy had given it to her — a token of his love, she'd thought. Now, she understood. He didn't want evidence of his extramarital affair floating around set, not even in the wastebasket. He knew she'd keep it hidden. Still was. The photograph was under her nightgown, and she didn't want Willy May to find it or the bottle of pink pills beside it.

Hilly slid the suitcase under the cot. "Don't worry about me."

Willy May tapped her foot. "Okay, but at least put on a pair of slacks and tonic."

She handed over linen pants and a bottle of Kokoda insect repellent.

"Slather up. Put some in your hair, too, or you'll regret it."

Hilly took the bottle. "What kind of place is this?"

"An island of bloodsuckers." Willy May laughed and swatted away a flying assailant. "Like I said, *moustique.*"

Hilly didn't see the humor. She changed into a T-shirt and her mother's pants. Too short for Hilly, they ended above her ankles.

She rubbed Kokoda on the skin that showed and greased it through her hair. It was pungent with camphor and made her nose run, but if that's what it took, so be it.

She climbed under the mosquito netting and the room went gossamer. When she closed her eyes, the sea air made her feel like she was docked in the hull of her childhood: mother, father, sister. Before she remembered to take the pill in her pocket, she was asleep. It was the first time she'd slept unassisted since her father's death.

Hours later, after the sun had set and the tropical frogs had commenced their *mo-mee, mo-mee* lullaby deep in the thicket of the jungle night, Hilly woke briefly to find her mother bedded beside her. She rose and unveiled herself from the mosquito tent. The light was bright. She was sure she'd find a full moon. Instead, a crooked crescent grinned down.

Swear not by the moon, the inconstant moon that monthly changes in her circled orb, lest that thy love prove likewise variable.

Her favorite of Juliet's lines. It felt truest.

A hundred fireflies twinkled outside her window while thousands more blinked on and off down the cliff's slope. Their flickers took on a rhythmic dance, and she understood why her mother had named the house after them. They made their own sparks, exchanging light in unique patterns of courtship. Males and females asking, *Will you love me?* A flash for yes. No flash for no.

Hilly gently cupped one of the insects and held it in her palm. How much simpler their ways were. If only humans could be so honest. She let the firefly go, and it took flight.

Hilly wondered where Guy was in the world. The thought of him tore her raw again. She gulped down the cry and berated herself for being a naive romantic.

"You okay?" asked Willy May from the bed.

Hilly turned sharply, surprised to see her awake.

Her mother patted the cot. "Come on."

She took a step forward but then hesitated. She didn't want to be treated like a child, and yet . . . part of her wanted to be exactly that again. But childhood only existed in hindsight. She couldn't say who she was or wanted to be now. Her head and heart were all thorned up.

What she knew was that when Willy May beckoned her, the yearning for Guy was quelled by an even stronger power: the longing to curl like a kitten beside her mother.

She pulled up the netting and crawled into the cot.

Willy May had never been one to coddle her and Joanne openly, but there was an unspoken understanding that sometimes it took all of them, bound together, to defeat the night. Willy May would come in the darkness when she or Joanne had nightmares, and they'd wrap themselves around her like vines.

Now, Hilly leaned her head into her mother's shoulder. Her soft skin pillowed against her cheek. Willy May inhaled and exhaled. Hilly listened to the vibration of it through their bodies as one.

"Mum . . . ," she whispered. She hadn't meant to say it aloud and she wasn't sure what to follow it with.

"Mm-hmm," Willy May replied in half sleep.

"I'm glad I'm here," said Hilly.

"Me too, honey," said Willy May. "Sleep now."

On the floor beside their beds, Hilly recognized a figurine. It was the goddess that she and Joanne had given Willy May on the Mothering Sunday that they'd spent in Santorini, Greece. The merchant who sold it to them said that the Amazon queen was the most admired mother of them all. Hilly hadn't thought of it in years. The sight of it plucked a nostalgic chord — not for that doll but another.

When she was very young, before they'd set sail on the *Stingray,* she'd had a miniature doll no bigger than her thumb. It was part of the dollhouse that she and Joanne received as a Christmas gift from Grandmother Michael. The dolls were hand-painted to resemble their family members. The mother doll had red lips, rosy cheeks, and a beautiful tuft of shiny corn-silk hair. Hilly had taken it and claimed the figurine had been lost in the garden. In truth, it was in her pocket even while the lie was being spun. Deceiving her sister weighed most heavily on her, but she wasn't like Joanne, who made friends easily. The girls in Hilly's school had called her names — *snobby, skinny, stupid.* When they teased her in the lunch canteen, she'd slip her hand into her pocket and hold the doll tight. It reminded her that she was her mother's daughter. There was beauty inside her, an expansiveness that she felt even if no one saw.

When her father died and her mother launched out to circle the globe, she'd left the doll in the carriage house with all the other Michael family mementos. A token of a bygone dream. But seeing the statuette made her realize that just because you left a thing, didn't mean it left you . . . and she was glad for that.

CHAPTER 13
MAKE IT PINK, MAKE IT BLUE

"We need to order you clothes." Willy May flipped through a Sears Wish Book.

Hilly had just woken from a nap and was eating buttered cinnamon toast on the veranda.

"You need more to wear than what you brought," Willy May continued. "What size are you?"

"Five feet eleven inches. Thirty-two, twenty-two, thirty-two," she answered on instinct, though the measurements were hardly accurate. They were what she needed to be on paper.

Willy May scribbled in the catalog margin. "I'll order a size up. You've got to leave breathing room in the tropics."

Hilly bit her toast, chewed, and swallowed. It hit like a stone in her gut. The catch-22 of going cold turkey off the pills. She had an appetite that her body didn't know what to do with. It hadn't bothered her so much before. Fashion photographers preferred for models not to eat, drink, or take bathroom breaks during shoots.

Hilly's makeup artist in Paris had been the one to introduce her: "Pinks get you up — energized! Blues bring you down — sleep. These are doctor prescribed, so they're safe. Everybody on set is taking them," she had assured. "It's the only way to go four A.M to four A.M."

Hilly was quickly hooked and considered the photographs with Guy some of her finest work. No wonder — she had been high as a shooting star and fallen just as quickly.

Sobriety was a struggle. She was hungry all the time. But the minute she ate, she felt queasy and had to take a nap. She'd spent her first week on Mustique eating and sleeping, eating and sleeping. Her mother attributed it to travel fatigue. She fixed her fried eggs and cinnamon sugar toast with fruit for breakfast, lunch, and dinner. In the hopes of expanding her diet, Willy May had ordered a shipment of supplies, which had arrived by ferry that morning.

The first box contained ketchup, Vienna sausages, bac-o-bits, toaster waffles, maple syrup, prunes, Bisquick, mixed nuts . . .

The second box was entirely filled with Charmin toilet paper rolls.

"The true island gold," Willy May had said. "I wouldn't recommend wiping with Colin's cotton unless you want to hatch a boll weevil in your cooch."

She did not.

There were also catalogs for their next order. Everything from electric hair-dryer bonnets and braided rugs to paisley wallpapers and casual fashions.

"I need your help making this place presentable."

Willy May had no concept of creating a home from scratch. Her single contribution to their house in England had been a color television set, placed beneath the oil-painted family portrait. Quite a stink was made about it. They'd grown up watching *Doctor Who* and *Gilligan's Island* under Grandmother Michael's disapproving gaze.

Here they had an entire villa to decorate. It was clear that her mother was overwhelmed. Hilly was keen on showing how her natural proclivities might be the solution. She spent a week flagging items and styles in the catalogs. The whole time she didn't put on a stitch of makeup or run a comb through her hair. Decorating gave her a purpose that had nothing to do with how *she* looked, but rather, how she transformed the outside to match her inner vision. A marked change and great relief.

She was proud of what she'd done and presented Firefly's design storyboard to Willy May. She wanted her mother to get a sense of all the items together.

"A kind of fairy-tale theme."

Willy May lifted an eyebrow.

"See? Each room has a story motif. One room will be all iridescent shells, another will be all hummingbirds, and another fireflies, of course. Each unique."

"*Mm,* sounds nice," said Willy May. "But what about the furniture? I appreciate what you're trying to do, but we need beds."

Hilly had picked out the home's accoutrements: bath mats and matching towels, chiffon curtains and fringed lampshades, dining room plates stamped with gold wings, colorful tablecloths and seahorse napkin rings. Stylish, modern things that Grandmother Michael said were frivolous and never let through her doors. But Hilly had neglected the beds.

"Let's focus on the essentials first, shall we?" said Willy May. "Titus knows where to find everything at a bargain." She fingered the edge of one magazine. "I appreciate your zeal but we need to be . . . somewhat thrifty."

Her mother hadn't given her a budget,

and she hadn't thought to ask.

"Oh," she said when it dawned on her. "I can be thrifty."

"Good girl. We aren't like the Tennants, but we can still have nice things."

Colin had returned the day before, bringing with him bolts of indigo and crimson silks fringed with gold and silver beads. His latest business venture was the creation of lavish party tents. The prototypes he planned to test on Mustique. Anne had apparently remained in Scotland with their children this go.

"There's a dinner party tomorrow night at the Cotton House," Willy May continued, "to welcome new residents building on the eastern shore. A doctor from New York. You may want to wash your hair, dear."

Hilly scratched her neck. Colin was important. His guests were important. But mostly, it was important to her mother, and she wanted to please her.

So, she collected her catalogs. "Yes, Mum."

Willy May smiled. "Go into my closet and pick something. My long dresses will be too short on you, but I have some others that might work."

The next day before dinner, Hilly shampooed with L'Oréal and couldn't help whispering, "Because I'm worth it," while she scrubbed.

It was the new ad campaign. Her agent had submitted her portfolio to the company's casting director but then never heard back.

She swiped her hand across the misty mirror so she could see herself: hair stringy and wet around her bare face; collarbone jutting out awkwardly; the shallows of her eyes were dark and puffy.

"Hello, Hilly," she said.

The steam fogged the mirror again. She ruffled her hair so that it took on a sexy wave across her brow, bit her lips to bring color, cocked her shoulder, and turned her cheek to her best angle. She swiped the mirror again.

"Because I'm worth it," she repeated in her deepest register before puckering her lips for the final camera close-up.

Yes, there she was: Galatea.

In the master bedroom, Willy May laid out two sheath dresses: one neon pink, one neon blue. A few years past their fashion prime but still pretty.

"Which one?" she asked aloud. It reminded her of the war between fairies in Disney's *Sleeping Beauty:* make it pink or make it blue. The result, in the film at least, had been a disastrous mishmash and future ruin.

A cat meow from under the cots set off a series of them: feeding time. There'd been a litter of calicos born at the Cotton House over the summer and Willy May had brought home the whole kit and caboodle. The tomcat was somewhere in the jungles of Mustique. But apparently the mother queen, Checkers, had belonged to a woman named Candace and her daughter Ada. There was an outbreak of fever and Candace had been stricken with a bad case. She came through but working the hours that Colin's full-time employment required was not sustainable. The pair decided it was best to return to family on St. John's. Willy May had offered to take in the cat for them. Unbeknownst to everyone, Checkers was carrying three more, two girls and a boy.

Hilly and Joanne had never had pets growing up. Mother Michael didn't allow so much as a finch to roost. *People and animals should not room together,* she'd said. *It isn't sanitary.* And on the *Stingray,* there'd barely been room enough for the four of them. The closest they'd come to a pet was a purple orchid whose roots they set in a bowl of water each Sunday to "eat." Whatever the reason, it stopped blooming and became a pot of garden-variety green leaves. Without the blooms to catch their attention, they forgot to feed it, and eventually, it died.

Hilly feared the same outcome for a pet. A dead plant was one thing. A dead dog or cat was unforgivable.

She watched Checkers roll awake from her nap, stretch, and then lead two of her little ones down to the kitchen, where Willy May kept the bag of kibble. It made Hilly glad that the kittens had her to look after them and made her wonder about maternal instincts. Not from the point of view of the mother — hundreds of people had written about that, hadn't they? But maternal instincts from the point of view of the child. When did a person know that her mother is her mother and being so, must love her? Was it there from inception like breathing or did it grow as they did? The old nature versus nurture debate. It went both ways.

Make it pink or make it blue. She held one dress up to her frame and then the other.

"Wear the blue," her mother said from the doorframe. She nestled a spotted kitten under her chin.

It was a small gesture, but Hilly had never seen her mother do it before. Not to any creature, not even to her or Joanne. So

211

potent with affection; she couldn't take her eyes away.

"We should probably go on and name these guys. I think they're here to stay," Willy May continued. The kitten batted gently at her cheek.

"Okay," said Hilly.

A scrap of paper with boxed *X*'s and *O*'s lay on the bed. An attempt by Willy May at gamesmanship.

"How about Tic, Tac, and Toe? Keeping with the familial tradition."

"I think Checkers would approve." Willy May winked. "Come on, Tic, let's go christen your siblings." They went down to the kitchen, where she poured the kibble into bowls, the sound causing the meows to crescendo and then immediately fall silent with dinner contentment.

Upstairs, Hilly continued to dress. She colored her face with Willy May's cosmetics, hiding the blemishes and painting on cat's eyes, rose lips, and apple cheeks. She feathered her hair with Velcro rollers and applied a swipe of Vaseline on her collarbones to make her skin shimmer. Last, she slipped on the blue sheath dress.

After feeding the cats, Willy May went ahead to the Cotton House to prepare for the party. Colin had declared mojitos the night's specialty so George had asked if she might bring extra mint from her garden.

It was the first time that Hilly had driven the cart herself and trivial though it might've been, the power of the acceleration underfoot and the wheel in her palms felt a measurable exploit after months of being led by the bit, like a show pony.

She revved the engine but took the roads at a leisurely pace. She wasn't in a hurry. The sun was beginning to descend into the ocean. By the time she arrived at the party, it would be gone. Another day over. Another night filling the sky with stargazers, staring down, staring up. It depended on your point of view.

Twice, she was so busy looking up at the purple twilight that she drifted off the marked path. One wrong turn, and she'd be in the jungle or tumbling down a hill. Mustique might've been three short miles, but so many significant events happened in the smallest of places. A boat was a castle. An island, a kingdom. A person could go off course anywhere.

Too soon, the bright lights of the Cotton House were unmistakable. She parked the cart at the pool house. When the purr of the engine died away, the twang of guitars, tinkle of glasses, and drone of conversation throbbed at her temples before she'd even entered. She sat a moment alone with her hand in her dress pocket.

She'd brought a pink pill. She told herself that it was only for emergency use. She'd done so well without. But sitting on the edge of Colin's dazzling estate, she felt the old anxieties rising. So, she gathered the saliva in her mouth, put the pink on her tongue, and swallowed hard.

Entering the party, a doorman announced: "Miss Galatea of Firefly."

Name and pedigree. The right ones held the world on a string. The rest were bobbles on it.

Heads turned, and for a fleeting moment, she felt the usual rush. Then, just as quickly, the audience turned away.

The drug took effect. Her heart beat fast. Her pulse raced with a thousand volts of confidence. She'd forgotten how good it felt.

She took a champagne coupe from the waiter and raised it to her approaching mother.

"Mum!" She drank the glass. She needed to dilute the pink with something or she'd pass out from the head rush.

Willy May's expression changed from welcome to concern.

"Hilly?"

Hilly didn't correct her on the name. Her tongue tickled where the pill had sat.

A bald fellow with a mischievous grin joined them. Leprechaun gold glimmered in his eyes, but that could've also been the candlelight.

"Colin," Willy May said. "This is my eldest daughter."

"Quite extraordinary," he said and tapped his chin with a manicured set of fingers. "It's amazing how the genetics manifest. So much of her beautiful mother and yet so dark and exotic! Her father's side must've been Welsh. The Spanish and Moors' influence."

Without waiting for a reply, he spun round to the crowd. "Galatea — our very own sea nymphette! She's joining us from her *Vogue* shoot in Paris."

He extended his bejeweled hand and led her to the banquet table, chattering away about something that passed through her like the vibration of a tuning fork. His plummy accent fell on her ears like a series of staccato notes instead of words.

A beauty, he said clearly, and she sighed.

She was seated without remembering how she got there. Colin introduced her to a couple across the table with matching suntans.

"This is Dr. Rob — we try to avoid surnames. Anne's rule. And one that I quite support. It makes things more intimate. Don't you agree?"

Hilly nodded. She hadn't asked for explanation.

"Dr. Rob is a Harvard-trained obstetrics surgeon, now practicing in New York."

Dr. Rob smiled hello.

"And his wife, Beatrice," Colin continued. "An American heiress and summa cum laude graduate of Smith College, if I have that correct?"

Beatrice took a beat to finish her wine. "Quite."

"Beatrice's parents and Anne's are old friends."

"Okay," said Hilly. She wasn't familiar with Beatrice, Anne, or their families.

Beatrice looked at her curiously and then raised an eyebrow at her husband.

The waiters approached.

Willy May sat to her left. "Hilly, are you okay?"

Colin overheard. "Are you unwell, dear?"

"Still a bit jet-lagged." Willy May nudged a glass of water forward. "Drink this."

Hilly obeyed but then drank the red wine, too.

"I'm *so* thirsty," she said. "Not used to

this island heat."

Willy May handed her a dinner roll.

"Is this the body and blood?" The chute between her mind and mouth was slippery.

Willy May looked horrified, but Colin laughed and so did the table guests.

"A pious she-devil, I like that."

The salad course was served: butter lettuce and baby carrots with their bushy green tops on. A feast for Bugs Bunny, she thought.

"What's up, Doc?"

Everyone laughed again, except Willy May.

She should audition for more comedic roles. They could be her career watershed. Hilly made a mental note to call her agent about it, but by the time they removed the salad plates, she'd forgotten.

The main course was some kind of red meat. Beef or lamb, rabbit or venison. Who could tell by looking? She ate and felt herself sobering up. The voices cemented into conversations.

Dr. Rob and Colin were discussing tennis when the dessert was served: a ruby ring of sangria Jell-O.

"Is there a court on the island?" Dr. Rob asked while wobbly fruit was spooned onto plates.

"Not yet. We'll have them start building one!"

"Do you play?" Beatrice asked Hilly.

"Not well."

"Well then, Rob must give you a lesson. He's an ace with a ball and racket. I've never enjoyed the game, myself. Too much exertion. I'm more of a spectator."

Dr. Rob leaned back in his chair and Hilly's gaze shifted with the movement. He winked at her and his wife watched.

Hilly inhaled sharply. Her stomach cramped.

Dr. Rob was inviting her to more than a ball game and his wife was keen on it. She looked to her mother, but Willy May was deep in conversation with Colin about the construction of a community tennis court.

I heard wrong, she told herself; *it's the pill.* Sometimes the pinks made her emotional, bringing fears to the surface. One of which was that she was little more than a passing amusement, no better than a bouquet of roses from the flower stand. When she curled up with age, she'd similarly be tossed in the trash for a fresh-cut bunch. She would mean nothing, be nothing. All she, Hilly Michael, truly had were images of a failed seductress named Galatea and the abiding suspicion that something inside her

218

was fundamentally puckered. A dropped stitch in the knitting of her person.

Once when she was nine years old, her father invited a group of his businessmen friends for drinks on the *Stingray*. They were at a port off the coast of California. She had begged Willy May to buy her a bikini, thinking it would make her look like Raquel Welch. Everyone in California was a celebrity. She wanted to be one, too. She was tall for her age, and with a handful of tissues stuffed into her tops, she looked positively Raquel-ian. She'd worn the new bathing suit that afternoon, lying casually on the boat while the men sipped their cocktails. She knew they were staring at her, and she liked it. Willy May had been in the galley fixing appetizers with Joanne. When her father went down to check on them, one of his guests had gestured to her.

"Harry better watch out for that one," he'd said. "She's going to be a handful with the fellas."

"A handful?" his colleague had replied. "Looks like she'll be *two*." And then he'd cupped the air like breasts, and the men had laughed.

Her father and mother had come back up with pigs-in-a-blanket and cheese cubes on toothpicks.

She never told anyone what the men had said. In the moment, she'd felt proud. Being admired felt so much like being loved. She'd wanted to be seen as desirable, objectified, pleasing. Part of her still wanted to. That was the deeper shame of it.

Dr. Rob spooned globs of Jell-O into his mouth. Sick to her stomach, she pushed her bowl away.

"Galatea is busy decorating Firefly for me." Her mother saved her.

Colin smiled. "Interior design is one of my passions! I'll put you in touch with my consignment dealer, Delaney. He helped me find the most magnificent boudoir set. It belonged to a Grecian princess — stolen by pirates who sold it to a collector in Barbados. It's my favorite. Do you have an idea of your style?"

"A bohemian water sprite theme," said Willy May.

"Lovely," said Colin. "The last time I visited you, it was nothing but wooden planks. The crew was down with that awful fever. Speaking of visions, have you seen the photograph?"

Willy May furrowed her brow. "Photograph?"

"Indeed. Your Patrick's photograph — with the Princess."

Hilly wouldn't have noticed the pronoun except that her mother blushed and broke out in a glisten.

"He's hardly *my* Patrick." Willy May waved to a barman mixing drinks. "Club soda on ice with a lime twist, please?"

"Photographer?" Hilly asked. Her mind hung on only one.

"Yes, Earl Patrick," said Colin. "A close friend of your mother's."

The barman brought the drink. The ice inside made the glass surface slick and dewy.

"I haven't seen it," said Willy May. "But I'm sure it's great."

"It's marvelous!" said Colin. "I'll have a print made for you to hang at Firefly."

Willy May drank with a nod.

"We'll have to have him come back and take another. Now that we have new residents." Colin lifted his glass to the doctor and his wife. Then, remembering Hilly, he swiveled. "You, too."

Willy May set down her glass with a sturdy *click* on the teak.

"I hear you have a son." She redirected the conversation to Beatrice. "Will he be joining you here? I'd love to introduce my daughter to eligible, young bachelors."

Hilly momentarily balked, but then realized her mother had observed the couple's innuendo. This was her warning shot.

"Rusty is five," Beatrice replied coolly. "I understand that arranged marriages are common for the British, but such things are frowned upon by Americans."

"Oh, but Willy May is an American!" said Colin.

"Yes," said Beatrice. "She should know better."

"I didn't realize he was so young. Innocence is not a thing to be squandered." Willy May pushed back from the table. "My apologies, Colin. We must be going. It's getting late."

"Must you?" asked Colin.

"I'm afraid, so." Willy May took Hilly's hand. "It was nice to meet you, Beatrice, Dr. Rob. Welcome to Mustique."

The couple smiled back cordially. The sparring match had ended in a draw.

"I'll come up to Firefly soon," said Colin and then he beckoned for the minstrels to play.

Outside the Cotton House, Willy May put the back of her hand to Hilly's cheek

"You're warm."

How could she explain truthfully?

"I'm better now, Mum."

Willy May shook her head. "I told you, there was a fever earlier in the year. People almost died. I'm not taking chances." She put an arm around her. "Home and straight into a bath."

Hilly leaned into her mother's hold. It felt nice for someone to lift her up, whether she deserved it or not.

CHAPTER 14
HILLY CAT

After the New Yorkers left to celebrate the American Thanksgiving, Colin came to Firefly. He was every bit as theatrical as the first night Hilly had met him. Maybe even more. He showed up in Bermuda shorts, a ladies' silk shirt printed in hibiscus flowers unbuttoned down to his navel, and a matching pink scarf tied in a bow.

"It's our latest Mustique fashion line. We're selling these pieces at the Cotton Cutie-que — that's my pet name for the boutique in the village. Does it meet your approval, Galatea?"

She smiled. "The person makes the fashion. The fashion can't make the person."

A nice quote when removed from the original context. A casting agent had rejected her with it, stating that a white man in a white suit could be Mark Twain or Colonel Sanders selling cheap chicken. The person mattered and not everyone was the right person for everything. Hilly knew this was true and yet . . . she couldn't stop wanting to be the right person for everything.

Colin preened at her response. It was the right one.

"I'm hoping to get you into some. You've got just the frame to show off our island trends. Built like a palm tree — or a champagne flute. Ooh, are those mimosas?"

Willy May had made a pitcher for his visit and handed him a bubbling glass now.

"Lovely." He sipped and licked the creamy foam from his upper lip. "Shall we see what you've done with the place?"

They led him through the rooms, where he crowed "Divine!" at every turn. Then he settled himself on a chaise longue with a cushion under his left side and the mimosa in his right hand.

"I must admit, I'm a little irritated with Arne and Oliver. They did a vastly better job here than on the Cotton House. Granted, they had to make do with the bones provided at ours, but this place — it's so stylishly modern. The way you've decorated. I knew you and Delaney would be an excellent match. Isn't he fabulous? All of his items are one-of-a-kind trophies."

Colin had introduced them to Mr. Delaney Archer, who ran a secondhand shop in

Barbados. Over the course of a few weeks, he'd outfitted each room according to Hilly's vision. The interior of Firefly was her utopia. The island and the house's framework might've been her mother's choices, but the inside was hers. She fashioned it with all the things she dreamed of and never had in England: teak and bamboo furniture, braided rugs, seashell lamps, cream linens, and rayon curtains that looked just as glamorous as any silk. Grandmother Michael would've scoffed and called it all kitsch. Maybe it was, but Hilly relished that she had chosen each item.

Colin lifted a groomed eyebrow at her. "Your fashion pedigree at work, no doubt."

"Thank y—" she began, but he'd already moved on.

"I need to go over to Barbados. My last collectible was a 1939 Louis Vuitton trunk that belonged to a Nazi general. Rumor has it that he kept his stash of women's negligees inside for his own private dress-up. I don't entirely believe it, mind you, but it's sensational to imagine." He laughed and then frowned. "I hate the idea that I'm missing something new at Delaney's shop. I'll have to wait for Anne. She's very particular about what I bring into the house — dust allergies." He drank the last of his mimosa. "But that's not what I'm here to discuss."

He extended the empty glass to Hilly. She hesitated, unsure if it was a request or a gesticulation. He set it down on the glass side table.

"I thought this was a social call to your neighbors," Willy May chided.

"Of course it is," said Colin. "But I also wished to discuss an opportunity that would allow the Mustique Company, as an enterprise, to be choosier about who purchases the remaining plots — who we invite to be our neighbors — and bring in a bit of extra capital. Not that any of us *needs* it."

"And what exactly is the opportunity?" asked Willy May.

"Renting your villa." He cleared his throat. "You know we lend rooms at the Cotton House as our social calendar permits. It was Titus's suggestion and a good one. I let him run the books when it comes to managing Mustique's properties. He's a whiz with numbers."

"Is Princess Margaret renting out Les Jolies Eaux?"

He spat a little spindrift into the air. "Heavens no! She's a princess. Her home is a royal residence. No, no." He laughed. "But it would be nice to direct the overflow of guests to someone trusted. Someone of a similar caliber. Like here."

True, they had six bedrooms with only three in use. But this was their home, not an inn. Hilly didn't like the idea of strangers walking over her rugs, eating off her plates, lounging on her settees, and certainly not sleeping in her beds.

"I'll think it over," Willy May told Colin as a means of dodging.

"Excellent. I need an answer in two days. John Bindon —" He turned to Hilly. "The actor, you know?"

She did, and her pulse fluttered.

She'd snuck into a theater with some other young models to see *Performance,* starring Mick Jagger. It was rumored that Jagger did the sex scenes for real, making the film as close to "the real thing" as Hilly had ever seen in living color action at the time.

John Bindon had portrayed a minor character named Moody in *Performance.*

"He's coming with a group of friends this Saturday."

Colin collected himself off the sofa. "I best go. I've called in extra staff. A nice boost for the local economy."

They walked him out to his mule cart.

"Oh! I brought you a housewarming gift — nearly forgot." He pulled a framed photograph from the back seat and handed it to Willy May. "Patrick's masterpiece! It turned out better than expected. We'll get the Earl back soon for another Mustique portrait. It's our new tradition."

Willy May began to decline, but before she could, he started the engine.

"Too-da-loo!"

His cart kicked up a haze through the jungle as he went.

Willy May shook her head, holding the frame. "How can we say no?"

"Maybe we aren't meant to," said Hilly.

John Bindon — Biffo, as he was called — was a popular actor, playing onscreen gangsters, crime bosses, bad boys, and the occasional villain. There were rumors that he was connected to the London mafia, but Hilly knew firsthand that people often liked to believe a person's performance was their identity. It gave them a sense of familiarity, one step closer to the starlight, true or perceived. What was certain was that Biffo had contacts with major film directors and the clout to make things happen. All she really needed was a good word. Someone to say she was more than a beauty. Someone to see her talent.

Preparations were made. On the day of Biffo's arrival, Colin hauled out trunks from the Cotton House cellar containing Victorian costumes. A theatrical welcome was a Mustique ritual. *Pride, pomp, and circumstance of glorious war!* According to Othello, it was the English way.

Hilly was given a six-tiered bell skirt. Snug. She'd put on a few pounds round the pool. Her breasts were plump, and her cheeks tanned. She was positively Gidget-like. Girl next door, some might even say.

Her mother refused to dress up, but Hilly had always enjoyed a bit of make-believe. This one seemed relatively benign. She'd taken theater classes in secondary school and been a player in the drama club productions. Her professional portfolio might've only consisted of *The Devils,* but one film was more than none. She hoped it could be the start of more. Biffo was a sign! And she was looking for signposts.

"We look like the court of Queen Victoria, like royalty," said Hilly.

"But you *aren't* royalty," Willy May corrected, "and neither are these men. Remember who you are and more importantly, who *they* are."

Colin arranged the players on the beach. Willy May stayed in the shade. The ferry came to the dock carrying ten men. No women. Hilly spotted Biffo from afar.

230

Shorter and stouter than he looked on-camera. The others were a head taller and circled him like rings on a bull's-eye. Their open-collared, polyester shirts shone slick under the sun.

An island violinist played the welcoming overture as one by one, Biffo's crew disembarked the ferry. Cotton House staff carried the luggage off to a waiting truck while Colin and ensemble received the guests.

"Welcome to Mustique." Hilly curtsied when the men reached her.

"And who's this?" asked Biffo.

"Galatea," introduced Colin. "A *Vogue* model and up-and-coming Hollywood star. Some of your men will be staying with her family at the Firefly villa. That's her mother over there."

Colin nodded to Willy May in the golf cart, fanning herself with an old copy of *The Sun.* The large-font headline read: U.S. SWOOPS DOWN ON MAFIA BOSSES.

"Charming." Biffo scratched the stubble of his jaw and moved on.

Hilly hoped she'd made an impression. If not now, then she must later.

Following closely at Biffo's heels were the large, looming figures carrying heavy brows and weary expressions. All save one.

"Hello, I'm Alexandre." He extended his

hand. "I'll be staying with you."

His accent was distinctly French. The familiar lilt of the romance language reminded her of Guy. Her ears rang at each upward turn of vowel.

"Welcome, Monsieur —" Hilly began.

"Call me Al. It's easier."

"*Al*. I'm sure you are tired from travel."

The intonation was that of her Grandmother Michael. She heard it and her shoulders straightened hard in similar Grandmother Michael pose. She was overcompensating, trying to demand respect. Did she want to be liked or feared?

Growing up, she and Joanne had played an ongoing game of Choices. The subjects were far-flung, ranging from *Chicken kabobs or beef?* to *Die in the desert or in the Arctic?* The question could be physical, *Pretty hands or pretty feet?*, or philosophical, *Impassioned love for a short time or cordial love for a lifetime?* They could change their minds if the question was asked again at a later date, but they had to choose in that moment. *Neither* and *both* were not permitted.

Hilly wanted to be liked. That was evident. Being feared didn't come as naturally to her as it had to Grandmother Michael. Though, in hindsight, Grandmother Michael had moments of tenderness, too.

As a young child, Hilly had a fondness for lemon drop candies. Grandmother Michael would give one to Hilly if she brushed her hair fifty strokes before bed. She loved the way the sugarcoated disk made her mouth pucker, and she slept with the lingering taste of summer in her dreams.

Then, for reasons she never understood, her mother accused Grandmother Michael of spoiling Hilly and pampering her vanity. The next night, Grandmother Michael announced that Hilly was too old to be bribed with sweets. She should brush her hair because if she didn't, it would get horribly tangled and they'd have to cut it off.

Fear.

Hilly would rather have liked her grandmother. Her shoulders slumped with the sweet-and-sour memory.

Al rubbed the stubble of his cheek, noticing her deflation. "You're right, it's been a long day for everyone."

Hilly reminded herself that this was not Paris, and he was not Guy.

"Long and hot. We've got coconut ice cream up at the house. Freshly made."

"Oh, *oui*? *Crème glacé* sounds like the cure."

He pointed to a man with pitted cheeks

flamed like elderberries in the humidity. "Tony and I are to be your guests. We'll get the boss settled first and then come up."

She nodded.

In a panama hat and cane, Colin led the group to a caravan of jeeps parked in a line by the palm tree grove. After they'd gone, the beach troupe disrobed.

"Glad that's over," said Joseph. "Leo, hand me one of those colas."

Leo popped up the lid of a cooler hidden behind a trunk. "Care for one?" he offered Hilly.

"Yes, please." Under the corset cage, droplets of sweat had pooled between her shoulder blades and done an agonizing shimmy down her lower back.

Leo passed round cold cans while they folded their costumes back into the trunks. Soda tabs zipped and fizzed.

Hilly guzzled hers.

Willy May had introduced her to a couple of the local people: her friend Titus, a woman named Naomi, but Hilly was still getting familiar with the Cotton House staff. Joseph was lead butler. Leo was a waiter. Kenton was Colin's personal assistant. Since meeting Dr. Rob and his wife, she'd found every excuse in the book to stay away from the brouhaha of Cotton House guests. Until now, when they were coming to her door.

Leo dropped a set of antique suspenders into the trunk. "White people got strange ways." Remembering Hilly, he turned suddenly. "No offense, Miss Galatea."

"None taken." She pointed to the trunk. "This is one of the stranger ones."

All the islanders nearby grunted in agreement. She found herself grunting, too, because she had to continue this strange charade back home. But then, didn't they all.

When Al and Tony arrived at Firefly with their duffel bags, the women showed them to their rooms. Tony was an attorney, so Willy May put him in the room with a quartz-top desk.

"Befitting a man of the law," said Willy May.

Hilly liked the piece because the stone had a pink glitter that matched the watery sunrise, not because of any functional use.

"I don't practice anymore," Tony was quick to correct and the silence that followed said not to ask why.

Al's room was actually the pool house, outside the main villa and down a little stairwell. Hilly had decorated it in a palm frond motif.

"It's perfect." He set his bag down on the floor. *"Merci beaucoup."*

"He seems nice," said Hilly on their walk back to the main house.

"Nice is as nice does."

"I thought that was 'handsome.' "

"Did you?"

She'd been burned by one Frenchman already. She wasn't about to put her hand in the fire twice.

"It's the saying, Mum. 'Handsome is as handsome does.' "

"Hmm," Willy May replied.

An hour later, Al and Tony met them on the veranda, where Hilly had scooped out homemade coconut ice cream into beveled-glass bowls.

"Thank you again for the hospitality," said Al.

"Your home is quite lovely," added Tony.

While brutish in looks, Tony had a meek nature. Wound so nervy tight, he could barely let loose to eat dessert.

Hilly picked a French rosé from the wine rack and uncorked the bottle. It smelled of cherries and roses. It reminded her of Paris. She brought it to the table to let it breathe. Let herself breathe, too.

She hadn't noticed under the glaring sun,

but Al's eyes were the color of rain.

"I came here from Paris," she told him.

His gaze twinkled with curiosity. *"Parlez-vous français?"*

"Non, pas beaucoup. I knew a guy . . . in France. He taught me enough to say that I don't know anything."

She hoped her mother didn't notice the break in her voice. It was Al and Guy and the emotive treble of the French accent through her. Memory had a way of tricking the rememberer.

Willy May stood and stacked the empty bowls. "I better wash up." She gestured for Hilly to stay and make sure the men didn't go wandering while also giving the hint that it was time to turn in.

Willy May went into the kitchen. The faucet ran. She switched on the radio and sang along to Elton John's "Honky Cat." An intimation that she was out of the room but not gone.

". . . I said, get back, Hilly cat . . ."

Willy May never sang lyrics correctly. It had embarrassed Hilly as a teenager. What did it matter, Willy May had argued, the song was the same.

"Changes gonna do us good . . . ," her mother crooned.

Tony popped two chalky antacids from a

roll in his pocket and then excused himself to bed, leaving Hilly and Al alone at the table.

She poured rosé into her cup.

"What part of France are you from?"

"Bourges. South of Paris."

The wine made everything drowsy, like seaweed moving underwater. She'd forgotten how nice it was to be so close to dreaming.

Since the night of Colin's dinner party, she'd been back on the pinks. At first, just one in the morning. Like a cup of coffee, she told herself. But without the blues to bring her down, sleep evaded.

"I knew a woman from Bourges," she told him. "She had two poodles and forbade anyone from feeding them scraps. I slipped them sable cookies when she wasn't looking, and they followed me everywhere. She thought they loved me."

He laughed and it fell on her like the rain. Refreshing and a little dangerous.

"My mother had a poodle when I was young. He was like a brother. He even ate off the table beside me. His name was Apollon."

"Al and Apollon. What did your father think of that?"

"I don't know. I never met the man." He

sipped. "I was the illegitimate son of a count and a laundress. She raised me in the trade. Me and Apollon."

"I'm sorry, I didn't mean to bring up . . ."

Al cleared his throat. "I'm not ashamed. Biffo helped me break into film."

She nodded. It was exactly what she hoped for herself — the breakout part, at least. Al certainly had the looks and charm. In a blink, she saw it: the two of them starring in a romantic epic on a deserted island. No set or costume budget necessary. All they needed was for Biffo to call in a favor with a director, François Truffaut, Michel Piccoli, or Francis Ford Coppola. He didn't have to be French, of course.

"You don't live in Bourges anymore, I take it."

He shook his head. "I moved to London. I needed to be there for the work."

"British film work?"

"No."

She saw the wheels of his mind turning.

"Biffo's crew provides protection to business clients," he explained.

On their drive up to the house from the beach earlier, her mother had handed her *The Sun* newspaper.

"Read this." She'd pointed to a story on the second page.

It said that the actor John Bindon was being investigated in connection with a Hounslow double homicide.

"Remember who these men are," Willy May had cautioned once more. "They are paying to stay with us, and that is all. Money can buy a lot of trophies, but it can't buy merit. Don't forget that, honey."

It was like what the casting agent had said about fashion not making a person right.

"What happened to innocent until proven guilty?" she had reminded.

Willy May had frowned. "That's what people say because it sounds good. Truth is in action and more often than not, the world will treat you as guilty until innocence is proven."

Now, her mother leaned her head through the kitchen doorway. "It's getting late. Best if we all turn in."

"Yes, Mum," said Hilly.

Willy May addressed Al. "As a guest in my house, I trust that my daughter can escort you to your room without my chaperonage." She tapered her eyes. "On your word as a gentleman."

Al bowed respectfully. "Of course, ma'am."

Willy May left. The kitchen radio clicked off.

"I think she's auditioning for Biffo's protection ring," Hilly joked to ease the tension.

"She'd get the job." Al finished his glass and stood. "She's doing what any good mother of *une belle fille* would."

Her cheeks warmed at the compliment.

She led him to his room dutifully. At the door, he kissed her hand.

"Bonne nuit, ma chère."

"Bonne nuit," she repeated.

Walking back by firefly light, she put her hand to her lips, tasting the sweet grape of wine and the bitter spice of aftershave.

A movement in the curtains of her mother's bedroom made her look up. Willy May was keeping watch.

CHAPTER 15
JUST A GIRL WHO CAN'T SAY NO

A week later, Colin arranged a sunset pool party. That same day, Willy May had a hot flash that turned into a nauseating migraine. By three o'clock in the afternoon, she was in bed with a washcloth over her eyes.

Hilly was tasked to shuttle Al and Tony to the Cotton House while her mother stayed home. She didn't mind. She enjoyed Al's company.

Did she find him attractive? It was hard not to. But any feelings were just that — *feelings* — and she'd learned well that they alone could not sustain a relationship.

Bacon-wrapped pineapple skewers, shrimp canapés, and Singapore Slings were passed around the Cotton House pool deck. The men laughed over some not-quite-so-funny story that Biffo had just told when Willy May zoomed in on a mule cart.

"I want to talk to the boss!" she demanded.

Colin set down his drink. "Shouting, shouting." He tsked and rubbed his temples. "Why the tizzy, Willy May?"

"I'm not in a tizzy. I'm straight *pissed off!*" In her hand was a pill bottle. Hilly gasped. Willy May opened the top and tossed the pinks directly at Biffo. The pellets bounced off his chest and skipped across the patio table.

"I found these at my place."

Biffo looked to Tony.

"I don't know nothing about those."

Al shook his head, too.

"I can only assume that those are yours." Biffo continued to puff his cigar.

"Your assumption would be wrong," said Willy May. "I found them mixed up in the towels so *I* can only assume that they belong to your men."

Hilly retraced her steps. She hadn't been sleeping. She had taken a pill when she got up. She'd needed them more and more often to accomplish all the things she wanted in a day.

This morning, she'd been collecting dirty towels when she saw that a little gold warbler had drowned in the pool. She'd grabbed the bottle for another dose before fishing out the bird and burying it in an empty Toastettes box. Then her mother asked her to freeze the wet washcloth for her headache, and she'd gone to do that. She was perpetually moving faster and faster. She couldn't remember when she'd put down the bottle. It must've been with the towels.

"I won't have drugs in my house — not on top of everything else." Willy May glared at Biffo. "I've been as hospitable as possible, but this is where it stops. We all have a limit, and you've reached mine." She took Hilly's arm. "Come on, honey."

"Mum, it must be some kind of misunderstanding."

She knew she should confess, but in front of everyone? The way they might look at her. And her mother — that anger was a tempest of fury. She'd learned long ago that once set into motion, it would not stop until it had run its course.

As girls in the midst of a sexual revolution, she and Joanne had been given matching bicycles. Still too young for cars, bicycles were a status symbol of major independence with her schoolmates. Anybody who was anybody her age threw caution to the wind from behind a set of handlebars. Extra merit for chrome spokes. The one rule her mother had was that they were not to ride in short skirts as a number of the girls were keen on doing, particularly when the secondary school boys were having rugby practice. Willy May had gone so far as to purchase pedal pushers.

"That's what they make these for," she'd told them. "So your knees don't get dirty while you ride."

Joanne being Joanne and two years younger had eagerly complied. She was one of the first in her elementary class to have a new bike by virtue of her older sister getting one.

While Hilly was glad for the gift, it was hard for her to enjoy given the hypocrisy of the rule assigned to it. Her mother wore miniskirts all the time. Not on a bike, but that was only because she didn't ride a bike. She had a car. Which left only one conclusion in Hilly's mind: this was about her mother wanting to control her freedom. So, she made it her mission to wear her skirt on her bike, even rolling her waistband to make the hem shorter.

She hadn't tried to hide her disobedience. Defiance without acknowledgment held little satisfaction. She'd anticipated getting caught, mused on how it would burn her mother to see her doing the very opposite of what she'd instructed. What she hadn't anticipated was the disproportionate extent of Willy May's anger.

Hilly had been pedaling home from school when a car of boys from the University of Gloucestershire pulled up beside her, whistling out the windows. She'd been flattered and let the wind catch her pleated skirt an extra beat. When suddenly came the goose-like honk of an approaching driver, her mother. Willy May had raced her car around the boys at such a speed that they all nearly crashed. She'd parked perpendicular on the road ahead and got out, red-faced and arms flailing like a maniac.

"She is a child!" she'd yelled at the university boys. They'd come to a halt at the road obstruction with apprehensive concern. "I have a mind to call the police and report you as perverts!"

The cheeky young driver dared to counter: "All respect, miss, but how do you know how old she is?"

Willy May marched over to Hilly and took the handlebars of her bike. "Because she's my daughter and she has just lost privileges. *All* of them. No bike. No television. No cinema. No vinyl records. No parties. No friends. Nothing. You are grounded forever," she'd growled. "Get in the car, Hilly, and roll down your darn skirt!"

Hilly had been mortified and stunned.

Her mother had ripped the bike from her hands and shoved the front wheel into the trunk. The back tire hung out over the bumper.

"I don't want to hear a word from you. Don't even try or I may do something violent," she'd said inside the car.

Her hands were trembling on the steering wheel and Hilly had obeyed for fear that her mother would make good on her threats. She'd expected her disapproval but thought it worth the price to prove that she could make her own choices. She hadn't expected such a reaction.

This felt like the same thing. Except she was an adult woman now.

Willy May turned to Colin. "If the authorities found these, do you know what they'd do? They'd ransack this whole island. There would be a reckoning for *all* of us, Colin."

Biffo picked up a pill and examined it between his fingers. "Flush them down the loo if you want. No need to get so emotional."

"Emotional?" Willy May bared her teeth in a strained smile. "Get your people out of my house. Stay away from my girl or I swear to God, I'll report you to Interpol myself."

At the mention of Interpol, Biffo smashed the end of his cigar into the teak table. A burnt ember flittered to the floor.

Silence curtained them.

After an endless minute, during which not even Colin dared a word, Biffo finally spoke. "It's been swell, but I think it's time we go."

"Well . . . ," Colin murmured, just loud enough to be heard, "perhaps with Christmas coming . . . ."

"Have my men's things sent down from Firefly. We won't trouble you any further."

Hilly followed her mother on shaky legs. She had done this. Those were her pills, and she hadn't taken responsibility. The lasting impression of her would be that of a wrongful accuser. She and her mother were yoked as one.

"Pack up, boys," said Biffo. "We're leaving in the morning."

What Willy May had bottled in front of the men, she let loose on the drive home. "Hoodlum trash! Common thieves! Con artists!"

Hilly remained silent. She went straight to her room and stayed there the rest of the night. No more pills to hold her steady. She was scared to be found with them and scared to be without.

Willy May went to bed early. Another migraine on the way. Hilly was silently grateful. She couldn't face her. She crept down to the kitchen for something to quell the nausea growing inside but the cold corn soup in the fridge turned her stomach further. So, she went back to bed empty and slept in fits of cramps, sweat, and anxiety.

Then, in the violet shade of morning, someone rapped on the door. Her vision blurred. Her stomach cartwheeled. She thought she might vomit if she moved too fast.

"I'm sleeping," she groaned, thinking it her mother; but then, she heard the singsong of his voice, lilting upward.

"Galatea? It's me, Al?"

She pulled her head from the pillow and saw that her nose had bled a little. She sniffed, touched the tip of it lightly, and wondered if she should be worried. She was chilled despite the warm temperature. Pulling on a robe, she carefully stood to answer.

She held the door ajar, and he leaned in but didn't push it.

"The ferry is going to be here soon. I came to explain."

Him explain? They were her pills.

"We've been here too long. It doesn't look good for the boss to be away from London — a vacation is one thing. Hiding is another."

"But aren't you hiding?"

"As much as you, *oui*."

"I don't know what you mean."

He double blinked at her.

"I've seen you taking the pills."

She shook her head. She'd been so careful. She only took them when she was alone. He couldn't have known unless he'd been spying. She pulled the robe collar up around her throat, feeling exposed and vulnerable. She didn't know Al, and she hadn't known Guy either. Not really. She only knew what the men chose to tell her and what she wanted to believe.

"You don't want your mother to know. Biffo understands. We'll keep your secret if you keep your mother quiet."

It felt like a threat. Blackmail of a sort. Intimidation at the least.

Fool me once, she thought, *shame on you; fool me twice, shame on me.*

"I'll make sure Mum doesn't say anything." She began to close the door. She wanted him out, gone, forgotten.

"Good. Here." He pushed a plastic baggy of tablets through the opening. "Dexies, right?"

She should refuse. She should hold her ground. She should use this episode to come clean. But her hands were shaking and the long day ahead hadn't even begun yet.

So, she took them.

From the pool deck, she watched Biffo, Al, and the rest board the ferry down below on Britannia Bay. It departed the dock and grew smaller and smaller until it was a black splotch on the horizon.

"It's for the best," said Willy May. She'd come out to the pool with her morning coffee. "He wasn't good for you."

Hilly didn't face her — couldn't.

The sky flashed chartreuse as the sun rose. A trick of the eye. A trick of Mustique. She was dizzy. Bile bubbled in her throat. She put a hand to her mouth, holding it in long enough to reach the ferns.

Willy May followed close, pulled strands of hair from her lips, and rubbed her back.

"Hilly, honey," she soothed, "is there something you want to tell me?"

"I'm not . . . ," she began but lifted her head too fast and nearly toppled over.

It came in sharp sobriety. Guy. Her first and only lover. She couldn't remember the last time she'd menstruated. It had been two or three months, maybe longer. Before she came to Mustique. Her cycles had always been irregular. She put a protective hand to the swell of her belly and behind her, Willy May sighed.

■ ■ ■ ■

PART 3
JOANNE

■ ■ ■ ■

CHAPTER 16
HANDLE WITH CARE

May 1973

Joanne had been amid her freshman year music theory exams at Dartington College of Arts when her residence hall director said she had a call from Willy May. It was 10:00 P.M.

"Hilly is having a baby. Can you come to Mustique?"

Her mother had forgotten the time difference. Not that it mattered. Life was lived on Willy May's clock.

Joanne stood in the dorm hall cradling the clunky pay phone. The mouthpiece smelled of cigarettes and boozy tears. Girls passed by in their quilted robes and Velcro curlers, readying for bed, and chattering fretfully about exams. Joanne had an eight o'clock test the next morning and still had to finish composing her final music project.

What else could she say but "Okay . . . as soon as school's finished."

Truth be told, she'd felt slighted when her mother launched out into the wider world; her father went on to another; her big sister, Hilly, jetted off to fame; and Joanne, always the good girl, was left behind. Nobody asked her to come with them. They'd simply gone.

It was easier to be angry with family for leaving than to feel their absence. Grandmother Michael had been the only one who remained steadfast. That must be love, she told herself. In accepting college tuition, she'd contracted herself to do her grandmother's bidding. She would inevitably be asked to play something on the piano at every dinner party, charity concert, and afternoon tea her grandmother attended — entertain old friends, all of whom had a bachelor son, nephew, or cousin that would be *a perfect match for such a girl.* She overheard her grandmother telling them that Joanne was the only respectable thing that came out of *Harry's marriage to the American* and that she was determined to see her granddaughter properly educated before she was wed. She wanted better for Joanne. A suitable match and nothing less.

"What should I tell Granny?" she asked her mother.

Willy May exhaled into the receiver. The

sound traveled across the miles and wires in a rush of static.

"Don't tell her anything. It's family business. She's made it clear that I'm not part of her family, so she's not part of our family. I'll send you a plane ticket."

"Okay."

Joanne wasn't easily flustered. Her sister always said she took after her father in that regard. The Michaels were coolheaded, while her mother was hot-tempered. Between her British father and Texan mother, the choice was to face the chill or the fire. There was little temperate ground between. Hilly had been her refuge.

She'd once known everything about her elder sister — knew that when she genuinely smiled, her nose crinkled like a cat's; the cadence of her breathing in deepest sleep; the ocean-deep shade of her eyes after she'd been crying; the differing tones of her voice when she was happy or sad, confident or afraid. But since Hilly had left home, the thread between them felt cut. Hilly had taken a stage name: Galatea. Joanne didn't know that person.

She hung up the phone, mulling over the magnitude of the news. *Hilly was having a baby.* She let that thought crescendo and decrescendo in her mind while standing perfectly still. She was not shocked that this thunderbolt had come from Hilly. All Joanne's life, her sister had made it her mission to defy convention. This was another case in point.

Joanne had never personally known a single, unwed mother, and not knowing things was one of her biggest pet peeves. A true catch-22. While she hated not knowing, sometimes the knowing was worse. Like now, she was cross with her mother for not telling her sooner about Hilly's baby but grateful that she hadn't, because how was she supposed to think about anything else?

She returned to her music composition final. She needed a coda to finish. She tapped her pencil to the meter. Usually, she could hear the piano notes in her mind and feel the keys under her fingertips. She couldn't this time. She was busy imagining how quiet it must be inside a womb and wondering if babies heard music in heartbeats.

She couldn't comprehend how this had happened. I mean, she knew the mechanics of how it happened. She meant figuratively speaking. It was a modern era. Women had options.

Joanne hadn't batted an eyelash when she told her GP that she was sexually active.

258

She wasn't brazen. She simply felt it medically responsible to be honest with her doctor. He'd suggested the birth control pill, and she'd been on it ever since. There were other preventatives, too. While her grandmother and mother spoke in metaphors when it came to sex (Granny: *It's the most holy union between husband and wife;* Mum: *It's how a flower and a bee make honey*), her sister had been the one to bring home a *Playboy* magazine so they could finally get clear answers. She knew!

So maybe Hilly wanted a baby.

She put down her pencil and tried that thought a beat. A whole new, unknown person was growing this very minute.

She checked the time: quarter to midnight. She wasn't getting anything accomplished. She turned off her lamp, wound the metal crank of her clock, and set the narrow arms for an early alarm. She'd get up when the music was fresh in her mind and thoughts of her sister had been put to rest.

As soon as exams finished, Joanne was on her way to Mustique. Willy May booked the airplane ticket and wired money for the boat ferries plus cargo charges. She'd asked Joanne to bring the last remaining box of her things from a storage locker near the Gloucester marina.

First, however, Joanne had taken the train north to Cheltenham to drop off her dorm belongings. Grandmother Michael was already on holiday in Scotland, avoiding the summer heat. She'd left a note with the groundskeeper inviting Joanne up to the cottage on Loch Lomond. Joanne sent her reply the day she left: *Sorry, Gran, I'm to Mum's on Mustique. I'll see you when I return. Love, Joanne.* By the time the letter reached Scotland, Joanne would be thousands of miles away, and there'd be nothing to be done.

She set out on the southbound train from Cheltenham to Gloucester; collected her mother's belongings and carted them, plus her luggage, the hundred kilometers back north to Birmingham airport. Naturally, Willy May hadn't thought of the topographical yo-yo of the errand.

Joanne was piqued until she opened the box. Inside was a record player and LPs of the Beatles, Nat King Cole, the Supremes, and more, alongside her childhood "Story and Songs" soundtracks. The glossy images of her favorite melodies made her go weak with nostalgia. *Peter and the Wolf, Snow White, Cinderella, Sleeping Beauty . . .* It was through these that she first fell in love with music.

When she and Hilly were young, her mother had ordered the fairy-tale records from the United States, seemingly a place of perpetual song and sunshine based on the items that arrived from there: packages of oranges, candies that whizzed and popped on your tongue, rainbow-colored T-shirts, glossy books, and vinyl records with tempos that made her heart skip in rhythm.

As the story went, they first knew of her musical affinity when four-year-old Joanne tapped her spoon against her dish to the rhythm of Verna Felton's "Bibbidi-Bobbidi-Boo." Recognizing her natural aptitude, Grandmother Michael insisted that Willy May allow her to advance in formal music training. Granny was the one to put a proper instrument in her hands and the rest, as they say, was history.

Joanne hadn't thought of those early songs in years and seeing them again left her awash with nostalgic glee. She retaped the box and wrote *Handle with Care* in fat black marker before checking it as plane cargo. With her parents, she'd sailed nearly every sea on the globe and flown in commercial jets a handful of times, but this was her first solo voyage. That changed everything.

The Clipper Class ticket couldn't have been more precious if it were made of solid gold. Her pleather seat might as well have been nubuck. Her welcoming washcloth was luxurious as a hot mineral spring. She barely slept the entire flight between feasting (spring chicken, mushroom caps, baby onions, and lardons braised in a red wine sauce), endless cups of Nescafé, and a widescreen showing of *Willy Wonka & the Chocolate Factory.* Joanne was still humming "Pure Imagination" when she landed in Trinidad to begin the multi-ferry hop to Mustique.

The ferry captain had invited Joanne to sit in his covered helm when he heard she was Willy May's youngest daughter. But it'd been such a beautiful day that she'd kindly told him she preferred the outdoors. The light was different here than at home. It pirouetted on the waves. The sound of the sea was distinct, too, like a piccolo versus an oboe. The sail from St. Vincent to Mustique played like a symphony across the horizon.

Her mother waved as the ferry came into dock. "Ahoy there!"

The Texas twang was like jingle bells and brought on a similar cheer. Joanne's heart lifted.

"Welcome to Mustique! Let me look at you." She put both hands on her shoulders and narrowed her eyes against the overhead sun. "You've filled out pretty as pie since the last I saw you."

Joanne hadn't felt like she'd changed much in the hour by hour, day by day, but when she added it up into a lump sum, she supposed she had. The last she saw her mother was during her orientation week at Dartington. Willy May had briefly returned to England. Hilly had been on the set of *The Devils.* So, for one of the first times in Joanne's memory, they were a duet instead a trio.

The two went to Cheltenham's Corner Curry restaurant and ordered braised lamb shanks with masala to share. Joanne told Willy May about the college courses she'd signed up to take and her dismay with Paul McCartney's band Wings. They talked of Hilly in Hollywood, the summer crickets, the constellations shining down, and stayed away from hard topics — past and future — afraid that the arrow forward or back might puncture the magic of the moment. The Corner Curry had turned off its lamps. Its sitar strings stilled. Karahis were taken off the flames. But they remained. The hours seemed weighted by a sustaining pedal.

Their two notes vibrated freely and resonated long after.

The masala sauce had splattered on the blouse she'd been wearing. A whole note of bright red, indelible as blood. It was still there. She hadn't tried to wash it out. The stain would be palpable proof of this memory, and the unspoken promise that no matter how much time or distance passed, her mother and she would find each other.

"I missed you, Mum."

Willy May cupped her cheek. "I missed you, too, Josie girl." She gestured toward a golf cart parked on the beach. "Your chariot awaits."

At the cart, she hefted the box of records into the back seat. "Thanks for bringing these. We've only had the radio and I wanted some real music around the house. We don't have a piano, but I'm working on it."

It warmed Joanne. Growing up, she'd cut out catalog pictures of instruments she'd seen at her music teacher's house. She taped them to the wall on her side of the shared bedroom with Hilly and practiced playing each on an empty milk bottle: blowing across the top for the woodwinds, knocking the side with a spoon for the percussions, strumming sideways for the strings, holding it up like a trumpet for the brass. She had the whole orchestra in her imagination. At the center of her vision board was the grand piano.

When she was eight years old, Grandmother Michael asked what she wished Saint Nicholas should bring her that year. She'd said a grand piano and lessons to play it. When they attended the annual Michaels' Christmas supper, beside the cranberrystrung spruce was the piano, dark and shiny as the Bristol Channel at night. Joanne had been ecstatic even while her mother had frowned for reasons that she never did understand.

"My friend Titus, you'll meet him," she continued, "is a guy who can do just about anything he sets a mind to. I wouldn't put it past him to show up with a baby grand prettier than the one you left at your gran's."

Joanne had never heard her mother speak like that. *Whatever one sets a mind to* was not an option. There were limitations to one's dreams, outward obstructions and inward deficiencies. One might set a mind to fly but unless one were born with wings, falling was inevitable. That was the reality of nature.

Was it the heat, the seawater, or Mustique magic? Joanne couldn't say for certain. But something had changed in Willy May.

On the drive through the coconut trees and black mangroves, Joanne listened to the way the wind whistled through the fingers of the palms overhead. A sweet, almost indecipherable note that rose and fell with the gusts while the birds chirped a colorful timbre and the breaking waves set the tempo.

Willy May parked at Firefly.

"I'll take your suitcase to your room," she said.

"I can do that —" Joanne began but her mother lifted a hand.

"Best you and your sister get reacquainted alone."

Hearing the whirl of the cart's approach, Hilly struggled to pull herself up from a chair at the top of the pool terrace. Her belly was round and heavy as a melon.

"I didn't know she was *this* far along," said Joanne.

"By my count, she shouldn't be due for another month. But she was rail thin to begin with so she looks bigger, I reckon. Pregnancies don't always follow formulas."

Didn't they?

"What did the doctor say?"

Willy May shook her head. "She refuses to see one. Colin — you'll meet him too —

brought over one of the other residents, Dr. Rob, an obstetrician. Hilly wouldn't let him near her, and I couldn't blame her."

There was a warning in the remark, but Willy May was out of the cart untying the box of records before Joanne could ask.

"She's had a tough pregnancy. Not that that's unusual. I can't say any of mine were easy. She's been . . . hormonal. On a positive note, she's barely gained twenty pounds. Most women would kill to have such a light load. My right arm alone weighed that much when I was carrying her."

"Isn't it dangerous not to have a doctor on hand? Doesn't she need vitamins, and, um, Dr. Spock books?"

"Women've been baking babies for generations without Dr. Spock," said Willy May. "Go on up to her. She can't do the steps anymore. She's been so excited to see you. We both have." She gave her wrist a squeeze before heading round to the villa's entrance.

Hilly had risen by then and gingerly waved from the terrace. Joanne climbed the steep stairs until the two were standing face-to-face. Hilly's hair was thin and limp. Her cheekbones were ghoulishly prominent. The half-moons under her eyes tinged green despite the tanning that kissed her nose and the tips of her ears pink. Raised bug bites dotted her arms.

"Hilly?" It came out like a question.

"Josie." She inhaled as she said it and waved over her protrusion.

"Wow," said Joanne. "Gosh, Hilly."

Her sister gulped hard, a wetness sprung to her eyes, and she reached for her hand. Joanne thought she was going to place it on the baby but instead, she threaded her fingers through like they used to do as girls.

"I feel bad that you're giving up your summer for me," said Hilly. "You might have a boyfriend or something."

"I don't."

Hilly leaned closer. The weight of it teetered her off-balance and Joanne embraced her steady. She didn't even smell the same — like vinegar and overripe fruit. It nearly made Joanne cry.

"I'm really glad you came," whispered Hilly.

They stood there a long while, neither one daring to let go until both of their heartbeats slowed and the threat of tears passed.

"Come on," Hilly said finally. "Let me show you the house. I decorated. Not much else I'm good for like this."

There was no discussion of the baby between them. For a little longer, they pretended to pick up where they left off, back when it was a reassurance that who they were to each other was the most important thing in the universe: sisters.

Hilly held on to the crook of Joanne's arm. They had to stop often for her to catch her breath and ended the house tour in Joanne's bedroom, near Willy May's on the upper floor.

"This room has the prettiest view. See?" Hilly pulled open the curtains. The scene was citrus bright.

"It's even better now with you here."

Joanne reached down and squeezed her sister's hand, noticing how spindly it was, how dry and rough her skin.

"I'm here, Hilly, I'm here."

That night, Hilly said she wasn't feeling well and went to bed early without supper.

"Does she do that often?" Joanne asked Willy May.

They were in the kitchen preparing hot ham and Swiss sandwiches.

"Only on her low days. Highs and lows. You know Hilly, she's always been prone to mood swings."

She did. Her sister was mercurial. That's part of what made her beautiful. But something felt different now. Joanne had attributed it to Hilly's "Galatea" persona, time apart, and the struggle of bringing a baby into the world. However, her gut told her that there was more.

She picked up a knife and slathered the toast with mustard.

"Is it really all pregnancy hormones?" she asked.

"Could be."

Willy May layered on slices of ham and then cheese.

"What else do you think?"

Her mother sighed and rubbed her forehead. "I think she's depressed. The guy, the baby's father, was a con man. We don't talk about him." She gestured to the toaster oven.

Joanne took the sheet tray of sandwiches to it, placing it under the electric coils with the door slightly ajar, watching for the broil bubbles, like her mother showed her as a child. Willy May could cook nearly anything in a portable toaster oven and usually did. Joanne did the same. It had made her a chef de cuisine of her residence hall.

"Does he know?" she asked, blinking hard.

The heat stung her eyes, but she had to keep a close watch. All it took was thirty seconds, less than a minute. A second more and the bread would char. She pulled out the tray.

"Maybe. Maybe not. That's your sister's secret to tell."

Willy May grabbed a bottle of M&B beer from the refrigerator and popped the metal top against the counter. "Beer?"

It was their family's brew. Michael & Boutler, although her grandfather had bought out the Boutler part fifty years ago.

"Still drinking that." Joanne smiled.

"Not often. Hard to get out here, but I ordered some for you." Willy May gulped. "Besides, I always liked your dad's beer. It was the rest of the family that I couldn't stomach."

"Fair enough."

Willy May passed her the bottle and she sipped, tasting the crisp coppery fruit of her legacy, a pale ale. The family beer was never consumed to excess any more than sacramental wine was drunk to inebriation. Cups of M&B had been more pervasive on their family's table than black tea, which their father had forbidden after sunset because of the caffeine.

They took their sandwich plates into the open living room where the record player had been unboxed on the glass coffee table. Joanne knelt to smooth a hand over the record jackets.

"I can't believe you kept these."

271

Willy May settled down on the ground with her back against the sofa. "Of course I did. They were your favorites."

Joanne sat cross-legged beside her and ran a hand over the cover of *Snow White: SEE the pictures. HEAR the record. READ the book.*

"Truth be told, *Snow White* used to give me nightmares! She loses her mother, is chased by a hunter trying to cut out her heart, and gets fed a poison apple. It's a horror story."

Willy May laughed. "Isn't every fairy tale horrific when you get down to brass tacks?"

"Now that you mention it . . . yes!" Joanne took a bite of her sandwich, savoring the salty ham and tart mustard. She hadn't had one of these in ages.

They bypassed the Disney records for Nat King Cole's *Love Is the Thing* LP. The gentle boom and fuzz of a record player needle landing on vinyl was nostalgic. The opening violins of "Stardust" made her close her eyes and lean back so the feeling of the purple . . . the music . . . the years . . . could fill her. Her eyes welled.

They listened to that record and two more. Finally, the stylus tripped at the end of Petula Clark, and Willy May gently lifted the tonearm away.

"It's late." She put an arm around her and kissed the side of Joanne's head.

The gesture was so motherly but so unlike *her* mother that it made Joanne's throat close up. She could count on one hand the times her mother had bestowed unsolicited affection. It wasn't that she was unaffectionate. She just showed it on the appropriately constrained occasions. A peck on the cheek hello and goodbye, to be specific. Anything outside of that was reserved for, well, extraordinary circumstances.

Like when Willy May told them that she was divorcing their father. She'd hugged and kissed Hilly and Joanne together then. Or once when Joanne was a girl, she fell off her bicycle and was nearly run over by a passing car. The driver had swerved to a halt meters away. Hearing the screeching wheels, her mother had run out from the house and scooped her into her arms.

In fact, Joanne couldn't recall a time when her mother had kissed or embraced her that hadn't been associated with panic, which made her panic now. What was going on? Something had unlocked her mother. Joanne was glad for it, but it cut her, too. Because after all these years, why hadn't she been able to do similarly? She was her daughter, after all.

One assumed that if a locksmith made keys, they would be able to open their own doors. But maybe that was the fundamental misperception — that creation gave one ownership. She and Hilly weren't keys either. They were their own doors with their own deadbolts. It seemed to Joanne that finding the key to one's lock might be the ultimate goal. After all, a door unlocked was a door unlocked. It didn't matter if the key came from within or without.

"You — you seem different here," Joanne dared.

The late hour cast dusty shadows and softened her mother's gaze. "Do I?"

Joanne nodded.

"Maybe I am." Willy May shrugged and slipped the vinyl back into its paper sleeve. "If we play them all at once, there'll be nothing for tomorrow and the day after."

Joanne didn't see it that way. Being familiar with a thing made it more special. As a child, she'd memorized every note and word on these records. When she closed her eyes, she breathed in the treble clef's risings and fallings. And suddenly, for the first time in her life, she yearned to know her mother similarly.

CHAPTER 17
MAGIQUE MUSTIQUE

Over the next week, Joanne felt as if she'd been given a crash course in Mustique 101. Colin hosted two suppers and three luncheons with a litany of revolving residents, potential investors, and well-to-dos. They reminded her of Gran's salons. At least at the Cotton House she wasn't obliged to play Bach's Prelude No. 1 in C Major for the hundredth time. She was free to mingle politely without committing names to memory. The one fixed neighbor was Titus, whom she immediately liked.

He popped by the house from time to time with fresh fruit from the islanders' groves. Hilly couldn't stand the smell of anything meaty. She gagged if Willy May so much as cracked open a can of Spam. Her preference was for Del Monte mixed fruit. So many empty tins, they'd begun using them to sprout seedlings. A dozen lined the pool patio with various herbs. Tender green

275

tips reached toward the sun. Titus brought fresh finger bananas, coconut, breadfruit, and pineapple. Hilly gorged herself but still looked rawboned. They were all worried that she wouldn't have the stamina for childbirth

"You said there's a doctor here?" asked Joanne.

"Dr. Rob is a resident. But he's not here now. He comes for Colin's birthday in December and stays through the winter."

She and Willy May were doing the laundry. While on the *Stingray,* her father had insisted that the girls learn the basics of washing and cooking. He tried to run the family's boat like a navy ship. Willy May was quick to remind him that he'd been a military pilot, not a sailor. He argued that quality standards were the same across the armed forces.

"But we aren't soldiers," her mother had said. "These are your daughters and this is our vacation. Let them swim and soak in the sun."

It had infuriated her father. To try to keep the peace, Joanne had made it her goal to ensure things were shipshape. So, while Hilly lounged on the upper deck in her bikinis and her father tinkered with the navigation maps, she'd helped her mother

276

do the chores — cooking and laundry, chiefly. More proof that old patterns repeated themselves.

Joanne scraped a T-shirt's underarms with a thumbnail. Sun-baked deodorant was ruthless on cottons. She gave up and left it to soak in the bucket. The air was heady with the aroma of LUX detergent and bubbles. She appraised the basket of dirty clothes. One load of laundry was nostalgic. A half a dozen was grueling.

"What this place needs is a washer and dryer."

"Talk to your sister. She's got the catalogs. Don't tell me how much she's spending, though. It'll put me in an early grave."

"She's done a nice job with the furnishings," said Joanne. "The house is beautiful."

"Despite all those back in England who wished the opposite, we haven't gone bankrupt yet!" Her mother winked. "If I'd known there was money to be made in boarding, I might've turned your grandmother's carriage house into a bed-and-breakfast."

"That would've put *her* in an early grave."

"I'm sorry I didn't think of it sooner," Willy May teased.

Colin's opportunity had proven to be a blessing in disguise. Joanne had been unaware of her mother's large expenditures until her arrival. Without Michael & Boutler Brewery supplementing her finances, Willy May's bank account was steadily declining. The unsaid was that Joanne and Hilly had trust funds. They were Michaels. Their blood ties were forged in sterling. Conversely, what Willy May received in the divorce settlement was all she had. Joanne worried about her mother's ability to maintain Firefly in the long term.

"You should increase the rates," she suggested. "Like real hotels. Higher rates in the popular months."

"Good idea."

"But no amount of money is worth hand-washing all of this." Joanne held up her chafed palms.

Willy May took them between hers with a squeeze. "These were meant to play music, not suds dirty towels. We'll order that washer and dryer. There's going to be a lot more to do when Hilly's little one is here."

Willy May stood to hang brassieres on the dry line, and Joanne moved on to the next item in the dirty laundry basket: one of Hilly's caftans. Without thinking, she slipped her hand inside the pocket to make sure there were no tissues or candy wrappers. Her fingers fumbled on a tablet.

She pulled it out. Chalky white.

"I need to grab something." She stood, cupping her palm to hide it.

Joanne was not a good liar. She left before Willy May could turn from the line and see that her face had gone hot, her upper lip sweating.

Alone, Joanne examined it. The pill was not white but a pale pink. The imprint of *3/0* was barely visible through the dissolution. She pressed her finger to it and then put it to her tongue. So bitter, it made her tongue tingle. She knew what this was: amphetamines. Her dorm mates had been passing them around all year.

"You okay?"

She jumped. Her mother had come up behind her.

"I — I —" she stuttered.

"Heat get to you?" Willy May put the inside of her wrist against her forehead. "Go have an iced tea."

Joanne obeyed and kept her breathing steady by imagining a metronome's click.

It all made sense now. Hilly's mood swings, her energy highs and lows, her emaciated appearance. She was strung out.

Joanne marched straight to her sister's bedroom, still cupping the remnants of the pill. She swung open the door without knocking and stretched out her hand.

Hilly was sitting on her balcony, fishing seeds out of a pomegranate. She torqued her neck to look over her shoulder.

"Hey," she said, licking her spoon.

Joanne came closer. "I found this in your dress."

Hilly took off her sunglasses and tapered her eyes. "What is it?"

Joanne brought her open palm inches from her sister's nose.

"I don't see anything but detergent powder."

"Is that the lie you're telling yourself? You and I both know that's not what it is."

Hilly pushed her hand away, and the tablet fell over the balcony railing.

"Well, at least you won't be taking that one."

"You don't know anything," Hilly said and brutally scooped into her pomegranate's core.

All her life, Joanne had held her tongue while Hilly said and did what she felt, when she felt it. Joanne was here because Willy May asked her to come — for Hilly. They were all walking on eggshells and trying to provide — for Hilly. Facilitating her sister's labor and delivery would fall on their shoulders, too, and afterward, the care of both mother and child. Joanne knew it even before it happened. She had always considered it her sisterly duty to look after Hilly. Her big sister hadn't inherited the Michaels' resilience as she had. When they were younger Joanne was the sister with the mettle. Hilly was fragile where she was strong. Beauty was often that way. It needed protecting. But Hilly's failure to appreciate — no, her sense of *entitlement* to Joanne's devotion was suddenly too much to bear.

Never in Joanne's life had she asked so much of anyone as did her sister. Hilly took, took, took, but never gave. Now, all Joanne was asking for was the truth and Hilly was denying her that.

"I know a junkie when I see one. It's so selfish. I mean, fine, get knocked up. Pill-pop yourself to death. Screw up your life if you want. But it's immoral to screw up a kid before it's even born."

Hilly's eyes went too wide for her gaunt face. They seemed to take up every spare millimeter.

"How dare you," she seethed. "You spoiled brat!"

"Me?"

"Yes, *you*. Everybody's favorite, Joanne. Always doing the right thing, never wrong. So talented. So kind. So selfless. You don't

281

have a clue. I would *never* hurt my baby."
She chucked the red rind over the railing
and stood, nearly falling sideways from her
girth.

Joanne reached to steady her, but Hilly
made her arms into an X across her chest.

"Don't touch me." Her eyes welled dark.
"I only take them when I need help — a
boost. I'm not you, Joanne. I can't be perfect."

"Hilly, I didn't mean —" she began.

"Everybody thinks they know. You don't
know . . ." Hilly's voice caught and the
sound speared Joanne like an angler's hook.

"I used to know, and I want to again."
Joanne dared to lay a hand on her sister's
arm. "I'm not perfect. Not even close. I'm
not judging you right or wrong. I'm worried
because those pills will hurt — *are* hurting
you and the baby. Do you have more?"

Hilly shook her head. "We had a guest.
He gave them to me."

"Girls!" came their mother's voice. She
was coming up the stairs at a pace that
made her pant. "Colin says they're writing
a feature on Mustique!" Reaching the
bedroom, she exhaled loudly with exertion.
"Oh good, you're together." She frowned
seeing their faces. "What's wrong?"

Hilly turned away.

"A misunderstanding."

Willy May held up a handwritten note like a royal proclamation. "*Gourmet* magazine is sending a journalist. She's coming this weekend, and Colin needs us to help impress. Just think — if this story hits the national press, property values will go through the roof! Tourism, too. This is the beginning. Colin is sure dozens of other major media will pick up the story. First *Gourmet,* next *Vogue*! But that's old hat for our Hilly."

She was practically giddy, waving the note around like a victory banner.

Hilly didn't turn around. So, it came to Joanne to answer. "Great, Mum."

The cats Tic, Tac, and Toe caught sight of a green-toed gecko and chased it to the corner, where it skittered up the wall, outwitting everyone. In the wake of their commotion, Willy May raised an eyebrow at her daughters.

"What kind of misunderstanding did you two have?"

"Nothing."

"We're fine."

Willy May looked from one to the other. "Whatever it is, make up. You're sisters first." She waved the letter at the cats, and they leapt *one-two-three* at the fluttering.

"Well, that's more of the reaction I was expecting. Let's get treats."

Joanne regretted saying what she had to Hilly, even if she believed it. You couldn't take back words and some, even true ones, were better left unspoken. She could've said it differently. She should've said it differently.

Janne from *Gourmet* arrived by private plane at Colin's insistence. He arranged everything to the T, though even he couldn't control the season. Summer on Mustique was painfully hot even by Caribbean standards. Nothing had a chance of producing under the blazing sun. The lettuces bolted and were bitter to eat. The herbs went to seed. There were no fish or fowl to be caught. Even the seaweed stopped washing up on the shore.

It would've all been fine if Janne had been a journalist for *Newsweek* or *The New Yorker,* but she was writing for *Gourmet* and no matter how many strings Colin pulled, he couldn't change her purpose: to write about Mustique's native foods. None of which were in season.

So, he ordered as much as he could from wherever he could find it. Frozen beef and poultry from the butcher in St. Vincent;

papaya, mangoes, and melons from St. Lucia; plantains and cornmeal from Barbados; scone mixes and teas from London; white bread, sugar, and cereals from America. Supplies came by the ferry-load.

It was decided that Hilly was too far along to participate in Colin's entertainment plans.

"She's in the final throes, poor dear," he told them. "Anne wanted nothing but silence and seclusion during the last days of her pregnancies. It's such an ugly time, isn't it?"

He shook his head mournfully, ignoring the proverbial elephant in the room. Colin didn't welcome *ugly* into his circle and certainly not when his circle was to be featured to the world.

"I would hate for her to overextend herself."

"Thank you, Colin," said Willy May. "Very considerate."

Colin wrote up an hourly agenda, the acts and scenes of his latest play. They were well rehearsed for the grand production. Washed and waxed, the jeeps were brought out to the tarmac and the mule carts tucked away in the pool shed. Janne was coming straight to the island's heart by plane. Upon landing, they shuttled her to the Cotton House

285

safari-style with Colin giving her the illustrious history of Mustique and the Mustique Company residents.

A massive nest of brown widow spiders was discovered in the largest trunk of Victorian costumes so the whole lot was retired, much to Colin's dismay. The death of the tradition was quickly cheered by the design and manufacturing of new Kwadril dresses and guayabera shirts. Colin was chuffed with himself when he saw the rainbow of fashions. He decided to continue that colorful spread to the table. For breakfasts, waiters served sliced watermelon, eggs seven different ways, and banana buns rechristened by Colin as Mustique Breads. Cereals and more colonial dishes (waffles, pancakes, and porridge) were available upon request. George was instructed to invent a signature drink that could be drunk from sunrise to sunset. Colin named it the Cotton House Special: an icy, sweet rum punch.

With a Special in hand, they took Janne down to the beach and displayed the snorkeling gear and skin-diving equipment, none of which anyone had used yet. They pointed out the beautiful reefs and protective coral bays; the gleaming white beaches and palatial swimming pools; the marble terraces, new tennis courts, garden fountains, and lawn games. All for the enjoyment of those privileged enough to be Mustique's guests.

The islanders were the dramatic chorus. When Titus laughed at one of Colin's jokes, the staff laughed. When Joseph frowned over a melted ice cube, they all frowned. It was quite a concerto, culminating in a daylong banquet scherzo.

"Our gourmet Garden of Eden!" Colin declared.

There was stuffed lobster, shrimp ceviche, roasted hens with breadfruit, pâté (chicken but presumed duck), marinated vegetables, steamed snapper in banana leaves, and more. None of which had come from Mustique, but the effort of assembling it all made it feel as if it ought to have.

After lunch, Colin insisted on a high tea. The staff had never served an estate-wide tea. Still, they were to give the impression that this sort of thing went on habitually. The guests were asked to move from the lunch table to the veranda, which was staged with bone china, silver spoons, and platters of scones, mangrove oysters, exotic fruits, and pots of English Breakfast brew. Janne broke out in a sweat that stained the underarms of her polyester frock.

Joanne wondered if she felt their collective eye on her. She couldn't imagine the pressure of that kind of attention, nor did she want to. It was a funny paradox of the elite. They all wanted the spotlight of celebrity, but once achieved, they bemoaned the loss of anonymity. Janne was no longer an individual but a figure: Luminary Food Critic of *Gourmet,* a public commodity. They all stood round watching her masticate, swallow, and smile. No surprise that she drank too much. It was impossible to be incognito in a fishbowl.

As dusk fell on her last evening, they gathered in the transformed dining room where the landowners awaited, seated at a long, candlelit banquet table so that the line of names could be read for Janne's journalistic notation. It was the finale and Colin had spared no expense. The profusion of dishes included jumbo shrimp cocktail, Madeira consommé, avocado soup, beef curry, poached whitefish, puddings, and the Cotton House Special through it all.

After dinner, they lit torchieres and dancers twirled them for show. The band played. A bonfire was ignited on the beach. Guests were given sparklers. Staff sent up paper lanterns to the moon. It was madness. It was marvelous. It was Colin's *ma-gique mystique,* but nothing about it seemed authentically Mustique. Not even to Joanne, who'd

288

only been there a short while.

By the time Janne's plane departed, every-one on the island was exhausted.

"So? How was it?" Hilly asked.

Joanne and Willy May sat along the Fire-fly's pool ledge, soaking their feet and watching a coqui frog swim the length like it was his own private kingdom.

"Let's just say, when it comes to fantasy, Walt Disney's got nothing on Colin."

Willy May laughed.

"What did I miss?" asked Hilly.

Joanne shook her head.

"I guess the proof will be in the pudding when that article comes out," said Willy May.

"Maybe the proof and definitely the pudding, but not the truth," said Joanne.

Colin called the stunt a grand success when the *Gourmet* issue finally arrived. THE MAGIC OF MUSTIQUE read the headline under a brilliant panoramic photograph of the island. The article listed in great detail all of Colin's culinary provisions, the history as he told it, and a wonderful plug for high-dollar vacationers to join the island revelry. His singular complaint was that there had been relatively few pictures of the food.

"Out of everything, they print a picture of

spotty bananas," he groused.

It spoke to the unspoken, Joanne thought. Janne knew those ripe bananas were just about the only thing that actually came from the island. She'd been onto them the whole time.

CHAPTER 18
THE ROLLING JAGGERS

It was the first day without tyrannical humidity so the women decided to roll their hair smooth. Joanne and Willy May were in culottes and tank tops with scarves tied over damp tresses set in barrel rollers. Hilly napped in the shade with hair swirled and pinned round her head in a doobie wrap. Dippity-do gel was the magic potion. Joanne loved the supple feel of it between her fingers, which made her linger in the task, relishing the way the product turned their dry strands to satin.

She was relieved that Hilly joined them. For a long while, she'd avoided Joanne, staying in her room on the claims of exhaustion and discomfort.

"I just want to sleep until this is over," she told them. "I'm miserable."

Joanne couldn't argue. She had no experience with how a woman felt pregnant. She could only hope that her sister had taken her pleas to stop using the amphetamines — for the child's sake if not her own. After the initial altercation, she wouldn't bring it up again. Hilly had felt attacked and her defense against pain had always been detachment. Joanne understood that and more. It was the way of siblings. They knew every chink in one's armor. But a chink in her own was that as much as Hilly needed her, Joanne needed Hilly. Knotted by sisterhood. She had to trust her to do the right thing, and she had to help Hilly feel like she could.

"Lookie here, lookie here!" Colin climbed the terrace steps waving a letter.

Willy May put a hand to the roller holding back her bangs. "Oh? Colin? We weren't expecting —"

"It's Mick Jagger!" Colin cut her off.

Hilly woke and covered her belly with a beach towel. "Mick Jagger?"

"He read the *Gourmet* feature in his dentist's waiting room and loved it! Aren't you glad we put forth the effort now?"

There had been so much leftover food in the wake of Janne's visit that Colin had solicited Titus's help in distributing the bread, sugar, and other perishables to the islanders. A feast of comestibles, which Colin would mention each time a staff member requested a day off, a raise, or any favor.

"I gave you *Gourmet* food!" Joanne had overheard him say.

A generous miser, a miserly giver. It depended on how one chose to look at it.

"No Sir Grapefellow in the handouts?" Willy May had joked over cups of coffee with Titus the week before.

"Not a purple crumb," replied Titus.

"Colin wouldn't give away his favorite."

"He puts little effort toward seeing the world from another person's shoes."

"I guess, why would he when his own are platforms, eh?"

"Literally and metaphorically," said Titus and Willy May nodded.

It had made Joanne glad to know that they saw the same injustices as she.

Now, Colin lifted the open letter into the air and took a theatrical stance. "Mick and Bianca are in Martinique and vastly under-whelmed by the service. So, I invited them to Mustique."

Her mother touched her rollers again.

Hilly's head snapped right and left. "No!"

The day before, Hilly had awoken in hor-ror to find her belly button popped out like a Thanksgiving turkey timer. Naomi, who moonlighted at the Mustique General Store, was better known as the island midwife and told Hilly it was a sign of a baby's impending arrival.

"Another musician — like you, Joanne," said Willy May. "Maybe he could give a nudge with industry contacts."

"He sings. I play instruments."

Her mother was aware of the difference. Never mind that Joanne didn't want inroads handed to her in any situation. That was something her mother and sister shared that she did not. Light Switch Syndrome: that's what she called it. They were always looking for the switch to turn everything on in a single flip. From what she'd experienced, the world wasn't wired for electricity. It was up to you to collect the twigs, find the flint, strike a stone, and build a flame.

"He plays the harmonica," countered Willy May.

"And apparently he's taken up the guitar," said Colin. "I only know because he's bringing the thing and asked if I had any extra strings. Still learning, he popped a few."

"Oh? This might be your opportunity, Joanne." Willy May smiled. "You could be his resident music teacher."

Joanne couldn't contain her eye roll.

Lately, Willy May had been hinting more

and more at wanting Joanne to stay on Mustique.

Nearsightedness was another way Willy May and Hilly were alike. They operated entirely in the present: what they felt, believed, and championed in this precise, singular, and utterly transitory moment. The past and the future were left on either side. It was a gift and a curse. Joanne was not like this. Yesterday and tomorrow were the castaways she carried.

Joanne, the reliable. Joanne, the trustworthy, the whole note pinning the meter to its place. Some people spent their entire lives striving to achieve such status. She felt stifled by it. It was one of the reasons Hilly's accusations of perfection had shocked her. If she came off as perfect, it was by virtue of being boxed into a frame.

Another gecko skittered across the ground. No cats in sight, it found a shady spot under the wicker sofa.

"I need your help, my dears," Colin proceeded.

"We don't have a room ready," said Willy May. "And I needn't remind you that Hilly could give birth at any hour."

Hilly grunted — with hope or fear. Joanne understood it as both.

"Can you imagine how distressing that

would be for your guests?" Willy May went on. "A laboring woman in the next room?"

Colin waved a hand. He didn't want to imagine.

"I don't need your rooms. We have enough at the Cotton House. I need your feminine wiles — your captivating company. We can't have Mick visit and find out it's nothing like the magazine write-up. Unmet expectation is responsible for ninety-nine percent of the world's unhappiness."

A red hibiscus on the nearby bush was shriveling. Colin broke it off the stem and tossed it into the thicket.

"Everyone loves the idea of a deserted island, but nobody wants to vacation on one. Not *really.*" He laughed, a beat too long.

No one laughed with him. Following was a corresponding beat-too-long silence.

Then, Hilly began to cry. "I don't want to miss meeting Mick Jagger."

She'd become increasingly maudlin in the last few weeks, sleeping most of the days away in a low funk. When she was awake, she wept at the drop of a hat. Once again, their mother chalked it up to hormones. Joanne didn't contradict her, but she surmised it might be the lack of amphetamines, too. She could only hope.

"It's because her career is over," Willy May had said and Joanne heard her mother's own regrets in it. "Galatea no more."

Joanne thought it tragic to grieve the loss of something as fleeting as beauty. But she understood that it had been both of their golden sashes. Her mother and her sister felt naked without them, making her glad that she'd never had one.

Willy May invited Titus over that night. She was doing so more and more often. At first there had been excuses: *he's bringing over fresh pineapple; he's getting me set up with an offshore account; I need him to help me move a bureau; I need his advice; I need him to . . .*

Tonight, it didn't come with any qualifiers, just a simple, "Titus is coming."

Willy May put on the record player, and they all sat in the living room playing Hearts over glasses of virgin sorrel stuffed with orange slices. Even Hilly joined in the card game. By the time they'd declared a winner, the fruit and their lips were dyed hot pink by the hibiscus flowers.

Then Titus put on the Ronettes' LP. The opening maracas of "Be My Baby" started shaking and he stood, extending one hand to her mother and the other to Joanne.

"Come on, ladies. This one's too good to

stay sitting."

Joanne felt the heat rush to her cheeks. For all her musical prodigiousness, she could not get her limbs to move correctly to the tempo she knew was there.

"I make the music so others can dance," she said, declining.

He narrowed his gaze in teasing disbelief, then turned to Hilly.

"Are you kidding? I could barely fan my cards over this thing." She motioned with both hands to her belly and giggled.

The sound made Joanne giddy. It'd been so long since she'd heard it.

Willy May stood. "Well, I love this song."

She took Titus's hand, and they swiveled and stomped their feet to the beat.

"We'll make 'em turn those heads . . . ," Willy May sang out, *"Whoa, whoa, whoa, whoa . . ."*

Willy May bungled all the words per usual and hummed her way through the verses, but they all sang along to the *be my*'s. It was surprising to see how well her mother danced — she had rhythm! And it dawned on Joanne that her music proficiency might not have been a freak gift of nature but inherited from her mother.

At the end, Willy May fell forward laughing into Titus's shoulder. Joanne would've thought nothing more of it than companion-ship had there not been a quiet moment when they pulled back in a close, open stare.

Titus's hands circled her mother's waist. One of Willy May's hands was round his back. The room fell silent as the needle dragged to the next track, "Walking in the Rain." When the storm cloud sound effects broke and Ronnie Spector sang out *I want him . . .* they parted, eyes cast briefly down to the floor. Joanne had looked away, too. The moment felt keenly intimate.

There had to have been at least a decade in age between her mother and Titus. As long a time as it took the Ronettes to become as famous as the Beatles and break up to anonymity. Ten years seemed chasmic to think about. Joanne was only nineteen. But if she let herself forget the years, the way they were in this hour seemed to add up just right.

A day later, Mick Jagger, his actress wife, Bianca, two-year-old daughter Jade, their nanny, and an assistant arrived by seaplane on Britannia Bay.

The staff was suited up in their new island costumes but that left the women of the Firefly without welcoming regalia. Willy May was thrilled, until Colin suggested that she and the girls wear cowboy hats and fringed gloves that he'd purchased for a Wild West–themed dinner party.

"He's hell-bent on trussing us up as American clowns," she grumbled under her breath.

Colin was adamant. "It's part of being on Mustique. You must. It's tradition!"

His tone was shrill, on the verge of anger. In response, her mother's breathing became more rapid. Underneath the temper, her mother was a pleaser. Joanne knew it as intrinsically as she knew her own bent nature, different but similar. The mother-daughter paradox. Her own pulse quickened, too.

A bolt of fresh island muslin had just been delivered to the Cotton House for Colin's inspection and approval. Joanne pointed to it. "What if we wore that instead?"

"How so?" he asked. "It hasn't yet been cut."

Joanne fingered the soft edge. She'd gone to a toga party with her hallmates at university. They'd used bedsheets and pillowcases. Easy costumes to put on and, more important, to take off.

"As Roman togas."

Colin's eyebrows arched with glee. "Like Venus and her nymphs. I love it." He unspooled a portion of the cotton. "The white fabric will stand out on the beach and allow us to show off the Mustique Company's textiles. You and your girls can model our fashions!"

He proceeded to wrap Joanne and Willy May in Mustique cloth and cinched their waists with silver satin ribbons.

"To distinguish you from the rest!" He topped off the outfits with glittering crowns of plastic gems.

And while her mother was still dismayed at having to dress up, the unsaid was that togas were a thousand times more tolerable in the island heat than cowboy duds.

Hilly had remained at Firefly under Naomi's watchful eye. She hadn't slept the night before, unable to orient her belly in a comfortable position. She'd walked the halls like a zombie. Joanne had stayed with her as long as she could but could not ease her sister's suffering.

"I need something to help me sleep," Hilly had begged. "Please, Josie, just for one night. There's a bottle of barbital in Mom's bathroom."

Joanne hated refusing her. It was clear she was in pain. Near dawn, Hilly's crying and pacing had done the job of ten pills. She lay curled in bed, asleep. Joanne was glad to see her rest.

Now, on the beach, an island man wearing a top hat pulled a violin from its sleeve — an instrument Joanne knew well but had not seen since she left England. She gasped at the sight of its shiny wood, curved peg box, and high throat scroll. With all the baroque features, it looked distinctly Klotz. But there were so many forgeries. The telltale would be the sound and even that was predicated on the hand that played.

On the first note of "Rule Britannia," Joanne broke out in chills. She was nearly weeping by the end. Did the violinist know the worth he possessed? Before she could reach him to ask, Colin intercepted her path with Mick Jagger in a flamingo-printed shirt unbuttoned to his navel.

"This is Joanne of the Firefly villa. She's a musical savant studying at Dartington College."

Instead of correcting him, she smiled.

"Joanne composes songs and is proficient in a wide variety of instruments," continued Colin.

"The piano, really," she clarified. "I don't sing. Not like you."

Mick ran a hand through his shaggy hair, and it feathered back in the breeze. "Hey — meet my girls."

Bianca Jagger was the most striking woman Joanne had ever seen. Her eyelashes looked like butterfly wings. Her lips were full and ripe as a plum. She thought she might be a little in love with her from . . .

"Hello." Bianca smiled. "This is Jade."

On her hip was a two-year-old with her same doe eyes and Mick's irrepressible pucker. She gripped Joanne's finger.

"Nice to meet you both."

Bianca turned over her shoulder to two figures: "This is our nanny, Nancee Helferb, and our assistant, Tim May."

They were silhouetted against the shine of the midday sun so Joanne only caught the outline of the nanny's straw sun hat and large diaper tote. She gave a tired "good day" and moved along quickly while the assistant lingered long enough for Joanne to shield her eyes.

"Thanks for having us," Tim replied.

An American. His voice was like the strike of a piano's middle C, neat and confident.

He bent closer. "You guys saved the summer from being a total disaster."

His words tickled her ear.

When he pulled back, she saw his face without shadow. *The Happiest Millionaire* was one of her favorite films growing up — it was the Technicolor and the alligators and the jaunty butler singing out tunes. Tim was dimpled and handsome like the musical's leading man, John Davidson. His gaze brought on the melody of the waltz song "Are We Dancing?" in her mind. Her knees went spongy, and she shifted her weight to make them solid again.

"Do you not find Martinique *magnifique?*" she asked and chastised herself, *You sound like an idiot.*

"*Au contraire, Mick l'a trop apprécié.*" Tim glanced over his shoulder to make sure his boss wasn't paying attention before pinching his forefinger and thumb together at his lips and pretending to hold a pipe. "*C'est le problème.*" He winked.

She restrained her laugh with a nod, impressed at his skill with charades and French. Most Americans knew English and . . . English. While she wouldn't profess herself fluent, she'd tried to pick up the language when Hilly went to Paris. She'd always been a quick study, languages and music came easily. For a short while, the sisters had fostered the idea of traversing Paris together. Hilly suggested that she come during her next school break. While she was busy modeling, Joanne could explore the cafés and hear the street performers of the Latin Quarter. Joanne had been thrilled by the idea and signed up for a conversational French class that semester; but then Hilly went directly to Mustique without sending word or warning. She assumed, like many things, that Hilly had simply forgotten her in the moment. Only later did she understand that Hilly's expedited departure had a weightier spur. She forgave her sister and was glad to have the French at her disposal now.

"*J'espère que tu es heureux ici sur la Mustique,*" she replied.

"*Très bon.*" Tim nodded with admiration. "I like your French in a British accent."

Joanne hadn't realized she had an accent, but then, one never rightfully heard the sound of one's own voice. A professor had explained the science of it: when another person spoke, the sound came by way of external air conduction. But when it emanated from one's own vocal cords, it was enhanced by deeper frequency vibrations through flesh and bone. So, *your voice* was a combination of sound carried along both paths.

"I like your American accent in French, too," she said.

"Is it that obvious?" He grinned. "I'm from Miami. How about you?"

She cleared her throat. "I wish I could say

it was something that interesting. My dad's family is from Cheltenham."

He smiled, and she found herself staring at his perfectly aligned teeth.

"Tim!" Mick called. "Need you, mate."

She was keeping him from his duties. "Sorry."

He shook his head. "For what?"

She didn't know. It was just what one said. "Sorry," she said again instinctively.

"You Brits and your 'sorry-sorry's."

"I'm only half Brit." She nodded to Willy May. "Mum's from Texas."

"A Yellow Rose?"

She didn't know what he meant so she shrugged with a laugh. "Sorry."

"Tim!" Mick called again. "Stop flirting and help me with the bags."

He blushed, and the color made his lips rosier. She guessed him to be Hilly's age.

"I hope we have the chance to talk more," he said. "In whatever language you like."

And then he jaunted over the sand to Mick's side and took up the handle of a guitar case. Mick clapped him on the back, nodded to Joanne with a grin, and then they were gone.

In his wake, the sounds crashed together like the roar of the sea, tumbling head over heels.

Colin drove the guests up to the Cotton House. She watched from the beach, curious how a young man from Florida came to be Mick's assistant on Mustique. After that, she wondered what his family was like, what was his favorite song, did he have a girlfriend, and more. In fact, every thought seemed to involve him, like a fermata of the mind. He was all she could see, hear, or think.

"Joanne — get the cotton outta your ears!" Her mother's voice came cymbal sharp. "I called you three times. Didn't you hear me?"

Joanne shook her head.

"Hilly's in labor. Naomi sent word with Kenton." Willy May nodded to Kenton, who'd returned with an empty cart to collect Colin's trunk of new costumes.

Joanne started to follow.

"Leave that crown in the trunk," said Willy May.

She'd forgotten she had it on. She'd forgotten she had any of it on: the toga, the sash, the tiara. How foolish she must look to Tim. But then, she recalled the ease of his smile and it made her smile, too.

"Come on," said Willy May from the driver's seat of their cart.

Joanne climbed in and Willy May throttled the gas.

"What's gotten into you? Your sister's having the baby!"

"Sorry," she said and even that had new meaning. She bit her lip to hold back the grin.

By the time they reached Firefly, Hilly had given birth.

Naomi said that the baby girl raced out on the first big push. The child was small, vastly underweight, and made no sound. Naomi had feared a stillbirth, so she gave the baby's foot a little pinch. It took a beat but then, she cried. They could tell it troubled Naomi.

"The baby is slow to respond to stimulation," she explained, while snapping her fingers at the child's ears and over her eyes. She slept on in the bassinette.

Joanne bit the inside of her cheek. She was pretty certain that Hilly had stopped using but maybe not in time. For a fleeting moment, Joanne wondered if she ought to say something of the truth . . . but she was hard-pressed to find the good it would do them now and worried it would alienate her sister more.

"She was just born," said Willy May, beaming down at her new granddaughter.

"The world takes some adjusting to."

Naomi nodded with pursed lips. "Hilly named her Windstorm — Windy."

The day was clear as a bell and unusually still, not a curtain fluttered.

"Windstorm?" asked Willy May.

"That's what she said. She's in her room. She told me to take the baby out so she can rest. If there's excessive bleeding, call me immediately. And make sure she eats and drinks. She needs it for breastfeeding." She collected her bag of birthing tools.

"Okay," said Willy May. "Thank you, Naomi. I'll go check on her."

Naomi paused again over Windy, assessing one last time before leaving. Joanne leaned in to where Naomi had just been to see if there were visible signs of . . . Joanne wasn't exactly sure.

Windy was pink as a rosebud and smelled milky sweet. She looked nothing like Hilly and nothing like her name. Her breathing was quiet but even.

Joanne gently lay the back of her palm against the baby's warm cheek. "Hello there, Windy," she whispered. "I'm your aunt."

It wasn't until she pulled away and stood that she saw the movement. Windy's right eyelash batted open, followed a moment later by her left, and then they closed again.

Windy's and Mick's arrivals on the same day was bad timing. Colin wanted to put on a show, but a show required a crowd and there were frightfully few audience members on a private island. Joanne had been given the duty of representing Firefly. She spent the mornings helping with Windy and the evenings at the Cotton House.

Colin loved games. At his first party for the Jaggers, he had the servers clear the table after dinner and place a series of items down the center: a peacock feather, an ivory comb, a tapered wax candle, a bowl of ice chips, a velvet glove, a wooden spoon, and more. Beside them was an Oxford English Dictionary.

"It's a game of senses." Colin held up a silk purple blindfold. "The rules are simple: One player is blindfolded while another player picks an item. You aren't limited to these here. The whole room is in play. Then we, the nameless chorus of sorts, pick a secret word from the dictionary that the Observant player must spell out using his or her chosen item on the skin of the Perceiver player." His eyes darted devilishly round the room. "The Perceiver must guess the word and the item. Guessed correctly, the team earns a point. The team with the most points gets a prize."

Guests tittered nervously.

"What's the prize?" asked Mick.

Colin raised an eyebrow. "That's the sur-*prize.*" He laughed at his own wordplay. "But I promise, everyone will want it."

More riddles. More games. Joanne had concluded that Colin communicated 90 percent in double entendres.

Colin cleared his throat and continued, "I've done us the liberty of pairing everyone so we can get the game started without all the sticky business of picking partners." He went round the table calling out name to name. When he reached her, she could've sworn she saw him wink. "Joanne and Tim."

Of course he did. This game of senses was a game within a game. Playing Cupid was Colin's ultimate favorite.

Colin and Bianca went first so he could demonstrate. Bianca's eyes were covered in an Hermès scarf.

Mick's famous lips puckered approvingly. Colin pulled on the velvet glove. Hugo's wife, Jinty, opened the dictionary and fanned the pages for Mick. He stuck his thumb in the *K*'s.

Jinty pointed silently at *kick*.

Colin frowned. "Really, can't we do better?"

She slid her finger down to *kilometer*.

"No science-y words and nothing more than two syllables. Come now, be practical."

Joanne swallowed her guffaw.

Jinty moved on to *kiss*, and Colin's eyes twinkled.

Silently, he lifted a velvet finger and touched the skin of Bianca's décolleté.

Bianca inhaled. "Ooh, soft as . . . *velvet?*"

"Correct," said Anne. "You've got it half right."

Colin continued gliding his finger: *K-I-S-S*.

"H? L?" guessed Bianca. "Is that an *S?*"

"Yes and no. *Feel* the letters. Concentrate, my dear."

Despite the rules stipulating that only the blindfolded Perceiver could speak, it was impossible for Colin to remain Observantly silent. Joanne was surprised that he'd not blurted out the answer already. If there was anything he loved more than playing games, it was winning them.

Bianca laughed and scratched at her neckline. "It tickles!"

"I think that's the point," said Mick, licking his lips.

Bianca pursed her own in concentration.

"Hiss? No . . . *Kiss!"*

"Yes!" Colin slipped the blindfold off and planted one on her cheek.

Jinty and Hugo clapped. "Well done!"

"Joanne and Tim, your turn," said Colin, with increased excitement.

Joanne's face flushed hot.

"Ladies always go first." Colin wrapped the silk around her eyes before she was ready and the room slipped to darkness.

A sliver of light shimmered from beneath the seam of the scarf so that she could barely see the shadow of movement — not enough to discern identities, just enough to be aware of the world beyond. With her eyes covered, it took a moment longer for her other senses to adjust. She focused on the smell of the menthol digestif being served, tasted the evening's treacle tart in the back of her throat, listened to the papery pages of the dictionary, and felt . . . there. Fully present.

The anticipation of Tim's touch sent her pulse galloping. A match lit in her body, and she began to burn in all the hidden nooks: between her breasts, behind her knees, in her earlobes, between her thighs. She knew all eyes were on her, including Tim's, so she tried to keep her breathing steady. Tried not to bite her lip or twitch or show signs of agitation. Because she was agitated. Highly.

When she finally felt the press of him, she jumped — so keyed up.

Colin chuckled somewhere to her left. "She's a flinchy filly."

Against the back of her shoulder blade, parallel to her dress's spaghetti strap, Tim moved something soft but fleshy, delicate but firm. So overwhelmed by the feel of it, she forgot that there was a word to decipher.

"I'm sorry," she whispered, breathless. "Can you write it again?"

"Hm-mm," he replied.

The vibration of it against her bare skin sent a wave of hot chills down her back that pooled between her legs in a silent bonfire. She could see the flames behind her eyelids.

"C?" she said, because she needed to say something and once more, she'd completely missed his marks.

He ran the item serpentine.

"S!"

She felt his head nod and suddenly, she wanted to guess right for him. Silly as it sounded, she wanted them to win together. She focused, visualizing his eyes, his lips, his face, the bulge of his biceps down to the sweep of his hand. She imagined her own on it, moving together: *S-T-A-R*.

"Star."

"Brava!" said Bianca.

"That's only half," reminded Colin. "She's got to guess the instrument."

Joanne leaned her chin toward her shoulder, toward Tim. So close, she could hear his breath moving in and out. Reflexively, she moved her own in tandem. He pressed the item to her skin and the edge of his fingernail caught her: a lightning bolt of pleasure and pain. Her breath gave way. She gulped to keep the sound inside and squeezed her eyes together beneath the blindfold.

Then it came: sweet honey. A fragrance.

"A flower." She inhaled. "Honeysuckle or jasmine, I'm not sure."

Bright light. The room climaxed into a cacophony of sounds, colors, and sensations.

Colin had undone the blindfold. "Clever girl!" He clapped.

Just behind her, Tim held the white jasmine blossom between his fingers. He'd plucked it from a vine crawling up the veranda wall.

Her hands were shaking. She squeezed her nails into her palms, leaving purple half-moons. Tim smiled at her in a way that made the cinders inside blaze again.

"We make a good team." He extended the little flower, and she unclenched her fists to accept.

"One point for Tim and Joanne," Colin continued. "Jinty and Hugo are up next!"

But Tim didn't move away and neither did Joanne, closer to one another now than the hour before. The game afoot.

They called it a night with the moon at its highest point. Mick won the most sets as Observer with Anne as Perceiver. The reward? A pair of cheetah-print tights. A bit anticlimactic, but Colin insisted.

"One can never have enough animals in the closet!"

Joanne and Tim agreed that had they known the prize, they might've tried to *lose*. Mick and Bianca were quickly off to their suite. So, Tim borrowed one of Colin's golf carts to drop Joanne at Firefly with plans of circling back to give Nanny Nancee an hour respite.

"Will I see you tomorrow?" he asked.

No hidden meaning: it was a question and a desire.

"Yes," she said. "You will."

She went to sleep conjuring the feel of his fingers tracing the word *tomorrow* over her body, gliding across the burning places, still ember warm to the touch.

■ ■ ■ ■

She was in love with Tim. It happened fast. She knew it because despite the incessant onslaught of sexual innuendos and the many secluded hours, they had not had sex. Instead, they talked.

He told her stories about being raised by his eccentric great-aunt Jasmin, who moved to Florida after World War II and collected wooden sleds; about meeting Mick through a British uncle on Jagger's legal team; about getting his business degree at the University of Miami and his dream of being a studio manager. This was his break into the industry. He was living his beginning right then, and she wanted it all for him.

In return, she shared things that she'd never told anyone: about her devotion to her grandmother Michael undeterred by the umbrage among family members and her father's infidelity. She told him her most hidden truth: that studying music was making her resent it. She didn't want to be a professional musician. She loved it too much. She wanted to protect it and keep it for her own pleasure.

"If not music, then what?" he asked.

"I like sharing what I know, so I'd say

317

something in education."

"Then do that."

Uncomplicated honesty. That's what Tim gave her that no one else seemed to allow themselves to do. It made it easy to trust his word, and she could say that about few others.

Each day when she left Firefly for the Cotton House gatherings, she wasn't entirely sincere in her guilt. For that, she felt sincerely guilty.

Nanny Nancee offered to care for both Jade and Windy while the Jaggers were on the island, but Willy May declined.

"Windy can't even hold her head up," she told Joanne. "You don't leave a newborn with a stranger. We aren't those people."

Joanne didn't know what kind of people her mother meant. Nearly all her friends in England had been raised by a nanny or governesses. She often thought she and Hilly would've been better off growing up with more stable child care, as Grandmother Michael had wished. It would've lifted the day-to-day burden from her parents and freed them to grow as individuals and a couple still in love. Instead, they seemed to attach themselves to Joanne and Hilly like barnacles on a whale's belly. But you couldn't build a life on your children's lives any more than a child could build its life on its parents'.

"Nanny Nancee is a professional, Mum," Joanne argued. "She knows more about child-rearing than we do."

"Joanne!" Willy May gasped.

That was the end of the discussion for Willy May, but it didn't solve the larger problem.

While Windy had found her voice, crying at the drop of a hat for reasons they never could rightly identify, it was clear that she was developmentally delayed. Physically, for certain. Joanne hoped that was the extent of it, but Naomi was not one to mince words.

"I am no pediatrician, but there are milestones — hand motions, vision focus, head movement. Windy is not as active as she should be. Try to engage her more and order more formula. She's still under-weight."

Hilly was little help. She'd barely touched her daughter. She refused to breastfeed even when her breasts throbbed red and nearly burst from the swelling. She let them stain her shirt while she cried softly to herself.

Joanne had crawled into bed beside her and lay nose to nose.

"What is it?" she'd asked. "You can tell me."

But Hilly had buried her cheek into the pillow and wept — the hurting too deep and wide for words. Joanne checked all her pockets and drawers for pills, afraid that she'd returned to using. But she found nothing. Her sister was clean. It made Joanne second-guess herself. Maybe Hilly needed medicine — prescribed. Maybe the drug use was a symptom of a more substantial medical issue. Joanne wasn't sure about such things. Most of her mental health knowledge was based on media bits related to Vietnam veterans, which seemed magnified with shame. But her sister hadn't gone to war. Not a physical one, at least.

"This isn't the life I wanted," Hilly said when they brought Windy into the room. "Please, take her away." Then, in the same breath, "Don't leave. I don't want to be alone."

One of them would always stay. How could they do otherwise?

"She wouldn't hurt Windy," Willy May said one morning.

Joanne heard the question in it. "No, not Windy."

They looked at each other silently. Hilly wouldn't hurt her child, but she was prone to impulsivity: actions that didn't mean to harm but did, just the same. Like the time

320

Hilly jumped overboard when they were girls.

It was right after they'd set sail from California. They'd been enrolled at The King's School in Canterbury for the coming term. Granny had argued that it was high time they submitted to a formal education like all the Michaels before them. How else were they to meet fellow young people of merit? Hilly believed differently. She said she'd rather die in California than go to boarding school on the opposite side of England. Then she jumped.

They threw out a life buoy on the quick and circled the boat around to pull her in. Their father called it foolhardy melodramatics.

"What about Cheltenham Ladies' College?" Joanne had suggested.

A handful of fellow Girl Guides attended. It was a local school of equal prestige but without boarding requirements. Her father had sternly waved her off, but when they got back to England, they matriculated there. It had been a turning point.

Joanne realized that the traditional hierarchy (father, mother, eldest child, youngest child) wasn't an absolute construct. Despite being the lowest in the pecking order, she had influence. She and Hilly were more than branches of their parents. They were vines woven together and stronger for it, but their actions affected each other. If Hilly died, Joanne was sure a part of her would die, too. If Hilly had an addiction, Joanne would battle it alongside her — not for propriety or perfection, but to save their sisterhood. Love was a choice, not an expectation.

"It's the baby blues," said Willy May. "We've got to help her."

They bought Similac by the boatload. Joanne was at her sister's beck and call, mothering Windy as her own for as long as she could. But she hadn't expected to fall in love. Now she was confronted with the difficult decision: her sister or herself.

"Come back with me," Tim said. "Marry me."

No bended knee, candlelight, or symphonies. He'd been dabbing a Q-tip dipped in calamine on her bug-bitten arms. Regardless of the hour, the mosquitoes were ravenous. She'd been covered in pink polka dots, smelling sweetly mineral from the lotion and sweaty sour from the day.

Behind Tim in the twilight, a verdant flash haloed his head. Joanne took it as a sign.

"I will. But I need to figure things out here."

They made love that night, understanding that it was not either of their firsts. They had both been with others. The bed in Tim's guest room had a creaky spring that they tried to keep quiet from the household. She accidentally elbowed him in the eye. He pulled her hair. The sheet tangled around their legs. They couldn't quite get the angle right. They laughed more than they kissed and smeared pink calamine lotion all over. It was possibly the most unsexy act she'd ever committed, and it was the best. Because it meant more than all the others. Because they came to each other with no shame and no secrets. Because she was making love to the man she loved. The rest would work itself out in time.

They decided that Tim would go back immediately with the Jaggers, and she would follow in a few weeks, making Colin's farewell dinner party feel more like a beginning than an ending.

From her closet, Willy May chose a powder-blue shift for Joanne. It had only been worn once by Hilly. While the dress fit Joanne to a T, it lacked the panache on her frame that it had on her sister's.

"Hmm." Willy May adjusted the neckline. "Maybe if we accessorize."

She layered on so many bangles that

323

Joanne felt anchored at the wrong end. Top heavy, she teetered on her mother's platforms.

"Can I at least go without heels?"

"Mum?" Hilly called from the other room.

"You decide, but take a lesson from Cinderella: bad footwear can ruin a night!" Willy May left Joanne to find a pair of flat, gladiator sandals on her own. Her relief was palpable.

"Thank God!" she exhaled, loud enough to wake Windy, who commenced crying. What the child lacked in pounds, she made up for in volume.

Joanne instinctively clapped a hand over her own mouth. Windy's cries would lead to Hilly's cries, and Hilly's cries would inevitably result in her staying right where she was all night. She wanted to see Tim. She needed to. This might not have been the life that Hilly wanted, but it was the life she had made. It was not Joanne's.

The German cuckoo clock that Hilly had purchased from Delaney struck the hour and a set of Bavarian dancers came out from their miniature door to spin. Joanne thought it out of place in the tropical setting. *She* was out of place in this tropical setting. It came to her as sharp as a bell, and she left before the final chime.

CHAPTER 19
TO EVERYTHING
THERE IS A SEASON

With the summer bank holiday's approach, Joanne wrote Grandmother Michael. She always came home from Scotland then for the Cheltenham carnival. Joanne explained that she would not be returning to Dartington College or England. Willy May didn't hide her enthusiastic approval, but the celebration was short-lived. At the same time, Joanne announced that she had accepted Tim's marriage proposal.

"Tim? Tim who?" her mother protested.

"Tim May," said Joanne calmly. "You know who he is, Mum, Mick's summer assistant."

Willy May often suffered from selective memory.

"You can't leave," said Hilly, wounded by the very idea. She was out of bed, a step in the right direction, but she continued to carry a blade of sorrow. "What do you mean, marry Tim? You barely know him."

"Mum and Dad knew each other for less time."

"Look how that ended up," cut in Willy May.

Joanne winced.

"It's not about how long you're with a person, Mum. When you love someone — *really* love them — you know."

"How do you know?"

The question was edged with sincerity.

"You just do."

Hilly held Windy close to her chest and the child fussed at her mother's tight grasp. "You guys could live on Mustique."

"That's not a bad idea," said Willy May.

It shocked Joanne that her family assumed the island could be her permanent home. Willy May and Colin were deluded by the same fantasy — that by controlling every element of their lives on Mustique, they could create utopia. That didn't make it Joanne's home, even if her sister was figuratively shipwrecked there.

"We're moving to America," said Joanne.

Willy May and Hilly stared at her speechless.

"Tim arranged it," she continued. "The Jaggers are coming back to sign purchasing papers on one of Colin's plots. They're going to Criteria Studios in Miami afterward.

I'm to fly back with them."

"No." Hilly's eyes welled. "Mum, don't let her . . ."

"I sure as hell won't!" Willy May brandished the point of her finger. "Tim isn't running off with my girl without a fight."

It was a compliment of sorts. Joanne knew her mother's history. Nobody had fought for her to stay in Texas. Joanne and Hilly had never known their maternal grandparents. By the time Joanne thought to ask why, Willy May said they were already deceased and explained the aggrieved separation. When she eloped with their father, her family had simply shut the door behind her. Communication cut. Past forgotten.

So now, fighting for her was Willy May's perverse way of loving, but Joanne was a person not a possession. She made her own choices.

"Tim is in Miami, Mum. You're welcome to come with me if that would make you comfortable, but there's not going to be any fighting. I'm going."

Willy May turned away, staring hard out the window toward the rippling horizon.

"What about Windy?" Hilly pressed her cheek against her daughter's head.

Joanne loved her niece as much as she loved her mother and sister. Staying didn't

327

prove or deny that.

"Naomi says she's finally catching up in weight, hitting milestones, and look at you, you're doing so much better. Trust yourself, Hilly."

"You're too young to get married," said Willy May. "You don't know what you're getting into. If he loves you, he'll wait."

"Wait for what, Mum? There's nothing to wait for. I'm older than you were when you got married. I'm not going to be a different person if I stay on Mustique for another year or two or five."

Willy May shook her head. "Mark my words, Joanne, you'll ruin your life if you do this."

"That's my risk to take. Tim is a good man."

"Do you *have* to marry him?" Hilly's eyes darted right and left. "I mean, are you in trouble — a baby? We could raise our kids here together."

She shook her head. "It's not like that. I don't have to marry him. I want to."

Hilly started to cry.

Joanne had never pressured Hilly to share the identity of Windy's father. It was her secret to do with as she wished. What Joanne knew was that whoever he was, Hilly had loved him, and he had used her cruelly.

Love meant loss to Hilly. The only love that she felt she could count on unconditionally was blood.

It broke Joanne's heart. She wished she could explain to her that love wasn't a vessel poured out until empty. It was living water, moving, quenching, filling everything it touched.

"I'm going," Joanne said. "I want you to be okay with that, but even if you aren't, my decision is made."

"Please, stay," begged Hilly.

"Don't ask me to do that."

Hilly pulled back her hand from Windy's bottom. "She's messed herself. I've got to change her." She turned away, shoulders trembling as she went.

Willy May picked up a baby burp cloth. "You've upset your sister. She's just come out of the postpartum depression, too."

Joanne wouldn't be responsible for Hilly's depression, her sobriety, or her happiness.

"She's stronger than you give her credit, Mum."

"If you leave . . ." Willy May's eyes narrowed so that Joanne couldn't see past her mascara. "Don't call me when you need money. You've made your bed; you lie in it."

"Is that what your mum and dad said when you left?"

Joanne hadn't meant it as a slap, but by the red of Willy May's cheeks, it might as well have been one. Her mother turned on her heel, still twisting the baby cloth. Her footsteps clicked against the tile floor like a metronome: *one-two, three-four, five-six, seven-eight.* Her bedroom door slammed and it was silent.

Joanne sat alone on the veranda with the blue ocean at her back. She breathed in deep, hoping that she wasn't making a mistake or being a bad daughter or sister. Then, instead of trying to give words to what she felt, she tapped a rhythm on the inside of her wrist, feeling the harmonic triad on the treble and hearing the stack of notes. It comforted her in the way that music always had.

When Joanne took her seat on the Jaggers' plane, the only person who came to say goodbye was Colin.

"See you all back soon!"

"Right on," said Mick. "Keep an eye on our new villa while we're away."

"Will do!"

The plane door closed and cut the Mustique sunshine into ragged yellow swatches on the cabin's walls. The engine purred. The propellers oscillated. The air-conditioning blew cold whooshing currents. The flight attendant brought mineral water in glass cups. Mick's lips moved but Joanne couldn't hear him.

Bianca turned to her. "Tim will be so happy to see you, Jo. Can I call you Jo?"

Nobody outside of her family called her by a diminutive. She didn't decline, though. One didn't decline Bianca Jagger while sitting on her private plane, drinking her mineral water.

As they taxied to takeoff, Joanne pulled down the window shade and closed her eyes. She didn't watch as the island became an emerald, then a pebble, then a speck, and then nothing at all. Instead, she listened to the static air conduction, scrubbing the scales clean and making way for the new harmony of her future.

Joanne and Tim married on a clear day in late September with the Floridian air smelling of lemons and vanilla frosting. Though they'd been sent an invitation, no one from Mustique came. But Grandmother Michael made the trek from Cheltenham. Wearing a floral pillbox hat identical to Queen Elizabeth's and her hair styled similarly, she had many of the American wedding guests whispering that it *was* Her Majesty. Tim had been Mick's assistant; Mick was a celebrity; he knew the royals; they all vacationed together on Mustique. It was plausible to onlookers standing behind her. For the rest of their lives, they would regale friends of the time they attended a wedding with the Queen of England.

Mick offered to escort Joanne in the absence of her father, but Joanne said she'd rather walk alone. They didn't bother with bride or groom sides. Everyone gathered on the dunes at sunset, and she came down the aisle to Andy Williams's "Where Do I Begin?" carrying a nosegay of daisies and buttercups.

She wore an ivory lace gown. No designer labels. No veil. She bought the dress off the rack from Saks. She'd found a pair of cream kitten heels that almost matched. It didn't matter. She kicked them off after the ceremony when they cut the almond cake and tossed the miniature Mr. and Mrs. toppers into the ocean for good luck. Tim didn't ask her to take his last name but she wanted to — wanted the fresh start. Jo May. She liked the staccato cadence of it.

Joanne wrote to Firefly, sending pressed buttercups from her wedding bouquet and news of her honeymoon at Disney's Magic Kingdom.

A telegram reply arrived:

CONGRATULATIONS. MAY HAPPILY
EVER AFTER BE YOURS.
— MUM, HILLY, WINDY

She read it backward and forward trying
to hear tone between words. She wanted to
believe it rang of genuine sentiment.

Later, she sent photographs of their home,
a bungalow in Coral Gables close to where
Tim was completing his final year of his
MBA at the University of Miami. A few
months after that, she wrote of her Siamese
cat, Violin, and corgi, Saxophone, who
seemed to be in love just like the Silly
Symphony *Music Land.* She didn't hear
from them.

But when she sent word that she was
pregnant, Hilly replied with a handwritten
note:

Wonderful news! The cousins need to
meet. We should have a visit. Love, H

Joanne answered immediately:

Yes, please! I'm due in October. How
about a phone chat? That might be easier.
We aren't living at the turn of the century!
Love you more, J

She waited a week after mailing her letter

to call, anxiously wrapping the cord around her hand so that it left a pattern of spiral indents. All it took was one hello to move forward. They could make this right. Her mother had been hurt and angry. They had parted on terrible terms. She shouldn't have brought up her grandparents in Texas. But it couldn't go on like this forever, could it? She was having a baby! She needed her mother and sister as much as they needed her when Windy was born. They had to see that. It had been over a year. It was time to reconcile.

With each successive ring, panic rose. Shrill as a piccolo. "Pick up, pick up," she whispered.

The call rang for so long that it was finally dropped and the operator came on.

"Ma'am, I don't think they're home. Try back later."

Easier said than done. It had taken her an hour to rally the courage to dial in the first place.

"Thank you," she said. Her voice was nasal, on the brink.

She hung up, hand still wrapped in the cord.

They must've been out — by the pool, in the garden, or at the Cotton House. Maybe they had guests or were busy taking care of

Windy. Her mind fixated on the possibilities. *They aren't avoiding me. They don't know it's me calling.* And then, alarm bells: *They won't know that I tried to call!*

It broke her. She wasn't the kind for emotional outbursts, but the baby and the hormones . . . Joanne empathized anew with Hilly's mood swings during her pregnancy. It was hard to keep it all in check.

Tim found her sobbing, strung to the kitchen phone line.

"Aw, hon." He unwound her and held her in his arms. "Did it not go well?"

"They didn't pick up," she bleated. "They're not home."

He kissed her. He knew how hard the separation had been.

"You can try again."

"Okay," she said.

He brought her a Fudgsicle from the freezer. They sat together until her hot grief cooled, and there was nothing left but a stick and a smear of chocolate on her fingertips.

Another week went by, during which she'd jumped at every telephone call and postman's knock, but not a word from Firefly.

So, she wrote again:

You are my family. I'm here whenever you want to talk. I love you, Joanne

It was strange to have a whole year vanish. She had no idea what had happened to them on Mustique. So much, she imagined, like her life. Time was fickle. It moved too slow for the young and too fast for the old, letting all between falsely believe that they had more of it than they could handle. That's how it cheated the living. Once wasted, time was lost for good and it never obeyed the plans for it.

Three days before her due date, Joanne gave birth to a baby girl with Tim's full lips and her blue eyes. She looked like a fairy born of a flower. Joanne named her Luanne Hilly May, a variation of her own name and her sister's. Lulu for short.

Holding her daughter for the first time, swaddled in a cloud of pink, she thought of Mustique and the women of her family. They were connected, even at their farthest points.

"You are loved by so many," she whispered. "Your grandmum Willy May, your aunt Hilly and cousin Windy and great-granny Michael . . ." She wanted her daughter to know all of their names from the very beginning.

■ ■ ■ ■

When the phone rang unexpectedly one muggy afternoon, Joanne almost didn't answer. She was nursing Lulu with her right hand and trying to eat an apple with her left. Having a snack: once a simple task, now a colossal undertaking.

They were installing new window air-conditioning units and the handyman was supposed to call on his way. So she couldn't ignore the clattering jangle standing between her and her hunger pains. She left the half-eaten core on the counter and carried Lulu, still latched, to the corded wall receiver.

"The Mays . . . ," she answered. A bit of apple peel wedged in her back molar, and she flicked her tongue momentarily to dislodge it. "Hello?"

"Josie?"

Her mother's voice was a surprise. She dropped the handset. Unable to balance Lulu and pick it up, she slid to the floor and cradled both.

"Mum?"

"Hi."

Emotion choked her.

"I hope it's okay that I called."

"Uh-huh." It was all Joanne could muster.

"I don't really have a reason except . . ." She exhaled and the pause seemed endless.

"It's okay," said Joanne, wanting to fill up the void with comfort, assurance, love.

Her pulse beat fast and Lulu felt the surge. She unlatched and gave a cry of concern. Her cheeks tinged scarlet.

"Is that her?" asked Willy May. "Lulu?"

"Yes . . . she's saying hello to her grand-mum."

Slowly, cautiously, like trees after a long winter, they began again.

■ ■ ■ ■ ■

PART 4
HILLY

■ ■ ■ ■ ■

CHAPTER 20
GOLD ON GOLD

November 1976

In anticipation of Colin's fiftieth birthday, invitations for an island-wide Golden Ball were sent out from London to Tokyo. Princess Margaret and her companion Roddy Llewellyn came to Les Jolies Eaux. Anne was in residence at the Cotton House hosting her sister Sarah, cousin Liz, Oliver Messel, and a legion of young models and actors. Colin proclaimed Mustique the modern Mount Olympus, the *beau idéal,* and everyone who was anyone, according to Colin, was sailing in.

So, the morning before the ball, the women of Firefly sailed out — just for the day, mind you, and just north to St. Vincent. Sailing once a week had become their routine. Willy May claimed it was to keep the *Otrera* seaworthy, but Hilly knew it was more. The salty air, sunshine, and exercise made them stronger, body and spirit.

341

Little Windy had filled out curvy and so had she. She was sober and had been since her sister confronted her. With a healthier appetite, she was surprised to discover that she had a knack for cooking more than the toaster oven recipes passed down from her mother. Willy May encouraged her culinary pursuits. With a nudge from Titus, George at the Cotton House agreed to be her chef mentor. He started her with *mise en place* prep, but she quickly worked her way up to hot appetizers and a handful of entrées. Colin initially balked at everything about her prepping his tuna canapés; but soon enough, it too became one of his party tricks: *even our food is prepared by fashion's elite — a* Vogue *model!*

Since Windy's birth, Hilly had withdrawn more and more from the island's public party scene. She didn't like being gawked at by Colin's guests. Large gatherings stirred old anxieties. She preferred to be with friends in the kitchen or with family at home.

Once a week, the women sailed over to St. Vincent to shop the markets, eat orange Creamsicles from the dock kiosk, and visit the local aviary. Windy was obsessed with animals and Creamsicles, interchangeably. She was different from the other children her age. One could not ignore the lisp of her *S*'s, *Z*'s, and occasional *C*'s. They came out as *th*. *Seashell* became *the-thell*. *Zebra* was *the-ebra*. *Dance* became *dan-th*. As her mother, Hilly found it endearing, but she knew the world was not kind to different. She was glad that Windy was still too young to attend school. She hoped that by the time she was, these hurdles would be behind her.

"Get her a wooden flute," Joanne suggested over the phone.

In Miami, she was taking night classes in music education to finish the degree she'd begun at Dartington College.

"I read that it could be effective in strengthening the palate and tongue of children with speech impediments. It's nothing to be ashamed of. Look at King George the Sixth."

It was so Joanne, proactive problem-solving. Hilly no longer resented her sister's optimism. It helped her find her own. So they ordered a recorder from the Sears catalog. The little flute quickly became something of a security blanket for Windy. She played it whenever her emotions transcended words that slipped sideways on her tongue. In that regard, Hilly was grateful that her daughter had found a means of expressing herself so early in life. She hoped it might save her from the years of bottled angst that she'd experienced.

Sometimes Hilly would find Windy asleep with the flute, clutching it so tightly that the holes had pressed red rings into her arms. Seeing the indentations, she would feel a throb of pain, as if the wounds had been inflicted on her as well. Carefully, so as not to wake Windy, she would move the flute aside, rub the rawness away, and leave her to rest without future repercussion. It was in those unexpected and seemingly insignificant moments that Hilly understood motherhood most. It made her look at Willy May with more compassion and appreciate that when she suffered so did her mother.

Hilly continued to battle bouts of depression and a chronic feeling of listlessness. But she was off the pills. Some might argue that she'd kicked the habit by default of a deserted island. There was no local pharmacy, and even a bottle of Midol at the general store passed under Naomi's surveillance. Still, it had not been easy. She honestly didn't know what she would've done if she'd been in London, Paris, or New York with money and access. Too much privilege could be more dangerous than too little.

Now, however, when her mood swung low,

she didn't self-medicate or try to hide her feelings. Her mother would take one look at her and know . . . like the press of wooden flute holes. They never spoke of the thing. That was a bridge too far for her mother. Instead, she would bring Hilly gingerbread and tea in bed while they listened to songs on the record player. Their LP selection had expanded to include Aretha Franklin, Elton John, Dolly Parton, Smokey Robinson, Barbra Streisand, and anything else they could get their hands on. The player was used so frequently that the needle had to be replaced twice.

They missed Joanne. She was the music in both their lives. While they talked on the phone occasionally and sent a handful of letters, it wasn't the same. Her absence was a vacuum that they filled up with whatever they could.

A twenty-five-inch color TV had been purchased from the United States and installed in the middle of the house where once stood a coffee table. It kept Windy happy — Hilly, too. They sat in front of the set through hours of programming: *Captain Kangaroo*, *I Dream of Jeannie*, *Lassie's Rescue Rangers*, and *Mister Rogers' Neighborhood*.

Hilly sometimes mentioned her sister dur-

ing reruns of *The Andy Williams Show.*
"Joanne would play that musical number much better."

"She sure would," Willy May would agree.

In passing, they discussed taking a long sail to Florida when Windy was older, and they didn't have lodgers at Firefly, after *Otrera*'s keel had been rebolted, when the weather was good. But there was always something . . . Windy would catch a cold. Colin would throw a party. More guests arrived. The forecast called for rough winds. It was enough to get through today. So they put it off to tomorrow, next month, next season, and the days spun into years. Joanne became an echo of a song they'd once sung.

Hilly spent the morning of Colin's Golden Ball in the Cotton House kitchen beside George learning to execute a proper Caribbean pig roast. This included forcing a bamboo pole through the length of the pig's body, salting it inside and out, preparing the firepit, and turning the meat over the embers every thirty minutes. It had taken nearly seven hours to get the job done. A lacquered red apple was placed in the pig's mouth and the animal was to be carried into the ball by Joseph and Leo. Colin wanted a spectacle.

An hour before the celebration was to

commence, Hilly returned to Firefly. She was in the kitchen mashing green peas for Windy's dinner when Willy May came in dressed to the nines.

Her mother did a little runway turn and her lamé gown shimmered in the lamplight. "Why haven't you changed yet?" she asked.

The question surprised Hilly. Her hand slipped and pea juice splattered across her T-shirt. "Why would I? I'm not going," she replied, wiping but only managing to smear the green. "I have Windy."

Hearing her name, Windy spun round in her playpen. *"Ma-man?"*

Willy May smiled. "Hey, baby girl. Mama's making you something good to eat. Do you see?"

Windy nodded excitedly and sang out, "Peeaa-thhh."

Willy May put a hand on a metallic hip. "Come on, we can have a girls' night out — wear pretty dresses, meet interesting people. Naomi said Windy is welcome over at her place with Fred. They're watching *The Wonderful World of Disney* tonight."

"That's very kind of her, but Windy and I are booked for a girls' night *in.*"

"Designer Carolina Herrera will be there," her mother baited.

Hilly might've been out of the industry,

but she still loved the art of it — the fashion and theater. Carolina Herrera was a trailblazer. Still . . .

"Mum, I'm done with all that. Look at me." She pointed to her stained shirt.

"Maybe you just need someone to give you another shot."

Instead of arguing, Hilly continued pressing peas through the mesh strainer. How was it that her mother knew her silent pains with a glance, yet still didn't recognize that she didn't want *another shot*? Could mother's intuition be selective, too?

"Don't send me into that bedlam alone." Willy May exhaled dramatically.

There was the nub of it. Hilly put down her bowl sympathetically. "Just because you live on their island doesn't mean you have to do the Tennants' bidding all the time. Stay home with us."

Windy took up her flute and blew a high-pitched squeal of approval.

"I promised Anne." Willy May shrugged. "And I'm already dressed."

When Willy May left, Windy began to cry. Though she had been too young to remember Joanne's departure, goodbyes of every kind broke her heart. Hilly tried to explain to her daughter that leave-takings were part of life. One simply had to carry on.

Saudade, one of her Cheltenham school-teachers had called it. The teacher was from Brazil and said the word originated with her people. They used it to describe the melancholy of missing things with an illogical fervor. For example: a person no longer present, a place unreachable, a time in life long past, a feeling that could not be replicated. It defied medical science. Music, literature, and art were the closest measure of the phenomena. Diminishing the sorrow was the best anyone could do.

She put on the *Cinderella* "Story and Songs" record that Joanne had brought and handed her daughter the wooden flute. By the time "So This Is Love" finished, so had Windy's tears.

They ate mashed peas with Vienna sausages for dinner. Hilly bathed and changed Windy into her Barbie nightgown. Then they watched the new episode of *Happy Days* and shared a cup of Yoohoo. Windy fell asleep with chocolate drool on her chin. *I should brush her teeth before bed,* Hilly argued to herself, and then, *Baby teeth fall out anyhow.* She couldn't bring herself to wake her.

A loud *pop* and *sizzle* did the job. A firework in the shape of a palm tree burst outside the window. Born and raised on

Mustique, Windy was accustomed to colored lights in the sky. However, unlike the island's nightly wink, Colin's green was garish bright and made their eyes sting.

"Ooo, eee, ooo-eee!" Windy mimicked the sound of the skyrockets.

They watched the popcorn of peonies, Roman candles, and waterfall sparklers rise to a bright *boom* and slowly fall to darkness, until all that remained were wisps of smoke like smudged writing on a chalkboard.

When it was over, they brushed their teeth with bubblegum-flavored toothpaste.

"Sleep with you?" asked Windy.

Windy was at the age when being swathed in her mother's bed and night lotion smells felt as luxurious as it got. Hilly remembered that yearning and the answer to her same question: *Not tonight, honey.* Last night, tonight, or tomorrow, Willy May's reply never changed, but hers could.

"Yes," she said. "You can sleep with me."

Windy giggled, raced for the bed, and plopped herself against the largest pillow. Hilly reached to turn off the bedside lamp, but Windy stopped her.

"Rara!" She pointed to the statuette of Otrera on the shelf. "Rara, too!"

The mythical queen of the Amazons was a favorite. Given that it was the family's boat's name, Windy assumed that a statue could be a living queen in the same way that animals, instruments, and other inanimate objects were personified in cartoons. During the bedtime retellings, Hilly had added that Otrera came to Mustique from England and found a home at Firefly. Windy liked that part best.

Hilly recalled her own childhood fascination with the statuette. It was her face. Otrera's was perfectly chiseled and unchanging, while Hilly's was growing in ways she didn't recognize. Some nights, she was almost certain that the goddess remained awake on their boat, vigilantly protecting her while she slept. It was make-believe, but the power of that had comforted her during the years when her nights were consumed by terrors, and she feared that something inside her was twisted up wrong. She wasn't like her charitable sister or her confident mother or any of the other cheerful people around her. She felt like a feather unseen on the ocean, one wave away from sinking and becoming part of the abyss forever. The statuette was something solid to hold on to.

Now, she pulled it from the shelf and laid it in the cotton sheets between them.

Windy kissed her finger and put it to Otrera's face. "G'night, Rara." She puckered her lips in the air. "G'night, *Ma-man.*"

She kissed her back gently. "Good night, Windy."

Hilly woke the next morning to Windy playing miniature house on the bedside. A wooden jewelry box was Otrera's table. Sewing thimbles full of papaya seeds and rice kernels were her breakfast. Barbie sat with legs splayed out, Queen Otrera's only guest.

Hilly yawned. "You're up early?"

"Rara 'ungry."

"Hungry? I bet you are, too."

Windy nodded and pinched a papaya seed to the statue's mouth.

It was nine o'clock. Usually by now, the house smelled of Willy May's coffeepot percolating for Firefly guests. They had two staying this week, Lady Anabel and Lady Victoria.

"Grandmum up?"

Windy shook her head. That was unusual.

"Come on, let's see what they want for breakfast."

She carried Windy to Willy May's bedroom door and knocked gently. No answer. Her pulse quickened. Willy May always came home. She pushed open the door.

"Mum?" she called, entering Willy May's

room with Windy on her hip.

A lump under the bedsheets gave her momentary relief but then Willy May drew down the sheet with Titus at her side.

"Oh, I'm sorry, I didn't realize."

Hilly turned her eyes to the floor and shuffled backward.

"Graa-Graa!" Windy called.

Willy May slipped out from between the sheets and into her robe. Titus started to follow but realized that wasn't for the best.

"Titi-th," Windy said. She was happy to see him.

"Good morning, princess," Titus replied, and then sheepishly looked to Hilly.

Willy May ran a hand through the wilds of her hair. "We — uh — Grandmum and Titus had a slumber party after Mr. Colin's party and — uh — well, yeah." She exhaled.

They were acting like teenagers. Hilly had never seen her mother so tongue-tied. It made her smirk. She'd long ago assumed that Mum was having relations with men. Willy May was a beautiful divorcée on an island renowned for romantic entanglements. It was the unmentioned given of Mustique. Hilly might've done the same if she'd been inclined. Postpartum depression, motherhood, and the *saudade* of Windy's father had quelled much of her libido. It'd been over four years since she'd been intimate with anyone. Frankly, she hadn't been attracted to most and hadn't trusted the rest. Or maybe it was herself she didn't trust. Whatever the reason, the impulse simply wasn't there. She couldn't deny that she missed the act, but it wasn't worth the emotional fallout.

Like this: Titus cleared his throat awkwardly in bed while her mother fussed and chattered in a sweat sheen.

"Do you know what a slumber party is, Windy-girl?"

Windy sucked her thumb, eyes searching for her flute. Hilly had left it in her room.

"A slumber party," Willy May continued, "is when your best friend sleeps over and you play records and games and stay up past your bedtime telling stories and . . ."

Uninterested in this "slumber party," Windy interrupted, "We th-ee fairy work."

"Fireworks," said Hilly.

Windy spread her fingers wide in the air. Willy May finally looked Hilly in the eyes, and Hilly smiled back reassuringly.

"If you and Titus want to have more slumber parties, we're okay with that, aren't we, Windy?"

Windy nodded into her neck and whispered, "Eggo?"

Hilly turned to her mother. "So long as Eggo waffles are on the slumber party menu."

Willy May exhaled. "Absolutely. You know they're Grandmum's specialty." She kissed both of their cheeks. "Give us a minute, and I'll be down to warm up the toaster oven. Lady Anabel and Lady Victoria stayed at the Cotton House. It's only the family this morning."

"Want me to brew a pot? I know you're a coffee man, Titus."

She winked at him over her mother's shoulder.

"I am, indeed," he said.

Hilly shut the bedroom door and didn't hold back the laughter snort. She'd noticed the spark between Mum and Titus when she first arrived but like all things familiar, she'd stopped noticing. She assumed that they either *had* and decided on friendship or *hadn't* because they were friends. Either way, it was her mother's life, just as she had her own to navigate.

Titus was a good man. She was happy for her mother.

Half an hour later, they were seated at the table: Willy May, Titus, Hilly, and Windy. Like a Norman Rockwell advertisement for coffee and Kellogg's. Her mother forked

355

waffles dripping with maple syrup while describing the fashions of the night before. Carolina Herrera's giant feather turban was her favorite.

Titus recounted how Colin transformed the beach by spraying the trees and grass with gold paint and constructing golden arches with palm fronds. He'd brought in generators to power the theater lights hung high in the trees so that the whole place was bathed in gold, gold, gold. Despite it being his birthday, Anne had apparently outshone him. She'd worn a dazzling gilt gown with her face and hands spray-painted to match. Princess Margaret wore a gold caftan and turban and was carried into the party by island men whose bodies had been oiled and dressed in gold tinseled cloaks.

And the pig roast — oh, the pig roast! — was the pièce de résistance, causing a number of women, and even a handful of men, to gasp aloud before sitting down to devour it.

Hilly was both thrilled and slightly revolted to hear it. She didn't regret her decision to stay home. Even now, she loathed to leave it, but she'd promised George that she'd help with the last event, a goodbye charity auction billed as a luncheon fundraiser. A portion of the monies was going toward the Grenadines chapter of Samaritans United, a humanitarian relief organization. A handful of their officials had come to represent the organization, and Colin arranged for sanctioned (read: *payrolled*) photographers to attend. He'd donated several of the Cotton House's paintings and furniture pieces and wanted his graciousness documented for the international press. It was the Mustique Sotheby's and an opportunity for guests to show their appreciation.

Creamy coronation chicken on baps were served beside a vast selection of crudités that stretched the length of the lawn tent. Hilly was particularly proud of the vegetables, which she had personally arranged in an artful rainbow down the buffet table. Feeling good-natured after their breakfast, she'd agreed to bring Windy to the luncheon and change into something suitable so they could sit together as a family. She wore a white bell-bottom jumpsuit with her hair ironed straight as a board, but that didn't stop her. As soon as she saw the waitstaff falling behind, she tied on an apron to help cut oranges and limes for drinks, more comfortable behind the bar than sitting in the crowd. She was squeezing fresh oranges for mimosas and wondering how much longer this thing would take when a young man stepped up to the bar.

"Any chance I could have one of those orange juices?"

"Just juice?" She turned to the voice and her breath caught.

He was beautiful. Dark-eyed with even darker hair. His skin was like a rich wood freshly buffed. His nose was bold in the most becoming way and when he smiled, his whole face opened like a door — to what, she was unsure, but wanted to come closer to find out. She was unable to look away, unable to speak, and unable to put words to why.

"Just juice," he clarified.

She poured it from the pitcher, and then poured herself one to cut the cotton in her throat.

"Perfect," he thanked her and returned to his seat at the front of the auction.

Titus passed by, on his way to help finalize the auction and tally the donation check.

Hilly put her hand on his arm to stop him. "Who's that?"

He followed her gaze and then grinned. "Why, do you fancy the look of him?"

She shrugged. "A new face."

"He's one of the Samaritans. I'll find out more."

"No, please I —" she began, but Titus was already off.

Hilly tidied the bar cart to steady herself before returning to her seat with a slice of coconut for Windy. In under a minute, the girl had chewed the sweetness out of the rind and left the shell on her chair, climbing into Hilly's lap to rest her hot head against her breast.

"Naptime," Hilly whispered to Willy May. "I should take her back to the house."

The last item of the auction was an old door that Colin had taken off the hinges and Oliver Messel had painted with a mural of a giraffe by a sea pine, neither of which could be found on Mustique. Still, it garnered the highest bid of the day.

"We'll all leave," said Willy May. "One at a time, so we don't disrupt."

Hilly and Windy went first. Despite their strategy, heads turned, including that of the young man on the front row. Hilly's skin prickled.

Titus waved her over to where he stood just behind the auction stage. "His name is Victor. A student studying medicine. I think he'd like to meet you."

Her palms went hot, her fingers cold. "What did you tell him?"

"Just the truth." Titus winked.

359

Which one? she thought. *The one where I'm a single mother trying to stay sober or the one where I'm a* Vogue *model living in a villa?* Truth was as similar and as different as the sun and the moon.

A *thwack* of the gavel and the auction was complete. A couple from Istanbul won the door mural.

"The Samaritans United and our esteemed hosts, the Tennants, thank you all!"

Colin held the handshake of the lead Samaritans United emissary while cameras snapped. Willy May was on her feet clapping alongside everyone else. Lost in the shuffle of milling guests, Hilly spun round to the very one she was hoping to avoid.

"You wouldn't leave without an introduction," said Victor.

Her stomach cartwheeled. "I'm Hilly."

"Nice to meet you, Hilly."

"Nice to meet you, Victor."

He smiled that big smile, and it dawned on her, he hadn't told her his name.

CHAPTER 21
MEN OF GOD

Hilly fell into loving Victor as naturally as salt in the sea. He was a medical student from the University of Puerto Rico doing a clinical rotation on St. Vincent. He'd received a Samaritans United scholarship so while the other students went home for breaks, Victor stayed to help with the volunteers.

"Have you ever felt like you've been launched on a course to a destination, but you aren't certain that's where you're supposed to end up?" he asked Hilly.

"Every day of my life," she said.

They were on the stone wall that separated Firefly's garden terrace from the pool. With feet dangling over the edge, the whole world stretched before them, blue on blue on blue, a sea of possibilities. She wished she could fly into them. But the reality was, if they leaned too far forward, they'd fall.

All through the spring, Victor had taken

the early morning ferry from St. Vincent to Mustique each Saturday to see her. He wasn't put off that she was a single mother. His own had been the same, raising him and his younger sister after his father passed away. He brought surprises for Windy. Little things: a pack of Juicy Fruit gum, an egg of Silly Putty, a Whistle Pop. Windy received each with great admiration. It was one of her innate strengths — immeasurable gratitude. She made the giver feel gifted by her exuberant reception. Even the remnants (gum wrappers, a plastic egg, a candy stick) were treasured on the shelf beside Otrera.

This visit, he brought a wooden cross no bigger than a bilimbi fruit. The only other crosses on Mustique were on the medical clinic doors or in the graveyard.

"My father died of typhoid when I was five years old. There were no doctors available when we needed one. My mother made God a promise: if he spared me, she would make sure that I grew up to be a doctor," Victor explained.

"My dad died of a heart attack," said Hilly. "Sometimes I wonder what my life would've been like if he was alive. Maybe I wouldn't have left England so soon. I wouldn't have gotten pregnant with Windy. I wouldn't be here."

"No use second-guessing the past. It'll never change. Fate doesn't obey the rules we try to pin on it. Maybe that's a good thing, because I doubt we would've met otherwise."

"Do you believe in fate?"

He nodded. "Don't you?"

"I'd like to. It'd be nice to be sure of something."

"Fate isn't a guarantee," he cautioned. "We still have choices."

Hilly thought it sounded nice to have a predestined life. As it was, hers was a blank slate, even to herself. She listened to Victor without interruption. She wanted to understand his conflict, but it was hard to fathom how a bright young man on the cusp of being a doctor could be questioning the trajectory of his life.

"Even after I finish these four years of medical school, I'll have four more years of residency. If I decide to specialize in anything, it's an additional one to two years of fellowship. That's eight to ten years before I am free to do the work I choose," said Victor. "People are sick and dying right now. They can't wait a decade for medicine, food, clothing, and shelter. They need someone to give them hope."

"Is that what you want to do — give

people hope?"

"I guess so. Does anything else really matter in the end?"

The end. Those were two words on the last page of storybooks. A way of controlling the characters, settings, and story worlds. A way of feeling satisfied: *Well now, that's The End.* A closed book cover. But was there really such a thing?

On a walk with Windy the weekend prior, they came upon a hollow tree, and Hilly made the mistake of stating the obvious aloud: "Looks like it's dead."

To which Windy had responded with a howl of sorrow. They had never directly spoken of death but somehow Windy inherently understood that it was the definitive goodbye. Nothing Hilly did, not even the wooden flute, comforted her.

Calmly, Victor had knelt beside her daughter and said, "Nothing ever really dies."

He pointed out that the tree's branches had become bird nests; that the roots turned to soil and fed the new baby seeds. Just because the tree didn't chronicle time with a growth ring didn't mean life stopped. There were forces greater than life and death. In a world where little was absolute, they could have faith in that. His words brought Windy peace. Hilly, too.

"In the end," she said cautiously after thinking it over, "love matters."

Victor smiled. "You're right. It does."

"Your mother loves you. That's why she wants you to be a doctor. Caring for people is a good thing."

He exhaled and picked a weedy vine growing up through the stone cracks. "But what if I'm supposed to do something else? Something I haven't found yet."

She nodded. That, she understood. She hadn't found her way either and unlike Victor, her options were limited. It made her head hurt to think about it. But the pain felt oddly important. She liked that Victor made her think harder than she had before. Like a muscle, his visits left her fatigued but stronger the next time.

He pulled a news clipping from his pocket. The *Vincentian* newspaper headline read: QUEEN ELIZABETH WELCOMES MAN OF GOD, EVANGELICAL PASTOR BILLY GRAHAM.

"Have you heard of this man?" he asked.

Hilly shook her head.

Money, politics, and religion: Those went undiscussed. They were frowned upon in dinner conversations and the rule extended beyond the table.

"The Queen is keen on Pastor Graham's

humanitarian work. Samaritans United has invited one of his men to speak next Sunday. It's made me wonder." He cleared his throat. "If perhaps I wasn't meant to join the ministry."

"You want to be a priest?" She balked at the thought.

"No, not a priest" — his eyes flickered to hers reassuringly — "but someone involved. There are many people who work in the church but aren't clergy. You don't see them in the pulpit, but they're important."

She felt nauseated. Leave it to her to finally be attractive to someone and he turns out to be the pious sort. Wasn't that just her bad luck.

"So you're telling me you want to give up on being a doctor to work in religion?"

"They don't call it 'work.' They call it 'a calling.'"

Even more confusing. "A *calling*? Who are you calling?"

He scratched the stubble of his jaw. Despite shaving each morning, it was always rough by noon. She could nearly tell the time of day by his chin. Its bearded shadows made her sad because she knew he would be leaving again soon.

"I'm called to the calling by God," he explained, "and then, I'm calling the people to God."

"What do you say? 'Hello, this is the office of God calling?' "

She couldn't help her cynicism. She felt like something was being taken from her — the version of Victor that she'd begun to hold close. The man she'd hoped to hold even closer as soon as the opportunity presented itself. It wasn't fair for fate to take that.

Victor laughed at her remark.

She frowned.

"The semantics are confusing." He cleared his throat. "Why don't you come with me and hear his message?"

"Come where and hear what message?"

"To the Crusade. That's what it's called. You could take the ferry over to St. Vincent and we could spend the day together. I'll show you where I study, where I live . . . introduce you to my friends."

She liked that idea. The day could lead to the night and perhaps his friends could help her convince him to stay the medical course and put this sanctimonious talk to bed.

"I'll have to ask Mum if she can watch Windy."

They left it at that.

"Victor is a sweetheart," Willy May said when he'd gone.

Hilly nodded and collected the dishes.

Willy May followed her to the kitchen. "Handsome and smart, too." She filled the sink with warm water and a squirt of Palmolive soap. "He's the total package, Hilly."

"He's thinking of quitting medical school," she said bluntly.

She wanted to illicit the same shock she felt. *Misery loves company,* wasn't that the saying?

Instead of reacting, Willy May circled the sponge round the plate. "A degree in medicine is a very fine thing to have. It comes with a built-in title. He'll be Dr. Victor for the rest of his life. No one can take that away. Doubts are normal. He just needs someone to say they support him no matter what. That's what all of us want." She rinsed the plate. "Have you ever considered going to university?"

"Me?"

Hilly hadn't thought it possible at this point. "How would I with Windy?"

Willy May wiped her wet hands on the apron. "There are remote courses. Titus has been telling me about them. We could figure something out. You're young, Hilly. You've got your whole life ahead of you — and Windy's, too."

Suddenly, the breath of opportunity felt

more burdensome than the lack of it.

"I don't know," she said. "That's a lot to think about."

Willy May winked. "Now you see Victor's predicament."

Before they could discuss more, Titus came up the veranda steps shaking his head and carrying a box of documents.

Willy May raised an eyebrow high. "Colin?"

Titus set the box down and pinched the bridge of his nose. "For years, I've tried to get the man to see his dollars with sense. Now he's nearly bankrupt in both."

She put her hands on Titus's shoulders and gently pushed him down in a chair. "Here, let me make you a coffee."

"He tells me that Hugo has it all worked out. Hugo tells me that Colin has it all worked out. When the truth is, nobody's got nothing worked out."

Titus went on to explain that staff weren't being paid. Anne had gone back to Scotland and instructed Colin to solve the island's financial crisis in her absence. But Colin was far more interested in the scandalous newspaper reports of the Princess's affair with Roddy Llewellyn.

The British press were becoming more and more intrusive. They came on water planes and by the ferry now that Captain Tannis had instituted a daily schedule. Colin stationed beach watchers to scan the barrier reefs for incoming snorkels and there was talk of constructing a castle wall around the whole island.

"Ludicrous," Princess Margaret had said just the night before while finishing a cigarette on the Cotton House lanai. "Are you proposing the Great Wall of Mustique, Colin?"

"Perhaps the Crown might subsidize?" Colin had countered.

At which Princess Margaret had cackled and Titus had groaned, because only he knew Colin wasn't joking. Instead of attending to his financial woes, he'd put all his eggs in one basket and handed it over to Titus while he busied himself with organizing an island-wide croquet tournament for the landowners.

Then it was Saturday again, and Victor was standing at their door. Island time was slippery as sand in surf, tumbling in and trickling out. Too fast and too slow all at once.

Knowing Windy's love of animals, he brought an egret feather. Hilly stuck it in her daughter's ponytail: "Lady Windstorm, the fairy bird of Mustique."

Victor didn't mention religion, but it hung between them. Finally, she mustered the courage to speak to Willy May about it while Victor played Connect 4 with Windy.

"Mum, Victor asked me to meet him on St. Vincent tomorrow . . . for church."

Willy May raised an eyebrow. "Church? I didn't know he was a churchin' kind."

"I don't know what that kind is, but he wants me to come with him to hear a pastor."

Willy May looked to where Victor dropped blue coins into a toy grid.

"Interesting. I suppose it shouldn't be a surprise. He's with Samaritans United. Your dad's family is Church of England. I came up Southern Baptist. Truthfully, I can't recall much of either. But it's good for a person to have a touch of religion. You've got to know what you believe before you know what you don't."

Windy gave a giddy squeal when Victor pointed out that she'd gotten four in a row.

"You 'connected four,' see?" he explained.

Too young for strategy, she'd thought herself a winner simply by stacking colorful coins.

"You'll miss the elephant," said Willy May.

"Elephant?"

"Colin's newest acquisition. A baby ele-

371

phant from Jaipur. He invited us to see it tomorrow. Not to worry. Church only comes once a week and the elephant will be here for . . . well, I hear they live seventy to eighty years."

"Those are the African elephants." The game complete, Victor brought Windy to where they sat, and continued, "Asian elephants live less than fifty."

"Oh," said Willy May. "I didn't know there was a difference."

He nodded. "Very slight but yes. It's in the ears. African elephants have large ears. Asian elephants have smaller ones."

"How would you know the difference if you'd never seen either before?" asked Hilly.

Victor scratched the stubble of his chin thoughtfully. "I suppose you wouldn't."

"An elephant would just be an elephant."

Hearing the word, Windy clapped her hands. "Horton!"

Hilly scooped her onto her lap. "You told her?"

"She overheard," said Willy May.

"Who's Horton?" asked Victor.

"You know, Dr. Seuss," said Hilly.

Victor shook his head.

"He's an elephant who hatches an egg."

Victor looked bemused. "That's absurd. You realize an elephant weighs an average of ten thousand pounds."

At which they laughed, while Windy fetched her copy of the children's book.

"El-fant," she said, her tongue skimming the letters like a stone on water. She pointed to the illustration of Horton perched on the bird nest.

Hilly thought of the books and records she'd cherished with Joanne: *SEE, HEAR, READ.* The commands had acted like a spell, bringing the voices to life and making her wonder if maybe, just maybe, the stories' magic could be real. Because then destiny and love and undeserved gifts could be real, too.

"I like Vic-*th*-or," Windy told Hilly before bed later.

"I like him, too," she replied and pulled the egret feather from Windy's hair so it wouldn't bend in the night.

Captain Tannis sailed from Canouan to St. Vincent, passing by Mustique at exactly 6:30 A.M. for anyone needing transport north. Hilly was the only one on the dock at that time.

"What's got you up early this morning, Hilly?" he asked.

"Church."

He gave no sign of an opinion, slurping

373

coffee from his thermos and motoring on. When she disembarked at St. Vincent, he said, "If you be praying to the Almighty, put in a good word for me."

She'd never really prayed before. The only prayers she'd seen were on television programs where the priests closed their eyes, lifted their hands, and spoke in a stream of Latin. If she was expected to do that, she'd get back on the boat and nearly did, if it hadn't been for the line of ticketed passengers glaring at her to move aside. She forced her feet, step by step, toward the shore where Victor waited.

He wore a pair of brown checked pants, a light blue guayabera, and a fedora pulled low on his brow. He was so handsome that it pained her. The desperate yearning to pull him into her cut like a knife. She didn't know how much longer she could stand not touching him or him not touching her.

"You look amazing," he greeted her.

She'd worn a new floral Gunne Sax dress with a shoulder-line ruffle. It covered all the tempting bits and so seemed perfect for church.

They went straight to the service, held under a white tent outside the Samaritans United building. Men and women of every age waited in a queue to be seated. She'd expected pews, golden crucifixes, organ music, and a crowned man in embroidered robes. But what she found were wooden folding chairs, a guitar player, a microphone stand, and a fruit box turned upside down as a pulpit.

"That's Pastor Charles," Victor pointed. "He's from Texas."

"Mum is from there."

She raised herself up and leaned around the people sitting in front of her so she could get a better look.

Pastor Charles's forehead was pink from the sun with a swath of gray hair that fell over his temples despite the shiny pomade. He stood at the front with two other men, patting them on the backs with one hand while he held a worn, black Bible in the other. Dressed as simple and clean as the setting: white-collared shirt, black slacks, belt, and brown boots. He didn't smile much, but when he did, it was inviting.

Hilly was dubious when he stood. She was ready to find some reason to dislike him.

"Hello," he said into the microphone, and the sound system squealed a pitch that made everyone in the audience rear back. He flushed. "Sorry about that."

Someone came up to adjust the settings,

gave the mic a test tap, and then handed it over.

"Well, now that all your eardrums are broken, I guess I can say just about anything."

A titter rippled through the crowd. Hilly felt for him. So many people staring, waiting for him to do, say, and be something inspiring or offensive, and judging every blink between. She knew that feeling. She decided to give him a chance.

The pastor told the crowd that he'd grown up in various foster homes. No parents and no God. But he always felt there was a supernatural presence to the world. He was called to the faith at twenty-two when a preacher in a revival tent said that it didn't matter that he came from nothing and had accomplished nothing. God loved him.

Then he told the story of Adam and Eve. Man created from dirt and woman from bone. Orphans in a secluded paradise. He read from Genesis:

" 'The Lord God made all kinds of trees grow out of the ground — trees that were pleasing to the eye and good for food . . . Adam and his wife were both naked, and they felt no shame.' "

It called to mind Colin's painted beach canvases. Scenes of a lush garden and a nude couple in love with each other, the earth, and the heavens. She'd assumed the decorations were to set the mood for Mustique's guests. She'd been wrong. They'd been repurposed from this . . .

"The story of Adam and Eve is the beginning of Creation and the end of Creation. Don't believe the world's lie that our lives are hopeless. Endings are human constructs. It's what people choose to believe. The stories passed on to the next generation are a retelling of a retelling with the original becoming less and less defined. Like a Xerox copy. So don't just take my word for any of this — go to the Bible and read it yourself. Starting with Adam and Eve. They are the original witnesses: No ending is 'the end.' The end of one thing is the beginning of another. I tell you, you have a soul inside your body that is more than this moment, more than the grass beneath your feet, or your troubled circumstances. God is love, and that love changes you from the inside out."

The guitar player strummed Norman Greenbaum's "Spirit in the Sky" and the people around her stood, sang, and clapped along.

Her head spun. Her pulse galloped. It was all so strange. The vicar's twice a year visits,

Easter and Christmas, had not expounded on more than baby Jesus in a candy-cane manger and grown Jesus rising from a chocolate Easter egg grave. Though she'd always hoped that a god of something existed, she couldn't honestly say that she'd ever felt one for certain. Now, this man spoke of love that didn't come by family lineage, rendered services, or beauty. He claimed there was something out there that saw her on Mustique, heard her voice, and read her innermost thoughts. It sounded like a fairy tale with a catchy song.

"*. . . friend in Jesus . . . spirit in the sky . . . friend in Jesus,*" they sang.

Pastor Charles hushed everyone. "The power is yours. Free love frees you to freely give love."

Free, frees, freely: each a different meaning.

He told the congregation to close their eyes and invited people to come to the front if they wanted *Jesus to save them.*

Hilly dug her fingernails into her palms and willed herself to close her eyes like the rest of the congregation. *Play along,* she told herself. But she couldn't. The storybook record played in her mind:

Snow White longed for the beautiful apple. . . . She barely had a bite in her mouth when she fell to the ground dead.

Beautiful apples, Tree of Knowledge, of Good and Evil, poisoned bites, and a handlebar-mustached savior singing happily-ever-after on his guitar: What was real and what was not?

She'd been in the dark for so long and she was tired of it.

"What did you think?" asked Victor.

The service had ended and the people filed out.

She blinked back tears that he misinterpreted as an epiphany. The opposite was true. She was more confused than ever and wished she had never heard any of this. She wanted to go back to that morning, when she didn't hope for some great love. Now, all she could do was think about it and felt more damned than ever.

Victor took her hand in his, threading his fingers through hers. They were intertwined, palm to palm, fingers rubbing gently and sweating in the creases. She felt the heat in all her between places.

"I want you to meet Pastor Charles and his son Jason. Pastor," introduced Victor, "this is Hilly."

"Hello," said the pastor, "it's nice to meet you. Victor told us you were coming."

"Pastor Charles and I know each other

well," said Victor. "I built houses in Puerto Rico with Jason last year."

Jason smiled. "Nice to meet you." He looked like a *Brady Bunch* son, all bangs and white teeth.

"Nice to meet you, too."

Tiny cream petals blew by on the breeze smelling peppery sweet. One snagged on Jason's shirt, and he tenderly lifted it to examine.

"Arrowroot blossoms," said Hilly.

Jason held it out on the tip of his finger. "Make a wish?"

She grinned. Dandelions to eyelashes, no matter where you came from, the wishing game was the same. "You caught it, it's yours to make."

He nodded and blew the petal back into the wind.

"Come on." Pastor Charles stepped forward. "They have doughnuts and coffee for the fellowship hour."

"That's when the congregation socializes," Victor explained.

"And eats," added Jason. "I'm always starving after service. I can only listen on an empty stomach for so long and then . . . somebody better pass me a plate or there's going to be fire and brimstone, for sure."

Pastor Charles gave his son a side-eye. "I

offered you an apple before we started. You can lead a horse to water but you can't make 'im drink."

"What verse is that exactly?"

"Gospel of Charles, chapter four, verse ten."

Hilly smiled. They had an easy way about them, father to son. She enjoyed being in their company and saw why Victor would, too.

"Pastor!" A woman handed him a glossy doughnut. "We saved the biggest one for you!"

"Aw, so kind. I'm not sure my waistline will bless me, but I'll pray the Lord absolves the calories." He took a large bite, flecks of sugar glaze snagged on his chin.

"I bet if you'd offered Jason one of *those* earlier, he might've accepted," said Victor.

"The Bible doesn't say that Holy Communion can't be sanctified by doughnut."

"Toeing the line, always toeing the line, son," teased Pastor Charles.

Jason handed a napkin to his father and a pastry to Victor.

He let go of her hand then, and she didn't know what to do with the emptiness. She balled her fingers into a fist.

"So, Hilly." Pastor Charles wiped his chin clean. "Victor tells us that you are from

Mustique. Is your family there?"

"Yes, my mother is a resident. She built a house — Firefly — on one of Colin Tennant's plots. I'm originally from England but Mum is from America. Texas, actually."

"Really?" He smiled. "What part?"

To be honest, she'd had so little to do with her American side. She had a name but no idea where it fit on an actual map.

"Limestone County."

"I'm not familiar," he said to her relief. "Texas is big."

"That's what I hear. Mum moved to England pretty young and never went back."

The pastor nodded a little sadly. "I lived in a lot of different places. It's hard to feel grounded when your roots keep pulling up."

"Yes," she said. "It is."

"Romans 11:17: 'But if some of the branches are broken off, and you, although a wild olive shoot, are grafted in among the others, you now share in the nourishing root of the olive tree.' "

The sudden segue into Scripture quoting made her uncomfortable. She steeled herself for criticism, religious castigation, or an attempt at conversion, at the least. Okay, so maybe she was the wild shoot. Broken. But the rest of it about the nourishing root, what was the hidden meaning there? He held her gaze and she, his. But all she saw was kindness.

Jason and Victor were lost in conversation about the West Indies win over India in the cricket Test series. It was her and the pastor and no place to hide.

"Would you like a Bible?" he asked.

"Oh no. I didn't raise my hand."

When he told everyone to close their eyes, she'd kept hers wide and seen that all who raised a hand of interest were given a Bible by an usher.

Pastor Charles reached under the fellowship refreshment table and pulled a Bible from a box. "Here."

She kept her fists balled. "I can't accept. I didn't ask Jesus."

Hearing the words come out of her mouth felt as foolish as saying that she didn't ask Santa Claus for a toy.

Pastor Charles took her hand and put the Bible in it. "God doesn't need you to love him for him to love you. Take it. It's a gift. Do as you wish with it."

And then, a group of church people came to his side, discussing his message and Samaritans United, and was Pastor Billy Graham really as tall as he looked on TV?

Victor slipped his hand back into her open one and pulled her across the crowded lawn to a quiet spot under a banyan tree.

"A Bible?" He pointed.

"Pastor Charles gave it to me. I tried to tell him no, but he said it was a gift."

Victor nodded. "That's how I met him years ago. He gave me one, too."

She spent the rest of the day with one hand in Victor's and the other holding the book, wishing she had brought a tote bag. She hadn't anticipated having stuff to carry home.

Victor showed her the dorm-style house where he lived and studied with his fellow medical students. They had lunch at the Sugar Bay Café with two of them, who said Victor was at the top of their class. Both were Canadian and talked the whole time about Yuichiro Miura and the documentary *The Man Who Skied Down Everest* and the toll extreme elements take on a body. Hilly had not seen the film, but she loved hearing them discuss the real-life adventure in a place so vastly different from the Caribbean. No costumes, scripts, or special effects involved. These were bold people doing bold things. It made her feel bolder, too.

There was no talk of religion or Pastor Charles among them so Hilly hadn't the occasion to bring up Victor's medical uncertainty. From their general demeanor, she guessed he had not given inklings of such, which made her think he might've only confided in her. If so, she would not break his trust.

She made him try a Creamsicle from the kiosk while they waited on the dock bench for the evening ferry.

"These are Windy's favorite," she explained. "I'd bring one back if it wasn't sure to melt."

And then he kissed her, lips and tongue of sweet vanilla orange, and she thought she might faint from the thrill of it. Clearly, he wasn't that churchy. His kisses were proof of good practice. The ice cream melted right off the stick and garnered the greedy attention of the seagulls. She wanted love to be like that — a consuming flap of wings.

Captain Tannis tooted his horn. He'd come into dock without her noticing, the two other passengers were waiting, and he was a man who kept to schedule.

"Good day?" he asked when she boarded.

Hilly smiled.

"Got a Bible, I see."

"Yes." She might've left it on the bench if Victor hadn't handed it to her.

"I've read some. The disciples were fishermen, you know."

"So I've heard."

Truth be told, she'd never actually read the Bible. It was hard to imagine any modern person who did, but apparently, there were those. She'd witnessed a whole tent full of them that morning. If that included Victor, she was keen to see what the fuss was about.

Warily, she opened the book: *In the beginning . . . the Spirit of God hovered over the waters and God said, "Let there be light . . ."* She read the whole two-hour ride home.

CHAPTER 22
IF ONLY I HAD WINGS

It took Hilly most of summer, but by August, she'd read the entire book. At the end, most of it was still perplexing, but it gave her insight into Victor's inner conflict and allowed her to speak more knowledgeably. Like medicine, religion was vastly mysterious.

"I don't see why you can't be a doctor *and* a man of God," she told Victor. "I didn't see anything that said you have to choose. Jesus' disciples continue their trades. The fishermen still fished. People have to eat. And I bet even the great 'I Am' wasn't above a bit of carpentry if a chair had a broken leg."

He laughed. "That's true."

"I mean, I appreciate that becoming a doctor is work and takes an insane amount of time. If you wanted to quit because of that, I see why. But making religion the excuse . . ." She shrugged. "I don't see how one infringes on the other."

He listened without reply, his gaze fixed on her arm where he ran thoughtful fingers along the bones between her elbow and wrist. The sensation brought chills.

"The radius and the ulna," he said. "Both are necessary for the wrist to turn and the hand to operate. If one is damaged, the whole limb suffers."

She turned her hand over and he slid his own into it, fingers laced.

"God knows, you're going to be a great doctor," she said.

He smiled and they kissed, parting just as Windy raced into the room with the crayon drawing she'd made: Hilly and Victor on one side, Willy May and Titus on the other with Windy playing her flute atop a palm tree between.

"It looks like we have a budding Frida Kahlo. Well done!" said Hilly. "Shall we hang it on the living room wall?"

Windy shook her head. "For Vic."

The *t* in Victor had given her trouble so he'd suggested she call him Vic. And he called her Win. They were the only two to call each other such, which instantly ingratiated him to Windy. They were both in love with Victor in their own way. Hilly hadn't anticipated how wonderful that shared devotion would feel.

Sure, she and Joanne both loved their parents, but sibling love came with a competitive side. Someone was always jockeying for favor. It wasn't so with Victor. The more he loved Windy, the more she loved him.

Now, he pulled her close. "Thank you, Win. It's beautiful."

The engine of Willy May's golf cart whirled to a stop, and she and Titus came up Firefly's terrace stairs in heated discussion. They'd been summoned to the Cotton House that morning for a meeting of the Mustique Company members. The rumors were true. The Tennants were nearly bankrupt.

"He doesn't want the Princess to know. But how are we to keep it from her?" Willy May asked Titus.

"There's a Venezuelan man, Mr. Hans Neumann," Titus explained. "He's offered to buy a majority of the island shares. Anne has given her blessing. Her loyalty was always to her family's estate in Scotland. Colin would never give up Mustique if the numbers weren't dire, and I have advised him that they are. I have three prospective buyers. After speaking with each, he believes Hans shares his '*beau*-topian vision.' "

Willy May stopped in her pacing with a

deadpan stare, and then she rolled her eyes. "And just what the hell does that mean?"

"It doesn't matter. If he sells out, then the Mustique Company and all the real estate thereunto would belong to the individual residents. You, being one. Mr. Neumann isn't going to move here and live. He'll do what the rest do. He'll come for holidays, drink the rum, soak in the sea, and then be on his way home as soon as he gets his first sun blister. This is the opportunity for Mustique to be practically self-governed. You, as owner of Firefly and a company stockholder, would finally have autonomy from the Tennants."

"Who says I don't have autonomy now?" barked Willy May. "I'm not their peasant!"

He tilted his head to the side and frowned. "Come now, Willy May. This isn't the time for ego. See reality."

By then, Hilly and Victor were on their feet. Victor offered to draw Windy some animal ligaments away from the brouhaha.

"El-fant and cat," she requested.

"I'm not sure I quite know the biology, but I'll do my best," he said and ushered her over to the crayon box.

Hilly mouthed *thank you* as they went. Windy shouldn't be privy to their financial worries or her mother's temper. God forbid

390

someone mention leaving . . . Windy would cry herself sick.

"This might not be the apocalypse, Mum," interjected Hilly. "Even the British Empire had to progress with the times. Anne and Colin aren't gods, no matter how much gold paint they spray on their faces."

It broke the tension. Willy May laughed and then shook her finger. "Don't repeat that."

"It will mean new people," said Titus.

It was meant as a positive, but Willy May took it as a negative. "We won't know who to trust."

She meant the media. Paparazzi had descended like locusts. They were disguising themselves as residents, potential investors, fake friends, and fraudulent well-wishers. Victor said he'd been stopped on the ferry by reporters asking if he had any insider information on the aristocrats of Mustique.

There was little Colin detested more than interlopers. He was on a witch hunt.

"He's implemented a new rule, you know," said Willy May. "Anyone arriving must have documentation of who they are visiting. We'll have to give Victor a note."

"Victor needs a hall pass?" Hilly shook her head. "Colin is off his rocker, Mum."

A silent agreement fell over them all.

"If the business deal with the Venezuelan goes through, the Tennants will return to the U.K. permanently. Then, hopefully, people will be less interested in Mustique. Between now and then, we must keep a steady hand on the tiller," said Titus.

Fate seemed to have other plans. The following week, a photographer posing as an ornithologist managed to get a roll of film back to England. On it were images of Princess Margaret and Roddy Llewellyn in UNDENIABLE, UNFORGIVABLE ADULTERY, as the headlines railed. The papers had a heyday. Every news source in the British Empire printed some blurry version of the photographs. Hilly had seen the two together and they were nothing as scandalous as the papers described. The Princess was always discreet. It struck Hilly — how something factual like a photograph could be changed by the words around it. One might know the sky is blue but find herself believing it was purple based on another's description. But then, sometimes the sky was purple. The context and source mattered.

By afternoon in London/morning in Mustique, the Cotton House phone was ringing off the hook, and Colin was sending messengers out to every resident instructing them to close their windows and doors, bar the outside world, and protect the Princess at all costs.

Overly dramatic, but very Colin. They could not deny the papers' pillory. Hilly had seen firsthand with her own parents' messy affairs, once printed in ink, a thing became history.

Panic crescendoed when the Queen telegrammed:

MARGARET. COME HOME. — ER.

Hilly happened to be at the Cotton House helping George mix milkshakes for Mr. Hans's welcoming breakfast when it arrived. Terrible timing. Mr. Hans was quickly ushered off to a tour of Endeavour Bay, while Dr. Rob was summoned to give Colin a diazepam shot for his nerves. The minute he left, Anne called, raising her voice loudly. The shrillness reverberated across thousands of miles of telephone wire. Everyone in the room could hear it through the handset.

"All fingers are pointing at us — and I am pointing at *you,* Colin!"

The couple had introduced Roddy to Princess Margaret in Edinburgh.

"He came on recommendation from Aunt Violet!" Colin defended. "Blame her if you must. She said he was a dim but affable gardener. How were we supposed to know he'd stir up this much trouble?"

Anne explained that all of England was talking about the affair. The images from Mustique were on every table from the royal court to the fishmonger's. It had even come to the attention of Parliament and the Houses, who were at that very hour discussing the immoderate expenditures of the monarchy through the pockets of British citizens. Tax dollars paid the Princess's allowance, which was being frittered away on an adulterous island.

"And to top it off, Tony is telling the press that Mustique was the greatest 'mustake' of his marriage. Playing the part of the poor, unwitting cuckold."

"That is ridiculous. We *all* know he is having relations with Lucy Lindsay-Hogg."

"It doesn't matter what we know is true. All that matters is what is *believed* to be true. The Parliament and Houses are considering doing away with the whole lot of us."

"The whole lot? What do you mean?"

"The *whole lot,* Colin! Must I spell it out? The Queen, the Princess, centuries of royal blood and nobility — all of us. Do you want history to say that the Tennants were the ones to turn the United Kingdom into a *republic*? Good God, the shame of it."

"We're ruined." Colin swooned and dropped the phone. "I need a gin. George — the gin!"

"Colin? Colin?" Anne shouted through the receiver. "Has the line dropped?"

Leo and Joseph stood beside Hilly staring at the handset. No one wanted to be on the other end of that.

"Someone should pick up," said Leo.

"Hilly," said Joseph.

"Me? Why not you?" she protested.

Joseph crossed his arms. Leo raised his eyebrows. There were unspoken boundaries of race, rank, and more. To not acknowledge those was cowardly. To not pick up the phone was equally so.

Reluctantly, Hilly took up the receiver. "Hello."

"Who is this?" asked Anne.

"Hilly Michael."

"Oh, thank God, someone dependable. It is my understanding that the Princess dismissed this telegram from Her Majesty. So, I need you to take it back over to Les Jolies Eaux and press upon her the direness of the situation."

"Right," said Hilly.

"Good girl. Now, put Mr. Colin back on."

George had poured him a couple fingers, and he'd gulped it bone-dry.

Hilly extended the receiver to him.

"Yes?" he answered weakly.

"The deal with Hans will be official by the end of this week. He's the new majority owner. Mustique is his problem now. Pack your bags and come home."

"Pack?" He picked up the Lakshmi statue and waved it around his room of collectibles. "But I wouldn't even know where to begin."

"Put your tunics and sandals in a bag, clasp it shut, and pick up the handle. Do you need me to instruct you on how to buckle your seat belt on the plane, too?"

"But — but —" he stammered. "You aren't suggesting that I fly. You know I have a phobia! Never mind that I can't leave everything."

"You can, you must, and you will. There are no other choices. Have you bothered to look past the front page of the newspapers? There's a hurricane headed that way. They're saying it's moving slowly, which makes it more dangerous."

"God help us." Colin clutched the statuette to his chest.

"I think he is. Perhaps the storm will sink

the whole island. I, for one, would not be sorry to see it go."

"You don't mean that, dear."

"I know exactly what I mean. Now, imagine that telegram was meant for you. Come home."

The line went dead. She'd hung up.

Colin set the receiver back in its cradle.

"Did we know about this hurricane?" he asked no one in particular.

Joseph nodded. "It's the season, sir."

"Quite. I'm usually in Scotland this time of the year. Anne's right. This is no place to be. We should leave at once." He set off toward his bedroom still holding Lakshmi. "Tell the Princess there's a diabolical hurricane on its way! We'll fly first thing in the morning. I'll suggest that Hans do similarly. I know the Princess hates the prop plane, as do I, but this is an emergency. We must obey Her Majesty."

Hilly took the mule cart over to Les Jolies Eaux.

Roddy answered the door bare-chested in tight swimming trunks that left little to the imagination.

"I have a message for the Princess from the Queen."

The Princess came from behind him. She wore a tasteful one-piece bathing suit and open silk robe; her hair was pulled back in a bright pink turban. "Again? What does she want now?"

Hilly held up the same telegram and watched the Princess's countenance fall.

"Oh, that." She shrugged. "Can't she use a telephone like everyone else? Such formality. It's all for show. Fine, fine." She motioned for Roddy to take the telegram. "Message received."

She pulled a slender cigarette from her pocket. Roddy flicked a striker, but she gave a small, definitive hand gesture that told him she'd do it herself. She sparked her golden lighter until the paper caught flame.

"It's all Tony's fault. The tabloids have upset her. Well" — she inhaled long — "I don't feel like going home yet." She exhaled longer. "I deserve a bloody holiday — for the good of my health."

Roddy tersely smiled back.

"Thank you —" She began to close the door, but Hilly dared to stop her.

"There's a storm coming, ma'am."

The Princess and Roddy shielded their eyes against the sun. Not a cloud in the sky. Searing blue from east to west, north to south.

"A storm?"

"Yes, Mr. Colin is packing to fly at dawn."

"And I take it he expects us to be on that awful plane?"

Hilly nodded.

"Hmm," she harrumphed. "Just like Mother Nature. She takes Lilibet's side here, too."

Roddy shifted his weight nervously. "If Colin thinks we should go, it's probably for the best. Safety first, darling."

She turned to Hilly.

"You and your mother are permanent residents. What say you? Should we all batten down the hatches and stay or tuck tail and run?"

If Hilly said *Stay* and harm came to the Princess, she would be blamed. If she said *Run,* the Princess would clearly be displeased. The only safe answer to God's anointed were his own words.

" 'If only I had wings like a dove, I would fly away . . . to my safe place, away from the wild wind and storm.' I believe that's from the Psalms."

She'd thought it one of the most poetic parts of the book.

The Princess stared at her like she'd grown a second head. The cigarette smoke rose serpentine-like. Then she laughed, and it cut the air sharply.

"You sound like my sister and her preacher

friend. Personally, I don't need salvation, but I'll take deliverance from the weather." She spun on bare heels. "Tell Colin we'll see him in the morning."

She didn't turn around again and Hilly was glad. She didn't want the Princess to see her smirk. No one had ever compared her to the Queen before . . . and she quite liked it.

CHAPTER 23
WINDS OF CHANGE

Colin's propeller plane took off the next morning.

Victor called Firefly to check on the women. "The hurricane's path has changed. It isn't projected to hit Mustique, but you must still take precautions."

The islanders had joined together to board up homes against wind, rain, and flooding. They had weathered many storms. None of which had sunk the island, despite Anne's wishes.

"We're ready," Hilly told Victor. "Mum stocked up on water, and there's enough food in the pantry to last a month. Wonder Bread has an eternal shelf life."

"The modern eucharist." He joked to ease the tension. "How about if the power goes out?"

"We borrowed one of Colin's party generators."

"Good. We're getting ready to go over to

Grenada."

"Grenada?"

She figured he'd do what everyone else was doing: hole up or leave. He'd completed his medical rotation but had remained on St. Vincent for the summer. She knew he'd stayed because of her. Now, however, with the hurricane's approach, she thought he'd go home to Puerto Rico.

"Samaritans United is sending a group of medical and relief workers to help those in the eye's path. Jason is here with volunteers and medical supplies from Texas."

Her mouth went dry. "Why would you go into the storm?"

"Why would I go anywhere else? You're the one who convinced me that I can help people now *and* do medicine. Here's an opportunity. They need us."

He meant Samaritans United, but she heard *us* as *we,* her and Victor. Her heart took the beat of a thousand drums. She understood it for the first time, then — the *calling.* Only it wasn't a sound but a feeling, a vibration through her bones. She was determined in a way she'd never felt before, awake and flying, and vitalized by a greater purpose.

"I'll take the evening ferry to you. Everyone on Mustique will be safe. Captain Tan-

402

nis will make his last pickup in two hours. Will you meet me at the dock?"

He didn't try to dissuade her. "I will."

She hung the phone back in its cradle. Where to start? A change of clothes seemed wise. She grabbed the muslin sack that they used to carry coconuts from the beach. She emptied it of hairy shell bits and packed cotton T-shirts, trousers, and some underwear. Good footwear was critical. All she had were sandals. She found a pair of Keds tennis shoes in the back of the closet.

"Mum, can I borrow your sneakers?"

Willy May looked up momentarily from feeding Windy a banana. "Yes, but why?"

"I'm taking the ferry to St. Vincent. Victor and the Samaritans United have a group going to Grenada."

Willy May batted her eyelashes once, twice, and then wiped her sticky fingers on a napkin. "No, I don't think so."

Hilly was so set on her course that she hadn't stopped to consider that Willy May would oppose her.

"They need volunteers to help," she explained.

Willy May broke off another mushy piece, and Windy gobbled it hungrily.

"I understand but you aren't going. Your place is here."

"The storm is headed west now. Mustique is safe."

"Exactly why you are staying put."

"Mum, are you saying that you don't want me to go?"

"I'm saying that you *can't* go."

It stunned Hilly. She wasn't a little girl anymore. She'd gone out into the world, made a name for herself, had a child. For good or for bad, she'd made choices. Like Victor said, that was the reality of fate — God — whatever one wished to call it: choice. Life was a steady accumulation of actions and reactions, ups and down, a seesaw of what was presented and what a person did with it. Hilly couldn't change her mother any more than she could change the past. But what *she* did in this moment would propel her forward. She was stronger than she'd been when she arrived. Mustique had given her a place to nest and grow and now, a high place to take flight. She was ready.

But looking back at Willy May in the kitchen, she saw that it was different for her mother. Firefly was her fortress and her exile. The only way Willy May knew to protect those she cherished was to try to keep them with her forever. It was love, twisted up tight and binding.

"You're doing to me what you did to Joanne. You can't force us to stay," she whispered. "Free, freeing, freely."

She knew better now. Love was its own sovereignty.

Willy May furrowed her brow. "Is that Bible stuff again? I've read it, too. 'Obey your mother' is one of the Ten Commandments. You want to *leave* us?"

Willy May stood, bumping Windy's hand. The last of the banana dropped to the floor. Hearing the word *leave* coupled with the lost banana, Windy wailed.

Hilly pulled her daughter out of the high chair and rocked her gently. "It's okay, baby girl."

Her hot face pressed into Hilly's chest, and the weight of each tear nearly made her set down her bag and stay. So she did what she wished her mother had done when she was a child. She didn't ignore the pain or pretend it wasn't there. She pointed at it to shed light on the truth.

"Leaving is hard, but sometimes it's good to leave. Think about Victor. You've gotten great at saying goodbye when he visits . . . why is that?" She turned Windy's chin up so their eyes met, mother to daughter. "Because you know he'll come back. And every time he does, it's like Christmas and your birthday all rolled together, right?"

Windy gave a weak smile.

"That's called a homecoming. It's a party you have when you see someone again. But you can't have it unless the person leaves. So see — there's no reason to cry when you know you'll have a homecoming when Mama comes back."

Windy sucked her sticky thumb. "B'nana?"

Hilly looked down at the ground. "Well, no, that's gone for good. But look —" She pointed at the full fruit bowl. "Lucky us, we've got more and bunches growing outside. Nothing is ever gone forever."

She heard Pastor Charles's voice echo and was glad she'd taken the ferry over to St. Vincent that day. She hadn't seen the pastor since or spoken with Victor about the religious message, but the decision to go had changed her irrevocably.

She kissed Windy's forehead. "You'll stay here and take care of Grandmum when I *leave*?" she said, testing the word gently.

Windy nodded and reached into the fruit bowl, choosing grapes over the finger bananas.

Her mother rose with a huff of exasperation. "I can't make *any* of you stay. You do what you want. But if something happens, I swear to God . . ."

She stomped out of the room.

Silently, Windy continued to pull and eat grapes from the stem. Hilly dropped a handful of chocolate Space Food Sticks into her bag in case she got hungry later, too.

Then Willy May's door swung open again.

"Here." She thrust a pair of thick orange wellies into Hilly's hand. "Those tennis shoes are crap."

Hilly could feel her mother's heartbeat pulsing through the air between them. She leaned in. Willy May held up a hand. Pushing away or reaching out, Hilly wasn't sure, but it divided them.

"Come on, honey, Grandmum will put on a story record for us. Say goodbye to Mama."

For a flicker, Windy looked panicked. She bit her bottom lip, gulped, and Hilly felt herself doing the same.

"Bye," Windy blurted, the word clear and confident on her lips.

It brought Hilly to tears. Her brave little girl.

"Mama loves you. I'll be back soon."

Windy nodded again.

"Be careful," said Willy May. She paused as if she were going to say more, but then marched out of the kitchen with Windy.

Without asking Hilly, Willy May called Titus to drive her to the dock, and she was grateful. When he started the golf cart for their departure, the billowy drapes of Willy May's bedroom moved. Hilly knew she was standing there, loving her in the shadows.

Victor met Hilly at the dock on St. Vincent and they held each other a long minute without speaking. He smelled of day-old deodorant and sweat, and his beard was so rough that it scratched her temple when he pulled her close. It was him in the raw, and she'd never loved him more.

"Mum's angry at me for leaving," she told him.

"I'm sorry." He sighed. "But I'm glad you're here."

So was she. Together, they joined the Samaritans United team. Medical supplies, food, blankets, and more had been loaded onto a cargo plane with the volunteers.

"Good to have you, Hilly!" Jason shouted through the deafening whir of the plane propellers.

Victor helped her strap into the cargo-net seating between himself and Jason.

"Chew this." He handed her a stick of gum. "And put these in." He passed her a pair of neon-orange earplugs, showing her how to roll them small between her fingers before inserting them.

As they expanded, the sound fell away to a resonance. Senses became tangled in concentration. Noise had a color that she could feel running beneath her stilled feet. It smelled of diesel fuel and tasted of white peppermint.

The flight was eerily smooth. Out the portal window, the sky was an incandescent purple. The stars shone bright and reflected off the midnight sea. So mythical a scene, she could nearly envision a Pegasus flying across the full moon.

They landed in Grenada.

Away from the roar of the plane's turbines, the wind held its breath and everything in creation, too. Silence was rarely silent until it was, and then the void was louder than a thousand sirens. That was Grenada in the hours before the storm. Piercing.

They unloaded the cargo boxes without a word. A slow, heavy shroud fingered the sky until the constellations were snuffed out. The volunteers gathered round a radio, listening to the weather reports and drinking coffee while there was still electricity.

"Now weakened from hurricane strength to a tropical depression, the system is moving west-southwest. All in its path are strongly advised to seek immediate shelter," warned the forecaster.

The first droplet fell a little after 8:00 A.M. A thick, sad thing like its heart had been broken. It plunked against the toe of Hilly's orange boot and rolled off to stain the ground. An hour later, the sky had ripped open to torrents. While the Grenada residents had readied their hillside huts for the wind, the sandy ground was not prepared for the height and force of the sea. The waves washed up high, clawing everything that came against them and taking away pieces bit by bit. Hilly helped stack sandbags with the volunteers. When the waters took those, they used what they could: rocks, tree branches, furniture.

"It's not working," Victor yelled.

The rain shot sideways through the air. When Hilly opened her mouth to speak, it choked her. Then the ground shifted. Victor felt it, too. She pointed down, and their eyes locked.

"Landslide!"

The mud sluiced down the hill, and she nearly with it. Victor grabbed her arms and pulled her up with him onto a concrete ledge. There, he brought her forehead to his, ran his thumbs over her cheeks.

"You're okay," he whispered and then, "I

love you."

He kissed her before she could say it back. But the force of their kiss left no doubt that she did. She stopped breathing. The world fell away. It was the two of them, sealed as one. The ground trembled.

"The whole hill is going!" called out Jason. "Everyone, get on rock!"

The volunteers clinging to the slippery slope skittered to higher ground. Then they all saw them: a mother and two children hunched under what remained of their roof. The mother clutched a crying child to each side. The mud, rain, and surf surged. They would be swept out to the ocean or crushed beneath the wreckage.

"Take Hilly!" Victor said to Jason, sending her to him like a kite in the wind.

She tried to turn back to Victor, but Jason held her on the high ground. All she could do was watch. *Stay,* she prayed for the first time in her life, *please, God, let the ground stay.*

And it did as Victor lifted each child to volunteers on the rocky protrusion. It continued to hold while he helped the mother up. Then he turned to her with a smile, and she let go of her bated breath. Her prayer had been answered.

"Thank God," she said to Jason.

A tidal wave crested.

White and dark.

It was over in under a minute. After it receded, she fought like a woman possessed, kicking and clawing her way forward.

"It's not safe!" Jason yelled. "Hilly!"

She put her hands into the hollow place where Victor had stood seconds before, soft beneath her fingers.

Why? she asked.

Why, she demanded.

Her hands sunk deeper into the earth, to her wrists, and then her elbows. Behind her, another wave was building. Above her, the rain continued to beat.

Take me, too, then.

The ancient myths, Bible stories, and sing-along fairy tales all came to uncompromising ends. Sacrifice was required.

Change me, she prayed. *I'm ready.*

■ ■ ■ ■

PART 5
WILLY MAY

■ ■ ■ ■

CHAPTER 24
EVERY DROP HAS A DESTINY

"Hilly . . ."

Willy May's throat squeezed tight. She was standing in Miami City Hospital with her daughter somewhere in the wings. The reception nurse shuffled a full deck of emergency charts. All of the hurricane evacuees with acute injuries had been med-evacked here. Family members of other patients huddled together behind her. So many tears shed, the room was salty as the sea.

"Hilly Michael." It came out as a whisper.

"Michael, Michael," the nurse parroted and flipped charts.

"What's her real first name — full, I mean?"

"That's her full, real first name. *H-I-L-L-Y.* She was evacuated with the Samaritans United in Granada two days ago. They said she's here."

The nurse moved to a stack behind her.

She flip-flip-flipped until her eyes caught on a chart. "Oh, sorry, we marked her as claimed." She cleared her throat. "She had visitors earlier who said they were family. Jo and Tim May."

"My daughter and her husband."

"And you are . . . ?"

"I'm Willy May Michael. Her mother."

The nurse didn't hesitate. Didn't ask for proof of identity or a birth certificate or even who had given her the information that Hilly had been admitted to the hospital. She scribbled her name in Hilly's file on the "Patient Next of Kin" line and sorted it back in the stack.

"I'll let the floor know that you're here. You can take a seat." She gestured to the waiting area, but there were no unoccupied seats. "Or stand. There's a cafeteria down the hall to the right. Closes at seven. Coffee's best before nine."

"Nine o'clock in the morning?"

She turned round to check on Windy, slumped over in a waiting area chair, fast asleep. She wished she could join her. It was 1:00 P.M., but they hadn't really slept for days.

"We came straight from the airport," she explained to the nurse. "We won't have to wait until tomorrow to see her, will we?"

They left Firefly as soon as the storm had passed and Captain Tannis could navigate the waters: Mustique to St. Vincent by ferry, St. Vincent to St. Lucia by propeller plane, St. Lucia to Miami by jet. The taxicab ride from the Miami airport to Miami City Hospital felt the most grueling of all.

The nurse's eyes softened. "Everybody has somebody here. We'll give you word as soon as we can."

Frenzied motion had brought them to this: stagnant purgatory.

Downgraded to a tropical storm, the wind and rain had still torn across the Windward Islands with unabating strength. No boats could sail to or from any island in the Caribbean. They were marooned in voyeuristic horror on Mustique, while power continued to flow to telephones, toaster ovens, and televisions. A marvel of modern technology. They could see the devastation clear as their ABC station without being able to put a toe outside their front doors.

From the living room at Firefly, Willy May had sat in front of the Zenith TV to watch footage from Grenada: flooded embankments, beachfront debris, and desperate attempts by helicopters to extract the wounded. Willy May prayed to catch sight of a woman in orange boots, and then prayed not to.

She'd kept Windy occupied at the kitchen table with a Magna Doodle board and a jar of maraschino cherries, giving her permission to eat as many as she liked. Windy drew magnetic houses and faces, erased with a swipe of the lever. A carnage of cherry stems piled beside the board. Her fingers were stained red.

When the phone rang, they'd both jumped, but she didn't move to answer. Fear tacked her in place.

"Graa," Windy had called. *"Ring-ring."* She'd sucked her sugary thumb.

Willy May had pushed her legs forward despite the buckle-and-pop in her knees.

"Hello?"

"It's Titus."

"Titus." She'd nearly fainted from relief.

"It's a swamp here at the Cotton House," he continued. "I wanted to make sure that you're okay?"

"Yes. We're fine. But we're watching the news and —"

"We received an emergency dispatch," he cut her off. "A man named Jason Charles. He led a Samaritans United team on Grenada. "He said that Victor . . . has been lost. A tidal wave from the storm surge."

The world tilted, and Willy May with it.

418

Not Victor.

"Hilly was beside him."

The phone receiver was suddenly too heavy to hold to her ear. It slipped into the crook of her neck and her whole body pitched forward. She steadied herself against the wall, clawing her fingernails into the damp stucco.

When Joanne left, Willy May's temper had flared. She'd been furious at her daughter for choosing to leave them, to leave her, to do the very thing that landed Willy May in a bad marriage with permanent regrets. But Joanne had been in no immediate peril. Life and death did not hang in the balance. Pride, loyalty, and the sense that she was unnecessary, yes, but she'd never been afraid that she'd actually lose Joanne forever.

Over time with a cooler head, she saw that she'd been wrong to react the way she had. Joanne married for love. She was happy. She and Tim were building a home, a new life. When Lulu was born, she reached out. Watching her daughters raise their daughters had shown her a way to be a better mother than her own, a better mother than she'd previously been. But too often her emotions worked faster than her wit. Old habits died hard. She should've done better.

She'd been worried about the storm, about Firefly, about the new majority owner of Mustique, and her financial woes. She'd snapped without giving much thought. Her impulsive Hilly had paraded into the room and said that she was going into the storm with a coconut bag slung over her shoulder and a pair of tennis shoes. Ridiculous. She'd almost laughed out loud and momentarily wondered if Hilly had nipped into the wine (or worse) again. Because this was completely crazy.

However, her daughter had challenged her with clear eyes and steady hands, and she realized suddenly that this was different. Hilly didn't need her anymore — for approval or permission. Willy May had long felt, even at a distance, that everything Hilly did was in an effort to gain one of those from her. The problem was, no matter how much approval or permission she gave, it was either not enough or too much. So Hilly's failures and struggles felt in many ways hers, too.

Lack of control made her angry, a defensive response more than an appropriate one. She'd blown up at Hilly and gone to her room. There, she'd stood before the sliding glass door of the balcony looking out at the darkening horizon. Her *Otrera* moored in

Britannia Bay. Macaroni Beach was empty and swept smooth by the building winds. She was right this time. Hilly and Windy needed to be protected. Here was real danger. But right and wrong weren't the point. Maybe they never were.

On the wall by the balcony, she'd hung a framed photograph of the girls and her on a holiday sail when Hilly and Joanne were small enough to fit under the wings of her arms. They were laughing so hard that all three heads bent toward each other. Harry must've taken the picture. She couldn't remember, but it was one of the few candids of them. How easy it was to build a story around a moment but forget the frame of reference.

It dawned on her that her own mother must've felt this — all of it. The anger, protectiveness, betrayal, love, and grief shaken up like a Magic 8-Ball, giving no more accurate answers. She imagined her mother standing at the window of their Texan two-bedroom, watching her leave. Not knowing where or why or how this beautiful thing she'd created could treat her so callously, could think so little of her that she'd go to such lengths to be free. It was indescribable heartbreak.

Willy May had touched the outline of

Hilly's head in the photo. Youth saw only the glimmering reflection of itself. But everyone had to grow up. Peter Pan was a fairy tale. By the end of his adventure, readers recognized the foolishness of clinging to eternal childhood. Life was not built for such. To everything there was a season. Hilly had grown and matured into a woman. Willy May had to allow her that. She had to love her in the going.

So, she'd grabbed the pair of Wellington boots from her closet. When she gave them to Hilly, the magnetic pull between them was strong. She had to push away, or she'd never let her go. Afterward, she'd stood by her bedroom window for hours, watching the waves come in and go out, until night fell and the low-hanging storm clouds hid the well of tears.

When Titus called the next day with the news from Grenada, it broke her.

She'd penciled down a Samaritans United contact number. The sound of the graphite against the paper was shrill as nails on a chalkboard. Windy had leaned her head against Willy May consolingly, but the heat of it made her whole body sweat and the smell of candied cherries turned her stomach.

"*Ma-man* home coming?" Windy had

whispered.

In a blink, Willy May's skepticism toward destiny and God and all things of myth turned on a dime.

"Yes," she'd told her granddaughter. "Mama will have a homecoming. But we've got to bring it to her."

The truth cut free from the tethers.

She'd dialed Joanne.

"Hilly's been evacuated to Miami City Hospital," she explained. I'm not sure if she's already there or if she's on her way, but she's alone. She needs us, Josie. We're coming to the States."

"Tim and I will go to the hospital now," said Joanne.

"I'll let you know when Windy and I get to St. Lucia and have tickets to fly out of Hewanorra International."

They'd packed suitcases.

Windy tried to fit all her books, dolls, and special shelf items into the bag.

"We don't have room, baby girl," Willy May explained gently. "You can bring one of each. The rest have to stay at Firefly."

What would she choose to bring with her? Hilly, Joanne, Windy . . .

"Titus." She'd called him back. "We're going to Hilly. Can you get ahold of Captain Tannis?"

"Yes," he'd said. "Leave it to me."

As soon as it was safe to sail, Captain Tannis traversed the choppy waters to Britannia Bay. Titus would look after Firefly, *Otrera,* and the cats. On the dock, he'd pulled her close and she let him — let herself stand in the folds of his embrace, smell the sun on his neck, and feel the warmth of his hands crossing her back.

She'd kissed him goodbye with Captain Tannis and Windy looking on.

"I wish you could come with us," she'd said.

"Me, too," he'd replied.

"I'll call you as soon as . . ." She wasn't sure how to finish. There were so many unknowns.

"You get to Hilly first."

She'd nodded and then, holding Titus's hand, she'd stepped off the dock of Mustique and onto the ferry. Her footing was wobbly on the water. She'd lost her sea legs.

The boat launched with a *chug,* and she watched as the island condensed into a droplet and then vanished into the sea.

CHAPTER 25
WHEN YOU'RE FAST ASLEEP

She'd just returned from getting Windy a can of Slice soda from the hall quarter machine when she heard her name called — not *Michael* but *Mum.*

"Joanne?"

Her daughter's cheeks were pink as peaches. Her lips sparkled glossily. Her blond hair had somehow grown blonder, the tips of it peeking out from beneath a paisley silk scarf. She wore a pair of flared blue jeans and a scoop-neck T-shirt emblazoned with a rainbow ABBA logo. The toddler on her hip pulled at the neckline, and she unconsciously slipped her thumb into the girl's fingers to keep them occupied.

Lulu was the spitting image of Joanne at that age, and Willy May felt an aching pull like she'd been threaded through her belly button. Before she could think of a reason not to, she lunged forward and pulled Joanne and Lulu to her. They smelled like honey biscuits and briny sun, and she inhaled deeper than she had in days, maybe years.

"Josie girl . . ."

"Mum . . ."

They whispered into the soft creases of each other's necks.

Joanne was wiping away tears when she finally let go. Lulu stared at them with concern. Her bottom lip trembled, but Joanne shook her head.

"These are happy tears, Lu. Happy tears are good. Mommy is seeing her mum. Remember, I told you about your grandmum — this is her!"

Joanne started to hand the child over, but she clung to her mother's neck.

"It's okay," said Willy May. "Don't force her."

"I'm sorry," said Joanne. "She's painfully shy." She exhaled worried frustration and then whispered, "This is Grandmum. You've heard her on the phone more times than we can count."

Lulu looked to Willy May but when she met her gaze with a smile, the girl hid her face again in Joanne's neck.

Windy tucked a hand into Willy May's. "Who that?"

"That's your aunt Joanne and cousin

Lulu," said Willy May. "And your uncle Tim."

Willy May hadn't initially seen him enter. He'd come in behind Joanne, pushing a plastic stroller and carrying a half-eaten box of Barnum's Animal Crackers.

Willy May nodded. "Hello, Tim."

"Willy May," he welcomed warmly. "It's good to see you. I wish it were on different terms."

She shook her head. "We're here, and you're here, and Hilly's here. Terms don't really matter."

Windy dropped her grip and held out her hand. She'd been schooled in polite introductions with the guests at Firefly. " 'Ello."

It was only then that Lulu lifted her head. Joanne set her down on the ground beside Windy.

"Hello, Windy," said Joanne. "I'm not sure you remember me. You were a baby the last time I saw you."

Windy canted her head to the side. "I hear you."

"That's right," said Willy May. "You heard Aunt Jo on the telephone. Just like Lulu heard us."

Windy nodded vigorously and her soda fizzed with the motion.

Lulu eyed it curiously.

"Say hello to your cousin, Lulu," Joanne pressed gently.

Slowly and with great thought, she turned to Windy: "Hi." She pointed at the can of Slice. "What's that?"

At two years old, her enunciation was clear as a bell. Beautiful, thought Willy May, and then, she felt a stab of remorse for Windy. Lulu's able tongue seemed to accentuate Windy's lisp. For a blink, Willy May was reeled back to when Hilly and Joanne were these ages. Two vines from the same branch. So different and yet so similar. Each with her own struggles to overcome and each thinking the other had the luck of the draw. She wished she could tell those past girls that they were made exactly so for a purpose and beautiful just as they were. She wished she could tell the present ones the same. But she was still trying to make sense of it all herself.

"*Th*-oda," Windy answered.

Lulu tottered over to Tim, took the cracker box, and rummaged two fingers in the wax paper. Locating a misshapen pink blob, she extended it to Windy.

"Trade?"

Windy eyed the offering suspiciously.

"It's a cookie," said Willy May.

"El-e-phant," Lulu said slowly but distinctly.

Windy chortled. "Horton?"

"Similar but not. Another elephant."

"Boop?"

She meant Bupa, Colin's elephant.

"No, another. A new elephant. One frosted in sugar that lives in the cracker box until you get hungry and then you eat it."

Windy's mouth hung open in awe and hunger. They'd had something of a lunch on the plane, but every leg of their journey had included food — it comforted. The traditional breakfast-lunch-dinner was all mixed up. No matter the time or the offering, Windy never turned down a snack.

The two children exchanged. Lulu guzzled the orange soda. Windy chomped the cracker. They watched each other, laughed, and were instantly friends. The adults watched them, sighed, and were momentarily eased. Childhood had that effect and was equally ephemeral. The somberness of their reunion returned.

"We've been here every day waiting," said Joanne. "They took our names and said they'd call us when Hilly was stable in the ICU."

Tim cleared his throat. "Why don't the girls help me put your luggage in the car?"

429

"We were going to find a hotel as soon as
. . . ," began Willy May, but she honestly
hadn't thought beyond getting to the hospital. She didn't want to impose.

"A hotel? But we made Lulu's room into
a guest bedroom for you."

Lulu cupped her mouth animatedly toward Windy. "A castle."

"Tim set up a tent in the living room. It
looks like a castle. It will be Lulu's first
slumber party," explained Joanne.

Windy's eyes widened, and she looked to
Willy May beseechingly. "S-*thhh*-slumber
party?"

Willy May was eager for a place to rest,
and she hadn't the energy to feign opposi-
tion.

"So long as we aren't a burden."

Joanne smiled.

Windy slung her backpack around to her
front, unzipped the seam, and pulled out
the miniature statue of Otrera. It had been
one of the special things she'd chosen to
bring along with her flute and box of crayons. She placed the doll in the cloth seat of
Lulu's stroller and got behind one of the
shepherd's hook handles. Lulu followed her
cousin's lead and took the other. They
started out at such a pace that Tim had to
skip to catch up. Outside, the Floridian sun

430

made their tiny shadows look ten feet grown.

Willy May and Joanne approached the hospital's reception station again.

"Hi," said Joanne, "we're back. Please, *any* information about my sister, Hilly Michael, would be greatly appreciated. We're desperate."

The nurse exhaled long, checked over her shoulder for her supervisor, and then picked up the phone.

"Hi, Jenny, this is Nurse Andrews at the front desk. I'm looking at the chart of one of the patients from Grenada. Twenty-six-year-old female. Hilly Michael. Any chance you could find her on the ward and give me a quick status report? . . . . Sure, I'll hold."

She put her hand over the mouthpiece. "I shouldn't be doing this." Her eyes swept to Willy May. "I have a daughter. She's forty-three now, but she still feels like a teenager to me. They never grow too old not to need their moms, right? I can only imagine what you're going through."

"Thank you," said Willy May.

Nurse Andrews returned to the phone. There seemed an extended amount of silence before she nodded.

"C648. Gotcha. I'll put a note in the chart. Thanks, Jenny." She hung up.

431

Willy May and Joanne leaned in.

"She's stable but unconscious. I don't know the details, but cerebral hypoxia is listed," Nurse Andrews said with clinical precision.

Willy May was grateful for the lack of emotion. She needed to hear it fact for fact.

"She nearly drowned. Apparently, one of the other volunteers, a Mr. Jason Charles, pulled her from the water and resuscitated her with CPR before the paramedics could get them off Grenada."

Willy May's stomach dropped. "What does that mean exactly?"

"She's in a coma," said Nurse Andrews. "She could come out of it today or in a week, six months or . . . never."

Joanne took her right arm. Holding her up or clinging on, Willy May couldn't tell.

"Can we see her?" she asked.

"Please," pleaded Willy May.

Nurse Andrews tapped a fingernail on the phone and then picked it up and pushed the floor call button. "Hi, Jenny, me again. If patient Michael is intubated and stable, the family can come up to see her, right?" She threaded her index finger through the loops of the cord and released it like a spring. "No, it's fine, they don't need a nurse escort. You guys have your plate full.

I'll give them directions and you can check them in at the ICU desk. They'll be up momentarily."

She hung up with a cat grin.

"Sixth floor. Take the elevator. It'll let you out at the desk and Jenny will sign you in. You're lucky, it's a visiting hour."

Without hesitating, they made a dash for the elevator. Tim would take care of the girls.

When the doors drew closed and the din of the waiting room fell away, Willy May took Joanne's hand. Something she only did with her girls when they were crossing the street as children, and she wanted them to hurry along. It had been a gesture of control not sentiment. Now, she squeezed her daughter's palm tight and hoped she felt all that she hadn't the words to say.

The metal doors reflected them, strong as hitch knots on a rope. Joanne pressed the button for the sixth floor and the elevator spirited upward. Willy May's stomach dropped with the acceleration, making it seem like they were falling while they rose. *So much of life was that way,* she thought.

Ping, ping, ping, ping, ping, ping.

The doors opened. A rush of sound spilled in: voices, coughs, ringing phones, pecked keyboards, shuffled papers, squeaky cart

433

wheels, and a symphony of *beep*s counting heartbeats, measuring breaths, tracking neurons . . .

A nurse stood from her desk when they exited.

"Michael?" she asked.

"Yes," said Willy May.

"I'm Nurse Alonso — Jenny." While her tone was detached, her eyes were welcoming. "Follow me."

They did, to the closed door labeled C648.

Nurse Jenny pulled the chart from the door, read quickly, then put it back and stood blocking their entrance.

"She's intubated, which means there's a tube down her throat so the machine can help her breathe. It's scary for a lot of family members to see a loved one like that. You may not recognize her. The brain has checked out from the trauma and lack of oxygen. Without all the facial muscles activated, it's rather like looking at the shell of a person. But she's there. She can hear you and feel you. So try to behave like you would if she were awake. Patients feel your emotions. She's not gone just . . . lost inside herself. But she's working hard to find her way back.

"Meantime, you can send her messages — hold her hand, play music, tell her stories. No food or flowers or perishables allowed. But being in the room does wonders for coma patients." She looked to her wristwatch and then gave it a tap. "ICU has set visiting hours. Four times a day. I'll give you the schedule. Unfortunately, this one is almost up so I won't keep you. If you have any questions, I'm at the desk."

Then she moved aside and walked back down the linoleum hall, each click of her heels distinct until they blended into the clangor.

Part of Willy May wanted to stay outside room C648. She didn't want to face the void, that "shell" of the person she loved so much. She wanted to turn around and sail back to Firefly, where the skies were blue and the tides were steady. But even Mustique was changed now. Hilly was part of it. Her presence was as felt as her absence. It was the equipoise of pain and pleasure that made life precious, inescapable as the sunrise and sunset. There was no place or person or construct that was singularly one or the other. She'd been a fool to think otherwise. She was a fool even now to hesitate at C648's closed door.

To love as a sustained action meant that Willy May had to stop thinking of herself first. That's where she'd gone wrong with her marriage, with her family in Texas, with her daughters; in truth, with everyone she had ever deeply cared for. She'd thought love was like the movies, plays, and storybooks — all glittering with blissful adoration and sealed with a kiss. A pageant to be won or lost. A crown and sash to be flaunted. It was none of that.

To love was to do the hard things. It was leading her daughters into the unknown with no guarantees except that suffering was inevitable. Love was being braver than she felt. It was giving hope when she doubted it herself and rising from her own ashes so that her girls would know it could be done. Love was not waiting another minute to be the mother she wished she'd had.

So, she stepped forward and opened the door.

On the hospital bed with wires and tubes hanging from her mouth, nose, and arms lay Hilly.

Nurse Jenny had been wrong. She looked every bit herself. Her hair had been washed and splayed out in a crown of dark curls. An IV bag of saline twinkled afternoon sunlight across her body.

Willy May ran a hand over her hair. "We're here, Hilly," she whispered. "We're here with you."

Hilly's cheeks were slightly pink from the warmth of the electric blanket tucked up beneath her arms. Willy May could nearly convince herself that she was merely sleeping. The sharp tang of disinfectant reminded her otherwise.

"Tomorrow, we'll bring Windy." Joanne's voice hitched.

It would be hard for Windy to see her mother like this — there but not. How would they help her understand? Willy May couldn't let herself imagine Hilly not waking up. It was too much for her own mothering heart.

She smoothed Hilly's knuckles below the IV line. "We can't let your hands get dry." She swallowed hard against the choke of emotion. "A woman's got to keep fresh, even in the hospital. I'll bring lotion."

The staccato note of the heart monitor was deafening.

Beep . . . beep . . . beep . . . beep.

Leave it to Joanne to rescue them. She turned the one note into a metronome by which she hummed "A Dream Is a Wish."

"Hmm-hmm, hmm-hmm hmm . . ."

Despite the painful lump in her throat, Willy May joined, too.

437

CHAPTER 26
THE CHOICE

The women came every day during the four ICU allotted visiting hours:

9 a.m. – 10 a.m.
1 p.m. – 2 p.m.
4 p.m. – 5 p.m.
7 p.m. – 8 p.m.

They briefly discussed taking shifts, but four hours out of twenty-four seemed too little with so much hanging in the balance. Hilly could wake up at any minute, the doctor explained, or she could be in a vegetative state the rest of her life. Time was the sovereign, and it would not conform to their wishes. So, they came together, sometimes with the girls and sometimes not.

Seeing her mother unresponsive with the machines and tubes for the first time, Windy had cried so hard that she hadn't even breath for her flute, and Willy May had nearly done the same.

But then Lulu put her arms around her cousin and said, "No cry, Windy. I love you." And Windy had leaned into that newfound security. Her tears had ebbed.

"She's like Sleeping Beauty," Joanne had explained, which made both girls draw near in wonder.

They strung paper drawings of palm trees, fairies, fireflies, stars, and moons around Hilly's bed. The waxy smell of crayons filled up the room. Windy stationed the Otrera statue on the windowsill. Willy May rubbed Hilly's hands and feet with plumeria lotion. Joanne brought in an electric keyboard on which she played show tunes, pop rock, radio ditties, childhood lullabies, classical piano, anything she thought Hilly would enjoy. "My Favorite Things" from *The Sound of Music* was a particular ICU hit. The medical staff and other patients' families started coming by C648 with requests.

The sixth floor was a world unto itself. Family members congregated in the hall to share heartaches and joys. Most patients were like Hilly, castaways in their bodies. The families treated each finger twitch and an involuntary eyebrow lift as the start of a miraculous recovery. They believed it was coming — needed to believe.

In C645 was Geraldine, a fifty-eight-year-old woman who had a stroke while driving to her aerobics class. She was the mother of three children, and her youngest daughter, Laura, had relocated from New York City to Miami to look after her. She came every day to exercise her mom's arms and legs in rhythm to their favorite songs.

In C632 was Jessica, a twenty-five-year-old who'd been in the passenger seat during a car accident. Her parents were moving her to an LTCH, a long-term facility. As a goodbye surprise, a handful of the nurses arranged for warm spa facials to be given to anyone who wished, patients and parents. Jessica's mother had cried, and Willy May had to excuse herself to get air.

Next door in C634 was Fred, a forty-two-year-old bachelor firefighter who'd suffered smoke inhalation and severe burns after evacuating residents from a burning apartment complex. He hadn't any next of kin so the sixth-floor families took turns visiting him, telling him jokes and funny bits from the newspaper.

"Headline says an alligator climbed into bed with a local politician. He rolled over in the dark and said, 'Good night, dear,' without noticing until his wife started hollering. Not sure which bed is colder — the one with the alligator or the one with the wife afterward!"

Willy May would imagine his laughter. He looked like a man with the big booming kind.

"I hope he wakes up soon," remarked a nurse one day.

Willy May learned then that the ICU couldn't accommodate coma patients forever. Either the families moved them to a private LTCH or they were sent to a state-funded one.

To everyone's great relief, Firefighter Fred woke up after sixteen days. His firehouse squad wheeled him out with fanfare. Even if he didn't consciously know Willy May, she missed him after he'd gone. It *was* possible to love someone without being loved in return.

Those inside the hospital spoke of the sixth-floor patients in present tense. They were a living, breathing blink away from a miracle. All of them. Conversely, those on the outside seemed to speak of them in the past. People didn't mean to be unkind; they'd simply moved on and didn't know how to address the out-of-sight, out-of-mind.

Even Tim would occasionally put his foot in his mouth.

"The first time I met Hilly, she was in a toga and crown. Your mom and grandmum, too. Like real princesses," he told the girls. "You would've loved her, Lulu."

It cleaved Willy May's heart. Not the memory but the remembering, the *would've*.

Without missing a beat, Lulu had replied, "I *do* love her."

Poor Tim immediately realized his error. Redness crawled up his throat. "Of course you do — we do."

Living so closely in their two-bedroom house, Willy May was privy to nearly every waking moment and so was surprised to find that Tim was as authentic as he appeared on paper. Few people truly were. He showered Joanne and Lulu with affection in a way that Harry never had with her or their daughters. And unlike her own in-laws, her son-in-law accepted that they would not always see eye to eye; what was most important was that they kept their eyes open. No turning a blind one and holding silent grudges. They squabbled like family and made up like family, maybe even better.

Tim's own mother and father had been musicians in a folk-rock group. He rarely saw them as a child and even less after they moved to Canada when Gerald Ford became president. They hadn't returned to the United States. Tim grew up with his great-aunt Jasmin in Miami. When she passed away five years prior, she bestowed her collection of snow sleds on Tim. Willy May promised to help him decorate the antiques with colored lights for the coming holidays. Windy and Lulu wanted the sleds to have plastic reindeer. One for each member of their family: Dasher, Dancer, Prancer, Comet, Cupid, and Rudolph, of course. They agreed that the most beloved reindeer would be Hilly's.

Willy May felt duplicitous in the planning; the truth was that she hoped the plans would not come to fruition. She wanted Hilly to wake up. She wanted to go home to Mustique. Every hour that Hilly remained unconscious was an hour closer to a persistent vegetative state. That was reality. The sands of time were not in their favor.

Willy May called Titus to check on Firefly, to hear news of the island, of Naomi and Fred, the cats, and anything else that took her mind away from here and planted it back there. Mostly, she called because she missed him.

"So." She sighed the word.

She'd just spent over an hour on Joanne's patio telling him the pros and cons of the LTCH options. The nurses had discreetly left the information pamphlets by Hilly's bedside. Willy May wasn't ready for this decision. She was having a hard enough time deciding how to manage the mornings, afternoons, and evenings. Hilly staying permanently was inconceivable. Because what did that mean for Windy? She wouldn't take her away from her mother.

She needed to talk to someone she trusted, someone who loved her family as much as she did. Someone she loved and who loved her, too.

"What do you think?"

The wind whistled in the background. She could nearly smell the coconut palms and fresh-cut pineapple.

"That is a very difficult choice," said Titus. "I think you must do what is best for Hilly."

"Perhaps Colin's private plane could —"

"She cannot come back here," he cut her off. "We don't have a modernized hospital, just the clinic. She needs to be there."

Old indignation rose up inside her. Not at Titus, but at God or whatever it was pulling the strings. She'd found a home for herself, a safe place for her daughter and grand-daughter, a good man. But now, forces outside her control were taking it away, and it wasn't fair.

444

She gulped down her panic. "It could be another month or a year or longer. I don't know . . ."

"Sometimes not knowing is the best way forward, Willy May."

While that was true in theory, she had responsibilities. Namely, bills that would not accept "not knowing" as payment. Mustique was her home and her financial security. She couldn't abandon it without ruin any more than she could abandon her daughters.

"Firefly can't sit boarded up. I can't afford it."

She'd openly shared the budgetary concerns of building, furnishing, and maintaining the villa. Operating it as an exclusive hotel to Colin's guests had been her saving grace. Titus had provided professional advice and helped her secure trusted staff. He'd taken over as general manager for the last month, but she couldn't task him with more.

"Do I need to sell it?" she asked.

He exhaled across the miles, and she closed her eyes wishing he were beside her.

"Yes," he said, and her heart plummeted. "A co-owner would help lift the financial burden. I know the perfect person."

She inhaled sharply. "Who?"

"Me."

She shook her head in disbelief and then stopped because, why not? He was the best businessman she knew and already living full-time at Firefly in her absence. He had become her partner in life, why not in this, too?

"They say not to mix business and pleasure." A thought she said aloud.

"Who said that?" Titus countered.

"You know . . . I don't have the damnedest clue." Willy May laughed.

He continued, "What's your price?"

She nearly cried. "What's your offer?"

"Fifty-fifty. Equal partnership. Do you approve?"

She loved him so much. "I do."

"Then it is so. For now, I'll take care of things here. You take care of things there."

It brought her relief and yet, the aching remained. "I miss you," she said. "I miss home."

"Home is never really a place," said Titus. "It's something you make inside yourself. I may not be where you are, but I am there."

She cradled the phone close. "Whatever cosmic forces brought you to me, I'm grateful."

"Then you should thank Candace!" He laughed. "She's the one who told Anne to send me with you to the village. She was afraid the white lady from Texas might fall off Toucan Hill if she tried to find it alone."

"Is that what she said?"

Willy May didn't recall Candace giving any indication that she doubted her ability to navigate the island. But then, her memory of those early months on Mustique was fuzzy. Her memory of the last month, too. Did it all even matter? History depended on who was telling.

"It was said with sincere fondness," reassured Titus.

They discussed a few of the immediate details regarding reopening the rooms to paying guests before hanging up. Like Hilly had told Windy, it *was* different saying goodbye when you knew there was hope for a homecoming. Still, she couldn't help holding the handset an extra beat.

She turned to find Joanne standing inside the open sliding glass door.

"You heard?" she asked.

Joanne nodded and looked down at the long-term-care pamphlets fanned across the patio table. "Tim and I have been discussing things, too. What if Hilly came here? We could bring in the equipment and hire a CNA to come to the house."

"This house — a two-bedroom?" Willy

May shook her head. "Tim has already been so hospitable with his space."

"You're right," said Tim, coming out through the door. "I can't even get a shave without pink bubblegum toothpaste in the sink." He smirked at Joanne. "I guess we'll just have to build on."

Willy May looked to Joanne incredulously.

"It was Tim's idea," said Joanne. "We have a little money saved up. It's not much but it's enough to pay for an addition. We have the yard space. And to be honest, I think it would be good for Windy and Lulu. The girls have gotten so close. Almost like sisters."

She teared up, and Tim reflexively put his arm around her waist. Somehow, it comforted Willy May, too.

"I understand." She appreciated where Joanne's heart was, but she wanted to make sure that they fully understood. "Are you saying you want Hilly and Windy to live with you permanently? Because that's a big responsibility. Your lives will completely change."

"We know," said Joanne, smiling at her husband. "Change is inevitable — good and bad. It depends on what you do with it, right? We're hoping that she wakes up, but if she doesn't, we'll still be together."

So where did that leave Willy May? Mustique or Miami — the choice was hers. A screw of anxiety began to turn within her just as the girls erupted onto the patio, panting from a game of sidewalk hopscotch. Seeing their smiling faces side by side, she realized that they had the same eyes, their mothers', hers. Undeniably different and undeniably similar.

Nothing in life was one or the other. Not really. Everything was both. It depended on how you looked at it. That was the choice.

CHAPTER 27
ROOT AND BRANCH

Tuesday afternoon, the week before they were to move Hilly off the sixth floor and into Joanne's home, they were surprised to find a young man by her bedside.

His back was to them. Hunched forward, he rested his forehead on Hilly's bare arm. His shoulders trembled.

"Let's give him a minute," whispered Willy May, and she and Joanne moved down the hall.

Luckily, they had not brought Windy and Lulu, who would've been the first to race into the room. The two were home with Tim finger-painting seashells collected at the beach.

"Who's he?" whispered Joanne.

"I don't know," said Willy May. "But clearly, he knows her."

"Is he from Mustique?"

"I never saw him before."

"Well, I don't think he's a kidnapper," said

Joanne. "If Jenny let him through the ward, she must've had a valid reason."

They made a beeline for the nurses' station. A junior male nurse was manning the desk.

"Hello," he welcomed them.

"Hi — yes, hello — actually, is Jenny around?" asked Willy May. "We're family of Hilly Michael in C648."

"Nurse Alonso is on a break," he explained. "Is there something I can do for you?"

"There's a man in my daughter's room," said Willy May, "and we don't know him."

The nurse stood quickly. "We are *extremely* careful about patient visitors." He took up a clipboard and scanned the names. "Everyone must sign in and they must —" His eyes stopped. "Oh." He turned the clipboard so they could read. "It's one of the Samaritans United. He's part of the pastoral staff that brought her here. Jason Charles. He's been a patient himself up on ortho's floor. Fractured his tibia. He was on crutches, correct?"

Willy May had only briefly glanced into the room. She hadn't seen crutches.

"He was sitting down," she said.

"But he was in plain clothes," said Joanne. "If he was a patient, wouldn't he be in a gown, like Hilly?"

The nurse took back the clipboard. "He was released today. He's on his way home to Texas, I believe. Now that he can fly."

And then from down the hall came Jason, hobbling on crutches with his leg in a cast. He stopped at their gazes and thumbed away the wet rawness under his eyes.

"I'm sorry," he said, "do I know y'all?"

His voice had a Texan twang that reminded Willy May of the boys who used to try to walk her home as a teenager. She'd pitied them with their little-town life and Gene Autry cowboy code. How disparaging she'd been. Ignorance could be ruthless.

"We're Hilly's family," said Willy May.

His face opened warmly. "Hello," he said, and then, remembering, his shoulders slumped. "I'm so sorry," he mumbled, biting his bottom lip.

The women flanked him.

"No apologies. You saved Hilly." Willy May took his hand with an assuring squeeze. "Thank you."

"I should've stopped her sooner. I should've . . ." His voice cracked and he covered his mouth with a balled fist.

Willy May shook her head. "Can't judge yesterday by today. If any of us knew what the future held, we might not have the courage to take a step. All we can do is put shoes on and be ready. The rest is *que sera, sera* — 'whatever will be, will be.' "

He lifted his face to her. "That sounds a whole lot like faith."

"I believe it's the Gospel of Doris Day." She winked. "From *The Man Who Knew Too Much*."

Joanne started humming the song. It did the trick of bringing him back from tears.

"When Hilly wakes up, will you tell her that I came? And when she's ready, will you ask her to be in touch? I left my number and mailing address. Also, the information for . . ." He gulped and his Adam's apple dipped hard. "Victor's family, if she wants to contact them."

Sweet Victor. Amid all the grief and worry, his loss seemed distant. She was ashamed to realize that. It was easier to imagine him on another island. Away but not lost. It reminded her of something Hilly said, about nothing being gone forever. That felt true. Because even though Victor was dead, she still felt him — his spirit.

"I'll make sure she gets everything," Willy May told Jason. "And I'll tell her that you were here."

When they returned to Hilly's room, they found a Bible. Not just any Bible, Hilly's

Bible. Willy May had seen it lying around the house enough to recognize the signature royal-blue cover. It stood out to Willy May because all the Bibles she'd ever known had been black leather-bound things that threw their weight like a slap. Hilly's was lighter. No gold-leafed titles or silver filaments. *The Bible* was stamped on the spine. Paper and ink. A cheap sacred text, she'd thought on first glance. Hilly said the preacher had given it to her for free. But everything had a price. A word might be gratis, but *the* Word was worth its weight in gold. A single article made all the difference.

Joanne stood in the room but neither spoke.

Willy May opened the book and Jason's contact information fell out of the front cover.

"Your visitor left you something," said Willy May to Hilly. "To find him when you're ready."

She picked up the note and slipped it between the pages for safekeeping. It landed in Corinthians and the exclamation caught her eye:

Behold! I tell you a mystery.

She read the words in a whisper:

" 'We shall not all sleep, but we shall all be changed, in a moment, in the twinkling of an eye, at the last trumpet. For the trumpet will sound, and the dead will be raised imperishable, and we shall be changed.' "

She took a deep breath and turned to Joanne.

"Do you believe this?"

"You didn't raise us to be particularly religious, Mum," said Joanne.

Willy May shook her head. "I mean, do you believe we can change — just like that?"

She hovered her hands over the words, paper and ink, she reminded herself. And yet, there was power. A spell or a prophecy, an incantation or a benediction, the semantics were the trick of it. Described one way as wicked, described another as righteous. No matter how the letters arranged themselves, what she felt was the same: a surge of courage toward her own honesty.

"I wasn't a very good mother to you when you were young," she said.

"I wasn't a very good mother to you and Hilly as adults either. I did so many things wrong. It's overwhelming to try to account for them all. Maybe going to Mustique was a mistake. Maybe I should've stayed in England and made a hard stand. If I had, Hilly wouldn't be here like this. You two have been through so much heartache that

I could've prevented if I'd chosen to do things differently. A mother's fundamental job is to protect her children, and I didn't do that."

The tears came and she didn't dam them up, make excuses, or run away.

"I want to believe we can change because I *want* to change."

Joanne's lips trembled. "Mum, you're human. That's what makes us changeable."

She knew humanity was flawed and full of doubt, but sometimes a person needed to point to the holes, the evidence, and be reminded that miracles were equally real. Sometimes a person needed to experience human touch to be changed.

Willy May pulled Joanne close.

"Mustique wasn't a mistake," said Joanne. "If you hadn't built Firefly, Hilly wouldn't have had a place to raise Windy. I wouldn't have come to Mustique and met Tim. We wouldn't have Lulu. Everything is connected."

Willy May pressed their foreheads together.

Then, unexpectedly, the uniform rhythm of Hilly's heartbeat changed. The monitor did a double beat and then another. The women turned. Hope and fear inextricably linked. A collective inhalation.

Hilly's eyelids fluttered. A sliver of light between her delicate lashes.

After eight weeks in a coma, Hilly awoke. Changed.

Traumatic brain injury was the official diagnosis. Memory recollection and story-books became part of their daily ritual. The therapist said it was critical to her recovery that they exercise her hippocampus: the center for episodic memories, emotion, learning, imagination, and recall. But she would never be the same Hilly she'd been before the injury.

She forgot words she used to know but now could only perceive their meanings. Simple things like *sky* or *wet* or *sleepy*. Aphasia, the doctors called it. Additionally, pronouncing *P*'s and *V*'s sometimes triggered a stutter, sometimes not. Windy offered her the wooden flute. With Joanne's help, Windy's lisp had become nearly imperceptible. She'd grown stronger from the musical practice and assumed the magic might work for her mother, too. They formed an unofficial family band, The Mustiques. Hilly and Windy on recorders, Joanne on the electric keyboard, Lulu on a ukulele, and Willy May on bongos. They'd wear feather fascinators and glitter eye-

457

shadow. No lead singer, they often didn't even have a musical score to follow, but that wasn't the point. The doing was — and they were grateful for it.

Because they hadn't earned these moments. They were gifts. In an alternate universe, they might not be having them. Victor and his family weren't. He was gone. Just as the former Hilly was gone and the what-could've-been of her love story — the what-could've-been of all their stories. They were connected and had been transformed root and branch. For the better, in some opinions. For the worse, in others. That was for history to decide.

Willy May stayed in Miami for another six months until the addition was completed and then she'd lived back and forth. They all did to some extent. Enjoying winter holidays and spring breaks on Mustique Island, the rest of the year in Florida.

Outsiders looking in might be tempted to envy their life without knowing the measure to which they had struggled and sacrificed. Their family might look to some like a fairy tale. Maybe it was . . . the dream and the nightmare. Beautiful and horrific. A bit of make-believe acted as glue. Because none of them could remember exactly how it all came to be.

Windy and Lulu listened to the tellings. Absorbing every detail. Adding their own tittles of whimsy.

"We eat cookie el-fants," said Windy. "Mama come home."

Because yes, they had eaten cookie elephants and Hilly had come home to them. For two little girls, it was the reality based on what they remembered.

At the end, no matter how many times it was told, the girls would ask, "Then what happens?"

Present tense.

"We don't know yet," Willy May would say. "We'll find out tomorrow."

ACKNOWLEDGMENTS

During the course of writing this book, our global community experienced one of the most harrowing tragedies of history, the coronavirus pandemic. The world changed. I changed. This book changed. I rewrote it four times. What started as a novel lark into the elite development of Mustique Island transformed during our quarantine chrysalis and was reborn as the book you have just finished reading. A book about family, about unseen roots and seen branches extending into the greater world.

There are so many I am grateful to for giving me the trust, guidance, time, and support to write the story that needed writing:

Mollie Glick, my fierce and loving agent. For believing in me. Always. Period. And being the first to stand beside me against all obstacles — external, internal, or a pandemic that shuts down the world. Thank you for the hours of phone calls just to check in, laugh, and commiserate. My love to your little men for sharing their big lives (and mom) with me.

As well, great thanks to Lola Bellier and Jamie Stockton; Michelle Weiner, my film agent; and the rest of my CAA family for all the support.

Rachel Kahan, my beloved, Beyoncé-bringing-the-"Hold-Up" editor. For encouraging me to write to discover and for shining your editorial flashlight on areas to probe deeper. I know this isn't the book that you thought you'd get, but thank you for having the confidence that it is the book that needed to be gotten. I am entirely grateful for your love and faith in me. Besitos round the house.

At HarperCollins: publicist Kelly Rudolph; production editor Rachel Weinick; Lainey Mays, Virginia Stanley, Chris Connolly at Library Love Fest; Jen Hart, Amy Wood, Lisa Sharkey (bell-ringer extraordinaire); Michael Fynan and Kim Racon at Harper Academic; and Corey Beatty, my whale of a marketing maestro at HarperCollins Canada.

Sam Edenborough, Nicki Kennedy, Katherine West, Alice Natali, and the rest of my unstoppable team at International Literary

Agency for sharing my work with every book-loving country on earth. We have a standing trivia pub date the next time I'm in London. Doc B is buying a round of pints.

Isabelle Felix, sensitivity reader par excellence. Your devotion to and care for this manuscript changed the course of its history. Thank you for giving me, the author, permission to not be perfect, and, in doing so, recognize my own areas to grow. Thank you even more for helping me elevate fiction for people of all colors. My prayer is that everyone will see, hear, and read themself in these and all my pages. Also — for the brilliant GIFs.

Beth Seufer Buss, Programs Director at Bookmarks, my local independent bookstore cheetah. B. Yang, no words can thank you for all your profound insight in reading the most shambolic first draft (ever) during the onset of a global lockdown with the coronavirus roaming the streets. You Lysol-ed, gloved, masked, and went to reading . . . that's a friend for life. I'm blessed to have you in my hometown, Winston-Salem, NC. We're going to grow very old together with our books and cats.

The rest of my Bookmarks indie bookstore family: Executive Director, brilliant planner, and friend Jamie Southern; Caleb Masters, Kate Storhoff, Lisa Yee Swope, Teresa, Mary Louise, Cat, Patricio, and Josie (we miss you), and all the other frontline booksellers who are the lifeblood of our business. I am so grateful for each of you. You are my tribe. . . .

That tribal circle encompasses author friends. I could not and would not walk this journey without you:

Paula McLain. Our crafty universe spun us into each other's orbits because it knew we needed Mc-soul sisterhood. I am joyfully indebted forever and ever, amen.

Jenna Blum. My eternal love lantern. Shine on, bright flame.

Christina Baker Kline. For being my phone-a-friend lifeline and made of fireproof/fire drill mettle. Thank you, dearest.

Mary Laura Philpott. I will meet you anywhere in the world to buy deodorant and Diet Cokes, find turtles, and defy the wonky stars with laughter.

George Saunders, who gave me the most vital piece of advice when my March 30, 2020, trip to Mustique had to be cancelled: "just Google it" and "carry on . . ." It was the go-ahead I needed to write the fictional guts out of this story. The book is infinitely more because of you, wise friend. Endless thanks.

Laura Dave, Therese Fowler, Jean Kwok — my early reader champions who read messy, unedited drafts and still had such loving words. Thank you for those and for the ones so generously bestowed in private. It takes a village of kindred spirits, and I'm grateful that you are part of mine.

Prayer warriors: Allison Pataki, Lisa Wingate, Martha Hall Kelly, Patti Callahan Henry, and Karen and Tim White.

Eternal cheerleaders and shoulders to lean on: Chris Bohjalian (Victoria for the photography inspirations and Jesse girl, too), Jane Green, Madeline Miller, Melanie Benjamin, M. J. Rose, Viola Shipman (aka Wade Rouse), and Gary Edwards.

I can never adequately thank the many bookstores, book clubs, podcasters, and readers to whom I owe mountains of appreciation. The following deserve special acknowledgment: Carol Fitzgerald, Greg Fitzgerald, Jenni Lai at the BookReporter; Robin Kall and Emily Homonoff at Reading with Robin; Jenny O'Regan, my bookaholic beauty; Carol Schmiedecke, for sending handwritten missives of the most beautiful creation; Susan (Sunshine Sister) McBeth at Adventures by the Book, for listening to this story premise on a car ride in 2019 and holding my secrets close for years; Andrea Katz and her loving Great Thoughts' Great Readers group; Pamela Klinger Horn of Literature Lovers' Night Out; the gracious gang at A Mighty Blaze; Anne Bogel (aka Modern Mrs. Darcy) of *What Should I Read Next?* podcast; Reg Banner, host of the Page Turners' Book Club of Winston-Salem, who faithfully sent letters of encouragement and loaned me his personal copy of the BBC documentary *Margaret: The Rebel Princess;* new BFF Ron Block; Meg Waite Clayton and all our Binderistas in the Binders Full of Novelists.

Christy Fore, J. C. Fore, and my honorary nieces Kelsey Grace and Lainey Faith. Love you beyond where flying unicorns roam. Sandy Poehling, God rest your gracious soul, for sharing your life, your daughters, Mommom Pauline, and your wonderland garden with me. Thank you to her husband, Dr. Gary Poehling, for sharing the family when every hour was direly precious. Sandy's spirit remains in our Winston-Salem community, an angel "wow-ing" us with every rose bloom.

Dr. Eleane Norat McCoy, mi mommacita. You awe me with your strength, resilience, love, and boundless capacity to renew your mind. What you hold before you now is so far from the scruffy bunch of pages I handed over four years ago. This finished novel is a testimony to *agape:* we can agree to disagree and still make the world a better, more compassionate, more inclusive place. Love is the only rule. You are my tree and I am your apple. I love you.

My McCoy men: Curtis, Jason, and Dr. Andrew McCoy, thank you for being lionhearted knights of the highest royal guard. Three of the only men that I would quarantine with, hug on, and sit within a yardstick of during an epic viral outbreak . . . but I would still wear my mask!

To mi abuelitos Maria and Wilfredo Norat, it's because of you and our family tree that I consistently return to the rich story ground of the Caribbean. My roots are in Aibonito, Puerto Rico, forever. Te amo y gracias por todo tu amor y cariño. Bendiciones y besitos.

My husband and best friend, Brian Waterman (aka Doc B), we didn't make it to Mustique in 2020, but (apparently) our Firefly reservations still stand! I love you for always being ready to jump on a plane, train, car, bike, boat, or simply lace up your sneakers and hit the trail. I could not climb life's mountains, cross the valleys, or sail the seas without you beside me . . . nor would I ever want to. You are my headsail, my anchor, and my rudder all in one. Thank you for believing with unflappable trust that where the future takes us is better than where we've been, and the divine winds will be in our favor.

AUTHOR'S NOTE

This book was loosely inspired by the true life of Billy Ray Mitchell, a Texan woman ahead of her time who married and divorced a British brewery baron, built her own boats, sailed to Mustique Island, constructed a home named Firefly, and lived there for a time with her grown daughters. She is one of the lesser documented founding figures on Mustique during the 1970s and a prominent face at the Tennants' publicly lauded soirees. I was captivated by her spirit, moxie, determination, reinvention, and never-ending quest for belonging. That all said, Willy May Michael and her family are wholly and unequivocally my invention.

Moreover, while many of the historical events mentioned in this novel occurred, I have taken liberties with the details, the timelines, the names of guests, and so forth in service to the narrative and to respect the privacy of the real people. One notably being the sale of Mustique Company shares to Hans Neumann, which had conflicting dates in sources. I have done my best to accurately depict the general time frames if not the exact dates. All historic errors are part of this book's imagined Mustique Island.

If readers are keen to learn more about the factual origins and events of Mustique, these are the references that greatly advanced my fictionalized creation:

- *Lord of the Isle: The Extravagant Life and Times of Colin Tennant* by Colin Tennant, the 3rd Baron Glenconner, and Nicholas Courtney
- *Lady in Waiting* by Anne Glenconner
- *Ninety-Nine Glimpses of Princess Margaret* by Craig Brown
- *Gourmet* magazine: "The Magic of Mustique" by Janne Chamberlain, October 1973
- *Margaret: The Rebel Princess,* a BBC/PBS two-part documentary

This story felt germane to the modern reader's struggle to understand our individual power as part of the collective: Who are we under the current defining governance?

How will history remember us? These are questions that I consistently ask myself as a Puerto Rican, an American, a woman, an author, a voice I hope readers feel compelled to ask the same during and after reading this story. Moreover, I hope they are emboldened to share their most genuine selves with each other.

ABOUT THE AUTHOR

Sarah McCoy is the *New York Times, USA Today,* and international bestselling author of the novels *Marilla of Green Gables, The Mapmaker's Children, The Baker's Daughter,* and *The Time It Snowed in Puerto Rico.* Her work has been featured in *Real Simple,* The Millions, *Your Health Monthly,* Huffington Post, Writer Unboxed, and other publications. She hosted the NPR WSNC monthly radio program "Bookmarked with Sarah McCoy" and previously taught English and writing at Old Dominion University and at the University of Texas at El Paso. She currently lives in North Carolina with her husband, an orthopedic sports surgeon; their dog, Gilly; and their cat, Tutu.

The employees of Thorndike Press hope you have enjoyed this Large Print book. All our Thorndike, Wheeler, and Kennebec Large Print titles are designed for easy reading, and all our books are made to last. Other Thorndike Press Large Print books are available at your library, through selected bookstores, or directly from us.

For information about titles, please call:
(800) 223-1244

or visit our website at:
gale.com/thorndike

To share your comments, please write:

Publisher
Thorndike Press
10 Water St., Suite 310
Waterville, ME 04901

475